KU-321-282

Shrine

Also by James Herbert

The Rats
The Fog
The Survivor
Fluke
The Spear
The Dark
Lair
The Jonah
Domain
Moon
The Magic Cottage
Sepulchre
Haunted
Creed
Portent
The Ghosts of Sleath
'48
Others

Graphic Novels

The City
(Illustrated by Ian Miller)

Non-fiction

By Horror Haunted
(Edited by Stephen Jones)

James Herbert's Dark Places
(Photographs by Paul Barkshire)

JAMES HERBERT

Shrine

MACMILLAN

First published 1983 by New English Library

This edition published 1999 by Macmillan
an imprint of Macmillan Publishers Ltd
25 Eccleston Place, London SW1W 9NF
Basingstoke and Oxford

Associated companies throughout the world

ISBN 0 333 76126 X

1 3 5 7 9 8 6 4 2

A CIP catalogue record for this book is available from the British Library.

Typeset by SetSystems Ltd, Saffron Walden, Essex
Printed and bound in Great Britain by
Mackays of Chatham plc, Chatham, Kent

Acknowledgements

The Author and Publishers gratefully acknowledge permission to include the following extracts:

From 'The Little Creature', 'The Ogre', and 'The Ghost' by Walter de la Mare, by permission of the Literary Trustees of Walter de la Mare and the Society of Authors as their representative.

From *Alice's Adventures in Wonderland* and *Through the Looking Glass* by Lewis Carroll, published by Macmillan Ltd.

Old Nursery Rhymes in *The Oxford Nursery Rhyme Book*, published by Oxford University Press.

From 'The Crystal Cabinet' by William Blake, 'A Slumber did my Spirit Seal' by William Wordsworth, 'Wake all the Dead!' by Sir William Davenant, 'The Hag' by Robert Herrick and 'Alison Gross' and 'Jemima' in *The Faber Book of Children's Verse*, published by Faber and Faber.

From *The Secret Garden* by Frances Hodgson Burnett, published by Frederick Warne Publishers Ltd.

From 'The Juniper Tree', 'The Three Golden Hairs of the Devil', 'Rumpelstiltskin', 'The Goose Girl', 'Fitcher's Bird', 'Hansel and Gretel', and 'Little Snow White', in *The Brothers Grimm: Popular Folk Tales*, translated by Brian Alderson, by permission of Victor Gollancz Ltd.

From *Peter Pan* by J. M. Barrie, by permission of Hodder and

Stoughton Children's Books, copyright © Great Ormond Street Hospital.

From 'The Little Mermaid', 'The Emperor's New Clothes' and 'The Snow Queen' by Hans Andersen in *Hans Andersen's Fairy Tales*, chosen by Naomi Lewis, published by Puffin Books, copyright © 1981 Naomi Lewis.

From 'On a Lord' by Samuel Taylor Coleridge, 'Three Witches' by Ben Jonson, 'Look Out, Boys' by Oliver Wendell Holmes and 'Kehama's Curse' by Robert Southey in *The Beaver Book of Creepy Verse* chosen by Ian and Zinka Woodward, published by Hamlyn Paperbacks.

From *Pollyanna* by Eleanor H. Porter, by permission of Harrap Ltd.

From 'Shadow Bride' in *The Adventures of Tom Bombadil* by J. R. R. Tolkien, by permission of George Allen & Unwin.

From 'The Two Witches' by Robert Graves in *Collected Poems* published by Cassell Ltd, by permission of Robert Graves.

From 'Grave by a Holm-oak' by Stevie Smith in *Collected Poems of Stevie Smith*, published by Allen Lane, by permission of James McGibbon, the executor of Stevie Smith, and the Publishers.

From 'The Curse be Ended' in *The Family Reunion* by T. S. Eliot by permission of Faber and Faber Ltd.

Shrine

Red blood out and black blood in,
My Nannie says I'm a child of sin.
How did I choose me my witchcraft kin?
Know I as soon as dark's dreams begin
Snared is my heart in a nightmare's gin;
Never from terror I out may win;
So dawn and dusk I pine, peak, thin,
Scarcely knowing t'other from which –
My great grandma – She was a Witch.

Walter de la Mare, 'The Little Creature'

Part One

Alice! a childish story take,
  And with a childish hand
Lay it where Childhood's dreams are twined
  In memory's mystic band,
Like pilgrim's wither'd wreath of flowers
  Plucked in a far-off land.

Lewis Carroll,
Alice's Adventures in Wonderland

1

Down with the lambs,
 Up with the lark,
Run to bed children
 Before it gets dark.

Old nursery rhyme

The small mounds of dark earth scattered around the graveyard looked as though the dead were pushing their way back into the living world. The girl smiled nervously at the thought as she hurried from grave to grave. They were molehills. Moles were difficult to get rid of; poison one, another moved into its lodgings. She had often watched the molecatcher, a round man with a pointed face, and thought he looked like a mole. He grinned as he delicately dipped stubby fingers into his baked beans tin and plucked out a strychnine-coated worm from its wriggling friends and relatives. He always grinned when she watched. And chuckled when he held it towards her and she jumped away with a silent shriek. His lips, ever wet, like his dosed worms, moved but she heard nothing. She hadn't for as long as she remembered. A shudder as the molecatcher mimed eating the writhing pink meat, but she always stayed to watch him push his metal rod into the earth then poke the worm into the hole he had created. She imagined the mole down there, snuffling its way through solid darkness, hunting food, searching for its own death. Digging its own grave. She giggled and couldn't hear her giggle.

Alice stooped and took withered flowers from a mud-soiled vase. The headstone against which the flowers had rested was fairly new, its inscription not yet filled with dirt nor blurred by weather. She had known the old lady – was she just bones now? – and had found the living corpse more frightening than the dead one. Could you be alive at ninety-two? You could move, but could you live? The time-span was incomprehensible to Alice, who was just eleven years old. It was hard to imagine your own flesh dried and wrinkled, your brain shrunken by years of use so that instead of becoming wise and all-knowing you became a baby. A hunched, brittle-stick baby.

She dumped the dead flowers into the red plastic bucket she carried and moved on, her eyes scanning the untidy rows of headstones for more. It was a weekly task for her: while her mother scrubbed, dusted and polished the church, Alice removed the drooping tributes left by relatives who thought those they had lost would appreciate the gesture. The flowers would be emptied into the groundsman's tip of rotting branches and leaves, there to be ritually burnt once a month. When this chore was completed, Alice would hurry back into the church and join her mother. Inside she would find fresh flowers ready to adorn the altar for the following day's Sunday services and, while her mother scrubbed, she would arrange the glass vases. Afterwards, she would dust down the benches, skimming along each row, down one, up the next, holding her breath, seeing how far she could get before her lungs exploded. Alice enjoyed the work if she could make it a game.

Once this was accomplished, and provided her mother had no other tasks for her, she would head for her favourite spot: the end of the front pew at the right-hand side of the altar.

Beneath the statue. *Her* statue.

More fading colours caught her eye and she skipped across a low mound – this one body length and not mole-built – to gather up the dying flowers. Tiny puffs of steam escaped her mouth and she told herself they were the ghosts of words that lay dead inside her, words that had never themselves escaped.

It was cold, although it was sunny. The trees were mostly bare, their naked branches seen for the twisted and tortured things they really were. Sheep, their bellies swollen with slow-stirring foetuses, grazed in the fields just beyond the stone wall surrounding the churchyard. Across the fields were heavy woods, sombre and greeny brown, uninviting; and behind the woods were low-lying hills, hills that were lost completely on misty days. Alice stared into the field, watching the sheep. She frowned, then turned away.

More flowers to collect before she could go inside where the air was not quite as biting. Cold – the church was always cold – but winter's teeth were less sharp inside the old building. She wandered through the graveyard, the tilted headstones no bother to her, the decomposed corpses hidden beneath her feet causing no concern.

The sodden leaves and branches were piled high, higher than her, and the girl had to swoop the plastic bucket back and swiftly forward for its wasted contents to reach the top. She reached for stems that fell back down and tossed them once more, satisfied only when they settled on the heap's summit. Alice smacked her hands together to dislodge the grime on her palms, feeling the sting, but not hearing the sound. She could once, but that was long ago. When she listened intently and there were no distractions, she thought she could hear the wind; but then Alice thought that even when no breeze brushed her cheeks or ruffled her yellow hair.

The small, thin girl turned and began to walk towards the ancient church, the empty bucket swinging easily by her side. Back, forwards, back, forwards, gleaming red in the cold sunlight. Back, forwards, back – and she looked behind her.

The plastic bucket slipped from her fingers and clattered to the ground, rolling in a tight semi-circle until it came to rest against a stained green headstone. Alice cocked her head to one side as though listening. There was a puzzlement in her eyes and she half-smiled.

She stood still for several seconds before allowing her body to turn fully, staying in that frozen position for several more long seconds. Her half-smile faded and her face became anxious. She moved slowly at first, making for the rough stone wall at the rear of the churchyard, then broke into a run.

Something tripped her – probably the corner of a flattened gravestone – and she tumbled forward, her knees smearing green and brown from the soft earth. She cried out, but there was no sound, and quickly regained her feet, eager to reach the wall and not knowing why. She kept to the narrow path leading through the cluttered graveyard and stopped only when she had reached the wall. Alice peered over, the highest stone on a level with her chest. The pregnant sheep were no longer munching grass; all heads were raised and looking in the same direction.

They did not move even when Alice clambered over the wall and ran among them.

Her footsteps slowed, her shoes and socks soaked by the long grass. She seemed confused and swivelled her head from left to right. Her small hands were clenched tight.

She looked directly ahead once more and the half-smile returned, gradually broadening until her face showed only rapturous wonder.

A solitary tree stood in the centre of the field, an oak, centuries old, its body thick and gnarled, its stout lower branches sweeping outwards, their furthest points striving to touch the ground again. Alice walked towards the tree, her steps slow but not hesitant, and fell to her knees when she was ten yards away.

Her mouth opened wide, and her eyes narrowed, the pupils squeezing down to tiny apertures. She raised a hand to protect them from the blinding white light that shimmered from the base of the tree.

Then her smile returned as the light dazzled into a brilliant sun, an unblemished whiteness. A holy radiance.

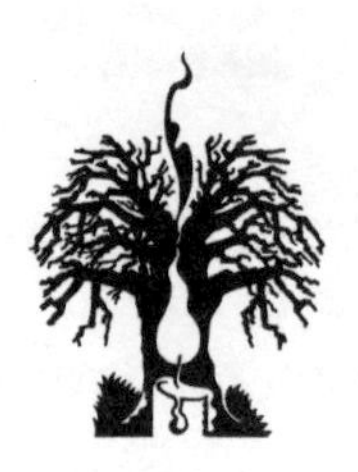

2

Another Maiden like herself,
Translucent, lovely, shining clear,
Threefold each in the other clos'd –
O, What a pleasant trembling fear!

William Blake,
'The Crystal Cabinet'

The white van slid to an abrupt halt and the driver's head came uncomfortably close to the windscreen. Cursing, he pushed himself back off the steering wheel and smacked the hardened plastic as though it were the hand of an errant child.

The van's headlights lit up the trees on the other side of the T-junction and the driver peered left and right, grumbling to himself as he tried to penetrate the surrounding darkness.

'Should be right, got to be right.'

There was no one else in the van to hear, but that didn't bother him: he was used to talking to himself. 'Right it is.'

He shoved the gear lever into first and winced at the grinding sound. The van lurched forward and he swung the wheel to the right. Gerry Fenn was tired, angry, and a little drunk. The public meeting he had attended earlier that evening had been dull to say the least, dreary to say the most. Who gave a shit whether or not the more remote houses in the locale went on to main drainage? Not the occupiers, that was for sure; a link-up with the sewage system meant higher rates for them. Nearly two hours to decide nobody wanted drains. They preferred their cesspits. As usual, Rent-a-Left had prolonged proceedings. A totalitarian sewer network was good for the cause, Fenn supposed. He hadn't intended to stay that long, hadn't even needed to. The fact was, he had fallen asleep at the back of the hall and only the noisy conclusion to the meeting had aroused him. The agitators were angry that the motion for had been defeated – good headline in that: 'LOCAL SEWER MOTION DEFEATED'. Too pithy for the *Courier*, though. Pithy. That wasn't bad either. He nodded his head in appreciation of his own wit.

Gerry Fenn had been with the *Brighton Evening Courier* for more than five years now – man and boy, he told himself – and was still waiting for the big one, the story that would make world headlines, the scoop that would transport him from the seaside town's local rag to the heart of the journalistic world: FLEET STREET! Kermit applause for FLEET STREET! YEEAAAY! Three years indenture at Eastbourne, five on the *Courier*. Next step: leader of the *Insight* team on the *Sunday Times*. Failing that, *News of the World* would do. Plenty of human interest there. Dig up the dirt, dole out the trash. File the writs.

He had phoned the newsdesk after the meeting, telling the night news editor (who hadn't been amused by Fenn's instruction to HOLD THE FRONT PAGE!) that the meeting had ended in near-riot and he had barely escaped with his vitals intact let alone his notebook. When the news editor had informed him that the office junior had just resigned because of an emotional crisis in his sixteen-year-old life, so the vacancy was available, Fenn had modified his story, explaining that the meeting really had been lively and maybe he should have left sooner but when the wild-eyed Leftie had rushed the platform and tried to stuff a turd (it looked like a dog's, obviously just used for effect) into the nostrils of a surprised lady councillor, he figured . . . Fenn held the phone away, almost seeing the spit spluttering from the earpiece. Excited pips brought the tirade to an end, and a fresh coin renewed the connection. The news editor had gained control by then, but only just. Since Fenn enjoyed the country route so much, there were a couple of little items he could cover in that area. Fenn groaned; the news editor went on. A trip to the local cop shop: find out if the boy scout impersonators (bob-a-job, once inside, pension books, loose money, small valuables, gone) were still impersonating boy scouts. Pop into the local flea-pit: were feminists still daubing the sexy posters outside with anti-rape graffiti and chucking runny tomatoes at the screen inside? On the way back, visit the caravan site at Partridge Green: see if they've got their power yet (the *Courier* had run a small campaign for the residents encouraging Seeboard to connect the site to the grid – so far it had taken six months). Fenn asked if the news editor knew what the bloody time was and was assured of course he bloody did and was Fenn aware that all his night shift had produced for tomorrow's editions was one RTA (Road Traffic Accident) and one diabetic poodle who went for check-ups in a bloody Rolls-Royce? And the RTA wasn't even fatal.

Fenn got mad and advised the news editor of his agitated state and informed him that when he returned to the office he would show the news editor just how mad he really was by shoving his copy spike right up his tiny arse, wooden end first, and by stuffing the nearest typewriter into the fat mouth which was always full of shit but never kind shit, then brain-drain the *Courier* totally by handing in his resignation. He told the news editor good, but made sure the receiver was resting on its cradle before he did so.

His next call was to Sue to tell her to expect him when he got there, but there was no reply from his flat. Then none from hers. He wished for Chrissakes she would move in with him permanently; it was a pain never knowing where she was likely to be.

Thoroughly morose, he did what he was paid for. The boy scout impersonators were now impersonating jumble-sale collectors (one old lady had even lost her false teeth – she'd left them on the kitchen table – but was understandably reluctant to talk about it). The flea-pit had been running *Bambi* for the past fortnight (expected trouble next week when *Teenage Goddesses of Love* and *Sex in the Swamps* were playing). He drove to Partridge Green and saw only candlelight through the caravan windows (he knocked on one door and was told to piss off so didn't bother with any more).

He scraped in to the nearest pub just five minutes before closing time and fortunately the landlord wasn't adverse to afters once the main crowd – two domino players and a woman with a cat in a wooden cage – was cleared. Fenn let it slip that he was from the *Brighton Evening Courier*, an admission that could have got him shown the door pretty promptly, or engaged in an informative after-hours drink. Landlords generally sought the good will of the local press (even the most drab were contenders for the Pub of the Year Award) unless they had some private reason for feeling bitter towards journalists (exposed marital upsets, too many voluptuous barmaids in the business, or reported unhygienic kitchens was usually the cause for their distrust). This one was okay, he even allowed Fenn to buy him a rum and pep, a gesture that had the reporter mentally scratching his head –

shouldn't the landlord be cosying up to him, not the other way round? He wasn't into investigative journalism tonight – Fleet Street and the world's wire services would have to wait until he was in the mood – so why the hell was he treating the landlord? Oh yeah, so he could drink after time, that was it. Fenn was tired.

Three pints and forty minutes of unexciting conversation later, Fenn found himself outside in the cold night air, bolts snapping behind telling him the drawbridge was up, the public house was no longer a refuge but a stronghold, built to resist the strongest invaders. He kicked the side of the white van before throwing himself into the driver's seat.

The vehicle was an embarrassment. It carried his newspaper's name, white lettering in a brilliant red flash, on both sides. Very discreet. Very undercover. The *Courier* had fallen out with their usual fleet hire company and now the journalists had either to use their own cars, for which there was no petrol allowance, or the one and only spare delivery van. Great for tailing suspected arsonists or dope peddlers. Great for keeping an eye on illicit rendezvous between well-knowns who should well-know better. Ideal for secret meetings with your favourite grass. Would Woodstock and Bernstein have met 'Deep Throat' in a fucking white van with *Washington Post* emblazoned on its sides?

The headlights barely pierced the darkness ahead and Fenn shook his head in further disgust. Bloody things were never cleaned. Christ, what a night. Sometimes the late shift could be good. A nice rape or mugging. The occasional murder. Brighton was full of weirdos nowadays. And Arabs. And antique dealers. Funny things happened when they all got together. Trouble was, many of the best stories never got into print. Or if they did, they were toned down. It wasn't the *Courier*'s policy to denigrate the seaside town's image. Bad for business. Great for family trade, Brighton. Mustn't scare off the punters. Unfortunately his earlier routine calls had produced nothing of interest. He always made the standard calls when he came on duty: police, hospitals, undertakers and fire stations were all on his regular list. Even the clergy merited a bell. Nothing much doing with any of them. The newspaper's *Diary*, listing events of the day (and night) which had to be covered, offered little to excite. If it had, he could have probably ducked out of tonight's council meeting; as it was, there wasn't much else to do.

Lights ahead. What town was that? Must be Banfield. He'd passed it on the way out. Not a bad little place. Two pubs on the High Street. What more could anyone ask? If the weather was nice on Sunday he might bring Sue out for a drink. She liked country pubs. More atmosphere. Real ale. Usually a fair selection of gumboots, polonecks, and tweeds. With the odd diddicoi thrown in to lower the tone.

He squinted his eyes. Bend ahead. So bloody dark. Whoops. Brake. Downhill.

The van levelled out at the bottom of the hill and Fenn eased his foot off the pedal. Sure these brakes are going, he told himself. Sometimes he suspected the delivery men sabotaged the vehicle as a mild protest against it being used by journalists. One day, someone was – *Christ, what was that*?

He jammed his foot down and pulled the wheel to the left. The van skidded, turning almost a full circle, front end coming to rest on the grass verge by the side of the road.

Fenn pushed the gear into neutral and briefly rested against the steering wheel. A sharp, quavering sigh later, his head jerked up and he swiftly wound down the window. He poked his head out into the cold night air.

'What the bloody hell was it?' he asked himself aloud.

Something had run out from the darkness straight across

his path. Something white. Small, but too big to be an animal. He'd almost hit it. Missed by a couple of inches. His hands were trembling.

He saw movement, a greyish blur.

'Hey!' he shouted.

The blur dissolved.

Fenn pushed the car door open and stepped out onto the damp grass. 'Hold up!' he called out.

Scuffling sounds came his way. Feet on gravel.

He ran across the road and was confronted by a low gate, one side open wide. His eyes were swiftly adapting to the poor light, and the half-moon emerging from slow-moving clouds helped his vision even more. He saw the tiny figure again.

It was running away from him along a path that was lined with trees. He could just make out some kind of building at the end of the path. He shivered. The whole thing was spooky.

It had to be a kid. Or a midget. Fenn tried not to think of Du Maurier's dwarf in *Don't Look Now*. He wanted to get back into the van. His jiggling sphincter muscle could lead to an embarrassment. But if it was a kid, what was it doing out at this hour? It would freeze to death in this weather.

'Hey, come on, stop! I want to talk to you!'

No reply, just slapping feet.

Fenn stepped inside the gate, called out once more, then began to run after the diminishing shape. As he pounded down the path and the building ahead grew larger and more visible, he realized he was in the grounds of a church. What was a kid running into a church for at this time of night?

But the figure, still just in sight, wasn't going to the church. It veered off to the left just as it reached the big cavern doors and disappeared around the corner of the building. Fenn followed, his breath becoming laboured. He almost slipped, for the path was muddy now, and narrower. He recovered and kept going until he reached the back of the church. There he came to an abrupt halt and wished he'd stayed in the van.

A dark playground of silent, still, greyish shapes spread out before him. Oh, Jesus, a graveyard!

The blur was skipping among them, the only moving thing.

The moon decided it had had enough. It pulled a cloud over its eyes like a blanket.

Fenn leaned against the side of the church, its flint brick-work rough against his moist hands. He was following a bloody ghost. It would roll into a grave at any moment. His instinct was to tiptoe quietly back to the van and go on his uninquisitive way, but his nose which, after all, was a news-paperman's nose, persuaded otherwise. There are no such things as ghosts, only good ghost stories. Walk away from this and you'll always wonder what you missed. Tell your friends (not to mention your pal the editor) you flunked out and they'll never buy you another drink. Go to it, Ace. His nose told him, not his brain, nor his heart.

'Hey!' The shout cracked in the middle and the H was over-pronounced.

He pushed himself away from the wall and strode boldly in among the grey sentinels. He blinked hard when he saw the conical-shaped mounds of dark earth at his feet. *They're making a break for it!*

He forced the explanation from himself. They're molehills, you silly bastard. His weak smile of self-contempt was per-functory. Fenn caught sight of the wispy figure flitting through the gravestones once more. It appeared to be making its way towards the back of the churchyard where large squarish shapes seemed to be lurking. Oh my God, they're tombs! It's a vampire, a midget vampire, going home to bed! Fenn didn't find himself too amusing.

He crouched, suddenly afraid to be seen. The moon was no friend; it came out for another peep.

Fenn ducked behind a tilting headstone and cautiously peered over the top. The figure was clambering over a low wall. Then it was gone.

Cold night air touched his face and he imagined lonely souls were trying to gain his attention. He didn't want to move, and he didn't want to stay. He didn't want to look over that wall either. But he knew he was going to.

The reporter crept forward, his knee joints already stiff from the cold. Dodging around the graves, doing his best not to disturb the 'not-dead-but-resting', he made for the back of the churchyard, towards the tombs standing like ancient, cracked supermarket freezers, their contents allowed to putrefy. He noticed the lid of one was askew and tried not to see the imaginary hand clawing its way out, skin green with age, nails scraped away, bones glistening through corrupt flesh. Cut it out, Fenn!

He reached the wall and knelt there, not overly-anxious to see what lay beyond. He was shivering, out of breath (kept forgetting to breathe in) and scared stiff. But he was also curious. Fenn raised himself so that his shoulders were level with the top of the wall, head projecting like a coconut waiting to be shied.

There was a field, slate grey and flat in the timid moonlight, and near the middle, some distance away, stood a contorted black spectre. Its multitudinous twisted arms reached skywards while the thicker lower limbs were bent in an effort to reach the ground from which it had sprung. The isolated tree provided a demonic relief in an otherwise dull landscape. Fenn's eyes narrowed as he searched for the little figure. Something was moving. Yes, there it was. Walking directly towards the tree. It stopped. Then walked on. Then – oh Christ, it was sinking into the ground! No, it was on its knees. It didn't move. Nor did the tree.

Fenn waited and grew impatient. The beer he had consumed pressed against his bladder. He continued to wait.

At last he decided if he didn't make something happen, nothing would happen. He climbed over the wall and waited.

Nothing happened.

He walked towards the figure.

As he drew near, he saw that it wasn't a midget.

It was a girl.

A little girl.

And she was staring at the tree.

And she was smiling.

And when he touched her shoulder, she said, 'She's so beautiful.'

Then her eyes rolled upwards and she toppled forward.

And didn't move again.

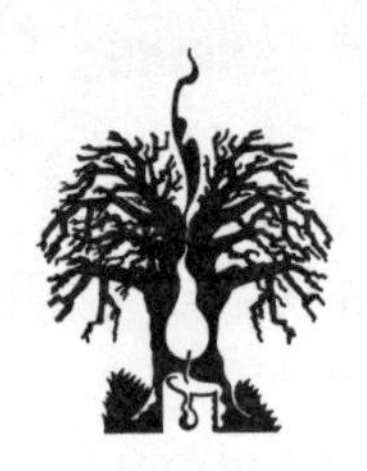

3

'Who are you?' he said at last in a half-hearted whisper. 'Are you a ghost?'

'No, I am not,' Mary answered, her own whisper half-frightened. 'Are you one?'

Frances Hodgson Burnett, *The Secret Garden*

Father Hagan lay there in the darkness, forcing his senses to break away from sleep's gooey embrace. His eyes flickered, then snapped open. He could just make out the thin glimmer of night through the almost closed curtains. What had disturbed him?

The priest reached for the lamp on the bedside table and fumbled for the switch. His pupils stung with the sudden light, and it was several seconds before he could open his lids again. He looked at the small clock, his eyes narrowing to a short-sighted squint, and saw it was past midnight. Had he heard something outside? Or inside the house? Or had his own dream disturbed him? He lay back and stared at the ceiling.

Father Andrew Hagan was forty-six years old and had been part of the Church for nearly nineteen of those years. The turning point for him had been two days after his twenty-seventh birthday when a mild heart attack had left him dazed, frightened and exhausted. He had been losing God, allowing the materialism of a chaotic world to confine his spiritual self, to subdue it to a point where only he was aware that it existed. Four years teaching History and Divinity in a Catholic grammar school in London, then three years in a madhouse comprehensive in the suburbs had slowly corroded the outer core of his faith and was chewing on the innermost part, the very centre of his belief which had no answers but merely KNEW. He had to retrieve himself. The closeness of death was like a prodding mother who would not allow her offspring to stay under the bedclothes for one moment longer.

He no longer taught Divinity in the comprehensive school, just History, and occasionally he took an English class; religion in that particular school was almost defunct. Humanity had replaced the subject and the young teacher of Humanity had been sacked in his second term for blacking the headmaster's eye. English had soon become Hagan's second subject. No longer able to discuss his faith every day with curious, albeit often bored, young minds, his thoughts of God had become more and more introverted, restrained by shackles of self-consciousness. The heart attack, mild though it was, had halted the gradual but seemingly irrevocable slide. Suddenly he was aware of what he had been losing. He wanted to be among others who believed as he, for their belief would strengthen his, their faith would enhance his own. Within a year he was in Rome studying for the priesthood. And now he wondered if the earlier corrosion had not left a seeping residue.

A noise. Outside. Movement. Father Hagan sat upright.

He jumped when someone pounded on the door below.

The priest reached for his spectacles lying on the bedside

table and leapt from the bed; he went to the window. He drew the curtains apart, but hesitated before opening the window. More banging encouraged him to do so.

'Who's there?' Cold air settled around his shoulders and made him shudder.

'Just us spooks!' came the reply. 'Will you get down here and open up!'

Hagan leaned out the window and tried to see into the porch below. A figure stepped into view, but was indistinct.

'I've got a problem – *you've* got a problem – here!' the voice said. The man appeared to be carrying something in his arms.

The priest withdrew and quickly pulled on a dressing gown over his pyjamas. He forgot about slippers and padded downstairs in cold, bare feet. Switching on the hall light, he stood behind the front door for a few moments, reluctant to open it. Although the village was close, his church and presbytery were isolated. Fields and woods surrounded him on three sides, the main road at the front being the link with his parishioners. Father Hagan was not a timorous man, but living over a graveyard had to have some effect. A fist thumping against wood aroused him once more.

He switched on the outside porch light before opening the door.

The man who stood there looked frightened, although he was making an attempt to grin. His face was drawn, white. 'Found this wandering around outside,' the man explained.

He moved the bundle in his arms towards the priest, indicating with a nod of his head at the same time. Hagan recognized the frail little body in the nightdress without seeing her face.

'Bring her in quickly,' he said, making way.

He closed the front door and told the man to follow him.

He turned on the sitting-room light and made for the electric fire, switching it on.

'Put her on the settee,' he said. 'I'll fetch a blanket. She must be frozen.'

The man grunted as he placed the girl on the soft cushions. He knelt beside her and brushed her long yellow hair away from her face. The priest returned and carefully wrapped a blanket around the still form. Father Hagan studied the girl's peaceful face for several moments before turning back to the man who had brought her to his house.

'Tell me what happened,' he said.

The man shrugged. He was in his late twenties or early thirties, needed a shave, and wore a heavy thigh-length corduroy jacket, its collar turned up against the cold, over dark blue trousers or jeans. His light brown hair was a tangled mess, but not too long. 'She ran across my path – I just braked in time. Thought I was going to hit her.' He paused to look down at the girl. 'Is she asleep?'

The priest lifted one of her eyelids. The pupil gazed back at him without flinching. 'I don't think so. She seems to be . . .' He left the sentence unfinished.

'She didn't stop when I called out to her, so I followed her,' the man went on. 'She ran straight up to the church, then round the back. Into the graveyard out there. It scared the bloody hell out of me.' He shook his head and shrugged again as if to relieve tension. 'Any idea who she is?'

'Her name is Alice,' the priest said quietly.

'Why did she run in here? Where's she from?'

Father Hagan ignored his questions. 'Did she . . . did she climb over the wall at the back of the churchyard?'

The man nodded. 'Uh huh. She ran into the field. How did you know?'

'Tell me exactly what happened.'

The man looked around. 'D'you mind if I sit down for a minute – my legs are kind of shaky.'

'I'm sorry. You must have had a nasty shock, her running out at you like that.'

'It was the bloody graveyard that shook me up.' He sank gratefully into an armchair and let out a long sigh. Then his face became alert again. 'Look, hadn't you better get a doctor? The kid looks done in.'

'Yes, I'll call one soon. First tell me what happened when she went into the field.'

The man looked puzzled. 'Are you her father?' he asked, keen blue eyes looking directly into the priest's.

'I'm a father, but not hers. The church is Catholic, I'm its priest, Father Hagan.'

The man opened his mouth, then nodded in understanding. 'Of course,' he said, managing a brief grin. 'I should've known.'

'And you're Mister . . .?'

'Gerry Fenn.' He decided not to tell the priest that he was from the *Courier* for the moment. 'You live here alone?'

'I have a housekeeper who comes in during the day. Otherwise, yes, I live here alone.'

'Creepy.'

'You were going to tell me . . .'

'Oh yeah. The field. Well, that was weird. I followed her in and found her just kneeling in the grass. She wasn't even shivering, just staring ahead, smiling.'

'Smiling?'

'Yeah, she had a big beam on her face. Like she was watching something, you know? Something that was pleasing her. But all she was looking at was a big old tree.'

'The oak.'

'Hmn? Yeah, I think so. It was too dark to see.'

'The oak is the only tree in that field.'

'Then I guess it was the oak.'

'What happened?'

'Then came the strange part. Well, it was all bloody – sorry, Father – it was all strange, but this was the ringer. I thought she might have been sleep-walking – or sleep-running to be more precise – so I touched her shoulder. Just gentle, you know? I didn't want to frighten her. She just went on smiling and said, "She's so beautiful," like she could see something there by the tree.'

The priest had stiffened and was looking at Fenn so intently that the reporter stopped speaking. He raised his eyebrows. 'Something I said?' he asked.

'You said the girl spoke. Alice spoke to you?'

Fenn was puzzled by the priest's attitude. He shuffled uncomfortably in the seat. 'She didn't actually speak to me. More like to herself. Is there something wrong, Father?'

The priest looked down at the girl and gently brushed her cheek with the palm of his hand. 'Alice is a deaf mute, Mr Fenn. She cannot speak, and she cannot hear.'

Fenn's gaze turned from the priest's face to the girl's. She lay there pale, unmoving, a rumpled frail figure, small and so very vulnerable.

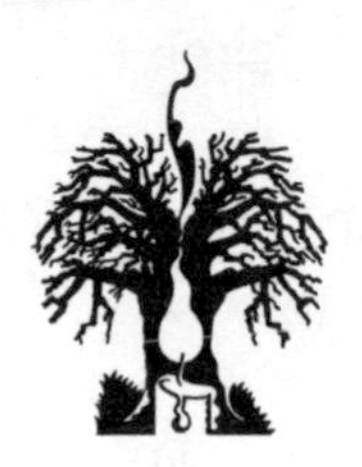

4

'But I don't want to go among mad people,' Alice remarked.

'Oh, you can't help that,' said the Cat: 'We're all mad here.

I'm mad. You're mad.'

Lewis Carroll, *Alice's Adventures in Wonderland*

A hand lightly cuffed Fenn's shoulder.

'Hi, Gerry. Thought you had the graveyard shift this week.'

He glanced up to see Morris, one of the *Courier*'s thirteen sub-editors, moving past him, his body half-turned in Fenn's direction but his stride hardly broken as he made for his desk.

'What? Yeah, you don't know the truth of it,' Fenn answered without elaborating. He turned his attention back to the typewriter, quickly reading through the last line he had just two-finger typed. He grunted in satisfaction and his index fingers rapidly stabbed at the machine once more. He ignored the apparent chaos around him: the clatter of other overused and badly-kept typewriters, the occasional curse or even less occasional burst of raucous laughter, the hum of voices, machines and odours. The hubbub would grow steadily through the day, building to a restrained frenzy which broke without fuss when the evening edition was finally put to bed at 3.45 p.m. Every trainee reporter soon learned the art of closing out the din, their thoughts, hands and black type on paper spinning their own frail cocoon of insularity.

Fenn's right index finger punched a last full-point and he ripped the paper with its three blacks from the machine. He read through it quickly, his smile turning into a broad grin. Shit-hot. Figure appearing like a white banshee in the night. Running out in front of the van. Chasing the apparition. Through the graveyard (could be a little bit more creepy, but let's not overkill). The girl kneeling in the field, staring at the tree. She's small, dressed in white nightgown. Alone. She speaks. Our intrepid reporter later finds out that she is – or was – a deaf mute. Terrific!

Fenn marched between crammed desks, his gleaming eyes on the news editor. He stood over the hunched figure and resisted the urge to tap a finger on the enticing bald dome before him.

'Leave it there, I'll get to it,' the news editor growled.

'I think you ought to read it, Frank.'

Frank Aitken looked up. 'I thought you were on the midnight shift, Hemingway.'

'Yeah, I am. Just a little special for you.' Fenn jiggled the copy in his hand.

'Show it to the sub.' The bald man returned to his pencilling out.

'Uh, just look through it, Frank. I think you'll like the story.'

Aitken wearily laid the pencil down and studied Fenn's smiling face for several moments. 'Tucker tells me you didn't produce last night.' Tucker was the night newsdesk editor.

'I came in with a couple of things, Frank, but not much happened last night. Except for this.'

The copy was snatched from him.

Fenn stuck his hands into his pockets and waited impatiently while Aitken skimmed through the story. He whistled an almost soundless, self-satisfied tune. Aitken didn't look up until he had read every word and when he did there was a look of disbelief on his face.

'What is this shit?' he said.

The grin disappeared from Fenn's face. 'Hey, did you like it or not?'

'You've got to be kidding.'

Fenn leaned on the news editor's desk, his face anxious, his voice beginning to rise. 'It's all true, Frank.' He stabbed at the paper. 'That actually happened to me last night!'

'So what?' Aitken tossed the typed sheet across the desk. 'What's it prove? The kid had a nightmare, went sleepwalking. So what? It's no big deal.'

'But she was deaf and dumb and she spoke to me.'

'Did she say anything to anyone else? I mean, after, when you took her into the priest's house?'

'No, but—'

'When the doctor got there? Did she say anything to him?'

'No—'

'Her parents?'

Fenn stood up straight. 'The quack brought her round to examine her while the priest fetched her parents. By the time they got there, the kid was asleep again. The doctor told them there was nothing wrong with her – slight temperature, that was all.'

The news editor leaned his elbows on the desk and said with belaboured patience: 'Okay, so she spoke to you. Three words, wasn't it? Were those words normal or slurred?'

'What d'you mean?'

'I mean if the kid was a deaf mute, she wouldn't know how to pronounce words too well. They'd be distorted if not incomprehensible, because she would never have heard them spoken before.'

'They were perfect. But she hadn't always been a deaf mute. The priest told me she'd only been that way since she was four years old.'

'And she's what now?' Aitken looked at the typed copy. 'Eleven? Seven years is a long time, Gerry.'

'But I know what I heard,' Fenn insisted.

'It was pretty late, you'd had a shock.' The news editor looked at him suspiciously. 'And probably a drink or two.'

'Not enough to make me hear things.'

'Yeah, yeah, so *you* say.'

'It's gospel!'

'So what d'you want me to do with it?' He held up the copy.

Fenn looked surprised. 'Print it.'

'Get outa here.' Aitken screwed the sheet of paper into a ball and dropped it into a bin by his feet.

The reporter opened his mouth to protest, but Aitken raised a hand.

'Listen, Gerry. There's no story. You're big and ugly enough to understand that. All we have is your say-so that the girl, after seven years of being deaf and dumb, spoke. Three words, kiddo, three fucking words, and nobody else heard them. Only you. Our star reporter, well-known for his vivid imagination, renowned for his satire on local council meetings . . .'

'Ah, Frank, that was just a joke.'

'A joke? Oh yeah, there's been a few little jokes in the past. The hang-glider who loved to jump off the Downs and float around stark naked.'

'I didn't know he was wearing a skin-tight pink outfit. It looked pretty realistic to . . .'

'Yeah, so did the photograph. The police weren't too happy when they tore around the countryside waiting for him to land the next time he was spotted.'

'It was an easy mistake to make.'

'Sure. Like the poltergeists of Kemptown?'

'Christ, I didn't know that old lady had a neurotic cat.'

'Because you didn't bother to check, Gerry, that's why. The clairvoyant we hired sold his story to the *Argus*. And you can't blame them for going to town on the joke – they're our biggest bloody rivals.'

Certain reporters in the near vicinity had grins on their faces, although none looked up from their typewriters.

'There's more, but I don't have time to go through the list.' Aitken picked up his pencil and pointed it in the general direction of the office windows. 'Now will you get out there and come back when your shift begins.' He hunched down to his pencilling and his shiny bald pate defied Fenn to argue.

'Can I follow it up?'

'Not on the *Courier*'s time,' came the brusque reply.

For the benefit of his eavesdropping colleagues, Fenn waggled his tongue in the air and tweaked his ears at the preoccupied editor, then turned and walked back scowling to his desk. Jesus, Aitken wouldn't recognise a good story if it walked up to him and spat in his eye. The girl had spoken. After seven years of silence, she'd said three words! He slumped into his seat. Three words. But what had she meant? Who was beautiful? He chewed his lip and stared unseeingly at his typewriter.

After a while he shrugged his shoulders and reached for his phone. He dialled the local radio station's number and asked for Sue Gates.

'Where the hell were you last night?' he said as soon as she came on.

'Get off it, Gerry. We've got no fixed arrangement.'

'Okay, but you could have let me know.'

He heard the long sigh. 'Okay, okay,' he said quickly. 'Can you make lunch?'

'Of course. Where?'

'Your place.'

'Uh uh.' Negative. 'I've got work to do this afternoon. It'll have to be a short lunch.'

'The Stag, then. In ten minutes?'

'Make it twenty.'

'Deal. See you there.'

He rang off, thought for a few moments, and went to the office telephone directory. He flicked through the pages, then ran a finger down a list of names, stopping when he found the number he was looking for. He soundlessly repeated it as he hurried back to his desk, where he dialled. No reply. He tried again. No reply. The priest must be out on his rounds or whatever priests did during the day. Housekeeper wasn't there either. St Joseph's seemed like a lonely place.

Fenn stood and pulled his jacket from the back of his chair, glancing towards the windows which ran along the whole length of the large office. It was a sunny day of a mild winter. He made for the door and almost bumped into the sports editor coming in.

'How goes it, Ace?' the editor said cheerily and was surprised at the low-growled response.

Sue Gates was late but, he had to admit, she was worth waiting for. At thirty-three, four years older than Fenn, she still had the trim figure of a girl in her twenties. Her dark hair was long, fluffed away from her face in loose curls, and her deep brown eyes could gain a man's attention across any crowded room on any enchanted evening. She was wearing tight jeans, loose sweater and a short, navy blue seaman's topcoat. She waved when she saw him and pushed her way through the crowded bar. He stood and kissed her when she reached him, relishing her lips' moist softness.

'Hi kid,' he said lightly, enjoying the spreading glow which swiftly ran through him and came to rest around the region of his groin.

'Hi, yourself,' she said, squeezing into the seat next to him. He pushed the already ordered lager in front of her and she reached for it gratefully, taking a long appreciative swallow.

'You eating today?' Fenn asked her. Sue often went a couple of days without touching a scrap of food.

She shook her head. 'I'll catch something tonight.'

'Going fishing?'

'Idiot.'

He popped the last of his cheese and pickle into his mouth and grinned through bulging cheeks.

Placing a hand over his she said, 'Sorry I missed you last night.'

Fenn had to gulp down the food before he could reply. 'I'm sorry I was ratty on the phone,' he counter-apologized.

'Forget it. I did ring the *Courier*, by the way, just to let you know I wouldn't be there. They told me you were out on an assignment.'

'I rang your place, too.'

'I was out . . .'

'I know.'

'Reg took me to dinner.'

'Oh, yeah.' His voice was casual. 'Good old Reg.'

'Hey, come on. Reg is my boss – you know there's nothing in it.'

'Course I know. Does Reg?'

Sue laughed. 'He's as thin as a drainpipe, wears glasses that look like the ends of milk bottles, is losing his hair and has a disgusting habit of picking his nose with his little finger.'

'It's the last bit that makes him irresistible.'

'On top of that he's married with three kids.'

'I told you he was irresistible.' Fenn drained his glass. 'I'll get you another while I'm up there.'

'No, let me get you one,' she insisted. 'You can reflect on what a wimp you're being while I'm at the bar.' She reached for his glass. 'Another bitter?'

'Bloody Mary,' he said smugly.

He watched her weave through the crowd to the bar and told himself how much he admired her independence – he'd told himself, and her, many times – and wished he was convinced of his own admiration. Sue had been married and divorced before she was twenty-six, her ex being an advertising man in London – high-powered, high-living, hi, girls! – something on the creative side of the business. After just one-too-many indiscretions on his part, Sue had sought a divorce. She'd had a good position with a film production company – she and her husband had met when her company was hired to make a TV commercial for his agency – but after her divorce came through, she decided she had had enough of advertising people, enough of London, and enough of men.

The big problem was that the marriage had produced a child, a son named Ben. He had been the reason for moving down to the south coast. Her parents lived in Hove, which was the other half (some said the better half) of Brighton, and they had agreed to become semi-permanent baby minders. Ben stayed with his grandparents most of the time, but Sue made sure they got together nearly every day and he moved in with her on most weekends. Fenn knew that she missed having the boy around all of the time, but she had to make a living (her fierce independence meant refusal of any maintenance, even for Ben, from the errant husband. Half the money from the sale of their Islington house was all she had demanded). She managed to get herself a job with Radio Brighton and had soon become a producer. But it took up a lot of her time and she was seeing less and less of Ben, which worried her. And she was seeing too much of Fenn, which worried her almost as much. She hadn't wanted to become entangled with another man; casual acquaintanceships were all she would allow, necessary only for those odd times when a weak body needed something more than a pillow to cling to. Those odd times had become more frequent since she had met Fenn.

He had urged her to give up her flat, to move in with him. It was ridiculous that they should feel so close and live so far apart (three blocks away, to be precise). But she had resisted, and still did; Sue had vowed never to become totally dependent on one single person again. Ever. Sometimes, and secretly, it was a relief to Fenn, for it gave him his own independence. Guilt hit him occasionally (the bargain seemed to be *too* much in his favour) but when voiced, she always assured him that the boot was on the other foot and it was she who was getting the better deal. A man to lean on when the going got rough, a body to comfort her when the nights were lonely, and a friend to have fun with when things were going right. A shoulder to cry on, a lover to spy on, and a wallet to rely on. And solitude when it was needed most.

What more could any woman ask for? Plenty, Fenn thought, but he wasn't going to prompt her.

She was back, handing him the thick red cocktail with an expression of mild disapproval on her face. He sipped the Bloody Mary and winced: Sue had told the barman to go *heavy* on the Tabasco. He noticed she was trying hard not to smirk.

'What are you doing here today, Woodstein?' she asked. 'I thought you'd still be tucked up in bed after your late shift.'

'I ran into a good story last night. Well, it kind of ran into me. I thought it might make the late edition but the Ayatollah had other ideas.'

'Aitken didn't like it?'

Fenn shook his head. 'Like it? He didn't even believe it.'

'Try me. I know you only lie when it's to your advantage.'

He briefly told her what had happened the previous night, and she smiled at the excitement that gradually began to blaze in his eyes as the story went on. At one point, when he was describing how he'd found the little girl kneeling in the field, cold fingers had touched her spine, making her shiver. Fenn went on to tell her about the priest, the doctor, then the arrival of the distraught parents.

'How old was the girl?' Sue asked.

'The priest said eleven. She looked younger to me.'

'And she was just staring at the tree?'

'She was just staring *towards* it. I got the impression she was looking at something else.'

'Something else?'

'Yeah, it's kind of hard to explain. She was smiling, you know, like something was making her very happy. Rapturous, almost. It was as if she were seeing a vision.'

'Oh, Gerry . . .'

'No, that's it! That's just what it was like. The kid was seeing a vision.'

'She was having a dream, Gerry. Don't exaggerate the whole thing.'

'How d'you explain her talking to me then?'

'Maybe you were dreaming too.'

'Ah, Sue. . . . Come on, I'm being serious.'

She laughed and linked his arm. 'I'm sorry, lover, but you get so het up when you think you're sniffing out a good story.'

He grunted. 'Maybe you're right. Maybe I did imagine that part of it. The strange thing was, I got the impression it wasn't the first time. When the girl's parents arrived, I heard the mother mumble something about Alice – that's the kid's name – going to the same place before. The priest nodded, but his eyes seemed to be warning her not to say too much in front of me. It was all kinda cagey.'

'Did he know you were a reporter?'

Fenn shook his head. 'He didn't ask, so I didn't tell him.' He sipped his drink thoughtfully. 'He wanted me out of the way, though. Couldn't wait to get rid of me once the mother and father got there. I pretended to be more shaken up than I really was, so he let me rest a while. Then, just before the parents took Alice away, he went through some ritual with her. Mumbled something or other and made the sign of the cross.'

'He blessed her?'

He looked at Sue quizzically. 'If you say so.'

'No. That's what you're saying. He must have blessed her.'

'Why would he do that?'

'A priest will bless a house, a holy medal, a statue. Even your car if you ask him nicely. Why not a child?'

'Yeah, why not? Hey, how do you know all that?'

'I'm a Catholic – at least I used to be. I'm not sure if I still am; the Catholic Church doesn't actually approve of divorce.'

'You never told me.'

'It was never important. I don't go to church any more, only at Christmas, and that's mainly for Ben's sake. He likes the ceremony.'

Fenn nodded knowingly. 'So that's why you're so wild in bed.'

'Creep.'

'Uh huh. That's why you're into flagellation!'

'Will you stop. The day I let you beat me—'

'Yeah, that's why I have to undress in the dark . . .'

She groaned and pinched his thigh under the table. Fenn yelped, almost spilling his drink. 'Okay, okay, I lied, you're normal. It's a pity, but it's the truth.'

'Just you remember it.'

He squeezed her thigh in return, but his touch was gentle as well as higher and further in. 'You're saying, then, that it would have been standard practice for him to bless the girl?'

'Oh, no, it sounds unusual to me under those circumstances. But not especially so. It may have been to reassure the parents more than anything else.'

'Yeah, could be.'

Sue studied his profile, and was aware that she loved him some days more than others. Today was a more day. She remembered when they had first met, over three years ago. It was at a party given by the radio station for one of their announcers, who was leaving to join the mother ship, Great Auntie BBC, in London. Some of the friendlier Press had been invited; Gerry Fenn was considered aggressive but friendly enough.

'You look familiar,' she had told him when he skilfully got

around to introducing himself. She had caught him looking her way several times before he edged his way round the room so that he could deliberately bump into her.

'Yeah?' he had said, eyebrows raised.

'Yes, you remind me of an actor . . .'

'Right. Who?' He was grinning broadly.

'Oh, what's his name. Richard . . .'

'Eastwood. Richard Eastwood?'

'No, no. He was in that space thing . . .'

'Richard Redford?'

'No, silly.'

'Richard Newman?'

'Dreyfuss, that's who. Richard Dreyfuss.'

His smile disappeared and his lips formed an O. 'Oh, yeah. Him.' He beamed again. 'Yeah, he's okay.'

They had talked, and he had made her laugh with his swift changes of mood, his sudden intensity broken by a wicked grin that would leave her wondering if he were not joking when he looked so serious. That was three years ago and she was still never sure.

He turned to face her, that same wicked grin on his face. 'You busy this weekend?'

'Not especially. I'll be seeing Ben, of course.'

'Could you keep Sunday morning free?'

'Sure. Any particular reason?'

His grin broadened.

'How would you like to go to Mass with me on Sunday?'

5

'Well I don't,' said the mother. 'I've got forebodings like there was going to be an almighty thunder-storm.'

The Brothers Grimm, 'The Juniper Tree'

Molly Pagett listened from the bottom of the stairs. It was a small, red-brick house, identical to all the others on Banfield's council estate, and movement in any of its rooms could be clearly heard from the bottom of the stairs. The familiar *bip bip* of Alice's Galaxy Invader came to her ears; her daughter spent hours playing the battery-operated game, shooting down the descending green aliens with an unerring skill that both baffled and impressed Molly. She went into the kitchen and filled the kettle.

At least Alice had put away her crayons for a while.

Molly sat at the fold-away table, her face, already thin, even more gaunt because of the increased anxieties of the past two weeks. Alice had been a constant source of concern for Molly Pagett since the usual children's illness at four years of age had left her daughter its unusual legacy; the effects of mumps had turned Alice into a deaf mute. Molly drummed her fingers on the table and resisted the urge to light a cigarette. Five-a-day was her maximum: one first thing in the morning, one halfway through the morning, one just before Len, her husband, arrived back from work, and two later in the evening while watching telly. Five-a-day was the most she could afford, but sometimes she smoked ten. Other times she smoked twenty. It depended on Len. He could be such a bastard.

Molly quickly crossed herself, an appeasement to God for the profanity, but not for the thought; that was well-founded.

Her frown increased when she remembered the night before. The priest had frightened her and Len, knocking on their door in the middle of the night, then standing in their hallway, his face white and anxious, a black-garbed messenger of bad tidings. Nonsense, she'd told him when he said Alice was up at the presbytery, a doctor taking care of her. Alice is safe in bed, Molly had insisted. She's been there since seven. Wanted to go up early because she was feeling tired.

Father Hagan had just shaken his head and urged them to get dressed and come with him; but Molly had run into Alice's room, knowing the priest wouldn't lie, just sure he was making a mistake. Her bed had been empty, covers thrown back, her doll hanging halfway out of the bed staring lifelessly at the floor. Len and the priest had followed and it was Father Hagan, not her husband, who tried to calm her. Alice was all right as far as the doctor could tell. She had probably been sleep-walking, that was all.

All the way to the bloody church? Len had asked, not caring that he was talking to a priest.

Father Hagan had told them to find warm clothing for their daughter; she was only wearing a thin nightie. By the time they had both hurriedly dressed, Len's mood had turned into one of anger for, being an atheist, he kept clear of churches (although he enjoyed the occasional funeral, which he regarded as a social event) and to be dragged out to one in the middle of the night – and a bloody cold night, too! – was not much to his liking.

Alice had looked so pale when they arrived there. Even Len stopped his sullen muttering. Yet she looked so peaceful.

The doctor told them he had found nothing wrong with her, but to keep her home for a day or two, make sure she got plenty of rest. If she acted strangely, or appeared not to be her usual self, give him a ring and he would pop round. He was sure there was nothing to worry about, though. Young children often went for midnight jaunts, whether asleep or otherwise; Alice had just jaunted a little farther than most.

Molly was still frightened. Why had Alice gone to the tree again? She had been frantic when her daughter had gone missing two weeks before. She had searched the church and its grounds, twice running down to the road to make sure Alice wasn't out there. In a panic she had run to Father Hagan's house and he had helped search the grounds again. It was the priest who spotted her daughter in the field kneeling before the tree. Alice had been smiling when they went to her, a smile that had vanished when she became aware of their approach. Then she had become confused, disorientated. They had led her back and, in sign language, Molly had asked her why she had gone into the field. Alice had merely looked puzzled, as if she didn't understand. She had seemed fine after that (perhaps a little distant, but that wasn't too unusual for Alice; it was easy to get lost in a world of silence) and Molly had tried to forget the incident.

Now, because of the previous night, the anxiety was back with a vengeance. And the fear was mixed with something else. What was it? Apprehension? More. Something more. The faint glimmer of hope . . . No, it was impossible. The man had been mistaken. He had seemed so certain, though.

She couldn't remember his name, the young man who had nearly run down Alice. He had been sitting in an armchair looking a little worse for wear when she and Len had arrived. The familiar stink of booze permeated the air around him (familiar to her because that same unpleasant odour was so much a part of her husband), although he didn't appear to be drunk. He said Alice had spoken to him.

The kettle changed its hissing tone and steam billowed out across the kitchen. Molly switched the gas jet off and dropped a tea bag into an empty cup on the draining board. She poured undiluted lemon squash into another cup for Alice and filed both with boiling water. Molly stood looking down at the swirling yellow-green liquid, thinking of her daughter, her only child, thinking that miracles never happened. Not to the Molly and Alice Pagetts of the world, anyway.

She put the cup and two biscuits into a saucer and made her way from the kitchen. As she mounted the stairs, her mind ran through a quick, silent prayer; but she dare not let herself hope. Alice would soon be back at the special school for the deaf in Hove, and Molly, herself, would be back at her part-time job as a home-help, and Len would be his usual disagreeable self, and everything would be normal again in the Pagett household. She prayed it would be so, yet she prayed also for something better.

Alice did not look up when Molly entered the bedroom. Even though she couldn't hear, her daughter could always sense when someone had entered a room, but this time she was intent on her drawing. The Galaxy Invader now lay on the floor beside the bed and her crayons were near at hand in a box on the bedside cabinet. Molly stood over her with the hot lemon drink and still Alice did not look up from the sketchbook.

Molly frowned when she saw the picture. It was the same one. The same one she had drawn day after day for two weeks. Molly had shown them to Father Hagan, who had dropped in earlier that morning and he, too, had made no sense of them.

Molly placed the cup and saucer beside the crayons and sat on the edge of the bed. Alice looked surprised when the yellow crayon was removed from her hand. For an instant, it was as though she did not recognize her mother. Then she smiled.

The rain was like tiny ice pellets striking at Father Hagan's face. He stood at the wall, looking into the field, watching the tree; the sky, after a bright start to the day, was now dark overhead, a thin haze of silver between the distant horizon and the brooding clouds.

Nothing happened. Nor did he expect it to. The tree was just a tree. A tired old oak. A silent witness to passing time. He could see the sheep grazing in a far corner of the field, their bodies yellowy-grey and bloated, concerned only for the next mouthful of grass and the growing heaviness in their pregnant bellies.

The priest shivered and pulled the collar of his dark blue raincoat tight around his neck. His black hair was damp, his glasses speckled; he had been standing there for five minutes paying no heed to the freezing rain. There was a feeling inside him that he could not grasp, a sense of unease that he could not define. He had not slept well the night before, after the doctor had left with the Pagetts and Alice, and the man called Fenn had gone. A peculiar loneliness had descended afterwards, leaving him feeling vulnerable, isolated. In his years as a priest, loneliness had become an acquaintance, and rarely an enemy. But last night, the solitude was total, his room a cell surrounded by impenetrable blackness, devoid of life, a deathly vacuity separating him from the rest of humanity. He had the terrifying feeling that if he left his bedroom and walked out into that darkness he would never reach its edge, that he would walk and walk and become lost in it, never to find even his room again. The sensation was suffocating and he was afraid.

He had prayed and prayer slowly forced back the contracting walls of fear. His sleep had been restless, more exhausting than if he had stayed awake, and the barest glimmer of morning had been welcomed with immense gratitude. He had shivered alone in his church, his early-morning devotions fervent, intense, and later, at morning Mass shared with four of his flock, he had begun to shake off the nagging unrest. But not completely; it still lingered through the day like an elusive tormentor, refusing to be identified, content to stab then hide.

The tree was withered; the years had made it a twisted thing. It dominated that part of the field, a gargantuan guardian, innumerable arms thrown outwards to warn off intruders. A grotesque shape disrobed of summer leaves, intimidating in its ugliness. Yet, he told himself, it was just a centuries-old oak, its lower branches bowed, bark scarred and dry, its vitality patiently stolen by time. But why did the girl kneel before it?

The Pagetts had always lived in the parish, Molly Pagett a staunch, if quiet, member of the Catholic community. She was paid for the work she did keeping the church clean, but the wages were minimal; she would have probably worked for nothing if Father Hagan had asked her to. He had not met

Leonard Pagett often, and he had reluctantly to admit that he cared little for the man. Pagett's atheism and ill-disguised dislike of the Church and churchmen had nothing to do with his feelings towards him, for the priest knew and respected many such people. No, there was something, well, not good about the man. On the rare occasions when Father Hagan had called at their home, Pagett had always appeared sullen, uncomfortable in the presence of the priest. And in turn, the priest felt uncomfortable in the presence of Pagett. He was glad Alice's father had been absent when he called in to see her that morning.

Alice. A good child, a curious child. Her disability had made her a solitary one. She was frail, yet seemed to carry an inner strength within that small body. She was happy at the church, helpful to her mother, respectful of her surroundings. Alice didn't appear to have many friends but, of course, her silence was frustrating to other children, who had little pity for such things. She appeared to be as intelligent as any other child of her age despite the cruel affliction, although she was often lost in her own world, in her own dreams, an obvious result of her disability. That morning she had seemed almost completely lost in that private domain, absorbed in her confused scribblings.

It was the memory of Alice's drawings that turned him back towards the church.

He walked through the bleak graveyard, his shoulders hunched against the stinging rain, his footsteps hurried. Molly Pagett had shown him more pictures drawn by the child over the past two weeks, and they had all looked similar to each other, mostly in yellow and grey, some with added touches of blue. Strangely, only one was different, although not in style; the colour had changed. It was in red and black. All had looked vaguely familiar.

Alice was no artist, but her illustrations endeavoured to portray a figure, a person dressed in white, the blue used infrequently, red just once. The figure was surrounded by yellow and it had no face. It appeared to be a woman, though the overall shape was not clear.

He entered the church porch, relieved to be out of the rain. He fumbled for the key to open the big oak doors, for the church was always kept locked nowadays because of increasing vandalism and theft. The holy sanctuary was only available to those in need at appointed times. The long key clicked in the lock and he swung one side of the double-doors open, stepping inside and closing it again. The thud echoed around the walls of the gloomy church and his footsteps were unusually loud as he walked to a side aisle after genuflecting and blessing himself.

He paused before beginning the journey to the front of the church, gazing at the distant frozen figure against a wall to one side of the altar. Could it be? Father Hagan became more certain as he approached the statue: the outstretched arms, the head slightly bowed to gaze at whoever knelt, sat or stood before it. The drawings made more sense when the image they represented was viewed.

Alice often sat here. Curiously, it came as no relief to identify the object of her obsessive drawings. Instead, it was a mildly unsettling sensation.

The priest stared up at the compassionate but stone face of the Blessed Virgin and wondered at the acute sense of despair he suddenly felt.

6

> 'I say, how do you do it?' asked John, rubbing his knee. He was quite a practical boy.
>
> 'You just think lovely wonderful thoughts,' Peter explained, 'and they lift you up in the air.'
>
> J. M. Barrie, *Peter Pan*

Sunday. Morning. Sunny. But cold.

Fenn pulled his Mini in behind a long line of cars, most of which were settled halfway on the grass verge beside the road.

'It's gone 9.30, Gerry. We're going to be late.' Sue sat in the passenger seat, making no attempt to get out of the car.

Fenn grinned. 'They don't make you wear sackcloth any more, do they?' He turned off the engine.

'I'm not sure I want to do this.' Sue's teeth chewed anxiously on her lower lip. 'I mean, it's a bit hypocritical, isn't it?'

'Why?' Fenn looked surprised, although his eyes were still smiling. 'Prodigals always get a good reception.'

'Cut it out, it's not funny.'

Fenn changed his tone. 'Ah, come on, Sue, you don't have to become a Born Again Catholic. I'd feel a bit lost if I went in there alone; I wouldn't know what the hell to do.'

'Admit it: you're bloody scared. What do you think Catholics do to agnostics? Burn them at the stake? And what makes you think you'd be noticed anyway?'

Fenn squirmed uncomfortably. 'I guess I do feel like a trespasser.'

'A spy, don't you mean? And how do you think I'm going to feel?'

He leaned forward and put a hand around her neck, gently tugging her towards him. 'I need you with me, Sue.'

She looked into his face, about to rebuke him for his blatant small-boy expression; instead she groaned, and pushed her way out of the car, slamming the door behind her.

Fenn winced but couldn't repress the chuckle. He locked the car and hurried after Sue, who was stamping along the tree-lined path leading to the church entrance. A few other late arrivals hurried along with them, the sound of organ music speeding their footsteps.

'The things I do for you, Fenn,' Sue muttered from the corner of her mouth as they entered the porch.

'Yeah, but they're not all bad,' he whispered back, a sharp elbow making his grin disappear.

The church was full and Fenn was surprised; he thought clerics were complaining about the fast-diminishing number of churchgoers. There were plenty here. Too many, in fact; he and the other latecomers would have to stand at the back. He watched as Sue dipped her hand into the font at the top of the centre aisle and admired her legs as she quickly genuflected. Remember where you are, Fenn, he told himself. He decided he would feel too self-conscious to follow her act and discovered he felt self-conscious not following it. Shuffling to one side, trying to look as unobtrusive as possible, he glanced around the church interior. The congregation ranged over all ages and all shapes and sizes. Plenty of kids, some with adults, others just with brothers and sisters or friends; plenty of women, mostly middle-aged or older, a few teenage girls here and there; and a good sprinkling of men, most of them family types, one or two groups of teenage boys among them. A hymn was being sung and mouths opened and closed, many not forming words – just opening and closing. The tune wasn't bad, though, and the overall effect of all the voices banded together by the rich strains of the wheezing organ was not unpleasant. Fenn hummed along with them.

The hymn finished and there was the rustle of closing books and shifting bodies, a muffled sound like a wave soaking the shore. The congregation knelt and he wondered what to do – the stone floor looked unreasonably hard. He snatched a look at Sue for guidance and was relieved to see her merely bow her head slightly. He did the same, but his eyes looked upwards, roaming over the heads of the people in front.

The priest's monotone litany drew his attention towards the altar and he barely recognized the man in his dazzling uniform of office, a white cassock and bright green and yellow vestment. Father Hagan had changed identity; he bore little resemblance in both character and appearance to the confused and anxious man in dressing gown and bare feet of a few nights ago. The transition was as dramatic as Clark Kent changing into Superman. Or Popeye after spinach. He wore his robes like a suit of holy armour and it afforded him a calm strength. Fenn was just a little impressed, but cynically reminded himself that fancy dress was the most camouflaging disguise of all.

Father Hagan's face was expressionless, his eyes cast down, almost shut, as he quickly went through the opening prayers. The congregation responded to his solemn supplications in an almost incoherent drone. Then both priest and worshippers prayed as one; and as they did so, Fenn noticed the priest's eyes were fully open, his head no longer bowed. He kept glancing to his left as though watching someone kneeling on that side of the church. Fenn followed his gaze but could only see rows of bowed heads. He shifted his position to get a clear view down the side aisle; still he saw nothing unusual. He turned his attention back to the Mass, interested in the service, but deriving no sense of well-being from it, no spiritual uplift. Soon he became aware of a growing frustration, a slight resentment.

Maybe he just didn't like being part of the gathering, part of a crowd that seemed – to him – to be mindlessly repeating words as though they were a magic formula, a collective petition of adoration. It began to unnerve him. Fenn neither believed nor disbelieved in the existence of God: either way, it meant little to him. Find your own morality, your own code; then stick with it. So long as nobody else got hurt (too badly) you were doing okay. If there was a God, He was big enough to understand that. It was man, mortal bloody man, who created the myths. What Supreme Being could encourage let alone appreciate this dogmatic repetitive ritual? What Almighty Power would encourage His own creation (whom, so the rumour went, He had created in His own image) to toady up to Him so they could have a slice of the heavenly action when their number was called? It didn't make sense.

Fenn glared defiantly towards the altar. There were lots of other things to toss in for debate. Like idolatry, theological misinterpretation, and naive symbolism. Like birth control, confession and penance and absolution. Like bigotry (who says you have to be a Catholic to get a foot in the gate?), ceremony, solemnization, and in-bloody-fallibility. Original

Sin, for Christ's sake! And not to mention the Church's view on fornication.

He began to smile at his own indignation. Nothing like a good church service to stir the emotions, for or agin.

As Father Hagan read from the Gospel, Fenn looked at Sue and surreptitiously reached for her hand, squeezing it softly; she ignored him, intent on the priest's words. He let his hand drop away, surprised.

The sermon began and Fenn paid scant attention, although he studied Hagan with interest. It was strange: the priest didn't look so invincible now. His face looked strained and he still glanced towards the side, at someone sitting in the front pew. Once again, the reporter tried to see for himself, and this time he could just make out the back of a woman's head between the shoulders of a man and woman sitting in the second row.

She was wearing a bright pink scarf. Maybe the priest didn't like pink.

Fenn shifted his feet, becoming restless. If he were a smoker, he'd be dying for a cigarette. Was it sacrilege to chew gum in church? He decided it probably was.

The priest's words seemed hesitant, as though even he were not convinced. But as he spoke and developed his theme, his words became stronger and Fenn could almost feel the sense of relief that passed through the congregation; they obviously preferred their sermons hard and unrelenting. Father Hagan's voice subtly rose in pitch, at one moment accusing and the next coaxing, then reassuring, returning to a more reproachful tone when things were getting too cosy. Fenn enjoyed his technique.

The service went on (to Fenn, on and on . . .) and he regretted having arrived for the full Mass. His idea was to soak up the atmosphere of the Sunday service, maybe chat to some of the people afterwards; but the prime purpose was to get to the priest. He intended to have a long talk with him when Mass was over, wanting to find out how the little girl was. Had she returned to the church? Had she spoken again? Now he wondered if he wasn't suffering too much for the sake of his craft.

He sneaked another sideways peek at Sue, feeling a trifle embarrassed by her obvious reverence towards the surroundings. Once a Catholic, always a Catholic. He hoped it didn't mean she was going to kick him out of her bed that night.

The church became particularly hushed. Father Hagan was doing something with a highly polished chalice, breaking what looked like a white wafer into it. The Communion, that was it. Drinking of wine, breaking of bread. Christ's blood and body. What did they call it . . .? The Eucharist.

All heads were bowed and the people standing around him sank to their knees as a tinkling bell rang out. He looked down at Sue in alarm and she motioned with her eyes for him to get down beside her. The stone floor hurt his knees.

He kept his head low, afraid to offend anyone – particularly HE WHO SEES ALL – until he heard movement around him. Looking up, he saw that people were stepping into the aisles and forming a double-line queue leading up to the altar rail where the priest waited with silver cup and Communion wafers. An older man wearing a white cassock attended him at one side. The procession of people shuffled forward and the organ wheezed into life once again.

Several people were sitting now and a few of those at the back of the church had risen to their feet, not prepared to suffer bruised knees any longer. Fenn considered their judgement to be sound and rose himself; Sue remained kneeling.

Singing began and the congregation moved down and

around, approaching the altar from the centre aisle, returning to their places by the side aisles. Fenn saw the pink scarf moving along the bench towards the centre and instantly recognized its wearer as the woman who had come with her husband to collect the little deaf and dumb girl from the priest's house a few nights before. The priest had been looking towards Alice's mother throughout the service.

The pink scarf joined the other bowed heads in the slow-paced procession and disappeared completely from view when the woman knelt to receive the host from the priest.

It was then that a small figure rose from the spot where the woman had been sitting throughout the Mass. She stepped into the side aisle and looked up at a statue before her; then she turned and walked towards the back of the church. Fenn recognized Alice. Her yellow hair was parted in the centre, two long plaits resting over her shoulders; she wore a maroon raincoat, a size too big for her, and long white socks. Her hands were clasped together tightly, fingers intertwined, and her eyes looked straight ahead and at nothing in particular.

Fenn stared, aware that something was wrong. Her face was pale, her knuckles white. He realized the priest had been watching *her*, not her mother.

And Father Hagan was watching her now.

The Communion wafer hovered tantalizingly above a gaping mouth, the receiver's tongue, draped over a lower lip, beginning to twitch. Alice's mother, kneeling beside her fellow-communicant, was too lost in her own devotional prayers to notice the delay in proceedings.

The priest looked as though he was about to call out and Fenn saw him visibly restrain himself. A few other heads were turning to see what was provoking such riveted attention from their priest, but all they saw was little Alice Pagett, the deaf mute, walking towards the back of the church, presumably to join the queue for Holy Communion. Father Hagan realized he was delaying the Mass and resumed the ceremony, but his eyes worriedly followed the girl's progress.

Fenn was curious. He thought of stepping forward to block her way but knew that would be stupid: she might just be feeling unwell and in need of fresh air. Yet, although she was pale, there was a look of happiness on her face, a faraway joy in those vivid blue eyes. She seemed to see nothing, only what was beyond her physical vision, and the notion disturbed Fenn. Could she be in a trance? She bumped into no one, nor were her footsteps slow or dream-like. He looked down at her as she passed, and half-smiled, not knowing why.

The organ played on and voices rose in communal worship, emotions high at this particular point in the Mass.

No one seemed to notice the other children leaving the pews.

Fenn looked from left to right in surprise. The kids – some no more than six years old, others up to twelve or thirteen – were slipping away from their elders and making their way towards the church exit, the infant exodus largely unnoticed because of the throng of people in the centre aisle.

Unlike Alice, there was nothing trance-like about these children. They were excited, some giggling, as they skipped after the deaf and dumb girl.

A mother realized her offspring was trying to make an escape (a common enough occurrence with this one) and swiftly caught him. His howl of rage and struggles to get free shocked the mother. People around her, other parents, began to realize what was happening. They were startled at first, then confused. Then just a little angry. One father forgot himself and called out after his departing boy.

Father Hagan heard the shout and looked up. He was just

in time to see the small girl in her maroon raincoat and long plaits pull open the church door and disappear into the bright sunlight. Other children rushed after her.

The voices grew weaker as people became aware that something was amiss. Soon only the plump nun at the organ, lost in her own rapturous praising of God's benevolence towards mankind, was singing.

Fenn suddenly became alert. Christ, he had almost been in a trance himself; it had taken an effort of will to snap out of it. He moved swiftly to the door and pushed one side open. The light stung his eyes for several moments, but a few rapid blinks allowed him to see clearly once more.

The children were running through the graveyard towards the low grey-stone wall at the back.

Fenn stepped from the porch and followed, his footsteps quickening when he saw Alice clamber over the wall. The other children began climbing over too, the smaller ones helped by their bigger companions.

A hand grabbed the reporter's arm.

'Gerry, what's going on?' Sue stared after the children, then at him as if he would know.

'No idea,' he told her. 'They're chasing after the little deaf and dumb girl. And I think I know where she's going.' He broke away, running now, anxious to get to the wall.

Sue was too surprised to move. Voices from behind caused her to turn her head; bewildered parents were emerging from the church, looking around anxiously for their missing children. The priest pushed his way into the crowd, saw Sue standing on the path leading through the graveyard, then looked beyond at Fenn's retreating figure.

The reporter skipped over fresh molehills, stumbling once but managing to keep his feet. He practically fell against the wall, his hands smacking its rough top. There he stood, drawing sharp breaths into his belaboured lungs, his eyes widening.

The girl, Alice, was kneeling before the crooked oak, just as she had on that dark chilly night less them a week ago. The other children were spread out behind her, some kneeling as she was, others just staring. Several of the younger ones were pointing at the tree, laughing, jumping little steps of delight.

Fenn's eyes narrowed as he studied the object of their attention. There was nothing else there! Just an old tree! It wasn't even beautiful; in fact, it was bloody awful. What was the fascination?

Someone bumped into him and he looked round to see Sue had caught up with him once more.

'Gerry . . .?' The question froze on her lips as she saw the children.

Hurried footsteps behind them, other bodies brought to a halt by the low wall. Fenn and Sue were jostled as parents pushed to see what had become of their offspring. A mild shock ran through the gathering crowd. Then a hushed silence. Even the organ had stopped playing.

Fenn became aware that the priest was standing beside him. They regarded each other for several moments and the reporter thought he detected a touch of hostility in Hagan's gaze, almost as if he suspected Fenn of having something to do with the phenomenon.

Fenn looked away, more interested in the children than the priest. He reached into his pocket and drew out a cheap, pocket-size camera; he clicked off four rapid shots, then leapt over the wall.

Sue, irrationally, tried to call him back; for some reason she was afraid, or perhaps just shocked, and it was the sense of fear that kept her quiet. The people around her grew restless when they saw him enter the field, and they seemed reluctant to follow. Scared, like her, or perplexed. Perhaps both.

He approached the first child, a boy of eleven or twelve in duffel coat and jeans. The boy was smiling, just as Alice had smiled that first night. He appeared to be unaware of Fenn, and the reporter waved a hand before the boy's eyes. A brief frown crossed the boy's features and he jerked his head aside, trying to get a clear view of the tree.

Fenn left him, went on to another child. A girl this time, squatting in the damp grass, a look of bliss on her face. He crouched beside her, touching her shoulder.

'What is it?' he asked softly. 'What can you see?'

The girl ignored him.

He moved on and watched a five-year-old clap his hands together and sink to his haunches with glee; two girls, twins, holding hands, both smiling; a boy of about thirteen, on his knees, hands held together before his nose, palms flat against each other, lips moving in silent prayer.

Another boy, this one in short trousers, his knees smeared with mud from where he had obviously fallen, stood hugging himself, shoulders hunched, a wide grin on his face. Fenn stood in front of him, deliberated obscuring his view. The boy stepped sideways, still grinning.

Fenn bent down so that his face was level with the boy's. 'Tell me what you see,' he said.

One thing was sure: he didn't see Fenn. Nor did he hear him.

The reporter straightened and shook his head in frustration. The little faces around him were all smiling. Some wept, but they still smiled.

He noticed the priest was climbing over the wall, others following his example. Fenn turned and walked swiftly towards the girl in the maroon coat, the deaf and dumb child, who knelt some yards before the other children, close to the oak tree. He moved in front of her, but to one side so that he did not block her vision of the tree. Crouching slightly, he aimed the camera and shot two more frames. Straightening he photographed the rest of the children.

Then he turned and photographed the tree.

The parents and guardians were among the children, claiming their charges, taking them up in their arms or hugging them close. A girl, not six yards away from Fenn, swayed, then fell into a heap on the soft ground before her distraught mother could reach her. Another younger girl followed suit. Then a boy. The five-year-old who had been clapping earlier broke into hysterical tears as his mother and father approached him. Many of the children began to weep, worried voices dispelling the uncanny silence that had prevailed as the adults tried to comfort them.

Fenn's eyes shone with bemused wonder; he had a story, a *great* story. He was witnessing the same kind of hysteria that had swept through a crowd of over three hundred children in Mansfield a few years before; there had been a mass collapse at the Marching Bands Festival. This wasn't on the same grand scale, but the events bore some similarity. These kids were being affected by whatever was going on inside Alice Pagett's mind. Somehow she was transmitting her own hypnotic state to them, making them behave in the same way! Jesus, some kind of telepathy! It was the only explanation. But what had induced *her* delirium – if delirium it be?

Father Hagan strode through the concerned families and swooning children, making straight for Fenn.

The reporter was tempted to snap off a quick picture, but decided it wouldn't be the right moment; there was something daunting about the priest, despite his worried manner. He slipped the camera back into his pocket.

The clergyman disregarded Fenn and knelt beside Alice Pagett. He put an arm around her, his hand covering one shoulder completely. He spoke to her, knowing she could not hear, but hoping she would sense the kindness in his words.

'Everything's all right, Alice,' he said. 'Your mother is coming, you're going to be fine.'

'I don't think you should move her, Father,' Fenn interrupted, crouching low again so he could look into Alice's eyes.

The priest looked at him in a strange way. 'Weren't you the man who brought her to me the other night? Fenn, isn't it?'

The reporter nodded, still watching the girl.

'What's your game, Mr Fenn?' Hagan's voice was brusque. He rose, pulling Alice up with him. 'What have you got to do with this business?'

Fenn looked up in surprise, then stood himself. 'Now look . . .' he began to say when another voice spoke.

'She wants us to come again.'

Both men were shocked into silence. They stared down at Alice.

She smiled and said, 'The lady in white wants us to come again. She says she's got a message, Father. A message for all of us.'

Fenn and the priest were not aware that the crowd was hushed again, that everyone had heard Alice's soft-spoken words even though it should have been impossible over the frantic hubbub of anxious voices.

The priest was the first to speak, his words hesitant. 'Who, Alice?' Could she hear him? She had spoken, but could she hear? 'Who . . . who told you this?'

Alice pointed towards the oak. 'The lady, Father. The lady in white told me.'

'But there's . . . no one there, Alice.'

The girl's smile wavered for a moment, then returned, but was less strong. 'No, she's gone now.'

'Did she say who she was?' The priest still spoke slowly, keeping his voice low, gentle.

Alice nodded, then frowned in concentration, as though trying to remember the exact words. 'She said she was the Immaculate Conception.'

The priest stiffened, blood draining from his face.

It was at that moment that Alice's mother, her bright pink scarf hanging loose at the back of her head, rushed forward and threw herself on her knees, pulling Alice to her and hugging her tight. Molly Pagett's eyes were closed, but tears poured from them to dampen her daughter's face and hair.

Wilkes

So the mother took the little lad and chopped him up in pieces, threw him in the pot and cooked him in the stew.

The Brothers Grimm, 'The Juniper Tree'

He closed the door, not forgetting to lock it. Then he switched on the light. It took no longer than two seconds to cross the small room and slump onto the narrow bed.

Kicking his shoes off, he laid his hands across his chest and stared at the ceiling.

'Fucking people,' he said aloud. *Treating me like scum*, he added silently.

His job as busboy in a trendy Covent Garden restaurant had not gone too well that day. He had spilt coffee, returned to tables with wrong orders, rowed with the barman – *who was a fucking poof, anyway!* – and locked himself in the staff toilet for twenty minutes, refusing to come out until he had finished weeping. The manager had warned him for the last time – *any more scenes and you're out!* – and the joint owners – *two fucking ex-advertising men not that much older than himself!* – had agreed.

Well he wouldn't go back! Let's see how they get on without me tomorrow! Bastards.

He picked his nose and wiped his finger under the bed. He tried to calm himself, repeating his mantra over and over in his mind; but it had little effect. Visions of his mother (as always, whenever he was angry) flashed into his mind, rudely elbowing his chosen soothe-word aside. It was because that cow had thrown him out that he'd had to accept such menial labour. If he had still lived at home he could have afforded to live on the dole like the other three million or so unemployed.

After a while he got up and went to a white-painted chest of drawers on the other side of the bedsit. Opening the bottom drawer he took out a scrapbook and carried it back to the bed. He turned the pages and, although it did not relax him, a different mood descended. He liked reading about them. Even now, nobody really knew why they had done it. The fact was: THEY JUST BLOODY WELL HAD!

He studied their newsprint faces, an impatient hand brushing away the thick lock of blond hair that fell over his eyes. He thought that one of them even looked like him. He grinned, pleased.

All you needed was the right person, that was all. It was easy if you found the right one. Someone famous, that's all it took.

He lay back on the hard, narrow bed and, as he considered the possibilities, his hand crept to his lap where it fondled his own body.

7

How cheerfully he seems to grin,
  How neatly spread his claws,
And welcome little fishes in
  With gently smiling jaws!

Lewis Carroll,
Alice's Adventures in Wonderland

Monday, late afternoon

Tucker used to love Monday stocktaking. Every empty shelf meant money in the bank. Every empty carton meant his bills could be met. Every empty freezer meant his smile was a little broader. But shelves, cartons and freezers were never so empty nowadays. Recession didn't stop people eating and drinking – they just didn't do it so well; the punters became careful with their money and particular in their choice. The profit margin on a tin of asparagus was higher than on a tin of peas, but the peasants were more interested in substantiality than taste. He understood their problem, for he was marking up new, dearer prices on virtually every product each week, but it didn't mean he sympathized. He had to eat, too, and when his customers ate less well, then so did he. Maybe not yet, but eventually he would have to.

However, there was still one small joy left to Monday stocktaking, and that was Paula. Paula of the lovely bum and thrusty tits. The face was a bit too fleshy, but when you poke the fire you don't look at the mantelpiece, he always told himself, the old adage a serious consideration to him, never an excuse or a witticism.

Rodney Tucker owned the one and only supermarket in Banfield's High Street, a smallish store compared to the usual chain supermarket, but then Banfield was a smallish town. Or village, as they liked to call it. He had moved there from Croydon eleven years before, his grocery shop having been forced out of business by the big combine superstores of the area. Not only had he learned from the experience, but the money he had made by selling the premises had enabled him to join the competition. Banfield was ripe for exploitation just then; too small for the big chains, but just right for the big individual (he had always considered himself a *big* individual). The two grocery stores in the town had suffered in the way he had suffered, although not as badly – only one had been forced to close down. Strangely enough, that particular shop had been turned into a laundromat, as had his own shop in Croydon. Recently, he had driven past his old premises and had noted that it had now become a porn video centre; would that happen in Banfield now that washing machines were as common as toasters? He doubted it, somehow; the planning committees of such places were notoriously hard to impress with the changes in twentieth-century retailing requirements. Strewth, it had been hard enough getting planning permission for his supermarket eleven years ago! Such towns and villages had their own way of carrying on. Even having lived in the area all these years, he was still considered an outsider. He knew most of the important men of Banfield, having dined with them, played golf with them, flirted with their wives – no matter how ugly – but still he wasn't accepted. You didn't just have to be born and bred in the area to be considered one of them: your father and *his* father had to be born there! It wouldn't matter one iota to him, except that he would like to have been elected to the parish council. Oh, yes, that would be nice. Lots of land going spare around Banfield, and he had many contacts in the building trade. They'd be very grateful to any council member in favour of giving certain plots over to development. Very grateful.

One hand rubbed his bulging stomach as though his thoughts were food set before him.

'Running low on grapefruit segements, Mr Tucker!'

He winced at the shrillness of Paula's voice. Add fifteen years and another four stone and Paula would be a replica of Marcia, his wife. It would have been nice to imagine that his attraction towards Paula was because she reminded him of his wife when she was younger, before years of marriage had exaggerated the weakness rather than realized the promise. Nice, but not true. Fat, thin, buxom, titless – it made no difference to Tucker. Pretty (he should be so lucky), plain, experienced, virginal (he could never be *that* lucky) – Tucker would take them all. Age? He drew the line at eighty-three.

Most of the bits he pursued had one thing in common with Marcia, though. They were all fucking dumb. It wasn't a qualification he demanded, far from it; it just helped his bargaining position. He was realistic enough to know that physically he didn't have a lot to offer: his girth was broadening by the month (despite lack of sales), and his hair, it seemed, was thinning by the minute (his parting was now just above his left ear, ginger strands of hair, some nine inches long, swept over and plastered down onto his skull). But: he had a quick mind, a quick wit, and the eyes of Paul Newman (a bloated Paul Newman, granted). Most of all, and an attraction he had to admire himself, he had a few bob. And it was an attraction he was never modest about. Expensive suits, made-to-measure shirts, Italian shoes, and a change of socks every day. Chunky gold jewellery on his fingers and wrist, chunky gold fillings in his teeth. A flash bright yellow XJS Jag to drive, a beautiful mock-Tudor house to live in. A fifteen-year-old daughter who won rosettes for horse riding and certificates for swimming; and a wife – well, forget the wife. He had a bit of cash and it showed. He made sure it showed.

Tucker knew how to give the women in his life a good time (forget the wife again) and because they were all fucking dumb, that was all they wanted. He could spot a schemer a mile off and had sense enough to stay well clear: no way did he want his comfortable boat rocked.

The dummies were just right: give them a good time in Brighton – a tasty meal, a spot of gambling in a casino or the dogs, disco afterwards – and round off the evening in his favourite motel on the Brighton road. If they were worth it, a trip up to London would be in order; but they really did have to be worth it. Paula merited two stays in the motel so far, but not a trip up to town. Shame about the face.

'Stacks of cannelloni!'

The voice didn't help, either.

Tucker sauntered down the rows of shelves, the smell of cardboard and plastic bags strong in his nostrils. Paula was on a small stepladder, clipboard in one hand, her other hand reaching up to examine the contents of a carton. The fashionable split at the rear of her tight skirt revealed the backs of her knees, not always the most sensual of sights, but on a late, wet, Monday afternoon, enough to tug a nerve in the shadowy regions below the overhang of his belly.

Sidling up to her, he placed a chubby hand against her calf muscle. His fingers slid upwards and she stiffened, annoyed because his heavy gold bracelet had snagged her tights.

'*Rodney!*'

He pulled the bracelet free and let his hand travel upwards once more. He stopped where the tights joined in the middle, forming, in collaboration with her panties underneath, an unbreakable seal, a nylon scab over a soft, permanently moist wound. The man who invented tights should have been strangled with his own creation, Tucker thought soberly. His fingers played with the round buttocks.

'Rod, someone might come in!' Paula pushed at his hand beneath the skirt.

'They won't, love. They know better than to interrupt while I'm stocktaking.' His voice still held faint strains of a northern whine, hinting at his origins before Banfield, before Croydon, and before London.

'No, Rod, we can't. Not here.' Paula began to descend the ladder, her lips pursed with resolution.

'It's never bothered you before.' He snatched his hand away lest his finger got crushed in the vice between her thighs.

'Well, it's a bit tacky, isn't it?' She turned away from him, clutching the clipboard to her breasts like a chastity shield and looking thoughtfully at the shelves around her as though concentration, too, was a protective force-field.

'Tacky?' He looked at her in surprise. 'What's that bloody mean?'

'You know perfectly well.' She moved away, ticking off items on the clipboard

Paula was Tucker's secretary-cum-supervisor-cum-easy-lay-ever-since-the-Christmas-Eve-after-the-store-closed-party. He'd taken her on three months before because she could type, add up without using her fingers, organize staff (she had worked one season for Butlin's as assistant to the entertainments manager) and had thrusty tits and looked knockout against the three spotty-faced youths and one failed double-glazing representative who had applied for the position. Paula was twenty-eight, lived with her widowed, arthritic mother, had a few boyfriends but no steady, and wasn't bad at her job. Since the Christmas-Eve-after-the-store-closed-party, their relationship had been highly pleasurable: drinks after work, a few nights in Brighton, a couple in the motel, swift titillating gropes whenever the occasion allowed. Like Monday stock-taking. What the fuck was the matter with her today?

'Paula, what the fuck is the matter with you today?' His words were whispered so that the cashiers in the shop could not hear, but his exasperation raised the tone to a squeal.

'There's no need for that kind of language, Mr Tucker,' came the stiff reply.

'Mr Tucker?' He touched his chest pointing at himself in disbelief. 'What's all this Mr Tucker? What happened to Rod?'

She whirled on him and the disdain in her eyes was intimidating. 'I think, *Mr Tucker*, we should keep our relationship on a strictly business basis.'

'Why, for f – ? Why, Paula? What's happened? We've had fun together, haven't we?'

Her voice softened, but he noticed her eyes didn't. 'Yes, we've had a lot of fun together, Rodney. But ... is that enough?'

Alarm bells began to clang in his head. 'How d'you mean exactly?' he asked cautiously.

'I mean perhaps I think more of you than you do of me. Perhaps I'm just a good screw to you.'

Oh yes, he thought, here we go. She's building up to

something. 'Of course you're not, love. I mean, you are, but I think more of you than just that.'

'Do you? You never show me!'

He raised his hands, palms downwards. 'Keep it quiet, lovey. We don't want the whole shop to know our business, do we?'

'You may not; I'm not particularly bothered who knows. I wouldn't even care if your bloody wife found out!'

Tucker sucked in his breath and felt his heart go *thump*. Oh no, he may have misjudged Paula. Maybe she wasn't so dumb. 'We could have a night up in London, if you like,' he said.

She looked at him as though he had slapped her face. Then she threw the clipboard at him.

He was more concerned with the clatter as it bounced off and then fell to the floor than any injury to himself. He bent to retrieve it, one hand flapping at her in a 'keep the noise down' gesture. A silent grope was one thing, an hysterical row that could be heard outside was another: it could demean his position as owner/manager – and word could also get back to Marcia.

He staggered against the shelves as Paula pushed by. 'You can finish the bloody stocktaking yourself!' she told him as she marched towards the door leading into the main shopping area. She paused at the door as if to adjust her emotions before stepping through. As she looked back at him he was sure there was calculation in those tear-blurred eyes, just behind the distress. 'You'd better think about our situation, Rodney. You'd better decide what you're going to do about it.'

She disappeared through the door leaving it open wide.

Tucker groaned inwardly as he straightened. He'd misjudged her. She wasn't so dumb. Her next ploy would be conciliation, get him panting again; then *wham!* – more histrionics, only more so. Something to really frighten him. Bitch! He knew the name of the game – he'd played it once before – but not whether the blackmail would be emotional or financial. He hoped it wouldn't be financial.

He emerged from the stockroom an hour later and his mood was even blacker than before. He had already known the weekend take was bad, but the untouched cartons piled high on the shelves always mocked him with the fact. Not much to re-order this week and the way things were going, there wouldn't be much the following week, nor the one after that. Strewth, Monday, bloody Monday!

The sight of his customerless shop and his three cashiers huddled together at one checkout increased his gloom. His shelf-loader was sitting in a corner reading a comic, index finger lost up to its first joint in his nose. Tucker turned away in disgust, too gloomy even to shout at the boy. He looked up at the office and saw through the long plate-glass window that it was empty; Paula had obviously gone for the day. Just as well. He was in no mood.

'Come on, ladies,' he said loudly, forcing himself to walk briskly towards the cashiers. 'Back to our tills, get ready for the rush.'

The three women in their green overalls looked up with a start. Hubble bubble, toil and trouble, he thought as he approached them. God, there were some ugly women in this village!

'Ten minutes to closing time, ladies. Word might get around there's threepence off the double-pack Kleenex this week, so be prepared for the stampede.'

They giggled self-consciously at his oft-repeated joke – he changed the product from time to time to keep the humour fresh – and one of the cashiers held something up in the air. 'Have you seen the early *Courier*, Mr Tucker?'

He stopped before them. 'No, Mrs Williams, I haven't. Been far too busy to read newspapers, as you well know.'

'We've made the big time, Mr Tucker,' another cashier said enthusiastically, causing her companions to giggle like croaky schoolgirls.

'Your syndicate's come up on the Pools, has it? I hope this doesn't mean you're going to leave the security of a good job just because you've become millionaires.'

'No, Mr Tucker,' Mrs Williams chided. 'It's about Banfield. We're on the map now.'

He looked at her questioningly and took the newspaper. His lips moved as he silently read the main story.

'It's the church just up the road, Mr Tucker. Didn't you hear about it yesterday? My sister's boy was there, you know. I don't go to church much myself, nowadays, but my—'

'You've seen the little girl, Mr Tucker. Alice Pagett. She's often in here with her mother doing the weekly shop. Deaf and dumb, she is . . .'

'Used to be deaf and dumb, Mr Tucker. They say she can talk and hear now. Some kind of miracle, they reckon . . .'

He walked away from them, quickly scanning the columns. It was a good story, although the reporter had obviously got carried away with himself. But it claimed to be an eyewitness account, that the reporter was present when it happened. 'MIRACLE CURE BANFIELD GIRL' the headline screamed. And underneath, the subhead asked: 'Did Alice Pagett see vision of Our Lady?'

He climbed the three steps to his office, studying the article, and closed the door behind him. He was still rereading the story when the three cashiers and the shelf-loader left.

Finally he reached into his desk, took a cigar from its pack, lit it, and stared thoughtfully at the exhaled smoke. His gaze returned to the paragraph which compared the alleged 'miracle' cure to the 'miracle' cures of Lourdes in the French Pyrenees. Tucker wasn't a Catholic, but he knew about the holy shrine of Lourdes. A gleam came into his eyes and, for the first time that day, excitement pierced his gloom like a laser through fog.

He reached for the phone.

Monday, early evening

The priest left the Renault and walked back to the white swing-gate he had just driven through. He pushed it shut, gravel crunching beneath his feet, wind, spiked with drops of rain, whipping at his face. He stepped back into the car and drove slowly up to the presbytery, eyes constantly flicking towards the grey-stone church on his right. The drive ran parallel to the church path, trees, shrubbery and a small expanse of lawn between them. It seemed appropriate that there should be a division between the two, one path leading directly to the House of God, the other leading to the house of His servant. Father Hagan sometimes wondered if his gate should bear a TRADESMEN ONLY sign.

He stopped the car and cut the engine. The church was just over a hundred yards away and its stout, weathered walls looked bleak, so very bleak, in the grey weather. Its image was mirrored in the newspaper lying on the passenger seat.

It was a bad reproduction, blurred at the edges, a hurriedly-taken photograph blown up as if to emphasize the photographer's ineptitude. Below it was an even fuzzier shot of Alice Pagett kneeling in the grass.

Father Hagan looked away from the church and down at the *Courier*. He didn't need to read the article again, for it seemed engrained on his mind. The story, so coldly objective in its telling, seemed wrong, distorted; yet it reported exactly what had happened yesterday. Perhaps sensationalism substituting for passion confused its truth. Had there been a vision? Had everyone gathered at the church witnessed a miracle? Was Alice Pagett really cured?

He smiled, but it was a guarded smile. Of the last question there was no doubt: Alice was no longer a deaf mute.

Hagan had just driven back from the Sussex Hospital in Brighton where the girl was still undergoing tests. Alice's sudden ability to both speak and hear had elevated her from being an interesting case to an extraordinarily interesting case. Years before, specialists, unable to find any physical malformation in Alice's ears or throat, had informed her parents that they believed the girl's condition was purely psychosomatic – her mind told her body she could neither hear nor speak, therefore she neither heard nor spoke. Now her mind was telling her she could. So, to the medical profession, there had been no miracle; just a change of mind. If there had been a 'miracle' – and there had been cynical smiles when the word was mentioned to the bewildered parents – then it was whatever had caused the change of mind. Even though the remark was flippant, it was something Father Hagan could accept.

The newspaper article had likened Alice Pagett's experience to that of a young French girl, Bernadette Soubirous, who claimed to have had a series of visions of the Blessed Virgin in 1858. The grotto, just on the outskirts of the small town of Lourdes, where the visions had allegedly taken place, had become a place of worship with four or five million pilgrims visiting the shrine each year. Many suffered from illnesses or disabilities and journeyed there in the hope of being cured, while others went to re-affirm their faith or merely pay homage. Of the former, more than five thousand cures had been recorded, although, after stringent investigations by the Catholic Church's own Medical Bureau, only sixty-four had been proclaimed as miraculous. But so many other pilgrims, not just the sick, were blessed by another kind of miracle, one ignored by medical recorders, but noted by the Church itself: these people received a renewal of faith, a calming acceptance of what was to be, an inner peace which enabled them to cope with either their own disability or that of loved ones. That was the true miracle of Lourdes. Intangible, because it was an intimate, spiritual realization, an enlightenment that could have no meaning to clinical registers, to medical 'score-sheets'.

Alice Pagett had undoubtedly undergone a profound emotional, *perhaps* spiritual, experience which had caused repressed senses to function normally once more. That, in itself, was the miracle. The real question for Father Hagan was whether or not it was self or divinely induced; no one was more wary than the Church itself of so-called 'holy' miracles.

He folded the newspaper under his arm and left the car. The evening sky had grown considerably darker in the last few minutes, as if the night was in a rude hurry to stake its claim; or had he sat in the car for longer then he imagined? His verger would be arriving soon to light the church for evening service and the priest would welcome the company. He let himself into the presbytery and went straight through to the kitchen. If he had been a drinking man – and he knew many priests who were – a large Scotch would have been very welcome; as it was, a hot cup of tea would do.

He flicked on the kitchen light, filled the kettle, then stood watching it on the gas ring, only vaguely aware that the longer he watched the longer the water would take to boil. His thoughts were of Alice.

Her mother was thrilled and tearful over the incredible recovery, her father still in a state of disbelief. Not only could Alice speak and hear perfectly, but there was a special radiance about her that was due to something more than just her physical mending.

Father Hagan needed to speak with the girl privately, to question her closely on her vision, to gain her confidence so that there would be no invention in her story; but privacy had been impossible that day. The local doctor had whisked the Pagett family off to hospital late Sunday afternoon. So stunned was he at the abrupt change in her condition that he insisted on an immediate examination by specialists. Alice had been kept overnight for observation and further examinations had been carried out all through the next day.

For someone who had been given back the power of speech, Alice wasn't saying much. When the doctors questioned her on the lady in white she professed to have seen, her happy face became serene and she repeated what she had told the priest.

– The lady in white said she was the Immaculate Conception (the difficult title had become easier for Alice to pronounce) –

– What did she look like? –

– White, shiny white. Like the statue in St Joseph's, but sort of glowing, sort of . . . of sparkling –

– You mean shimmering? –

– Shimmering? –

– Like the sun does sometimes when it's a hazy day –

– Yes, that's it. Shimmering –

– And what else did she say to you, Alice? –

– She told me to come to her again –

– Did she say why? –

– A message. She has a message –

– A message for you? –

– No. No, for everyone –

– When must you go back? –

– I don't know –

– She didn't tell you? –

– I'll know –

– How? –

– I just will –

– Why did she cure you? –

– Cure me? –

– Yes. You couldn't speak or hear before. Don't you remember? –

– Of course I remember –

– Then why did she help you to? –

– She just did –

A pause then, thoughtful, bemused, but good-willed. The medical staff were obviously pleased for Alice, but something more was affecting them. Her quiet serenity was infectious. A psychologist, familiar with Alice's case, broke the silence.

– Did you like the lady, Alice? –

– Oh yes, yes. I love the lady –

Alice had wept then.

Father Hagan left the hospital, confused, hardly touched by the elation around him. By that time the story had broken and he was stunned when he saw the banner headline in the *Courier*. It wasn't just the attention his parish church would now undoubtedly receive that worried him so much, nor the publicity that would pursue Alice – it was a small price for her to pay weighed against the loss of her affliction – but it was the comparison with the miracle cures of Lourdes. Hagan dreaded the circus such news would create. And there was something more. A sense of foreboding. He was afraid and did not know why.

The kettle was steaming when he left the kitchen and went to the phone in the hallway.

Monday, late evening

'How was the lamb, Mr Fenn?'

Fenn raised his wine glass towards the restaurateur. '*Carré d'agneau* at its best, Bernard.'

Bernard beamed.

'And yours, Madam?'

Sue made approving noises through the *Crêpe Suzette* in her mouth and Bernard nodded in agreement. 'And a brandy with your coffee, Mr Fenn?'

Normally he allowed his clients plenty of time to relax between courses, but by now he knew Gerry Fenn could never relax until the whole meal was over and a large brandy was placed before him.

'Armagnac, Sue?' the reporter asked.

'No, I don't think so.'

'Come on. We're celebrating, remember?'

'Okay. Er, Drambuie, then.'

'Very good,' said Bernard. He was a small, neat man, who took a genuine interest in his customers. 'You're celebrating?'

Fenn nodded. 'Haven't you seen the evening edition?'

The restaurateur knew that Fenn was referring to the *Courier*, for the reporter had written a small piece in the newspaper on his restaurant, The French Connection, a few years before when he and his business partner (who was also the chef) had first opened in Brighton. It had provided a good boost for business at that time, for the seaside town was saturated with restaurants and pubs, and from that time on the reporter had become a favoured client. 'I haven't had a chance to look at the papers today,' he said apologetically.

'What?' Fenn feigned surprised horror. 'You've missed my big scoop? Shame on you, Bernard.'

'I'll catch it later.' The restaurateur smiled, then disappeared upstairs to ground level where the small bar was. Almost as if they were working on pulleys, a waiter descended to the basement area to clear away the dessert plates.

The restaurant was on three floors, sandwiched between a picture framer's and a public house, such a narrow building that it looked as if it had been hammered into the position it occupied. To Fenn it was the best restaurant in town, to be used only on special occasions.

'You're looking pretty smug, Gerry,' Sue said, one finger running around the rim of her wine glass.

'Yep,' he acknowledged with a grin. The grin disappeared when he saw she was frowning. 'Hey, it was a good story.'

'Yes, it was. A little over the top, though.'

'Over the – ! Christ, what happened was over the top!'

'I know, Gerry, I know. I'm sorry, I'm not getting at you. It's just that, well, I can see the whole thing getting blown up out of all proportion.'

'What do you expect? I mean, that was a weird thing that happened out there. A deaf mute suddenly cured, claiming she had a vision of the Immaculate Conception. Some of the other kids say they saw something, too, when I spoke to them afterwards. That is, the ones I could get to – their parents scooted them away so fast I had a hard job catching any of them.'

'I was there, remember?'

'Yeah, I do. You didn't look too clever, either.'

Sue toyed with the napkin in her lap. 'I had the strangest feeling, Gerry. It was . . . I don't know . . . dreamy. Almost hypnotic.'

'Hysteria. Didn't you notice it was flying around yesterday? The kids picked it up from the girl. Do you remember that story a few years back? The Marching Bands Festival in Mansfield? Three hundred kids collapsed together in a field while they were waiting to take part in the contest; after a pretty thorough investigation the authorities put it down to mass hysteria.'

'One or two of the investigating doctors disagreed. They said the children could have been suffering from organic poisoning. And traces of malathion were found in the soil.'

'Not enough to cause that kind of result, but okay, let's call that an open-ended conclusion. Anyway, there are plenty of other cases of crowd hysteria to prove it happens, right?'

She nodded, then said, 'So you think that's what this is all about. Mass hysteria.'

'Probably.'

'That didn't come over too strongly in your story.'

'No, it was more implied. Look, people want to read about the paranormal nowadays. They're sick of wars, politics and the failing economy. They want something more to think about, something that goes beyond mundane human activities.'

'And it sells more copies.'

Fenn was prevented from voicing a sharp retort by the return of Bernard.

'Armagnac for Sir, Drambuie for Madame.' Bernard's smile wavered as he sensed the sudden icy atmosphere.

'Thanks, Bernard,' Fenn said, his eyes not leaving Sue's.

Bernard melted away to enquire how things were on the next table.

'Sorry again, Gerry,' Sue said before Fenn could form his reply. 'I don't mean to pick a fight.'

Easily appeased, Fenn reached across the table for her hand. 'What is it, Sue?'

She shrugged, but her fingers entwined in his. After a few moments, she said, 'I think it's that I don't want the whole thing cheapened. Something wonderful happened out there yesterday. Whether or not it was some kind of miracle isn't important; it was just something good. Didn't you feel that? Didn't you feel something warm, something peaceful washing over you?'

'Are you serious?'

Anger blazed in her eyes. 'Yes, damn it, I am!'

Fenn gripped her hand more tightly. 'Hold it, Sue, don't get upset. You saw I was busy; I didn't get the chance to feel anything. I noticed one thing, though: one or two of the people – those not worried about their kids – were pretty cheerful over what had happened. They were grinning all over their faces, but at the time I thought it was just general amusement at the kids skipping Mass. They weren't laughing or joking, though, just standing around looking happy. Maybe they felt what you did.'

'Hysteria again?'

'I'm not ruling it out.'

'You don't suppose this little girl, Alice, really did witness a visitation?'

'A visitation?' The word startled Fenn momentarily. He shifted uncomfortably in his seat, then reached for the brandy. He sipped it and allowed the liquid to singe the back of his throat. 'I'm not a Catholic, Sue. When it comes down to it, I guess I'm not anything religious-wise. I'm not even sure there's a God. If there is, He must be tuned to another channel. Now, can you really expect me to believe the girl saw God's mother?'

'Christ's mother.'

'Same thing to Catholics, isn't it?'

Sue let it go, not wanting to confuse the debate. 'How do you explain Alice's words? The Immaculate Conception. Not many kids could pull that one together, particularly if they'd been deaf for most of their lives.'

'She shouldn't have been able to pronounce anything coherently after all those years, but that's another argument. She could have picked up that label in any religious textbook.'

'And the drawings. In the paper, you say that Alice's mother had told you her daughter had been drawing pictures of Our Lady over and over again since her previous vision.'

'Yeah, she said that. That was about all I got out of her before the priest interfered. He whisked them away before I could get much more. But that doesn't prove anything, Sue, except that Alice was obsessed by the image. And *that* she could get from any book on Catholicism. There's even a statue of Mary in the church itself.' Fenn paused, drinking his brandy as the waiter poured coffee.

When they were alone again, Fenn said, 'The point is this: Alice had a vision, to her it was real; but that doesn't make it real for everyone else. My personal view is that she's a suitable case for a psychiatrist.'

'Oh, Gerry . . .'

'Wait a minute! For her to speak so clearly and so well after all these years, she must have been hearing words, sounds, for most of the time.'

'Unless she remembered them.'

'She was four years old when she was struck deaf and dumb, for Christ's sake! There's no way she could have remembered.'

Diners on the next table were looking their way, so he leaned forward and lowered his voice. 'Look, Sue, I'm not trying to knock your religion – although I didn't know you cared so much until now – but have you any idea of how many cases there are each year of people claiming they've seen God, angels or saints? Yeah, and even the Blessed Virgin. Any idea?'

She shook her head.

'No, neither have I.' He grinned. 'But I know it's on a par with UFOs. And there are plenty of murderers who commit the act because "God told them to". Look at Sutcliffe, the Yorkshire Ripper. It's a common enough phenomenon.'

'Then why are you building it up to be something else?'

He flushed. 'That's journalism, babe.'

'It's sickening.'

'You're in the media business too.'

'Yes, and sometimes I'm ashamed. I want to go home now.'

'Ah come on, Sue, this is getting out of hand.'

'I mean it, Gerry. I want to leave.'

'What's got into you? I'm sorry I took you to the bloody church now; you're going holy on me.'

She glared at him and for one gulp-making moment, he thought she was going to hurl her glass at him. Instead she wiped her lips with her napkin and stood. 'I'll see myself home.'

'Hey, Sue, cut it out. I thought you were staying with me tonight.'

'You must be joking.'

Fenn looked at her, amazed. 'I don't believe this. What's got into you?'

'Maybe I'm just seeing you for what you really are.'

'You're being bloody ridiculous.'

'Am I? Perhaps you're right, but it's how I feel at the moment.'

'I'll get the bill.' Fenn drained the brandy, then began to rise from the table.

'I'd rather see myself home.' With that she pushed her way past the table and clumped up the stairs.

Fenn sat, too confused to protest any more. He reached across the table for the untouched Drambuie, raised it towards the other diners who obviously found him fascinating, and drained it in two swift gulps.

Footsteps on the stairs made him turn in the hope that Sue had relented.

'Everything all right, Mr Fenn?' Bernard asked anxiously.

'Terrific.'

Monday night

He puffed his way up the hill, occasionally muttering to himself about the perplexing instability of the female character. His 'celebration' dinner had started out well enough, but the more he discussed the Alice Pagett story with Sue, the quieter she had become. She had a changeable temperament, volatile at one moment, tranquil, or even indifferent, the next. The trick was to predict her moods (and he cared enough to make the effort) and bend with them. Tonight, though, he had been unprepared for her attack. Unprepared and still mystified.

Why the hell had she been so offended? Had going to Mass on that particular Sunday morning brought about the resurgence of her past religious ideals? Why should it? She took Ben to Mass at Christmas, and there were never any sudden religious metamorphoses then. So why now? It had to be because of the kids; maybe she just didn't want to see them exploited. And maybe she was right.

But it was his job to report news, right? And Jesus Christ, that *was* news. Even the Nationals wanted it. There was no question: the story would be his ticket to Fleet Street.

With relief he finally stopped outside one of the street's rising (or descending – it depended on which way you were going) terraced houses, a two-storey, excluding basement, Regency house, walls painted flaky white, window frames and door flaky black.

Fenn inserted the key, his hand shaking slightly from pent-up frustration rather than the few pints he had consumed in the pub next door to The French Connection. He closed the door behind him and trudged up the staircase to his first-floor flat, hoping that Sue would be waiting for him, more than sure that she wouldn't.

The ringing phone hurried his steps.

8

'Will you, won't you, will you, won't you,
   will you join the dance?
Will you, won't you, will you, won't you,
   won't you join the dance?'

Lewis Carroll,
Alice's Adventures in Wonderland

The size of the Crown Hotel was in keeping with the village itself: small, intimate, the kind favoured by weekend lovers. The plaque on the Reception wall told Fenn it was once a sixteenth-century coaching inn which had been extensively refurbished in 1953 when additional bedrooms were added. The oak-beamed dining room comfortably seated fifty people and the hotel's sixteen bedrooms were all well appointed, some with private bathrooms and all with television and radio. The sign also informed Fenn that the management knew he would enjoy the good food and friendly service and had great pleasure in welcoming him to the Crown Hotel. Thank you, he acknowledged silently, but I don't think I'll be here that long.

He noticed the bar to his left was open and decided that 10.35 was a little too early for a beer. The smell of morning coffee wafted through and the occasional elderly couple wandered in from the street and disappeared into the bar, the aroma a subliminal siren's song for geriatrics.

'Mr Fenn?'

Fenn turned to see a grey-haired but youngish-faced man smiling at him from a doorway further down the hall.

'Mr Southworth?'

'I am indeed.' The grey-haired man stepped into full view, one arm raised towards the open doorway as an invitation for the reporter to join him within. Fenn gave an appreciative nod towards the pretty receptionist who had summoned the hotel manager for him, considering a wink a little too frisky in full view of her employer.

'Very good of you to come, Mr Fenn.' Southworth offered a firm hand to the reporter which he shook briefly before entering the room. Another man rose from his seat and stuck out his hand towards Fenn's midriff. He shook the chubby hand and resisted wiping the transferred dampness against his trouser leg.

The hotel manager quietly closed the door, walked around a large, leather-topped desk, and sat. He wore a black suit with a light grey waistcoat and grey silk tie; on closer inspection his face did not look so young, although the skin was smooth save for giveaway line-clusters around his eyes and the corners of his mouth. Fenn and the second man sat on two straight-backed chairs facing the desk.

'This is Mr Tucker,' Southworth said.

Mr Tucker nodded and for one uncomfortable moment Fenn thought he would have to shake the sweaty hand again; but the paunchy man merely nodded in his direction, his smile having little affiliation with the gimlet eyes shrewdly sizing up Fenn.

Southworth continued the introduction: 'Mr Tucker has

been a resident of Banfield for . . . what, Rodney . . . ten years now?'

'Eleven,' Tucker corrected.

'Yes, eleven years. A very highly regarded member of the community, if I may say so.'

Tucker preened and Fenn secretly winced at the ingratiating smile on the blubbery lips. He noted the heavy gold chain on the thick wrist, the rings, one a sovereign, on the fleshy fingers, and wondered how many extra pounds they added to the already overweight load.

'Very nice of you to say so, George.' There were the barest traces of a northern accent in Tucker's voice. He turned to the reporter. 'I own the local supermarket.'

'That's wonderful,' Fenn replied.

Tucker eyed him for a moment, not quite sure how to take the appreciation. He decided the reporter was sincere. 'I read your marvellous story in the *Courier* last night, Mr Fenn. First-rate bit of journalism.'

'Obviously that's why you wanted to see me this morning.'

'Yes, quite.' Southworth said. 'As you can imagine, the news was all around town by Sunday evening, but it was your report which has given the news a greater prominence in the region. For that, we are grateful.'

'That may be premature.'

'I'm sorry?'

'You may find a lot of unwelcome visitors to the town in the next few weeks now that the Nationals have got hold of the story too.'

Fenn noticed the look that passed between the two men. Tucker's eyes gleamed briefly, but Southworth's remained impassive.

'Weeks, Mr Fenn,' the hotel manager said, 'but unfortunately, not months.'

'Unfortunately?'

Southworth leaned back in his chair and picked up a fountain pen lying on the desk top; he coolly appraised the reporter while he toyed with the pen. 'Let me be perfectly frank with you, Mr Fenn. I had heard of what took place up at St Joseph's, of course, but had not given the story much credence, or even, I'm afraid, too much attention. I had, naturally enough, assumed that the story was wildly exaggerated or just – to put it bluntly – misinformed. But when Mr Tucker rang me yesterday evening and I took the opportunity to read your account of the occurrence, I must admit to giving the matter further thought. In the subsequent meeting with Mr Tucker, I became convinced that this event might well develop into major proportions.'

'Give it a couple of weeks, as I said, and it'll blow over. The public are pretty fickle when it comes to news; they like it fresh.'

'That's precisely the point.'

Fenn raised his eyebrows.

Southworth leaned forward, his elbows resting on the desk, the pen still held between the fingers of both hands like a delicately poised bridge across a ravine. His words were slow, measured, as though it were important that their meaning be received in the correct spirit. 'The world, I need hardly tell you, is in grave recession. Economic problems are not just confined to individual countries any more; the concern is global. But it's individual *people* who are suffering, Mr Fenn, not continents, nor countries. The common man has to bear the brunt of world management failure.'

Fenn shifted in his seat. 'Er, I don't see the connection . . .'

'Of course not, Mr Fenn. I do apologize. Let me be more direct. We are a small town – a village, really – in a small country, and it's we, the small villages and towns, that suffer under unfortunate government economic policies. Nobody subsidizes our local industries or businesses because, individually, their loss is insignificant when compared to the big combines or Nationalized Industries. Our local businesses are dying, Mr Fenn. Banfield itself is slowly dying.'

'It can't be that bad.'

'No, I may be over-emphasizing to make my point. It isn't that bad, but, given a few years, it will be. Unless the decay is stopped.'

'I still don't see what this has to do with what happened on Sunday.' But Fenn had begun to; the idea was just starting to glimmer through.

Tucker moved his bulky frame around in his seat and drew in a deep breath as though about to speak. Southworth hastily cut in, as though fearing his colleague's expression of their thoughts.

'You may have seen enough of Banfield by now to have formed some opinion of the place, Mr Fenn.'

'I can't say that I have. I've driven through it once or twice before, but until a week or so ago when I almost ran down the Pagett girl, I hadn't really given it a second thought.'

'And now?'

'It's a nice enough place. Quite pretty . . .'

'But unexciting.'

'Yeah, you could say that. There are plenty of other towns and villages in the south that are prettier, more traditional.'

'And more attractive to the tourist trade?'

Fenn nodded.

'That's exactly it. We, as a community, really don't have too much to offer. In summertime this hotel is quite a busy place, but my guests use it only as a base for travelling around the Sussex countryside or visiting Brighton and the other south-coast resorts. The benefit to Banfield is minimal. Yet I personally would be willing to invest more money in the village if I thought it would yield a reasonable return. I know Mr Tucker feels the same way, but is also reluctant to throw away good money.'

'It's not just us, Mr Fenn,' Tucker spoke up at last. 'There are plenty of other businessmen around here looking for a good investment.'

'I'm sorry, I'm not with you. What kind of investment are you talking about?'

'For myself,' said Southworth, 'I would very much like to open a new hotel. A modern one, with more amenities than the Crown can offer. Perhaps even a motel on the outskirts; that would be most suitable for the amount of passing trade we receive.'

'And I'd like to open more shops,' said Tucker enthusiastically, 'maybe a couple of restaurants – you know, the cheaper kind where parents on a day-trip can afford to take their kids.'

'And there is plenty of local land waiting to be developed,' said Southworth. 'The village could grow, spread outwards, become a real town.'

And make you and your friends some money in the process, Fenn thought ruefully. 'Okay,' he said, 'I see what you're getting at. I'm still not sure what all this has to do with me, though. When my news editor rang me last night he said you, Mr Southworth, wanted to see me personally, that you had more information on the Banfield "miracle" – your words, I believe, not his. As you wouldn't pass anything on to him, he decided it might be important for me to turn up this morning. Was he right?'

Again, a look passed between the two men; this time it was cautious.

'We found your account of what happened at St Joseph's a

first-rate piece of journalism, Mr Fenn. Accurate in detail, and imaginative in the questions it posed.'

Tucker made agreeing noises.

Oh yeah, Fenn thought. 'What questions?'

'Well, comparisons really. It was that which caused Mr Tucker to contact me in my role as chairman of the parish council. You compared Banfield to Lourdes. In fact, you posed the question: Could Banfield be another Lourdes?' He placed the pen on the desk top and smiled sweetly at the reporter.

'I admit I got a little carried away.'

'Not at all, Mr Fenn. On the contrary, we feel it was a very perceptive remark.'

The metaphorical light bulb above Fenn's head flashed brightly. He could see where it was all leading, but wondered what part he was to play. 'There's been more than one so-called miracle at Lourdes, Mr Southworth. In all seriousness, I hardly think Banfield qualifies, do you?'

'Oh I think it does. Look at Walsingham and Aylesford, both towns in England. They have become shrines to many thousands of pilgrims each year. As for Aylesford, nobody is quite sure whether or not a visitation from the Blessed Virgin ever took place there at all; many believed it happened in France. Also, there have never been any spectacular miracles in either of these towns, yet the mystique is there, the people flock to them in the true belief that they are holy places. At least we have evidence that something quite extraordinary happened at St Joseph's, something that enabled a little girl to hear and speak after years of silence.'

'Extraordinary, yes, but not necessarily a miracle,' Fenn broke in.

'Do you know one of the best definitions of a miracle: "A divinely ordained exception." I think that's rather appropriate in this case.'

'"Divinely ordained"? Don't you need some evidence of that?'

'The Church does, of course. But the girl claimed she saw the Immaculate Conception; why should she lie?'

'And why should you believe her?' Fenn came back quickly.

'I think it's irrelevant whether we do or do not. Perhaps as a Catholic myself, I'm more ready to believe than Mr Tucker here is, but as I say, that's beside the point. The fact is, many thousands – who knows, perhaps millions if the story is circulated wide enough – will believe. And they'll want to visit St Joseph's.'

'Giving a dying village a new life.'

'Is that so wrong?'

Fenn paused before he answered. 'No, it may not be wrong. But you'll forgive me if I say it sounds a little cynical on your part.'

Tucker could contain himself no longer. 'This is the real world we're living in, Mr Fenn. Opportunities come along, you have to grab at them.'

Southworth looked embarrassed. 'Come now, Rodney, it isn't quite so black and white as that. I deeply believe, Mr Fenn, that something – I hesitate to use the word, but I feel it's necessary – something *divine* has taken place at the church. Something ordained by God. And if that is so, there has to be a reason. Perhaps the real miracle is that Banfield has been given the chance of a rebirth, an opportunity to save itself from oblivion. And a chance for the people themselves to regain their beliefs. It was Shaw who wrote, "A miracle is an event which creates faith"; why shouldn't faith be created or renewed here?'

Fenn was confused. Southworth appeared to be sincere, yet openly admitted he would benefit financially if Banfield became revitalized. The fat man, Tucker, made no bones about his motives: he was in it for the money. But what, exactly, did they want of him?

'I appreciate your frankness, Mr Southworth, but I'm still not sure why you're telling me all this.'

'Because we would like you to write more on what will become known as the Banfield Miracle.' Southworth's eyes fixed on Fenn's and his expression was serious, almost grave. 'Your story has already created enormous interest. I don't know if you've had a chance to visit St Joseph's this morning . . . ?'

Fenn shook his head.

'I went to see Father Hagan myself earlier,' Southworth continued. 'He wasn't there, but his house was under siege from a small army of your journalist colleagues.'

'From the Nationals?'

'I believe so. I spoke to them but, unfortunately, I'm very much in the dark about this incredible event. There wasn't too much I could tell them.'

I'll bet you managed somehow, Fenn mused to himself. 'Well, you can be sure the "Banfield Miracle" will get good coverage now. Maybe too much.' He was a trifle aggrieved that the big boys were muscling in on what he regarded as his scoop, but knew – and had known – it was inevitable.

'I'm sure it will – for a day or so. As you say, the public is fickle when it comes to news, and so is the Press itself.'

Tucker broke in once more: 'This is too wonderful a story to be allowed to die in a couple of days, Mr Fenn.'

The reporter shrugged. 'There's nothing you can do about it. Unless, of course, something else happens . . .'

Unless something happens, unless something happens! What was wrong with this idiot? Tucker's left heel did an impatient jiggle on the red patterned carpet. He had tried to persuade

Southworth to deal with the biggies, not mess around with the local rag. The Nationals could give maximum publicity *now*, when it was hot; Southworth was *too* worried about declining interest afterwards, when nothing more happened up at the church. He'd insisted that a steadily built and maintained awareness would give more sustenance to a long-term plan, whereas massive, sensationalist coverage would only benefit in the short term. By patronizing the *Courier* they would, hopefully, ensure that sustained interest. The newspaper was, after all, a reflection of local affairs: it had a duty towards its audience (and to itself in terms of circulation figures) to consistently report (and, of course provide) any such newsworthy stories that would generate interest (and trade) in the area. But was this man Fenn taking the bait or was he too pea-brained to see the possibilities?

'There's the problem,' Southworth was saying. 'There is no guarantee that anything else *will* happen at St Joseph's. Which is why we felt the *Courier* will give the incident and its consequence more coverage than any of the other media. We can promise you, personally, Mr Fenn, every cooperation, any assistance, you might need.'

Fenn was silent.

'We do realize,' said Tucker, 'that your paper probably isn't over-generous with your expenses, so we would expect to help you out . . .'

His words trailed off at the icy glares he received from both the reporter and the hotel owner.

'I'm sorry, Mr Fenn,' Southworth said quickly. 'What Rodney is trying rather clumsily to say is that we would not want you to be out of pocket on this matter. Indeed, as a member of the parish council, I shall propose the setting up of a special fund to cover any expenses on the development of this, um, project. It could cover initial promotional material, personal expenses incurred by council members, and any extra miscellaneous costs.'

'And I'd come under any "extra miscellaneous" costs?' asked Fenn.

Southworth smiled. 'Precisely.'

To Fenn, it didn't smell any sweeter than the way the fat man had put it. He leaned forward, elbows on knees.

'Look, Mr Southworth, Mr Tucker, I work for the *Courier*, it pays my salary, and my news editor tells me what stories to cover. If he wants me to write obits for a month, that's what I'll do. If he wants me to cover garden fêtes for the next month, I'll do that, too. If he wants me to spend time delving into the strange happenings at the local church of a little country village, I'll be only too happy.' He took a deep breath. 'What I'm saying is, my editor calls the tune. He pipes, I dance. I'm independent to a degree – and that's a small degree – but there's no way he'll let me waste time on a story he considers to be defunct. Now, like I said, if something more happens, then I'll be back like a shot.'

Southworth nodded. 'We appreciate your position. However—'

'There are no howevers to it. That's it, that's the way it is.'

'I was merely going to say that the girl, this Alice Pagett, mentioned that the figure she allegedly saw has asked her to return.'

'She didn't say when.'

'But if she has another . . . another visitation, you would consider that newsworthy.'

'I'm not sure. A prepubescent girl's hallucinations don't warrant too much attention.'

'After what happened on Sunday?'

'That was Sunday. Today's Tuesday. Tomorrow will be

Wednesday. Things move on, Mr Southworth, and we live in an apathetic age. What you need is another miracle, then maybe you've got a continuation of the story. For the next few days Banfield will get all the attention it needs, so my advice to you is to make the most of it now. Next week, it will be dead news.'

Fenn rose to his feet and Southworth rose with him. Tucker remained sitting, a mixture of disappointment and ill-disguised contempt on his face.

Southworth walked to the door and opened it for the reporter. 'Thank you for coming by, Mr Fenn, and thank you for being so frank.'

'Right. Look, if anything does happen, I'd like to know.'

'Of course. Will you be going up to the church?'

Fenn nodded. 'And I'll have a look around the village, get some reactions from the people.'

'Very good. Well, I hope we'll see you again.'

'Right.'

Fenn left the room.

Southworth closed the door and turned to face the fat man.

'So much for involving the bloody local Press,' Tucker said scornfully.

Southworth crossed the room and sat at his desk once more. 'It was worth a try. I'm afraid he got the impression we were trying to bribe him into writing the story.'

'Weren't we?'

'Not in the true sense of the word We were just offering financial assistance.'

Tucker grunted. 'What now?'

'We – I – make sure the parish council becomes interested in our scheme. If not, all we can do is hope – as Mr Fenn put it – something else happens.'

'And if it doesn't?'

The sun shone through the window in dusty rays, highlighting one side of Southworth's face in a golden hue. 'Let's just pray it does,' he said simply.

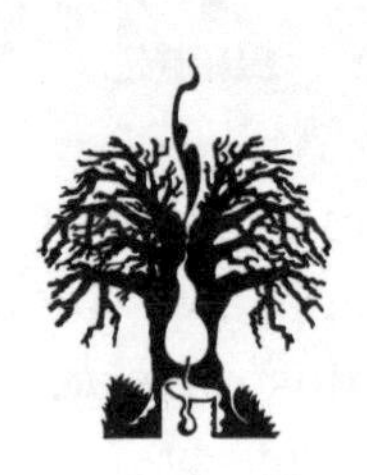

9

And see ye not that braid braid road,
    That lies across that lily leven?
That is the Path of Wickedness,
    Tho' some call it the Road to Heaven.

Anon, 'Thomas the Rhymer'

Bishop Caines regarded the priest with concerned eyes. 'I have grave misgivings about this whole matter, Andrew,' he said.

The priest found it difficult to look directly into his bishop's face, as though his gaze would see what lay beyond his own eyes. 'I'm worried too, Bishop. And I'm confused.'

'Confused? Tell me why confused.'

It was dark in the bishop's study, for the two windows which overlooked the tiny garden faced away from the morning sun. The deep wood panelling of the walls added to the room's sombreness and even the glow from the fire seemed muted.

'If – ' he struggled with his own words, ' – if the girl really did . . . really did see . . .'

'The Blessed Virgin?' The bishop frowned at the priest.

Father Hagan looked up briefly and said, 'Yes. If she did

and was cured because of it, then why? Why Alice, and why at my church?'

Bishop Caines' tone was clipped, impatient. 'There is no evidence, Andrew, none at all.'

'The other children – they saw something.'

'No evidence,' the bishop repeated slowly, and his finger-tips pressed against the polished surface of the desk. He forced himself to relax, aware that the parish priest somehow irritated him, and was even more vexed, not contrite, because of it. 'The Church must tread warily in such matters.'

'I know, Bishop, that's why I was so reluctant to bring it to your attention. When I read the newspaper report yesterday I knew I had no choice. Foolishly, I had imagined that the incident would be contained.'

'You should have contacted me immediately.' The bishop strove to keep the harshness from his rebuke, but did not succeed.

'I phoned you as soon as I saw the *Courier*'s article. It seemed so exaggerated.'

'Was it? The girl was cured, wasn't she?'

'Yes, yes, but surely not miraculously?' The priest looked at his superior in anxious surprise.

'How do you know that, Andrew?' The bishop's words had softened, for he had no desire for the man before him to be afraid. 'The child claimed to have seen the Blessed Virgin after which an incredible transformation took place. The girl could speak and hear.'

'But you said that was no evidence of a miracle.' The priest looked away again.

'Of course it isn't. But while we have to reject the proposition as we see it now, we must not close our minds to the faint possibility. Do you understand that, Father?' He didn't wait for a reply. 'It has to be looked into thoroughly before a judgement can be made. There are strict guidelines for such matters, as you well know.' The bishop smiled thinly. 'Some say our guidelines are too strict, that we eliminate all aspects of faith. But that isn't entirely true; we endeavour to eliminate doubts. The rules we follow for the discernment of a miracle date back to the eighteenth century, and they were laid down by Pope Benedict XIV, a man who had many progressive interests. He realized the jeopardy in which the Catholic Church could place itself by proclaiming miracles that later could be proved false by scientific means. In an age such as ours, where technological advancement is continually explaining "phenomena" in rational, scientific terms, the need to follow those rules is even greater.'

The priest's eyes were too intense and Bishop Caines wondered why. There was something wrong with the man, something – what? Unbalanced, perhaps? No, too strong a word. Father Hagan was disturbed by the peculiar happening in his parish, on his own church's doorstep, no less. And he was – yes, just a little frightened. The bishop forced a smile, an encouragement for his priest to open his heart.

'Would these rules apply to Alice Pagett?' Hagan asked.

'They would have to, should we decide to take the matter further,' Bishop Caines replied, maintaining the smile.

'Please tell me what they are, Bishop.'

'I don't think it's necessary at this stage. This whole matter will be forgotten within a month, I can assure you.'

'You're probably right, but I'd like to know.'

Bishop Caines curbed his impatience, then sighed. His eyes searched the ceiling as though scanning the corners of his own memory. 'The affliction or illness has to be very serious, impossible or extremely difficult to cure,' he began. 'The health of the person concerned should not be improving, nor should the nature of the illness be one that might improve by itself. No medication should have been given. At least, if it has, its inefficacy must be clearly established. The cure has to be instantaneous, not a gradual improvement.' His eyes dropped towards the priest again. 'The cure shouldn't correspond to a crisis in the illness brought about by natural causes. And, of course, the cure should be complete; there should be no recurrence of that particular illness.' He stopped speaking and Father Hagan nodded his head.

'It would seem almost impossible to establish a miracle,' the priest said.

'Yes, it would, but I have to admit the rules have been stretched just a little in the past. Generally though, they are adhered to.' He smiled again, and this time his warmth was genuine. 'That's why some of our best miracles get away.'

The priest did not respond to the humour. 'Then it would be too soon to make any judgement on the child?'

'Much too soon, and very unwise. Father, I'm a little perturbed by your seriousness. Is there something else troubling you?'

The priest straightened in the chair as though surprised by the question. He did not answer straight away. He shook his head, then said, 'It's just the change in Alice herself. Not the fact that she can now hear and speak, but in her manner, her disposition. Her personality has changed.'

'And so it should after such a wonderful cure.'

'Yes, yes, I know. It's something more, though, something . . .' His words trailed off.

'Something you can't define?'

Father Hagan's body seemed to slump into itself. 'Yes. It's more than just elation. She's serene – as though she really has seen the Mother of God.'

'It's not an uncommon apparition, Andrew. Many have claimed to have seen Our Lady and, of course, there is a great cult of Mariologists. But psychologists say that children can often see what is not there. I believe the term is "eidetic imagery".'

'You're convinced she was hallucinating?'

'At the moment I'm not convinced of anything, although I tend to lean towards that theory. You say the girl's favourite statue in your church was that of Mary. If her affliction truly was psychosomatic, then perhaps it was an hallucinatory vision which effected her cure. Even the Church cannot deny the power of our own minds.'

Bishop Caines glanced at his wristwatch and pushed his chair back, his portly shape making the action an effort. 'You'll have to excuse me now, Father; I have to attend a meeting with our financial committee. It's the time of month I dread.' He gave a short laugh. 'It's a pity the Roman Catholic Church cannot run on faith alone.'

Father Hagan stared up at the bulky figure, aware for the first time that black cloth hardly symbolized holiness. He was embarrassed by the thought: he knew his superior was a good man, infinitely better than he, himself. Why then, had the thought jumped into his head? Was it just part of his own self-doubt, the unease that was insidiously gnawing on his beliefs? His head ached, buzzed with thoughts that were unformed, fleeting – attacking. The urge to lie down and cover his eyes was almost overwhelming. What in God's name was happening to him?

'Andrew?'

The voice was soft, tender almost.

'Are you all right, Father Hagan?'

The priest blinked, seemed bewildered for a moment. 'Yes. I'm sorry, Bishop, my thoughts were miles away.' He stood as Bishop Caines approached the desk. 'Are you not well, Andrew?'

The priest tried to calm himself. 'I may be coming down with a cold, Bishop, that's all. The weather is so changeable.'

Bishop Caines nodded understandingly and led the way to the door. 'You're not too worried over this matter?'

'I'm concerned, naturally; but no, I think it's just a chill.' Or a sense of foreboding. 'Nothing to worry over.' He stopped before going through the open door into the outer office and faced his bishop. 'What shall I do, Bishop? About the girl?'

'Nothing. Absolutely nothing.' Bishop Caines attempted to look reassuring. 'Keep me informed of developments, watch over the situation carefully. But have no part in the hysteria that may well arise during the next few days. And keep away from the Press – they'll exploit the situation to the full without your help. I'll need a full report for the Conference of Bishops which will be held within the next two months, but only as a matter of record. I'm sure it will all have been long forgotten by then.'

He patted the priest's arm with an affection he hardly felt. 'Now you take care, Andrew, and remember to keep me informed. God bless you.'

He watched the priest walk through into the outer office and ignore the secretary who bade him goodbye. He waited for the other door to close before he said, 'Judith, would you be a dear and find me Father Hagan's file. And then let the finance committee know I'll be five minutes late.'

Judith, his secretary, a quiet but capable woman in her early fifties, was not even curious about the request. She never questioned anything her beloved Bishop Caines asked of her.

The bishop sat at his desk again, fingers drumming on the desk top. Was it all nonsense? Had Father Hagan exaggerated the situation? The priest had joined the diocese thirteen years before as an assistant priest in Lewes, and then on to Worthing as active assistant priest. Banfield was his first parish as senior priest. Was it proving too much? His work had been exemplary, and while his devotion to the Church was not remarkable among his peers, his conscientiousness was; where every secular priest would try if possible to visit at least four or five parishioners during the day, and spend ten or fifteen minutes with each, Father Hagan would visit the same number, but spend at least a half-hour with them; he taught for two mornings at the local convent school; he joined in with many local organizations such as the Self Help Group, the Liturgy Group, the Youth Group, as well as attending the monthly fraternal meetings of all the Banfield ministers – the Baptists, Anglican, Evangelical Free Church, and the Christian Fellowship (quite a few for such a small place). And these were just fringe activities outside his normal duties. Perhaps it *was* too much for a man with a weak heart.

A light tap on the door, and Judith was placing a buff file on the desk before him. He smiled his thanks and waited until she had left the room before opening the file. Not that there were any guarded secrets contained within; it was just that peering into a man's background was like peering into his soul, and both should be done in private.

There was nothing surprising, nor anything he'd forgotten in the file. The schools he had taught at, six years in Rome studying for the priesthood after his heart attack, ordained in Rome, returned to England. Then Lewes, Worthing, Banfield.

But wait – there *was* something he had forgotten. Father Hagan had spent six months in a parish near Maidstone on his return from Rome. His first assignment, as it were. Six months as assistant priest in Hollingbourne. Only six, then moved on. It wasn't significant; young priests made frequent shifts to where they were most needed at any particular time.

Why did it concern him now? Had he already begun to lose confidence in his priest's ability to cope with a difficult situation, one which could so easily escalate into a major phenomenon . . . if handled correctly? A miracle cure in his diocese. Something extraordinary, proven beyond all doubt. Bishop Caines was a pragmatist; the Holy Roman Catholic Church would not be harmed by such a miracle in these cynical and anti-religious times. The Holy Roman Catholic Church would benefit by it.

Imagine: a holy shrine in his diocese . . .

He pushed the thought away, ashamed of his own vanity. But it lingered. And soon he knew what he had to do. Just in case . . . just in case it really had been a miracle . . .

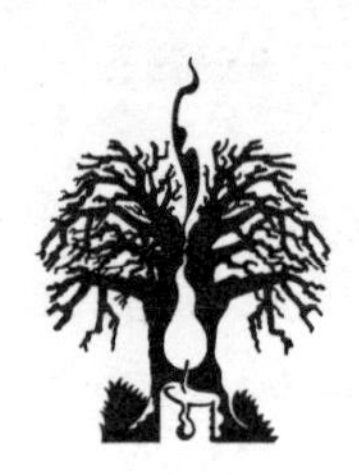

10

Once he was across the water he found himself at the gates of Hell. It was all black and sooty in there and the Devil wasn't at home, but his grandmother was sitting there in a big armchair.

The Brothers Grimm,
'The Three Golden Hairs of the Devil'

Bip bip bid-dip . . .

Molly Pagett's eyes flickered. Opened. What was the sound?

Her thin body lay stiff in the bed, her husband sprawled leadenly beside her. She held her breath, listening, wanting to hear the sound again, but dreading hearing it.

. . . bip bip bip bid-dip bip . . .

It was faint. And familiar.

She drew the covers back, careful not to wake Len. Her dressing gown was laid across the end of the bed and she drew it across her shoulders to keep away the chill of the night. Len grunted, turned over.

. . . bid-dip . . .

The sound, the familiar sound, was coming from Alice's room. Molly sat on the edge of the bed for a few moments, collecting her thoughts, shooing away the remaining dregs of a restless sleep. The day had been long, a confusing mixture of joy and anxiety. They had wanted to keep Alice overnight in the hospital again, but Molly would not consent to it. Somehow she felt their tampering, their tests, their probing – their endless questions – would undo the miracle.

. . . bip bip . . .

And miracle it was. There was no doubt in her mind. The Blessed Virgin Mary had smiled on their child.

. . . bip . . .

Molly rose from the bed, pulling the dressing gown tight around her. Quietly padding to the open door, fearful of waking Len, she stepped into the hallway. She had left the door open just in case Alice cried out in the night – the *joy* of having Alice cry out in the night! It was a sound Molly had not heard since her daughter was very small. How she had listened in those early days, alert for the slightest whimper, the beginnings of a cry. Molly would scamper up the stairs, or rush along the hallway, in a panic which her husband could only scoff at. But then he had never appreciated just how much the new baby had meant to Molly. Alice had filled a barren, empty life, an answer to years of prayer. God, through the divine intercession of Mary, Mother of Jesus, to whom Molly had fervently prayed, had blessed her with marriage and child.

How cruel, then, to smite the child so young. (And how disappointing the marriage.)

. . . bip bid-dip . . .

Now once again, Our Lady had intervened. The affliction had gone, just as suddenly as it had come. Molly's faith in the Blessed Virgin had not wilted during the years of trial, and she had encouraged Alice to worship Mary as she did. If anything, her daughter's adoration for Christ's Mother was even greater. And the years of devotion had been rewarded.

Molly stood outside Alice's door. Silence for a while then –

. . . bid-dip bid-dip bip bip . . .

The excitement of the last two days had been too much for Alice: it was the middle of the night and she could not sleep. She loved to watch the luminous green invaders descending the black screen of the microchip toy, destroying them with a quick stab at the red button, flicking a switch with the other hand so that her spaceship scuttled from side to side, dodging the invaders' deadly bombs. Now she could hear the machine, hear the computered pipes of victory when the last invader had been vanquished from dark plastic space. It must seem like a new toy again to her.

. . . bip bip . . .

But she had to sleep. The doctors had insisted that she rested. And Molly did not want a relapse. That would be too harsh of God . . .

. . . bip . . .

She pushed open the door.

. . . bi –

Molly was not sure that she had seen the small green light vanish on the far side of the room. It had been just a flicker in the corner of her eye, and it could have been nothing at all. She looked towards Alice's bed, expecting to see her daughter sitting up, eyes wide and happy, Galaxy Invaders in her hands. All she saw in the street light shining through the curtains was the little shape beneath the bed-clothes.

'Alice?' Molly realized how naturally she had called her name, how swift was the acceptance of her daughter's returned senses, as though she had never really accepted their loss. 'Alice, are you awake?'

There was no sound. Nothing from the child, nothing from the machine.

Molly smiled in the gloom and moved towards the bed. Little faker, she scolded silently, teasing your mum.

She bent over her daughter, ready to tickle her nose and end the pretence. She stayed her hand. Alice really was asleep. Her breathing was too deep and her face too much in repose for her to be faking.

'Alice,' Molly said again, softly, touching her shoulder. The child did not stir.

Molly lifted the covers, searching for the electronic toy, expecting it to be cuddled in Alice's arms. It wasn't there. And it wasn't on the floor beside the bed. But it had to be nearby, Alice couldn't have scooted across the room to get back into bed before she had entered. It wasn't possible.

Molly knelt and ducked her head to floor level, peering beneath the bed. No plastic shape lurked there.

She remembered the green fading light.

No, that was ridiculous. Just not possible.

But she looked anyway.

The electronic game was lying on the small dressing table on the other side of the room, its switch in the OFF position, its screen black and lifeless.

Molly knew she hadn't imagined the familiar sound. She also knew it could not have been in her daughter's hands. And there was no one else in the room. Just shadows and the sound of Alice's steady breathing.

11

> 'Could you keep a secret, if I told you one? It's a great secret, I don't know what I should do if anyone found it out. I believe I should die!'
>
> Frances Hodgson Burnett, *The Secret Garden*

Fenn rolled over in the bed and his own groan brought him awake. His head seemed to continue rolling.

'Oh, Jes . . .' He winced, one hand fumbling towards the throbbing lump that common sense told him really was his forehead. His fingers hardly eased the pain at all.

Turning onto his back, a hand over his closed eyes, he endeavoured to control the spinning sensation. Another groan developed into a low, self-pitying hum, a sound which was in perfect harmony with the higher-pitched hum melodying around inside his head. A full minute later, the cadence began to ease and slowly, experimentally, he eased back the shutters over his eyes. It was another half-minute before he lifted his hand.

The ceiling settled down when he stopped blinking and he considered sitting up in the bed. Consideration over, he lay there and groped a hand towards the bedside table, careful not to lift his head from the pillow, nor turn it in any direction.

The searching fingers could not find his wristwatch and he cursed his necessary habit of keeping the alarm clock as far away from the bed as possible (necessary because it was much too easy to turn off the bell and go back to sleep; he found the distance covered to find the bastard was enough to arouse him from his usual morning-zombie state). Where the hell was his watch? He couldn't have been that drunk last night. On the other hand, he could well have been.

Fenn sighed, screwed up his courage, and let his head slide towards the edge of the bed. Head hanging over, blood beginning to pound at the slab of concrete inside like waves against a sea wall, he stared at the floor. No watch there. But one arm was hanging over the edge too, hand bent back limply against the floor.

'Stupid, stupid,' he muttered when he spied the leather strap around his wrist. He twisted his arm and squinted at the watchface. Six minutes past eleven. It had to be morning; that was light coming through the closed curtains.

He drew himself back towards the centre of the bed, resisting the urge to lie down again. Head resting against the headboard, back propped up by the pillow, he tried to remember how he had come to this state. Beer and brandy was the answer.

He scratched his chest and mentally – the physical act would have been too painful – shook his head at himself. You gotta cut it out, Fenn. A young drunkard could be fun, an old one just a bloody bore; and you're not getting younger. Journalists had the reputation of being big drinkers, and it wasn't true. They were *enormous* drinkers. Not all of them, of course; just those he knew personally.

Fenn tentatively pushed himself further up in the bed. He called this slow method of reclaiming the day 'gradual resurrection'.

Memories of the night before came filtering through and he grinned once or twice, but ended up frowning and lifting the bedclothes to inspect his lower body as though suspecting something might be missing. He grunted with relief; still there although it was making no big thing of it. What the hell was the girl's name? Boz, Roz, something like that. Or it might have been Julia. He shrugged, not really caring. So long as I'm not pregnant, he told himself.

He eased the covers away, using his feet to kick them towards the end of the bed. Then slowly, and ever so carefully, he teased his body from the bed. His head weighed more than the rest of him and the trick was to keep it balanced on his shoulders as he made towards the window. He drew the curtains, sensible enough to keep his eyes closed against the glare which he knew would hit the room; the sun was especially partial to his bedroom at that time of day. He stood there, allowing the rays to warm his body, the worst of the day's coldness blocked by the glass. When he finally opened his eyes he saw a woman trudging up the hill outside, pushing a supermarket trolley laden with shopping before her, staring up open-mouthed at his naked body. Her stride did not break, although her progress was slow, and her head swivelled round in an almost *Exorcist* turn. Fenn faded back into the room, smiling sheepishly and giving the shopper a friendly little wave to show there was no menace in him. He hoped her head would not lock into its unnatural position.

Once out of the sunlight, coldness staked its claim with tiny, itchy goose-pimples, and Fenn grabbed his dressing gown from the end of the bed. It was short and loose, ending well above his knees, and looked much better on Sue. It had looked pretty good on Boz, Roz – or was it Anthea? – last night, too, but not as good as on Sue. Even that drunk he had noticed and noted.

He went into the kitchen and filled the kettle, staring at the running water as though fascinated, but not really seeing it. He switched the kettle on and then ran both hands through his rumpled hair. I need a cigarette, he told himself, and was relieved he didn't smoke. The note was propped up against the cornflakes packet and he pulled out a chair and studied the message for a few seconds without touching it. It was a telephone number and signed 'Pam'. Oh yeah, *that* was her name. He briefly wondered whether she had tried to wake him before leaving the flat. Probably had, not knowing it would take a major earthquake to rouse him after a drunken binge. Only Sue could do it with sneaky groping hands, but then she had a technique all her own. He laid Pam's note down on the table and tried to remember what she looked like. He remembered remarking to Eddy, his drinking-buddy from the sports page of the *Courier*, 'Nice face, shame about the legs,' when they saw her and a friend in the club, but couldn't recapture her image. The legs, though. Yeah, they were coming back. They'll crush your little head, Eddy had warned him; and Eddy hadn't been far wrong, he now recalled. He gingerly touched his ears and wondered if they were as red as they felt. Could ears bruise? He went into the bathroom to check.

When Fenn returned to the kitchen, satisfied at least that his ears had not been pressed flat against the sides of his head, but not too pleased with the bleary-eyed reflection that had sneered at him from the bathroom mirror, the room was filled with steam. He had taken time to ease the punishment on his bladder, senses suddenly sharp for any strange tingling sensation as the liquid flowed; you could never be too sure with girls you didn't know. And some that you thought you did.

Jesus, he missed Sue.

He poured the boiling water into a cup, only remembering to add coffee when he was settled down at the kitchen table again. It burnt his lips when he sipped, but at least it was a clean, stinging pain, not like the droning ache in his head. He dipped his hand into the cornflakes packet and ate some, reflecting sombrely that it was just as well he was working the night shift; he was in no fit state this morning.

He looked around the small kitchen and shuddered. He would have to make an effort today; he couldn't go on living in such a pig-sty. Maybe he was a little untidy, but this mess was ridiculous. Time to get yourself back together, Fenn. No woman was worth it. Are you kidding? he answered himself. Every one was worth it – well, maybe with just a few exceptions.

Fifteen minutes later he was still brooding over his third cup of coffee when the doorbell rang.

He leaned out of the kitchen window and saw Sue standing in the street below. Either his hangover cleared instantly or racing emotions swamped the ill effects. She looked up and waved.

He found it difficult to speak for a few moments, then stuttered, 'Use your . . . your key, Sue.'

'I didn't like to,' she called up.

She fumbled in her shoulder-bag, then stuck the key into the lock. Fenn drew his head back inside, scraping the hair on the back of his head painfully against the frame. He rubbed the skin and couldn't stop smiling. He hadn't seen her for nearly three weeks, not since she'd walked out of the restaurant. They'd had several strained telephone conversations, but that was all. It had taken her absence to make him realize how hooked he was on her. He leaned against the cooker, still smiling, relieved, expectant.

'Oh, shit!' The smile vanished.

Fenn scooped up the note still lying on the kitchen table and considered swallowing it; he shoved it into his pocket instead. Running into the lounge, he did a quick survey of the room. No incriminating evidence there. Then into the bedroom, lunging at the bed, scouring it for fallen hairgrips, strands of hair coloured differently to his own, smudges of lipstick or eyeshadow on the pillows. He made sure there were no other stains either. Sighing with relief, he allowed himself a few moments to collect his thoughts. Then Christ, did she smoke? He couldn't remember. No ashtray beside the bed. The lounge! There'd be cigarette butts smudged with lipstick in the lounge! He ran back in just as Sue opened the flat door.

'Sue,' he said, sniffing the air for the stale aroma of cigarettes. The air seemed to be okay if just a little alcoholic.

'Hello, Gerry.' Her smile was not a full one.

'You look terrific,' he said.

'You look awful.'

He rubbed his unshaven chin, feeling awkward. 'How've you been?'

'Fine. You?'

'Pretty good.'

He stuck his hands into the pockets of the robe. 'Why the hell didn't you return my calls?' He tried to keep his voice level, but the last word was on the ascendant. 'For Christ's sake, three weeks!'

'Not quite. And I've spoken to you a couple of times.'

'Yeah, you just haven't said anything.'

'I haven't come to argue with you, Gerry.'

He stopped himself from a retort, then said quietly: 'You wanna coffee?'

'I haven't got long. I'm on my way to the university to tape some interviews.'

'A quick one.' He went into the kitchen and reboiled the kettle. He was fortunate to find one cup that was clean at the back of the cupboard.

Her voice came through from the lounge. 'This place is a mess.'

'The maid's day off,' he called back.

When he returned she was sitting on the settee, calmly watching him. He felt a tightness in his chest; she looked good. He placed the two cups on the glass coffee-table, then eased himself down into the other end of the small sofa. A two-foot gap separated them.

'I called round once or twice,' he told her.

'I've been spending a lot more time at my parents with Ben.'

He nodded. 'How is he?'

'Boisterous as ever.' She sipped and pulled a face. 'Your coffee hasn't improved.'

'Nor has my disposition. No shit, Sue, I've missed you.'

She stared into her cup. 'I needed a break from you. You were becoming . . . a little too much.'

'Yeah, I know. It's a habit of mine.'

'I needed a breather.'

'You said. Nothing personal, right?'

'Stop it, Gerry.'

He chewed on his lip.

'And maybe you needed a break from me, too,' she said.

'No, babe, I didn't.'

She couldn't help asking. 'Have you been seeing anyone?'

He looked squarely into her eyes. 'No. I haven't wanted to.' His ears tingled sorely for a few guilty seconds. He cleared his throat and said, 'How about you?'

Sue shook her head. 'I told you, I've been busy with Ben.'

She sipped her coffee again and he moved closer. He took the cup from her hand and placed it back on the saucer. His fingers travelled to her neck, beneath her hair. He kissed her cheek, then turned her head with his other hand to reach her lips.

She was soft, yielding against him, returning his kiss with an emotion that matched his; but then she was pulling away, one hand held against his shoulder.

'Please don't. That's not why I'm here.' She seemed to have difficulty in breathing.

He ignored her and tried again, a feeling that was more than just desire strong within him.

'No, Gerry!' This time there was anger.

He stopped, having problems with his own breathing. 'Sue . . .'

Her glare stopped his words. And further action. Fenn struggled to contain his own anger. 'Okay, okay.' He turned away from her in a heavy sulk. 'What the hell have you come for, Sue? Just to collect some of your things?'

He heard her sigh. 'Not to upset you, Gerry. I didn't want that,' she said.

'Who's upset? I'm not upset. I may break out in pimples any moment now, but that's just late puberty. Christ, how could you upset me?'

'You're such a bloody baby!'

'Go ahead, turn on your charm.'

She had to smile, despite herself. 'Gerry, I came to tell you about the church. The church at Banfield.'

He looked at her curiously.

'I've been back. I've taken Ben there on Sundays.'

He opened his mouth to speak, but couldn't find anything to say.

'It's wonderful, Gerry.' Now her smile was full, and her eyes were shining with excitement. The transition was so swift it took Fenn by surprise.

'So many people are flocking to St Joseph's,' Sue went on. 'People are bringing their children, their sick, their handicapped. It's almost like a pilgrimage to them. And the happiness – it seems to hit you before you even reach the church grounds. It's unbelievable, Gerry.'

'Hey now, wait a minute. I thought it had all died down. I've rung the priest there – this Father Hagan – and he told me nothing more has happened. No more miracles, no more apparitions. Certainly nothing newsworthy or the Nationals would have been swarming over it like flies over a shit heap.'

'You have to be there to see it! Of course there's no more physical miracles, but the miracle is the atmosphere itself. That's why I came today, Gerry. I want you to see it for yourself. I want you to experience it.'

He frowned. 'But I'm not a Catholic, Sue.'

'You don't have to be, that's the joy of it. You only have to *feel* to know it's a holy place.'

'But why should the priest lie to me?'

'He didn't lie. Nothing is happening in the material sense; he told you the truth. He doesn't want the situation exploited, can't you see that?'

'And do you?'

'Of course not.'

'Then why are you telling me?'

She took his hand and clasped it tightly in both of hers. 'Because I want some of that cynicism knocked out of that silly head of yours. If you could just see for yourself the effect the place has on people, I know you'll begin to have some beliefs yourself.'

'Wait a minute. You're beginning to sound like a religious freak. You're not trying to convert me, are you?'

She surprised him by laughing. 'I don't think the Holy Ghost Himself could do that. No, I just want you to bear witness—'

'Oh, definitely a religious—'

'Just see for yourself.' Her voice had become quiet.

He drew in a deep breath and sank back against the sofa.

'What about the girl, Alice? Is she still going to the church?'

'That's the other thing you have to see.'

'What do you mean?'

'It's hard to say.' Her words were slow, deliberate, as though her thoughts were deep. 'She seems to have changed.'

'In what way?'

'It's difficult to describe. She seems – I don't know – older, more mature. There's a special kind of aura around her. Some people weep when they see her.'

'Ah come on, Sue. It's just some kind of hysteria. They've heard the story – their minds are doing the rest.'

'See for yourself.'

'Maybe I should.' He had to admit, he was becoming curious about the whole affair once more. The contact with Sue might bring them back together again, too. 'I could go there this afternoon,' he said.

'No. Wait 'til Sunday.'

He looked questioningly at her.

'Come to the Mass with me, when the crowds will be there.'

'You know it could have fizzled out by then. The place might be empty.'

'I doubt it. But there's another reason I want you to come

on Sunday.' She got to her feet, looking at her watch. 'I've got to go or I'll be in trouble.'

'What? What are you talking about? You can't just leave.'

Sue walked to the door. 'I'm sorry, Gerry, I really do have to go. Pick me up on Sunday morning at my place. Ben will be staying with me so we can all go together.' She opened the door.

'But what was the other reason?' he asked, still sitting perplexed on the sofa.

'There's a rumour that Alice has told the priest and her mother that the Lady wants to see her again. On the 28th. That's this Sunday.'

Sue closed the door quietly behind her.

12

You parents all that children have,
And you that have got none,
If you would have them safe abroad,
Pray keep them safe at home.

Old Nursery Rhyme

This Sunday was different. It was cold, drizzling, and miserable. But Fenn's senses keened to the excitement in the air as a rat's nose twitches at the scent of distant blood.

Sue had been right: it hit you before you reached the church grounds. The first signs came as he drove through the village High Street: there was a bustling activity that was unusual for a Sunday morning in any town, village or city, particularly on a cold and damp one. And most of the people were heading in the same direction. Traffic, too, was far heavier than normal.

Ben, in the back seat, had become quiet, which was a relief at any time. His arms were resting against the back of the front passenger seat, his face close to his mother's. Fenn quickly glanced at the eight-year-old boy and saw an expectant look in those large brown eyes; Ben's mouth was open and half-smiling as he stared ahead through the windscreen.

'Are you beginning to feel the atmosphere, Gerry?' Sue asked, looking past her son's head at the reporter.

Fenn muttered non-committally. He wasn't prepared to admit anything yet. He slowed the car as they approached a zebra crossing and the gathering on the pavement waved acknowledgements as they scurried across. Small children clutched their parents' hands, the elderly hung on to sturdier companions. A middle-aged man in a wheelchair came last, pushed by a younger man: their similarity in appearance indicated they were father and son. The cripple smiled at Fenn, then looked over his shoulder at his son, urging him to push faster.

Once the road was clear, Fenn eased his foot down on the accelerator, aware that traffic had built up behind him. The traffic moved off in convoy, Fenn's Mini at its head.

He glanced into his rearview mirror, surprised at the swift build-up he had caused. 'I hope we're not all going to the same place,' he commented.

'I think you're in for a surprise,' Sue replied.

He was passing groups of people along the roadside now, the houses on either side becoming fewer until there were only fields and trees. Even the steady drizzle could not dampen the cheerfulness that seemed to exude from the walkers.

Soon there were cars parked by the roadside, all driven half onto the grass verge.

'I don't believe this,' Fenn said as they were forced to drive past the church entrance.

'I said you'd be surprised.' There was no hint of smugness in Sue's voice.

He scanned each side of the road, looking for a space. 'Has it been like this every Sunday since?'

'No. It's been crowded, but not like this. The rumour has obviously spread.'

'You didn't tell me how you heard about it.' He swerved the Mini to avoid an opening door. Two metal sticks stretched out from the other vehicle's interior, followed by two ill-controlled legs. The driver was just emerging to assist his invalid passenger as Fenn's car passed.

'I was here at the evening service last Wednesday. I overheard some parishioners talking.'

Fenn risked a quick look at her. 'You were at evening service? In the week?'

'That's right, Gerry.'

'Right.'

He pulled in behind the last vehicle in the line. 'I guess this'll do,' he said ironically. The Mini bumped onto the verge and another car pulled up in front almost immediately. 'Okay, Ben, time to get wet.'

The boy was already pushing at the back of his mother's seat, eager to get going. Sue stepped out and pulled the passenger seat forward, allowing Ben to scramble through. Fenn slammed his door shut and pulled up the collar of his raincoat. 'Fine day for a bloody carnival,' he muttered under his breath. He tucked his hands into the coat's large pockets, conscious of the bulky object in one: this time, after moans from the *Courier*'s picture editor, who hadn't liked his last pocket-camera efforts, he had borrowed an Olympus. *If* (and it was a big *if*) anything happened, he was going to be prepared. In his other pocket he carried a micro-cassette recorder, a Christmas gift from Sue. They set off towards the church, Sue's arm linked through his, Ben racing ahead.

More vehicles were slowing, then stopping just beyond his. The gate to the pathway leading up to the church was crammed with people and Sue had to grab Ben, holding him close to prevent him from being jostled. Fenn stared around at the eager throng, bemused and becoming excited himself with their mood. Even if nothing spectacular happened – and he was sure it wouldn't – he now had a nice follow-up story to the previous one. It might take a little exaggeration on his part to say that St Joseph's was being besieged by pilgrims, believers and the just-plain-curious, but it wasn't too far from the truth. He shook his head in wonder: what the hell did they all expect to see? Another miracle? He suppressed a chuckle, delighted now that Sue had persuaded him to come. It wasn't going to be a complete waste of time.

The three of them, Fenn, Sue and Ben, squeezed through the open gateway, bunched together by the shuffling crowd. Fenn noticed that a young girl on his left, no more than fifteen or sixteen, was trembling visibly, then quickly realized her spasmodic movements were something more than just excitement. The tight drooping of one side of her mouth gave him a hint, for he had seen the disorder before. Her movements were clumsy, her hands and arms twitching uncontrollably; she was flanked on either side by a man and woman, presumably her parents. If he was right, the girl was suffering from a form of chorea, most probably St Vitus's Dance, for he had seen exactly the same symptoms in a young woman he'd interviewed in a Brighton hospital when covering the story of the hospital's imminent closure because of government cuts. It was an assignment he hadn't enjoyed, for the sick always made him feel unhealthy, but at least his article, with its many poignant interviews from the patients, had helped cause a stay of execution for the hospital. Its future was still uncertain, but that was better than positively no future at all.

He stood aside, allowing the small group more room for

manoeuvring, and the father smiled gratefully. Once through the gate, the queue thinned out, although the line stretched up to the church doorway itself. There were several among the throng who, like the young girl, were helped along by others. They passed a small emaciated-looking boy in a wheelchair, chattering happily to his surrounding family, his eyes, large and bulging, shining with some inner exhilaration. Fenn saw the smiling sadness in the face of the boy's mother; and there was hope in her expression, too, a desperate hope. It made Fenn feel uncomfortable, as if he were a voyeur into the private misery of others. Not just that, though: he was about to be a witness to their disappointment. He could sympathize with their desperation, but could not understand their gullibility. What had happened to little Alice Pagett had been a fluke of nature, an accidental triggering off of something in her brain that had over-ridden other, disobedient nerves, returning senses that she had never really lost physically; these people now thought the same chance process could happen to themselves or those in their care. It was, he had to admit, strangely moving. And he began to feel anger, for he resented having his protective wall of cynicism breached by such blatant stupidity, and that anger was turned towards the Church which nourished and encouraged such ignorance. His rancour had become seething indignation by the time they reached the porch.

Inside the church it was crowded, the rows of pews full to capacity. Fenn had expected it to be so because of the activity outside, but was nevertheless surprised by the size of the congregation. And the noise, the steady murmur of whispered conversations. A peaceful silence, he had always assumed, was the prerequisite of any church when not responding to the service taking place, but it seemed today the collective tenseness was difficult to contain.

Looking at his watch he saw that it was still sixteen minutes before the start of the Mass. If they had come any later, they would never have got inside the door.

Sue dipped her fingers into the font, making the Sign of the Cross in a quick, fluid movement and encouraging Ben to follow suit. The boy reached into the receptacle, but his ritual was slower, more solemn. One of the men obviously designated as ushers to control the inflowing crowd politely gestured for the three of them to move to the left of the church towards a side aisle where those unable to find seats were standing. Fenn resisted, for he already knew from which vantage point he wished to view the proceedings. He took Sue's elbow and guided her towards the right. The usher opened his mouth to protest and decided it really wasn't worth it.

Sue looked at Fenn in surprise as he urged her towards the spot they had occupied on his previous visit. There were a few disapproving stares as they jostled their way through, Ben anxiously clinging to his mother's coat, but they reached the right-hand aisle without hindrance. She was puzzled as Fenn stood on tiptoe, craning his neck towards the front of the church, then realized he was looking for Alice Pagett, whom he no doubt assumed would be sitting beneath the statue of Our Lady again. There was no way of telling if she was there, for the aisle was too full. Sue noticed there were more wheelchairs alongside the benches and emotion swept through her, feelings aroused in her that had been held in check for many years. Those emotions had been growing over the last three weeks and now she felt them unleashed, flowing through her and outwards, joining with others, uniting. She wasn't sure what these feelings were, but they had much to do with compassion, love for others. She felt like crying and knew she was not alone in that feeling. There was an anticipation inside her that exulted yet frightened her.

Even now, she was still uncertain as to whether or not Alice's cure had been miraculous, although she wanted to believe with all her heart. After years in a spiritual wilderness, clinging by only a thin thread to her religion, something had happened here at this church which had drawn her back, the absorption gradual at first, the link still tenuous, until her own will had strengthened the renewed acceptance. She had witnessed something extraordinary, be it a miracle or not, and that impression had rekindled her trust. And *that* was the feeling she shared with so many others gathered in St Joseph's church. *Trust.* It pervaded the air like the accompanying smell of incense.

She hugged Ben close and tenderly touched Fenn's arm, loving them both and wanting their love.

Fenn turned and winked and a small unpleasant shock made her hand drop away. The rushing compassion coursing through her almost stumbled to a halt, tripped by his wink of reality. No, not *her* reality, but *his*. His insensitivity, his mocking attitude. His only reason for being here was because there might be a story in it, a sequel to a feature that had enhanced his journalistic reputation. She thought he had come because he loved her and wanted to please; she had persuaded him because of her feelings towards him, wanting him to share her own acceptance. That one small gesture of his had dispelled her sentiment, made her realize they were two very different people, for it had contained the destructive contempt, no matter how lightly or how humorously disguised, of the detractor, the person who would never believe – never *trust* – because to do so would influence their own self-seeking opportunism. At that moment – and this was why her emotions had stumbled – she despised him.

He frowned as she stared at him, recognizing the sudden hostility in her eyes and confused by it. Sue averted her gaze, leaving him wondering.

More people were crowding in from behind, forcing them to move further down the aisle. Fenn tried once more to see the front bench, but there were still too many heads blocking his view. His initial excitement was now beginning to fade, the waiting and the claustrophobic atmosphere of the packed church taking effect. The tension was still around him, but he no longer shared it, or at least, not its particular brand of tension; his feelings were more of sharp curiosity. He examined the faces of those sitting in the benches. Were they all from the village or had word spread further afield? He recognized some, for he had spoken to them before on the day Alice had been cured. His gaze stopped on a particularly familiar face, this one seen only in half-profile, for the figure sat on the other side of the centre aisle, near the front. It was Southworth, the hotel owner. Well, Mr Southworth, it seemed, had been wrong: interest hadn't completely died away. Maybe it would after today, though. The punters were expecting too much, and they could only be disappointed. In fact, he wouldn't be at all surprised if there were some angry scenes after the service.

Fenn looked for the fat man, Tucker, whom he had met with Southworth at the hotel, but he was either hidden from view or not present. A disturbance at the back of the church drew his attention.

The doors were being closed, much to the annoyance of those still outside. Heads were turning as the dispute grew louder and a dark-suited man, wearing the unobtrusive collar of the modern-day cleric, rose from the front bench and strode purposefully up the centre aisle towards the source of the trouble. He was tall, well over six feet Fenn estimated, even though his shoulders were stooped, and he was painfully thin. Yet his face, with its high forehead and prominent nose, showed strength, a fact further confirmed by his vigorous stride. The priest's cheeks were sunken, his cheekbones high ridges on shadowed valleys, and his skin had a jaundiced look that betrayed a past illness; yet even that failed to detract from the strength.

When he reached the end of the aisle, he raised a hand as if to gently scythe a way through the crowd gathered there, and Fenn was surprised at its size; from where the reporter stood, it looked as though the priest's fingers could easily wrap themselves around a football. It may have been an exaggeration in Fenn's mind, but the congregation back there seemed to agree, for they parted before the advancing limb like the sea heeding Moses. He followed the tall man's progress, for he was easily seen above the heads of others, and wondered who he was and why he was there. Within seconds, the priest was walking back down the aisle, the disturbance behind having settled, the doors of the church left open wide, despite the chill, and Fenn had a chance to study the man's face in more detail.

His eyes were cast downwards, the lids heavy, giving the appearance of being completely closed. His jaw was firm, though not prominently so, and the upper lip slightly protruding, spoiling what otherwise would have been dauntingly strong features. His brow was furrowed in deep lines, and further wrinkles were etched sharply around his eyes, curling both upwards and downwards like the splayed ends of a wire brush. His eyebrows were grey and full, like his hair, shadowing his eye-sockets. His stoop was more than fatigue or negligent posture; the spine was curved unnaturally, though not badly. The priest genuflected, then took his seat once more. Fenn had the distinct feeling of just having witnessed a magnetic storm in human form. He realized, too, that the buzz of hushed conversation had come to an abrupt halt while the priest was on the move. The whispers began again now that the intimidating figure had disappeared from view.

The crowd at the rear swelled into the centre channel and the three ushers forced their way through to form a human barrier, preventing the overflow from filling the aisle completely. Fenn was intrigued by everything that was happening and already regretting not having followed up his story in the ensuing weeks. Evidently an undercurrent of interest and speculation had developed in the area, culminating in today's little turnout. They wanted to see the trick done again. Maybe a bit more this time, though. We've had the triple somersault, now let's see the quadruple. That was why they had brought their sick along. Great trick last time, but what's in it for me? Or: Sorry, missed the last show – can we have a repeat?

His story, the angle, the view it would take, was already forming in his mind and it had much to do with gullibility, superstition, avarice – and, yes, maybe even duplicity. The meeting with Southworth and Tucker, whose motives leaned more than overtly towards exploitation, gave a good indication of what could be behind the spreading rumours. They had tried to recruit him into their campaign and had been disappointed, but probably not discouraged. And how culpable was the Catholic Church itself? Just how much had they done to dispel the story of a miracle? Or had they encouraged it? Fenn felt grimly satisfied: there was the makings of some nice investigative journalism here. Not enough to set the world on fire, but controversial enough to sell a few extra copies in the southern counties. Then he glanced at Sue and fingers of guilt pushed at his thoughts.

Her head was bowed, her hands clasped tightly on Ben's shoulders. She was praying silently, a small frown of concentration on her forehead. Even Ben was still, lost in his own thoughts.

Fenn was perplexed. Sue was no fool and certainly not naïve as far as religion was concerned. At least, not since he had known her. So why this change? What had happened to bring her back to the Church so swiftly and with such conviction? And how would she react to the exposé he was already planning? He tried to shrug off the uncomfortable guilt: perhaps his story would bring her to her senses. He hoped so, because there was no way he could back off now he'd bitten the bait.

The tinkling of a bell startled him and a general movement swept through the church as those in the congregation lucky enough to have seats stood, and those already standing came to reverential attention. A door to the left side of the altar had opened and Fenn could just see movement between the heads of those standing at the front. The organ sounded its first chords, a brief clue as to which key the hymn was to be sung in, and throats were cleared and breaths drawn in. The start of the hymn was ragged, but quickly gained a unified momentum.

The priest mounted the two steps to the altar and turned to face the congregation. Fenn was surprised and a little shocked by the change in Father Hagan's appearance. The man seemed to have aged, to have become almost bowed. His eyes had the strange luminous quality of someone who was near death through hunger, and his skin had become sallow, stretched across his cheekbones. His tongue flicked across his lips in a nervous gesture and Fenn noticed that the priest's eyes flitted around the church in swift movements as though the very size of the congregation was unsettling to him. Hagan's vestments were no longer a shield; they merely emphazised the frailty beneath them.

Fenn leaned closer to Sue to make a comment on the disturbing change in the priest, but realized she was too absorbed in the service itself to notice.

Throughout the long Mass – drearily long, to him – he studied Father Hagan, gradually becoming aware that the man's deterioration was not as drastic as he had first supposed (or it could have been that the priest was regaining more of his previous stature as the Mass continued). It might also have been the fact that Fenn had not seen him for some time, and the sudden confrontation had heightened the aspects of change.

At the sign of peace, when everybody present shook their neighbour's hand and bade them, 'Peace be with you,' Fenn offered his hand to Sue. She looked at him coldly before taking it and her grip had no firmness. When she released him, he held on, squeezing her palm in an effort to make some mental contact. Her eyes dropped downwards and it seemed as though a shadow crossed her features. Fenn could only stare until a tiny hand tugged at his raincoat and he looked down to see Ben thrusting his hand upwards, waiting to shake.

'Peace be with you, Ben,' Fenn whispered, glancing again at Sue. She was watching the priest on the altar.

The Mass continued and, after the Eucharist Prayer, Fenn's interest switched to the congregation itself. Those wishing to receive Communion surged forward with undignified (and perhaps unholy) haste, causing a bustling bottleneck in the centre aisle. Invalids in wheelchairs, others on crutches, came forward, and Fenn could not help but feel sorry for them. Their desperation was obvious and it renewed his anger to see them exploited so. There were children in the queue, none younger than seven years old, but several not far past that age. They were eager and wide-eyed, probably not understanding exactly what was going on, but caught up in the excitement of it all. A youth of seventeen or more was being led towards the altar as if he were a five-year-old, and his shuffling gait explained why. The boy was severely retarded and Fenn could see the brimming hope on his mother's face.

Father Hagan's expression was one of anguish as he surveyed the long treble line of worshippers and the reporter grudgingly sympathized. He felt sure that none of it was the priest's doing and that Hagan was just as appalled as he, himself.

There were several nuns among the slow-moving procession, their heads bowed, hands clasped tightly together. The hymn being sung reached its conclusion, the verses running out long before the queue, leaving only the noise of scuffling feet and echoing coughs. Returning communicants were pushing their way along side aisles to their seats, causing those standing to crush against their neighbours to allow them through. A small figure suddenly appeared before Fenn, and the reporter winced when he saw the boy's hands were covered in unsightly verrucas. In the centre aisle another child, this one a boy also, was being carried towards the priest, his legs wrapped in a heavy blanket. It was the same child whom Fenn had seen in the wheelchair on the path leading to the church. The boy, coaxed by the man holding him, opened his mouth to receive the Host and the priest's eyes were filled with fresh sadness.

The procession went on, a constant human stream that seemed to have no end, and twice there was a delay while Father Hagan prepared more wafers. Finally, his reserves were depleted and the priest was forced to announce the fact to those still waiting.

Fenn took grim amusement in their disappointment as the

remains of the queue shuffled mournfully back to their places. It was like a bloody pub with no beer, he told himself.

The Mass ended soon after and the congregation looked around at each other as if expecting more. The priest and his white-frocked entourage disappeared into the sacristy, and the sense of anticlimax was almost tangible. Murmurs ran around the church and heads peered towards the right-hand side of the altar, to the pew beneath the statue of Our Lady. The whispers came back over the rows of seats: the little girl wasn't there. Alice Pagett had not attended Mass that morning. There were a few audible moans, a few muttered complaints, but because they were in the House of God, most of the congregation kept their grievances to themselves. They left the church, clearly feeling they had been let down, but having no recourse to take (which increased their frustration).

People were pushing against Fenn, and Sue looked up at him questioningly, ready, herself, to leave the church.

'Take Ben out with you, Sue, and I'll meet you back at the car,' he told her.

'What are you going to do?' she asked as she was jostled from behind.

'I just want to have a few words with the priest.'

'You can't go into the sacristy, Gerry.' She was almost forbidding him to.

'They gonna burn me in oil? Don't worry, I won't be long.'

Before she could protest further, he eased past her into the advancing crowd.

It was hard going, but churchgoers were not generally arrogant as a crowd and they made way for him where they could. The benches were emptying and he used one as a channel to reach the centre aisle. He stopped briefly to catch a closer look at the statue of the Madonna, the stone image that had fascinated Alice Pagett so, and briefly considered taking a quick photograph. Deciding it might be better to snap a few later when the church was empty – he didn't want to upset anyone present, especially the clergy – Fenn resumed his journey.

Once in the main aisle, the going was easier, for the crowd was more concentrated towards the church exit by now. He crossed the front of the altar, heading for the door at its side, finding it slightly ajar. He hesitated before entering. There were voices coming from inside.

'. . . why, Monsignor, why do they listen to these rumours? What have they expected—'

'Calm yourself, Father. You must behave as on any normal Sunday by going to the door of your church and conversing with your parishioners. If you wish to discourage them from such idle wishful-thinking, then show them that everything is normal.' The second voice was deep, commanding.

Fenn pushed open the door, deciding not to knock first. Father Hagan's back was to him, but the other cleric, the tall dark-suited man with the hunched shoulders, was facing the doorway. He stopped in mid-sentence, staring at the journalist over the smaller priest's shoulder. Hagan turned and his features stiffened when he saw Fenn.

'What do you want?' he asked, the hostility evident in his voice.

Not one to be easily intimidated, Fenn stepped inside. He smiled in pretended apology and said, 'I wondered if I could have a few words, Father.'

'I'm sorry, but you're not allowed in here,' the priest snapped back.

The altar-servers, three boys and a man, who had been

busy removing their cassocks, stopped and looked at the priest in surprise, his sharpness alien to his normally mild temperament.

Fenn held his ground. 'It won't take a minute.'

'I want you to leave right now.'

The reporter's smile dropped away as he returned the priest's icy glare. It was the older priest, the tall one, who quickly stepped in to break the deadlock. 'I'm Monsignor Delgard,' he said. 'Is there something we can help you with?'

'He's a reporter,' Hagan interrupted as Fenn began to reply. 'It's largely due to him that this fuss has been created.'

The older priest nodded and said pleasantly, 'You are Mr Fenn? The man who found Alice in the church grounds when this affair began? I'm very pleased to meet you, young man.' He offered his huge hand, which the reporter took cautiously. In fact, the cleric's grip was firm but surprisingly gentle.

'I didn't mean to barge in . . .' Fenn said and the priest smiled at the lie.

'I'm afraid we are rather busy at the moment, Mr Fenn, but if we could be of some assistance later?'

'Could you tell me why you're here at St Joseph's today?'

'Merely to assist Father Hagan. And to observe, of course.'

'Observe what, exactly?'

'You saw how many people attended Mass today. It would be silly for the church to pretend the congregation has not placed some special significance on this particular Sunday.'

'But have you, Monsignor?' The tape recorder in Fenn's pocket was running, flicked on by his thumb.

The priest hesitated, but he was still smiling. 'Let me just say we did not expect any phenomenon to occur. We are more concerned with our parishioners—'

'There's more than parishioners outside,' Fenn broke in. 'I'd say they've come from a larger area than Banfield.'

'Yes, I'm sure that's the case,' Hagan said coldly, 'but that's because your newspaper ran a grossly exaggerated story which played on the public's susceptibility.'

'I only reported what happened,' Fenn retorted.

'With some of your own speculation. And I might add, speculation that barely hid the cynicism behind it.'

'I'm not a Catholic, Father. You can't expect—'

'Please.' Monsignor Delgard stood firmly between the two protagonists, his big hands held at chest level as if to hold back their remarks. His voice was not raised, its tones barely hardened, but it was a voice to take notice of. 'I'm sure this discussion should continue – you must have your questions answered, Mr Fenn, and you, Father, may benefit from listening to a more objective view of this whole affair – but now is neither the time nor the place. I suggest you leave, Mr Fenn, and return some time later today.'

It was hardly a suggestion, more of a command. and one which the reporter reluctantly decided to obey. It would be better for the sake of his story to have Hagan's cooperation rather than his antagonism, and their conversation at this point was going nowhere useful. However, always one to turn a situation to his advantage, no matter how small, Fenn said, 'If I come back this evening will you give me an hour of your time?'

Father Hagan opened his mouth to protest, but Monsignor Delgard spoke quickly. 'As long as you like, Mr Fenn. We won't restrict your time.'

Fenn was taken aback. He'd expected half-an-hour, maybe twenty minutes. 'It's a deal,' he said with a grin, then pulled open the door.

The church was almost empty and it seemed much darker. He realized the rainclouds had become heavier, the light outside shining through the stained-glass windows poor and diffused, having no thrust. He closed the sacristy door and crossed the front of the altar towards the statue of the Madonna. The pupil-less eyes of the white statue gazed sightlessly down on him, its stone lips bearing the slightest traces of a benevolent smile. The sculptured hands stretched downwards, palms outwards, symbol of the Madonna's acceptance of all who stood before her.

It was just a block of stone to Fenn, a skilful effigy but one that had no meaning for him. The blank eyes were disturbing because they were blind; the look of compassion was meaningless because it was hand-made, not heart-felt.

He narrowed his eyes. And the statue was flawed. There was just the faintest hairline crack barely visible in the poor light, running from beneath the chin down one side of the neck. Nobody's perfect, he silently told the Madonna.

He was reaching inside his raincoat pocket for the camera, having decided it was as good an opportunity as any to photograph the statue, when running footsteps made him turn. A young boy of fifteen or sixteen was hurrying down the centre aisle, making for the altar. He did not seem to notice Fenn as he swung around the front bench and headed for the sacristy door. He thumped against the door with the flat of his hand, then burst in.

Fenn quickly hurried over and was just in time to hear the youth breathlessly say: 'It's Alice Pagett, Father. She's here.'

'But I instructed her mother to keep her away today,' came Father Hagan's voice .

'But she's here, Father. In the field, by the tree! And everybody's following her. They're all going into the field!'

13

'The Magic is in me – the Magic is in me. It's in every one of us.'

Frances Hodgson Burnett, *The Secret Garden*

When Fenn entered the sacristy he caught just a glimpse of the two priests and the boy departing through another door leading to the outside. The altar-boys and the older altar-server were still too surprised to move. The reporter ran through the room, following the three who had just left. Outside he found himself in the section of graveyard at the back of St Joseph's; the two priests and the youth were hurrying along a narrow path between the graves towards the low wall dividing the church grounds and the field beyond. He hurried to catch up, the eager gleam back in his eyes.

He veered off when he saw that the wall was crowded with people, many of whom were anxious to see into the field, but reluctant, for reasons of their own, to enter it. A section of wall towards the corner of the graveyard was clear, and it was this he made for. The two priests were trying to push through the jostling onlookers, but were having difficulty in reaching the wall. Fenn scuffed the top of a molehill with his shoe as he raced towards his chosen spot. The grass was damp and slippery and twice his feet nearly slid from under him. He was soon at the wall, leaning over it, catching his breath. Then he was on the wall, balancing on its rough, uneven top, fumbling for the camera in his pocket, fingers trembling.

Alice, wearing a blue plastic raincoat, was standing before the tree, staring up at its twisted branches, the light rain spattering against her upturned face. The clouds were dark and heavy, their full load having not yet been shed; the horizon was silvery white in contrast. The others stood further back from the girl as though afraid to approach her, afraid to go too near the oak. They stood in small groups, silent, watching. More were climbing over the wall, cautiously moving forward, but never beyond the groups behind the girl. Fenn saw the crippled boy, the one who had received Holy Communion earlier, being lifted over the wall, then carried through the waiting people towards the little girl. Just five yards from her, his father knelt and gently laid the boy on the ground, adjusting the blanket around the frail body to keep out the dampness.

A young girl was led forward and Fenn recognized her from her clothes: she was the same girl he'd made way for at the church gate, the one suffering from chorea.

Others were pushing their way through, bringing children with them, or supporting adults. Soon the groups were less obvious as the space around them filled, and the sick were laid on the grass, no one caring about the ground's wetness, or the chill in the air.

Fenn estimated there had to be at least three hundred people present, many now in the field itself, the rest still nervously lingering behind the wall as though it were a shield. All were hushed.

He could feel the tension and almost wanted to shout against it. It was building, passing from person to person, group to group, a rising hysteria that would reach a peak before breaking. He shivered, for it was uncanny, eerie.

He focused the camera, trying to keep his hands steady. His vantage point on the wall gave him a good overall view and he hoped he had chosen the correct aperture for the dim light. The Olympus had a built-in flash unit, but he was reluctant to use it: he felt that the sudden light might somehow upset the mood of the crowd, might break the spell they appeared to be under. Spell? Get a hold of yourself, Fenn. It was no more than the atmosphere created at football matches or pop concerts. Just quieter, that was all, and that was what made it so spooky.

He clicked the button, first photographing Alice and the tree. Then her and the crowd behind. The people at the wall next. Good shot, you could see the apprehension on their faces. And something more. Fear. Fear yet . . . longing. Christ, they were *yearning* for something to happen.

He saw the two priests climbing over and took a quick shot. The picture could be great when blown up and cropped in around Father Hagan's head, for he had rarely seen such an expression of pure anguish on another man's face before.

The priests moved through the gathering, but even they did not go beyond the fringe of people forming a ragged semicircle around the girl. Fenn jumped to the ground and made his own way towards the oak tree, approaching from the side, affording himself a good view of what was taking place. His shoes and the ends of his trouser legs were soaked by the time he reached the edge of the crowd, yet he did not feel the discomfort. He, like the others, was too fascinated by the diminutive figure standing perfectly still, gazing up at the tree. From his position he could see Alice's profile and her expression was one of sheer happiness. Many of the children were smiling too, their joy not altogether shared by the adults with them, although even they were not showing the same fearful apprehension of moments earlier. At least, those nearest the girl were not. Fenn caught sight of Alice's mother kneeling close to the group who had brought the crippled boy into the field and wasn't sure if it was just rain on her face or if she was crying. Her eyes were closed and her hands were gripped tightly together in a gesture of prayer. The scarf she wore had fallen back onto her shoulders and her hair hung damply over her forehead. Silent words formed on her lips.

And then everything became unnaturally still.

Only the falling rain convinced Fenn that the world had not ground to a stop.

There were not even any sounds. No birds, no bleating of sheep on the far side of the field, no traffic noise from the nearby road. A vacuum.

Until the breeze ruffled the grass.

Fenn shivered, for the sudden draught of air was more chilly than the drizzle. He pulled his raincoat collar tight around his neck and nervously looked around, the feeling of some unseen presence unreasonably strong. There was nothing there of course, just the field and its bordering hedge. To his left was the crowd, the wall, the church; to his right the tree . . . the tree . . . Beyond . . . the tree . . . He could not focus beyond the tree.

The wind – for it was no longer a breeze – was rustling through the bare branches, stirring the deformed limbs, making them sway as though they were slumbering tentacles suddenly come to life. The rustling became a low howling as the grotesque limbs shifted.

The onlookers' clothes were whipped by the wind and they clung to each other or held up their arms against it. Several began to back away, plainly frightened, while others stood their ground, also afraid yet curious – and for some, desperate – enough to stay. Many dropped to their knees and bowed their heads.

Strangely, Fenn felt his own legs grow weak and it became an effort to keep himself erect. He saw Father Hagan begin to stumble forward in an attempt to reach the girl, but the other priest caught his arm and held him back. Words passed between the two clerics, but they were too far away and the wind was too loud for the reporter to hear. He lurched, feeling as though something had pushed him from behind. He could feel muscles in his back stiffening and his windblown hair had become brittle.

But it passed. The low howling ceased, the wind died. The rain continued its drizzle, no longer blown off course.

The people looked relieved, several blessing themselves. They looked around at their neighbours, each seeking comfort from the presence of others, turning to their parish priest for reassurance. Father Hagan could offer none. His skin looked even more pallid as he stared at Alice Pagett.

Her arms were stretched outwards towards the now still oak and she was speaking, although no one present could catch the words. She was laughing too, joy almost visibly radiating from her small body. Yet there was nothing at the tree, no form, no movement, nothing at all. A gasp ran through the onlookers, a gasp that became a moan.

Alice's feet were no longer on the ground. She hovered two or three inches above the tallest blade of grass.

Fenn blinked, not believing what he was seeing. It just wasn't possible. Levitation was just a trick performed by conjurers under contrived conditions. But there were no such conditions here, just an open field. And no conjurer, just an eleven-year-old girl. Jesus Christ, what was going on?

He felt an electricity running through him, a sharp,

tingling flush that somehow jumped from his body to others, linking them all in a binding blanket of static. He was mesmerized by the girl, not sure if he were hallucinating, still refusing to accept the evidence before his eyes. Vaguely, somewhere in the more sane region of his mind, he was reminded of the camera in his pocket; but he could not find the strength nor, more importantly, the desire to reach for it. He shook his head, partly to clear it, partly to feel some physical sensation. The dream, the hallucination, the telepathic illusion, was still there in front of him, refusing to obey that part of his brain that insisted it was all unreal. Alice Pagett was standing above the ground and the grass was gently swaying beneath the soles of her feet.

Minutes passed and nobody dared move or speak. There was an aura around Alice that, although it could not be seen, could be felt. A radiance that, if it *were* visible, would be brilliantly white, golden-hued at its periphery. Her position did not fluctuate; she neither rose nor descended. And her body was immobile, arms still outstretched, only her lips moving.

Not many of those gathered there remained standing. Fenn's legs began to give way completely and it was not reverence for what was taking place that caused him to sink to the ground. It was weakness, a peculiar tiredness that assailed him; it was as though his body were being drained of energy. He felt so numb, so cold.

He crouched on one knee, a hand resting on the earth to keep himself balanced. The priests were still standing, although the monsignor had Father Hagan's arm tightly gripped as if supporting him. They appeared confused, bewildered by the incredible spectacle and, Fenn thought with some grim satisfaction, they too now looked afraid.

He turned his head to look at Alice once more and saw

that she was sinking, slowly, slowly descending, grass blades bending beneath her feet, a pliant cushion before she touched earth. She was down and she turned to look at her audience, a rapturous smile on her face.

At which point the miracles began.

A tiny boy ran forward, his outstretched hands a mass of grey-black lumps. He fell at Alice's feet, holding his hands aloft so that those watching from behind could see their ugliness. His tearful mother tried to join him, but her husband held her back, not knowing what was going to happen, just praying that it would be good for his son.

The girl smiled down at the boy and the blackish verrucas, with their edges of grey, began to fade.

The mother screamed and broke free, rushing to her son and hugging him close, tears streaming from her eyes to mingle with the rain in the boy's hair.

A cry from the crowd and all eyes turned in the direction of the teenage girl whose facial muscles could not be controlled, whose limbs twitched spasmodically and incessantly. She had been kneeling with her family group, but now was on her feet, her expression serene. Although she moved cautiously, there was no trembling, no twitching; she stared down at herself, examining her hands, her legs. The girl came forward, slowly but surely, her chest beginning to heave with her joy. She knelt at the feet of Alice Pagett and wept.

A man stumbled forward, pushing through the kneeling people, his eyes clouded with cataracts. They cleared a path for him, guiding him forward with gentle pressure on his arms, urging him on, praying for him.

He fell before he reached the girl and lay sobbing, his face wretched with longing. The opacity in his eyes began to clear. For the first time in five years he began to see colour. He began to see shapes. He began to see the world again, only his tears now blurring his vision.

A young girl, who attended the same hospital as Alice and whose parents had been given new hope ever since the latter's sudden cure, asked her mother why the man on the ground was crying. The words were not too clear, but the girl's mother understood them. To her they were the most beautifully formed words she had ever heard, for her daughter had not spoken in all the seven years of her short life.

Many in the crowd were collapsing, sprawling on the ground, or falling against those nearest to them, like marionettes whose strings had been cut. Fenn was forced to sit, his supporting knee giving way. His eyes were wild, looking from the girl to the crowd, the girl to the crowd, the girl . . . to the tree . . .

Another cry, becoming a wail, from among the rain-soaked people. A woman's moan of anguish.

Fenn's eyes scanned the crouched bodies and came to rest on the blanket-wrapped bundle lying on the fringe of the semi-circle. The boy was sitting upright; his eyes shining with some new-found understanding. He pushed the blanket aside and hands reached to help him. He didn't need their help though. He was rising, his movements stiffly awkward like a newborn lamb's. He was on his feet and the hands steadied him. He moved forward, ill-balanced but coping, staggering and eager to reach the girl. His father and another man quickly stood beside him, taking his arms. He walked, using the adults for support, but the motion coming from his own legs. They helped him forward and it was not until he was within touching distance of Alice Pagett that he allowed himself to sink to the ground. He half-sat half-lay there, his knees together, thin legs almost hidden in the grass, his upper body upright, his father holding onto his shoulders.

They gazed at the girl with adoration on their faces.

Fenn was stunned. His strength was returning although he did not yet feel steady enough to stand. Jesus Christ, what happened here? *It just wasn't possible!*

He looked towards the two priests, one dressed totally in black, the other in the robes of the Sunday service, green and yellow, white beneath. Father Hagan had already fallen to his knees, and the tall priest, the monsignor, was slowly collapsing beside him. Fenn could not be sure if they were suffering the same debilitating weakness that had assailed his own body, or if their gesture was one of homage. Father Hagan bowed his head into his hands and rocked backwards and forwards. Monsignor Delgard could only stare wide-eyed at the girl standing in the field, her small body so vulnerable beneath the black twisted tree that towered over her.

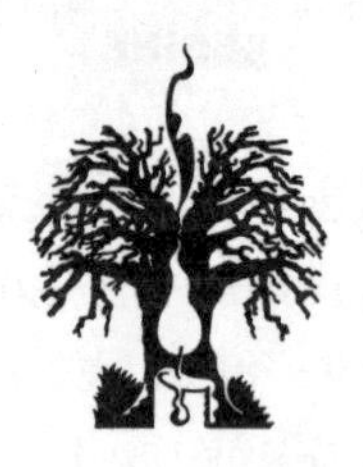

14

'She's as tender and sweet as a fat little lamb. Yum, yum! She'll make a tasty dinner!' She drew out a bright sharp knife, which glittered quite dreadfully.

Hans Andersen, 'The Snow Queen'

Riordan wearily shook his head. *It made no sense.* In his thirty-eight years as a farmer, nothing like this had ever happened before. Not to his livestock. He motioned the lorry to back further into the field, then nodded to his farm labourers to get busy with their shovels.

The vet came over and stood by him, saying nothing, his face haggard. The call from Riordan had come in the early hours of the morning and when he, the vet, had arrived he knew there was only so much he could do. Even those he had cut from their mother's stomachs, those he believed were well-formed enough to cope with premature birth, had not survived. It was inexplicable. Why should it happen to all of them at the same time? There had been a disturbance in the field the day before – an incredible event from all the confused accounts he had heard – but the pregnant sheep had been far away from it all, in a different section of the field. He sighed and wiped a hand over his tired eyes as the labourers scooped up the tiny glistening corpses on the shovels and tossed them into the back of the lorry. The sheep, the mothers the vet had not been able to save, were picked up by stiffened legs and swung onto the waiting vehicle.

Riordan looked at the grey church in the distance and wondered how people could worship such an ill-natured God. Farming was a hard life: you expected failures, mishaps – even tragedies. Crops could be ruined, animals could, and always did, have accidents or illnesses from which they perished. It happened to farm workers, too. But you never expected, could never be prepared for, something like this. There was just no sense to it.

He turned his back on the field and watched the heavily-laden lorry pull away.

Part Two

'I wonder if I've changed in the night? Let me think: was I the same when I got up this morning? I almost think I can remember feeling a little different. But if I'm not the same, the question is, Who in the world am I? Ah, that's the great puzzle!'

Lewis Carroll, *Alice's Adventures in Wonderland*

15

'When I used to read fairy-tales, I fancied that kind of thing never happened, and now here I am in the middle of one!'

Lewis Carroll, *Alice's Adventures in Wonderland*

'Good Lord, are you unwell, Andrew?'

Bishop Caines stared at the priest, shocked by the change in the man. He had looked ill when the bishop had spoken to him just a few weeks before, but now his physical appearance had deteriorated alarmingly. Bishop Caines moved forward and took the priest's hand, then indicated towards an armchair opposite his desk. He looked questioningly at Monsignor Delgard, but the tall priest's expression remained impassive.

'I think perhaps a small brandy might do you some good.'

'No, no, I'm fine, really,' Father Hagan protested.

'Nonsense. It'll give you back some colour. Peter, the same for you?'

Delgard shook his head. 'Perhaps some tea?' he said, looking directly at the bishop's secretary who had shown them into the study.

'Yes, of course,' said Bishop Caines, returning to his seat

behind the desk. 'Both for me, I think, Judith. I may need it.' He smiled at his secretary and she left the room. The smile dropped as soon as the door closed.

'I'm extremely disturbed, gentlemen. I would have preferred that you came to me yesterday.'

Monsignor Delgard had walked to the study's leaded window overlooking the secluded garden. The weak, late-February sunlight settled into the far side of the neat, partly-shadowed lawn, unable to draw the moisture from it, sparkling off the dew. It had rained heavily during the night and throughout the preceding afternoon; the sun looked as though it were still recovering from the soaking. He turned towards the portly bishop.

'I'm afraid that was not possible.' His voice was low, but the words filled the dark, wood-panelled study. 'We couldn't leave the church, Bishop, not after what had taken place. There was too much hysteria.'

Bishop Caines said nothing. He had assigned Monsignor Delgard to watch over the younger priest and his church, to control any situation that might arise over this girl and her apparitions; his role was to observe, influence and report. Peter Delgard was a priest not unused to incidents of the alleged paranormal or supernatural, his reputation for bringing sanity to insane situations renowned in ecclesiastical circles. He was a quiet, remote man, sometimes intimidating in his intensity; yet one knew instantly that he was a man of compassion, someone who shared the suffering of others as if the burden were his own. His authoritative quietness did little to reveal this side of his nature, but it was present in his aura as clearly as it must have been in Christ's. The bishop trusted Monsignor Delgard, respected his judgement, acknowledged his wisdom in matters that were often too bizarre for his own sensibilities to accept; and he was a little afraid of the tall priest.

Delgard was looking out of the window again. 'I thought, too, that Father Hagan needed some rest,' he said.

Bishop Caines studied the priest in the armchair. Yes, he could see that: Father Hagan looked as though the shock had been too much. His flesh was greyer than the last time; his eyes were dark, a look of desperation in them.

'Father, you look drained. Is it because of what happened yesterday?' he asked.

'I don't know, Bishop,' the priest answered, his voice almost a whisper. 'I haven't been sleeping too well over the past few weeks. Last night I hardly slept at all.'

'I'm not surprised. But there's no need for it to cause you such anxiety. Indeed, there may be much to celebrate.'

The bishop became aware of Delgard watching him. 'Don't you agree, Peter?'

A brooding silence, then, 'It's too soon to know.' The monsignor's stoop seemed more pronounced as he slowly strode from the window and sat in the study's other armchair. He regarded Bishop Caines with eyes that saw too much. 'What took place is quite inexplicable, beyond anything I've ever witnessed before. Five people were cured, Bishop, four of them no more than children. It's somewhat early to say how complete were their cures, but as from two hours ago, when I checked with each one, there had been no relapses.'

'Of course, we cannot accept these cures as miraculous until the medical authorities have made a thorough examination of those involved,' Bishop Caines said, and there was a carefully subdued eagerness in his tone.

'It will be a long time before the Church can even accept them as cures, let alone "miraculous",' Delgard replied. 'The procedure before such a proclamation is made is lengthy to say the least.'

'Quite so,' the bishop agreed. 'And properly so.' He found Delgard's stare disconcerting. 'I managed to reach the Cardinal Archbishop last night after you telephoned me. He has reiterated my own feelings that we must tread warily: he has no desire for the Roman Catholic Church in England to look foolish. He wants a full report before anything is announced to the media, and any statements must come directly from his offices.'

Hagan was shaking his head. 'I'm afraid it's beyond our control, Bishop. The reporter, Gerry Fenn, was there again yesterday. We haven't yet seen the early edition of the *Courier*, but you can be sure the event will receive full coverage.'

'He was there? Good Lord, the man's intuition must be incredible.'

'I think not,' Delgard put in. 'Apparently the rumour that Alice was to receive another "visitation" was spread around Banfield long before Sunday.'

'I forbade her mother to bring her,' Hagan said just as the door opened and Judith entered with a tray of drinks.

'I think that was unwise.' Bishop Caines nodded for his secretary to leave the tray on a small table at the side of the room. He waited for her to leave before he spoke again. 'Most unwise. You cannot forbid people to come to church, Father.'

'I thought it best that Alice stay away for a while.'

'Best for whom?'

'For Alice, of course.'

Delgard cleared his throat. 'I think Father Hagan was concerned over the traumatic effect the child's obsession was having on her.'

'Yes, that was one reason. The other is that I don't want St

Joseph's turned into a fairground!' His voice had become strained, almost strident, and his two colleagues looked at him in surprise. Delgard appraised him with troubled eyes.

Bishop Caines rose with an audible sigh and went to the tray of drinks. He handed the brandy to the pale priest. 'It's a little early for this kind of beverage, I know, but it will do you good, Andrew.' He noticed the priest's hand was trembling as he took the drink and quickly looked across at Delgard. The monsignor's face was impassive, although he, too, was watching Father Hagan.

Bishop Caines turned back to the small side table. 'No sugar for you, Peter? No, I remember.' He gave the tea to Delgard, then placed his own and the brandy on the desk. 'Tell me more about this reporter,' he said as he took his seat once again. 'Just how much did he see?'

Hagan sipped his drink, hating the taste and the burning it caused to his throat. 'He saw everything. He was there from the beginning.'

'Well, no matter. The news would have soon got out. What we must consider now is how we should proceed. Where is the girl, this Alice Pagett?'

Delgard spoke. 'I thought it best that she and her mother should move into the convent in the village for a few days; there she cannot be bothered by the Press.'

'Her mother agreed?'

'She's a devout Catholic and willing to follow our guidance. Her husband, I'm afraid, is another matter. I doubt he'll let us keep Alice there for long.'

'He's not Catholic?'

Father Hagan managed to smile. 'Most definitely not. An atheist.'

'Hmn, that's a pity.'

Delgard wondered at the meaning behind the bishop's

remark: was it a pity that the man did not believe in God, or that as a non-Catholic he could not be so easily manipulated by the Church? Delgard did not enjoy having such suspicions about Bishop Caines' motives, but he knew the man was ambitious. Even men of the cloth were not without that stain.

'I think perhaps I should see the child and her mother,' the bishop said, sipping his brandy thoughtfully. 'If Alice really has been blessed, there could be certain consequences to the Church in England.'

'An upsurge of religious fervour?' Delgard said bluntly.

'A return to the Faith for thousands,' replied the bishop.

Father Hagan looked quickly from one man to the other. 'You mean St Joseph's could become a shrine?'

'Surely you realized that?' said Bishop Caines. 'If this girl really did have a vision of the Blessed Virgin, then pilgrimages will be made from all over the world to worship at the place of the Visitation. It would be a most wonderful thing.'

'Yes, it would,' said Delgard. 'But as I said earlier, there is a long and extremely thorough process to be gone through before any such declaration can be made.'

'I'm well aware of that, Peter. The first thing I must do is bring forward the Conference of Bishops and place all the information we have before them. I shall ask for the Apostolic Delegate to be present so that the matter can be brought to the Pope's attention without delay and perhaps discussed at the next Synod in Rome.'

'With respect, Bishop, I feel we may be moving too fast,' said Hagan, clenching his brandy glass tightly. 'We have no proof at all that Alice really saw Our Lady, or that the cures were miraculous.'

'That is what has to be ascertained,' the bishop quickly replied. 'Whether we like it or not, the news will spread rapidly. I dread to think of the sensation this man, Fenn, will make of it. Five cures, Andrew, *five.* Six counting Alice Pagett's own recovery. Do you not realize the excitement it will cause, not just among Catholics but in the hearts of all people who believe in the Divine Power? Whether or not St Joseph's is declared a holy shrine will be quite irrelevant; people will flock to the site in thousands out of sheer curiosity. That is why the Catholic Church must control the situation from the beginning.'

Father Hagan seemed to shrink into himself, but the bishop would not relent. 'There are many precedents,' he continued, 'the most famous being Lourdes. There was tremendous resistance by the Church authorities in accepting that Bernadette Soubirous had truly seen the Immaculate Conception, and it wasn't just the overwhelming evidence of miraculous cures and Bernadette's obvious integrity that influenced their final judgement: it was public opinion itself. The Church could not disregard the situation because the people – and they were not just local people – would not allow it. Do you realize how many thousands flock to the shrine to Our Lady in Aylesford each year? And there is no evidence at all that an apparition of the Virgin Mary appeared there. In fact, the Church authorities do not even suggest it. Yet pilgrims visit every year from all over the world. The same applies to the other shrine at Walsingham. If people want to believe, then no edict from the Church will persuade them otherwise.'

'Are you saying we should acknowledge Alice's story?' asked Hagan.

'Absolutely not. The whole matter will be carefully looked into before any official statement is made. What I am saying is that we must act swiftly to govern whatever else happens at St Joseph's. Don't you agree, Peter?' He glanced at the tall priest whose eyes were downcast.

He spoke slowly, his words measured. 'I agree that the

situation will develop of its own accord. We have already had experience of that with the large crowd that gathered at the church yesterday. Even this morning, before the news has broken in the Press, and on a working day, there was a large gathering. In a way, it's a relief to be here away from them. Nevertheless, I feel we must not yet offer any encouragement.'

'No, no, of course not.'

'We must first interview each one of the persons apparently cured yesterday. Their individual doctors must also be approached for permission to examine their medical records. I think we will easily gain permission from the patients themselves, so the doctors in question should have no objection. I propose the immediate formation of a Medical Commission, one that is independent of the Catholic Church, which can investigate fully the medical histories of these six fortunate people – I include Alice, of course. With the enormous interest that will generate from yesterday's spectacular . . .' a wry smile '. . . I see no problem in that respect. Indeed, I imagine an inquiry would be instigated without our bidding.'

Bishop Caines nodded and avoided looking directly into the monsignor's penetrating eyes.

'Also,' Delgard went on, 'if we are to follow the example of Lourdes, I feel we must consider organizing our own Medical Bureau on the site of the shrine.'

Bishop Caines could no longer contain his eagerness. 'Yes, that would be sensible. So many alleged miracles have been dismissed in the past because of lack of scientific or medical data.'

'We must be fully aware, Bishop, that therein lies the danger to the Church itself. It could leave us open to ridicule if logical and sound reasons are found for what happened. At this very moment one of the Catholic Church's greatest mysteries may well be explained away by science, and the beliefs of millions will suffer because of it.'

'You mean the Shroud?'

'Yes, the Turin Shroud. Thermographic investigation, infra-red spectroscopy, radiography, electronic microscopy and chemical analysis – all these scientific means have been used to prove or disprove that the image on the length of linen discovered in 1356 is that of Christ. As yet, nothing conclusive has emerged from any of those tests. Needless to say, the Church is regarded with some suspicion for not allowing a further vital – according to the scientists – test. I refer to carbon dating.'

'But that would require destroying a fairly large section of cloth,' Bishop Caines protested. 'We could never allow that.'

'Methods of testing have been considerably improved since permission was last sought. No more than 25mg of material would be needed. Yet still we say "no" and the public wonders just what it is that we're afraid of.'

'All the more reason we should not suppress our findings on this matter. I think we have nothing to fear, although I'm in full agreement about proceeding cautiously.'

'I . . . I think we're making a grave mistake.'

The two clerics turned towards Father Hagan. He was leaning forward in his seat, hands clasped tightly together.

Bishop Caines was alarmed at the distress on the priest's face. 'Why do you say that, Andrew? What is it that's troubling you?'

The priest rubbed a hand against his temple. 'It's just a feeling, Bishop. I don't know why, or what it is, but I feel things are not right. There's an atmosphere about the church . . .'

'Do you feel this . . . this atmosphere, Peter?' the bishop asked.

Delgard paused before answering. 'No, I'm afraid I don't. At least not the kind that Father Hagan is evidently referring to. Yesterday there was a tension in the air that was almost tangible, but it was caused by the congregation itself. I've experienced mass hysteria before, but cannot positively say it was the same. I'm sure scientists will theorize on mass hypnosis, collective hysteria, mass suggestion, and they may well prove to be correct. I know I fell to my knees to worship what was before me.'

'The child?'

'What she represented. Or appeared to represent.'

'Then you felt her holiness?'

'I can't be sure. A weakness seemed to overcome the whole crowd, not just Father Hagan and myself, but I just cannot remember my emotions. I can only remember the weakness, the incredibility of what had just taken place. Perhaps a psychologist could explain the phenomenon. Or a parapsychologist.'

'I meant the atmosphere at St Joseph's,' said Father Hagan quietly. 'It feels so cold.'

The bishop gave a little laugh. 'It is winter, you know. The church is bound to feel cold.'

'No, it's not just a physical coldness. And it isn't confined to just the church; it's in the grounds, in the presbytery.'

'You appeared to be under some strain the last time I saw you, Andrew,' Bishop Caines said, not unkindly. 'It was one of the reasons I asked Monsignor Delgard to help you – that, and because of his experience in such extraordinary matters. Frankly, your health seems to have suffered considerably since last we met. Are you sure your general disposition does not account for these strange feelings you have?'

'I'm sure. I admit I haven't been in the best of health lately, but I think that, in itself, may be due to present circumstances.'

'I don't see how, unless it's the publicity that's upsetting you. If that is the case—'

'No!'

The bishop blinked in surprise.

'I'm sorry, Bishop,' the priest apologized. 'I didn't mean to raise my voice. Please forgive me. But there is something more, something happening that I don't understand.'

'We are all aware of that, Father,' said Bishop Caines, keeping the irritation from his voice.

'I don't just mean with Alice Pagett. There is something more . . .'

'Yes, yes, you have already said that. Can you explain exactly what you mean?'

The priest slumped back in his seat and closed his eyes. 'I wish I knew,' he said after a while.

'Then I think it best—' A gentle rapping on the door interrupted his words.

'Yes, Judith?' the bishop called out.

The secretary peered around the door. 'A call from London, Bishop. It's the *Daily Mail*, I'm afraid. They say they would like a statement from you on the incident at St Joseph's in Banfield yesterday.'

'Well, gentlemen,' the bishop said, 'it seems the story has broken nationally. Put the call through, my dear, then contact His Eminence for me when I've finished.'

He lifted the receiver and Delgard was not sure if his smile was one of resignation or anticipation. As the bishop began to speak, Delgard noticed that Father Hagan's hands were clenched around the arms of his chair. Clenched so tightly that the knuckles showed gleaming white through the pallid skin.

16

'I can't explain myself, I'm afraid, sir,' said Alice, 'because I'm not myself, you see.'

Lewis Carroll, *Alice's Adventures in Wonderland*

Tuesday, mid-morning

Southworth smiled as he poured himself a sherry. He filled the glass almost to the top. Normally a half-glass was adequate, a private mid-morning treat he occasionally allowed himself; but today there was something to celebrate.

An emergency meeting of the parish council had been called the previous evening because of the new 'Banfield Miracles', the astonishing cures that had taken place at St Joseph's on Sunday. And not just cures: many claimed they had seen Alice Pagett levitate. Southworth, who had also been there, wasn't certain of that aspect, for his view had been somewhat restricted by those in front of him, but he was ready to believe almost anything after the breath-taking cures. The child's levitation could have been imagined, such was the intense feeling running through the crowd, but there was no imagining the healing of the invalids. Even now, even though he was an eye-witness, it was difficult to accept.

Fortunately, there was no question of fraudulence. The five who had been cured had genuine illnesses, all confirmed by their own doctors, and further guaranteed by the medical records from the hospitals they had attended. Those illnesses and debilities had disappeared completely in all but two cases: the man whose cataracts had cleared still did not have perfect vision, although the morning report was that his sight was steadily improving; the crippled boy still had difficulty in walking unassisted, but this could hardly be otherwise with his wasted leg muscles – his condition was expected to improve as his legs grew stronger.

Southworth sipped the dry sherry and glanced over the newspapers spread before him on his desk. The story was now worldwide news. Banfield was literally crawling with media people. Press, television, magazines – all wanted the story. The village was bustling in a way it never had before, nor had ever expected to. It was alive! The residents were bewildered, but the world knew of their existence! And they, the villagers, were responding to the sudden attention. Not just responding, but thriving on it! Of course, there were those who found the publicity unwelcome, those who preferred their cosy, stagnating privacy, but they were in the minority. An indication of the high excitement generating through Banfield was conveyed at the council meeting on Monday evening. Never had he seen his fellow-members so active! And so willing to listen to plans of expansion.

There was no question but that St Joseph's would become a shrine after last night's news broadcast and this morning's headlines, even if the Catholic Church refused to proclaim it as such. The publicity alone would undoubtedly attract pilgrims, tourists and thrill-seekers to the area in their thousands (one councillor, the manager of one of Banfield's two national banks, was carried away with the whole idea enough to estimate the number in millions, a reckoning that drew guffaws from his fellow-members, although secretly not entirely rejected by them). Southworth ventured that the Church would be forced into making concessions and might even relish the situation. What more could any religion ask for than a present-day miracle to perpetuate the Faith? He knew the bishop of the diocese, Bishop Caines, personally, and would arrange for a meeting to discuss recent events. He would also broach the subject of how they could combine forces to meet the human deluge that must surely descend upon the area.

Southworth had spoken with the bishop that morning and had been surprised at the eminent cleric's general receptiveness to the council's proposition. Yes, he understood absolutely the need for agreement between the parish council and the Church in the coming months, and he would endeavour to cooperate fully with any plans put forward by them provided they did not entail cheap exploitation or pertain to any activities which would infringe on the dignity of the Catholic Church itself. Southworth was more than pleased with the statement, albeit somewhat pompous, and assured Bishop Caines that the council had no intention of commercializing what must be considered a most holy event. The bishop warned him without hesitation that it could not yet, and perhaps never would, be proclaimed a 'holy' event. Indeed, the whole matter would require lengthy examination to determine the validity of Alice Pagett's vision and the cures that had ensued within a religious context. His Eminence, the Cardinal Archbishop, had expressed deep concern and urged caution.

Bishop Caines went on to suggest that a meeting between members of the council, Monsignor Delgard, whom the bishop had appointed overseer at St Joseph's, and Father

Hagan might prove fruitful at this early stage. They would report back to him and he in turn would report to the Conference of Bishops.

Southworth had thought that to be an excellent idea. In fact he would stage two meetings: one informal, between him and the two clergymen in which he could appraise their attitudes (and perhaps he would invite the reporter, Fenn, along too); another, larger meeting involving the rest of the council. In that way he could smooth the path first – certain colleagues on the council were a little too earnest with their ideas. Like Rodney Tucker, they were non-Catholics and inclined to forget the sensitivities of the religious. Most of the councillors were long-standing members of the community, their family histories, as did his, tracing back through the centuries to the beginnings of the village itself, in the fourteenth century. It had been known as *Banefeld* then, a community formed by those who had fled the horrors of the Black Death, which had become rife in the more densely populated towns. Those early settlers had thrived on the rich agricultural land of the area and had stayed, content to ignore the changing face of England, like so many other small communes. Nothing world-shattering had ever happened in Banfield; perhaps a few minor misdeeds through the centuries, but nothing of any great consequence. But now the village had the opportunity to rise from obscurity, a chance to save itself from the oblivion it was slowly and surely sinking into. And the council members knew it – even the old 'keep the-world-away-from-our-door' diehards were aware. Those with family names entwined with Banfield's inglorious and uneventful past saw the chance, not just to revive the mouldering corpse, but to inject it with a life far more brilliant than it had ever experienced, and so to re-establish their own history.

And all were excited by the prosperity this dramatic and awesome incident could bring them.

Southworth smiled again. It was difficult not to.

Wednesday, early evening

She pulled the covers up to her neck and lay there staring at the ceiling, waiting for him to come out of the bathroom. That was one of Rodney's good points: he was clean. He always washed himself before and after. His *mind* wasn't as clean, but that didn't bother Paula too much; her own thoughts could be just as raunchy.

She rubbed her hands over her stomach, the feeling sensuous, almost as enjoyable as if it were another's fingers probing the flesh. Paula, still single, knew well the pleasures of her own body. She checked her nipples to see if they were erect, wanting to be at her most desirable for her employer, tweaking them both for full projection. The toilet flushed and she became a little impatient with Rodney's ritual. Keep cool, Paula, she told herself, tonight wasn't the night for upsetting him. Tonight was progress night. She'd given him enough to worry about over the past few weeks, now was the time for a little mercy, a little loving, a little giving on her part. It was a fine balance, keeping him anxious and keeping him interested.

He was in a buoyant mood, for his plans were going well. The village was stirring, at last awakening to the big world beyond its semi-rural confines. Things were moving and Tucker was moving with them.

Paula's fingers probed lower, sliding their way through tough dark hair like snakes through undergrowth, middle finger, the leader of the pack, finding the dip below. She opened herself, knowing Rodney liked to find her wet and waiting, and caught her breath at the stab of pleasure. There was something sordidly exciting about making love in a motel bedroom, the kind of self-abasement that went with self-abuse, and Paula was partial to both. She would have preferred a candlelight dinner for two, followed by a night of love in a plush hotel suite, energy and ideas sustained by an ice-bucket containing Dom Perignon (there were several things she could do with a linen towel packed with ice). But failing that, a gin and tonic and a motel fuck had some merit.

She heard Rodney splashing at the bathroom sink and worked a little more vigorously at herself, only too aware that her employer was not the most lingering of lovers. Too many times she had lost the climax race to him; nowadays she made sure she had a head start. She moaned a little and closed her eyes.

Tucker watched her from the open doorway, enjoying the view. He loved her to do it to herself, so long as she held back on the best bit for him. It saved him a lot of preliminary work.

Paula confused him, for her moods seemed to change from day to day. It was worrying too: on her really bad days there was more than just a hint of hysteria in her actions. When she shouted at him she didn't seem to care who heard and twice she had suggested that it night be better in the long run if Marcia found out about their affair. She was fed up with being treated like a trollop. He wondered how the hell else you treated a trollop.

But today and yesterday she had been all sweetness and light and genuinely pleased at his personal good fortune (or imminent good fortune). Maybe she had just caught the village's carnival atmosphere. Or maybe she wanted a part in his new schemes.

Tucker's freshly washed penis indicated its impatience by pressing uncomfortably against his underpants. Never one to keep a personal friend waiting, he made for the bed where Paula's movements were becoming a little too frantic. She opened her eyes and smiled lasciviously at him, her hand slowing to walking pace.

'Enjoying yourself?' he said, unbuttoning his shirt and placing it neatly over his trousers draped on the back of a nearby chair. The ginger hair on his floppy chest stuck through his string vest like stuffing from an old sofa.

'Just waiting for you, lover,' she replied and slowly drew back the covers for him. She allowed him a titillating glance at her naked body, then let them fall back over her. 'Take your vest off, lovey,' she said as he clambered in next to her. Paula didn't relish having the criss-cross pattern all over her breasts and stomach.

He squatted in the bed and struggled out of his vest, the released blubber swimming around the waistline of his underpants for a second before finding its level. My God, Paula thought, it was like being fucked by a whale.

Switching off the wall-light on his side of the bed, but leaving hers on, he wriggled down under the blankets. Without preamble a cold hand closed around her right breast like a metal claw in an amusement arcade's lucky dip.

'Wait, Rod,' she said pleadingly. 'There's no rush.' Paula squirmed against him to make sure he realized there was no rebuke or rejection in her words. 'Besides . . .' she giggled '. . . I've got a little treat for you.'

Tucker's ears pricked up and his penis took a new interest. Paula's 'little treats' were usually worth delaying the action for.

Her hand roamed around his chest, over his belly, then round to his fleshy back. Delicate fingers surfed through the tidal wave of fat to swoop down beneath the stretched elastic of his underpants and splay out over his buttocks. He nuzzled her neck in appreciation.

She murmured something and he said, 'What?'

'I said, did you see Southworth this morning?' Her teeth chewed his nipple.

He grunted and she took it as an affirmative.

Paula drew away when he said nothing more and looked into his face.

'Well?' she said.

'Well what?'

'What happened at the council meeting? What was decided?'

'Oh bloody hell, I don't want to talk about that now.' He yelped when she dug in her long fingernails.

'You know I'm interested in your affairs, Rodney.'

'You *are* my affair, precious.'

He yelped again.

'You know what I mean,' she scolded. 'You've got ideas, Rod. You could do things in this town.'

'That's true enough. Anyway, I think it's all set.' He turned onto his back, sex forgotten for the moment, ambitions elbowing the physical need aside.

'They've given the go-ahead for another shop?'

'No, no, they don't move that fast. But they're listening to Southworth now; he's shifting them off their backsides. And the way it's going, my lovely, it might mean more than just another shop. It might mean a bloody big supermarket, bigger than the one I've already got.' He chuckled and she joined in.

'So you'd probably need me to run this one on my own, then, so you could get on with organizing everything,' she said slyly.

'Uh. Well, yes . . . I suppose I would. It's early days though, pet. You know, anything might happen.' She couldn't see the frown on his face.

Too bloody right it could, Paula thought. Tourism was going to hit the town in a big way if this shrine business came off, and a lot of money was going to be made. She knew Tucker well enough to realize he would be at the front of the queue, arms spread wide to receive the benefit. And she intended to be there right alongside him, Marcia Tucker or no Marcia Tucker.

His frown was replaced by a smile as he went over the meeting with Southworth in his mind. The hotel owner wasn't one for over-exuberance, but even he couldn't contain his delight. New development plans would be pushed forward to the Horsham District Council over the next few months with an incautious speed that had never before been allowed. Expansion – rapid expansion – was a necessity. The village was already jammed solid with sightseers and even if another 'miracle' never occurred again, the legend was already born. The incredible amount of worldwide publicity had seen to that.

He chuckled again. It was only because the motel manager knew Tucker would not require the room all night that he had kept it free for him. The motel was packed, almost every room taken by media people, the rest by tourists, and he and Paula had to be out by ten so that a camera crew from Holland could move in.

'What are you laughing at?' Paula asked, giggling herself.

'Just the thought of glories to come, my darling. Banfield won't know what's hit it.'

She wasn't cold, but Paula shivered. It was almost as if something icy had touched her. She shrugged off the peculiar feeling.

'You won't be too busy for me, will you, Rod?' Her voice was wheedling again and her hand was tugging at his underpants.

'You, my love? No way. I'll always have time for you.' He moaned as she yanked the pants down and lifted his fat bottom so that they would go all the way. Physical need was back on top again. 'Hey, what's my special treat?' he reminded her.

Paula sat up, her thrusting breasts bouncing together with the sudden movement. Tucker couldn't resist nipping at her well-rounded bottom as she turned from him and stretched down beside the bed. She gave a little screech and wriggled her rump; he kissed it better, wondering what she was reaching for.

She came up with a paper-wrapped bottle and he guessed its contents immediately. He couldn't stop grinning as Paula unwrapped the Freezomint. 'Have you been raiding the store again?' he asked without malice.

'I know you don't mind me helping myself to this, Rodney. Not when it's for your benefit.'

She unscrewed the top and took a deep swig of the *crème de menthe*, gargling it around her mouth and throat until they were coated with the green liquid. She swallowed, then drank again, her tongue burning as she wriggled it in the cold, stinging liquid. Her eyes were seductively half-closed when she placed the bottle on the bedside unit and Tucker's were wide open in anticipation.

His penis, short but stocky, was already tingling, but he knew it was nothing like the shocking tingling it would feel when her lips and tongue closed around it.

He was smiling again, as she lowered her head towards his body. All in all, it had been a good day.

Thursday, early morning

Alice stood in her nightdress staring out of the window. The sun hurt her eyes although there was little warmth from it. Behind her, the bedclothes on the nun's cot were rumpled as though her sleep had not been easy. As yet, there were no other sounds in the convent, for the sun had not long risen. Soon though, the nuns would be gathered for prayer in the room used as a chapel and Alice's mother would be among them, thanking God for the honour he had bestowed upon her and her daughter.

There was no expression on Alice's face.

Only twelve nuns lived in the convent, for it was merely a large house, acquired ten years before from a retired theatre actor who had moved abroad to sunnier climes. Its walls were painted cream, doors and window frames white. A high brick wall assured the nuns their privacy and beyond the heavy black gates, which were as high as the wall itself, was a spacious yard where they parked their Morris 1100 and minibus. The minibus was used during the week to collect the village children who attended the Catholic school four miles away and in which the nuns taught.

The high gates, solidly forbidding, and the surrounding wall had been a formidable defence against the hordes of reporters that had descended upon Banfield during the past week, for it had soon become known that little Alice Pagett was being kept at the convent for her own privacy and protection.

The convent was situated at the southern end of the town, close to a sharp bend where the main road turned left for Brighton and another, minor road continued straight on into the Downs. A garage was on the bend itself and the nuns knew the proprietor was hiring out the offices above to camera crews and photographers so that they could film over the convent wall. There was little the nuns could do about the situation but pray that Alice's mind would not be too disturbed by the frantic attention.

Alice's spartan room overlooked the courtyard at the front of the convent. Apart from the small bed, it contained only a chair, a straw rug, and a small sink in the corner. A plain wooden crucifix hung on the wall. Two of Alice's favourite dolls shared her bed at night, but each morning her mother found them thrown into the far corner of the room.

Molly Pagett slept next door, close to her daughter, and had spent most nights since moving in with the Sisters lying awake mumbling prayers and listening for any disturbance in Alice's room. Her eyes were red-rimmed through lack of sleep and her face and stance seemed to have aged ten years since the miracles had begun. A woman always devoted to the Church, it had now become her obsession.

Alice did not appear to feel the chill as she stood at the window, nor did the birds that swooped into the courtyard interest her.

She hated the convent, hated its sparseness, its lack of comfort. And she disliked the dull greyness of the nuns' habits. She was frightened of the doctors who tested and probed her, who examined her body and asked her questions, questions, questions. And she was tired of the questions from the priests, from the nuns, from . . . from . . . just about everybody who spoke to her.

She wanted to leave this place.

She wanted to go back to the church.

She wanted to see the tree.

A movement below caught her attention. The cat had leapt from the high wall into an empty flower bed at the courtyard's side. It stalked lazily across the damp cobbles, the birds having already flown. It stopped. Looked up. Saw the small figure in white watching it.

It sat and gazed upwards.

For the first time in days Alice smiled. Her hand unconsciously touched her side and rubbed at the small lump six inches below her heart. The doctors had shown great interest in the strange protuberance at first and her mother had explained it had always been there, although very tiny, and nothing to worry about so her local doctor had said. They had agreed it was nothing to worry about and did not mention nor probe it again.

But it itched now and was bigger, though not much, than before. Alice rubbed at it as she watched the cat and her smile did not seem that of an eleven-year-old.

17

A slumber did my spirit seal;
  I had no human fears:
She seemed a thing that could not feel
  The touch of earthly years.

William Wordsworth

'Hey, come on, Sue, open up!'

Fenn put his head against the door and listened. He knew she had to be in there because he had rung from the call box on the corner just a few minutes earlier and put down the phone as she'd answered. Twice that week Sue had hung up on him and twice she had been out when he'd gone to her flat. It had given him no satisfaction to hang up on her in return, but he wanted to see her. It was time to stop frigging around. If she really wanted to end it, fine – but she would have to tell him to his face.

It had been a heavy, glorious week. The *Courier* had syndicated his personal story of the 'Banfield Miracles' to most of the Nationals both in Britain and abroad, while magazines, periodicals and television companies were offering substantial amounts for follow-up stories and interviews. In just four days he had become what could only be termed as a 'media figure', the Alice Pagett phenomena inextricably linked with his own name, for it had been his first-hand coverage of both extraordnary events – the first vision and miracle experienced by Alice herself, and the subsequent five miracles on the second Sunday – that had caught the attention of millions around the world. He was riding high and enjoying the journey.

There was movement inside.

'It's me, Sue.'

Only silence.

'Come on, Sue, I only want to talk.'

The door-chain being slid back, the latch being turned. Sue peering through a six-inch gap.

'There's nothing much to say, Gerry.'

'Oh yeah? That's your considered opinion?'

'Have you been drinking?'

'Sure.'

It looked as if she was going to close the door again, so he put his hand against it.

'Sue, let's just talk a little. I promise to leave within ten minutes if you want me to.'

For a moment she was undecided and he lifted his eyebrows in a silent 'please?'. Sue disappeared from view and with relief he pushed open the door. He followed her down the short hallway into the lounge. As always the room was comfortably neat, lit by a small lamp which cast intimate shadows. He saw she was in her dressing gown.

'Bed so early?' he asked. 'It's only just gone ten.'

'It's late to call on someone,' she replied, sitting in an armchair. He realized she had carefully avoided the sofa. He was about to sit on the arm of her chair when she shook her head and pointed at the sofa opposite. With a sigh, he obeyed.

Neither one spoke for several moments, then Sue said, 'You're making quite a name for yourself.'

He cleared his throat, hating the awkwardness. 'I was lucky enough to be on the spot. It's a reporter's dream.'

'I'm glad you're reaping the benefit.'

'We went through this before, Sue. It's my job.'

'I'm not being sarcastic, Gerry. I really am pleased for you. And I like the way you've written your features; they've been factual, no gloss, no exaggeration. Not like your first story.'

'There was no need for exaggeration. The truth was spectacular enough.' He leaned forward, resisting the urge to kneel at her feet. 'So what is it, Sue? Why haven't you wanted to see me, to speak to me? What the hell have I done?'

She looked into her hands. 'I'm not sure if it's you or just me. I've found my faith again, Gerry, and I don't have time for anything else.'

'You mean being a Catholic excludes being in love with someone.'

'Of course not. I just think you're probably not the right one.'

'Oh terrific. Excuse my wicked ways, but we seemed to get along pretty fine until you started with this church business.'

'That's just the point! I've changed. But you haven't.'

'Why the hell should I? I'm not a bloody Catholic!'

'You were witness to one of the most shattering and marvellous things that could happen on this earth. Why hasn't it meant anything to you?'

'How d'you know it hasn't? You haven't seen me all week. Today's Thursday; I could have sent in my convert's application forms since Sunday!'

'Stop joking, Gerry. I read your articles, I know nothing's changed.'

'You said you liked them.'

'Yes, and I said they were factual. *Cold* and factual, an impartial observer's account.'

'What did you expect?'

'I expected you to be moved by what you saw! I expected you to be spiritually moved!'

Fenn's eyes widened in surprise. He shook his head. 'I don't get it.'

Her voice softened. 'That's just it. You really don't understand, do you?'

He remained silent.

'Everyone else present that day underwent some deep, emotional experience; I know, I've spoken with many of them since. They believe they witnessed a divine act of God, healing miracles that proved His existence beyond any doubt, and their lives have taken on a new order because of it. Yet you feel nothing. You can't deny what took place, but it has no effect on you. What's wrong with you, Gerry? What makes you so . . . so unreachable?'

'I'm not so sure it's just me. I haven't had a chance to get near Father Hagan during the last few days – he's avoided all contact with the Press – but he doesn't look too happy.'

'Couldn't you see the poor man was overwhelmed by it all? Six wonderful miracles. The levitation of a young child who saw the Blessed Virgin. In his parish! Have you any idea at all of the magnitude of what's happened? Father Hagan is still in a state of shock and his own humility will see he stays that way for some time to come. So don't dare compare his reaction to yours – because with you there's been no reaction at all except to seize the opportunity to make a name for yourself.'

'That's unfair.'

'I know it's unfair and I'm not blaming you for that. I just wish there was something more, some indication that your cynicism had been, if not broken, then at least pierced.' She was weeping freely and he felt a flush of irrational guilt.

He went to her, kneeling on the floor, gently taking her wrists and pulling her hands away from her face. She looked at him and there was sheer misery behind the tears.

'Oh, Gerry . . .' she said, and then was in his arms, head buried against his shoulders, her body shaking.

His throat felt sticky and there was a heaviness dragging at his chest. Sometimes a woman's crying could make him cold, could numb his emotions so that he was accused of having no feelings, an accusation that was often true but only in relation to that particular woman or situation. Fenn had learned to guard himself, to protect his own sensitivities against the demands of others, past hurts, rejections, perhaps forgotten but their marks indelibly made. With Sue there was no such protection. He hugged her tight, close to tears himself.

'I'm sorry,' was all he could think of to say.

'It's not your fault, Gerry,' she said softly. 'You can't help the way you are. Maybe I'm wrong in wanting you to be different.'

'I love you, Sue.'

'I know you do, and I wish you didn't.'

'It's impossible not to.'

'Have you tried?'

'All the time. It's no good, though, I'm hooked.'

She pulled away slightly. 'Gerry, I'm not sure any more how I feel about you.'

That hurt. God, it hurt. He hugged her back to him. 'It's because of everything that's happening, Sue. Things're moving too fast, it's confusing. Just don't make me into the anti-Christ, eh?'

'It's just that I'm seeing you differently. Oh, I've known your failings—'

'Failings? Me?'

'I've known them and chosen to ignore then. Now, though, we seem to be in conflict with each other . . .'

'Not me with you, babe.'

'Then why can't you feel the same way? Why is it just a launching pad for your own career, a way to make money?'

This time it was Fenn who pulled away. 'Let me tell you something,' he said. 'I'll agree I'm taking full advantage of a fantastic story that just happened to fall smack into my lap. Any reporter worth his salt would do the same. But there are others using the Banfield Miracles for their own purposes too. You know, after Alice saw her first vision and I wrote the feature, a guy called Southworth contacted me. He's the owner of the Crown Hotel in Banfield, a councillor and, from what I can gather, owns quite a lot of property in the area. He and someone called Tucker – another of Banfield's fat cats – wanted to hire me to exploit the situation with follow-up articles, keeping the place in the public eye, drumming up more interest than was warranted at that time. Oh, they were a little more subtle with their proposition than that, but that was the strength of it! They wanted to start the carnival there and then.'

He rested back on his heels. 'You might be pleased to know I turned them down.'

'It doesn't mean anything. Two men out of a—'

'Have you been into the village lately?'

'Of course. I've been to St Joseph's—'

'No, not the church. The village itself. All the merchants can talk about is the money that's going to come pouring in. A lot of the property-owners are applying for planning permission to turn their premises into souvenir shops, tea-shops, restaurants, bed-and-breakfast – anything that will bring in money from the tourists that are already flocking in.'

'Now you are exaggerating.'

'Am I? You should take a close look. A kind of insanity has hit Banfield and it's easy to see why. For the first time in its history, the village is the focus of world attention. Maybe it's because we're all sick of hearing nothing but violence, wars and depravity, maybe it's because when something good happens, something that restores our faith in goodness itself, we go overboard. Everybody loves a miracle because it transcends this rotten stinking world we live in. Don't forget this is the age of science, where everything is becoming explainable. Religion is nothing but wish-fulfilling stories for the masses, love is only body chemistry, art is a surge of conditioned reflexes. And now we've got something that really is inexplicable. Something today, in this time!'

'But you're saying the village only wants to make money from it.'

'Sure it does. It doesn't mean they don't believe in the miracles.'

'But they can't all be thinking that way.'

'In cash terms? No, of course not. There are plenty who love what's happening for its own sake, who feel proud their Banfield's been chosen to play host to the Madonna.'

She listened closely for a hint of sarcasm, but found none.

'Yeah, they're happy and more than over-awed. Stunned and grateful. There'll be the few who'll want nothing to do with it, maybe some who'll move away, but they'll be in the minority. The rest, I figure, will wallow in the glory.'

'There's nothing wrong in that.'

He shook his head. 'No. But wait and see the competition to tell the media their own personal stories. How they've known Alice Pagett since she was a baby, how she came to their shop once a week for sweets, how they're distant cousins twice-removed, how their piles miraculously cleared up one day when they passed St Joseph's, how their migraine disappeared when Alice smiled at them. You may think chequebook journalism is an overworked phrase, but wait and see just how many personal accounts of the Banfield Miracles are sold to the newspapers. And wait and see how many "close" friends the Pagett family are going to have, all with intimate details of their private lives. The whole personality of the village is going to change, Sue, as well as its appearance.'

She was staring at him, for the first time realizing the commercial aspect of the mystical experience. For someone whose profession was journalism, she had been remarkably naïve; or perhaps too spiritually involved.

Fenn hated to disillusion her further, but went on, anxious to vindicate his own motives. 'Pretty soon, you won't be able to get near the church without being bombarded with religious junk. Madonnas in snow storms, Madonnas that light up, Sindy Doll Madonnas, rosaries by the thousands, postcards, crucifixes, medallions . . . you name it, it'll be on sale.'

'The Church wouldn't allow it—'

'Huh! The Church will be part of it.'

'That's not true.'

'Do you really think the Catholic Church, with its steady loss of followers and general disenchantment among its worshippers, can afford not to take advantage of something like this? Young priests are leaving, some to get married, women are demanding to be allowed into the priesthood, the Vatican itself is criticized for hoarding its vast wealth and not using it to feed the starving, to help the underprivileged, criticised for not condemning the violence in Northern Ireland more strongly, openly mocked for its out-dated views on birth control, divorce, and plenty of other topics which seem to have no relevance to today's society. The Church needs its miracles to bloody survive!'

Sue flinched and he checked his growing anger. 'Look, when Pope John Paul was shot in '81 – shot six times, mind, an old man pumped with bullets – Catholics by the millions turned back to their faith. Even non-believers felt grief. When he lived, when he *miraculously* recovered, everyone – everyone who was not insane or just plain evil – had a new respect for the Papacy. The world was reminded of the ultimate triumph of good. Well now the Church has got something even more grand: six cures, all witnessed, a possible levitation, and a Visitation. There's no way they won't take advantage of it.'

'Father Hagan won't allow it to be exploited.'

'Father Hagan will be over-ruled. I don't know too much about Bishop Caines, who's the governor of the diocese, but from what information I've managed to gather this week he appears to be an ambitious man. Oh yeah, they have that kind in the Church hierarchy, you know. Apparently he's already sought authoriazation to buy the field next to the church and the farmer who owns it is willing to sell. Seems he's been down on his luck lately.'

'It makes sense to make the field where Alice had the vision part of St Joseph's.'

'Yeah, makes perfect sense. Church ownership of the field will be necessary to accommodate all the visitors who're going to flood the place. I'll bet you the bishop will be accommodating in other ways, too, as this thing snowballs. He's already arranged a Press conference for tomorrow.'

'That's hardly surprising with all the public interest.'

'Well, we'll wait and see how he handles it. How much he refutes, how much he evades and how much he encourages. It should be pretty telling.'

'You'll be there?'

'Would I miss it?'

She sighed and lay back in the chair, wiping at her damp face with the back of her hand. He straightened his legs and leaned over her, conscious of her knees against his groin. 'Sorry for the diatribe, babe, but I wanted you to understand that I'm not the sole passenger on this particular bandwagon.'

Her hand cupped his cheek. 'I still don't trust you, Gerry.'

He groaned aloud.

'Perhaps the miracles have changed us,' she said. 'Brought out the worst in some, the best in others.'

'Maybe some are more gullible than others.'

Her hand froze on his face. 'Meaning?'

He shrugged. 'Maybe some have been taken in by a phenomenon that has no mystical basis whatsoever.'

'"The Power of the Human Mind" theory again?'

'Could be. Who's to say otherwise?'

'Your ten minutes are up.'

'There you go again, not prepared to listen to any other argument. Does all that's happened suddenly make me an enemy, Sue, a child of Satan you have to close your ears to? We used to have long, rational debates at one time, for Christ's sake. With all this deep, religious feeling you're going through, shouldn't you love me even more?'

She didn't answer.

'Okay, let's forget the other alternative for now and accept that the so-called "miracles" have a religious context. Seems to me that Jesus Christ hired twelve pretty good PR guys to spread the Word, four of whom wrote a worldwide best seller. His life story. I guess you couldn't call me a twentieth-century disciple, but isn't there some kind of saying in the Good Book about using the best tools available? Could be I'm one of the tools.' He raised his eyebrows.

Sue was frowning, but Fenn knew he'd scored a point.

After a while she pulled his head down towards her and he was grinning against her chest.

'I'm confused, Gerry, still confused. But maybe I've had my head in the sand. It could be that our beliefs are not allowed to be insulated or introspective any more.' She kissed his hair. 'Your cynicism might even be a healthy thing, who knows? It's so easy to get carried away with it all.'

He held his tongue, not wanting to spoil the mood. Raising his head to look into her eyes, he said, 'All I ask is that you don't lock me out. You might not approve of my approach to the subject, or my appraisal of it, but you can be sure it's honest. And I think that's something you can at least respect.' He kissed her chin. 'Right?'

She nodded, then kissed his lips and he was acutely aware that her abstinence had made her very, very hungry.

It was dark, the curtains drawn.

Fenn lay there, puzzled for a few seconds. Where the hell was he? Then he remembered and relaxed. He smiled in the darkness, remembering their love-making. Christ, Sue had been almost frightening in her intensity. Her physical need for him had seemed to surprise even herself. He wasn't complaining, though; exhausted, but not complaining. He felt her moving in the bed.

Had she disturbed him with her restlessness? He moved towards her, touched her back, and was alarmed at how hot she felt. He pushed close, his arm going around her and becoming damp with her stickiness. Her body jerked and her head twisted into the pillow.

'Sue?' he whispered.

She murmured something, but did not waken. Her limbs were trembling.

Fenn gently shook her shoulder, wanting to wake her from the nightmare, but not wanting to frighten her.

She twisted towards him, still asleep, her breathing rapid, shallow. 'It isn't . . .' she murmured.

'Sue, wake up.' He felt her face, her neck and her breast. She was soaking.

He quickly reached over and switched on the bedside lamp. She pulled her head away from the light, still murmuring. He could hardly hear the words, but it sounded like, 'it isn't . . . her . . . isn't . . . isn't . . .'

'Sue, wake up!' He shook her more fiercely and suddenly her eyes were wide open. Staring.

The fear in them was alarming.

Abruptly, they seemed to cloud over and she blinked several times. She recognized him. 'Gerry, what's wrong?'

He breathed a sigh of relief. 'Nothing, babe,' he said. 'You just had a bad dream.'

He switched off the light and settled down again, holding her in his arms. She was asleep almost instantly.

But he stayed awake for quite some time.

18

'The devil told you that! The devil told you that,' shrieked the little man, and in his fury he stamped his right foot into the ground, right up to his waist, then, foaming at the mouth, he grabbed his left foot in both hands and tore himself apart right down the middle.

The Brothers Grimm, 'Rumpelstiltskin'

DAILY MAIL Has the Vatican an 'official' statement concerning the Banfield Miracles?

BISHOP CAINES The only 'official' statement we can issue at this very early stage is that the Holy Roman Catholic Church acknowledges that a series of what can best be described as extraordinary cures have taken place in the grounds of St Joseph's—

DAILY MAIL Forgive me for interrupting, Bishop, but you just said in the grounds of St Joseph's. Surely it was in the field next to the church?

BISHOP CAINES That's quite correct, but in such close proximity that it could be considered within the church property. I should perhaps inform you that agreement for the purchase of the land by the Church has already been reached and that the necessary documents will be signed within the next day or two. However, to return to your original question: The six extraordinary cures – alleged cures, I should say – which have occurred at St Joseph's will be scrupulously examined by a specially-formed Medical Bureau and their findings passed on to the International Medical Committee. No announcement, no proclamation, and no assertions will be forthcoming until the International Committee is satisfied that every aspect of the six individual cases has been fully investigated.

REUTERS Will the International Committee you refer to be the same committee that examines the cures at Lourdes?

BISHOP CAINES Yes.

CATHOLIC HERALD But the Committee can only recommend that the cures be declared miraculous.

BISHOP CAINES That's correct. As bishop of the diocese in which the cures took place, the final decision as to whether or not the cures are declared miraculous is mine alone.

THE TIMES Have you a view right now?

BISHOP CAINES I have not.

THE TIMES None at all? Even after having talked with Alice Pagett and the others most closely concerned – your own Parish priest, for instance?

BISHOP CAINES I find the whole matter intriguing, to say

	the least, but I cannot possibly make any judgement at this stage.
WASHINGTON POST	What would, then, Bishop Caines, constitute a miracle in the eyes of the Church?
BISHOP CAINES	A cure that is medically inexplicable in the present state of science.
DAILY EXPRESS	When will the Medical Bureau be organized?
BISHOP CAINES	It's being organized right now.
DAILY EXPRESS	And how will it operate?
BISHOP CAINES	Well, it will consist of at least twelve medical men—
JOURNAL DE GENEVA	All Roman Catholics?
BISHOP CAINES	No, most certainly not.
DAILY EXPRESS	But will it be an independent body?
BISHOP CAINES	Absolutely, although the director of the Bureau and several members will be employed by the Church. Others will be gathered from interested medical and scientific research units. Medical records of each cured person will be examined and the individual's own GP and the hospital under which they are receiving treatment will be consulted. They will, naturally, undertake their own thorough medical examination of each cured person and a dossier will be kept. Their findings will eventually be passed on to the International Committee, who will make the final recommendation.
ASSOCIATED PRESS	What will be the criteria? For a miracle, I mean.
BISHOP CAINES	Perhaps Monsignor Delgard would like to answer that?

MONSIGNOR DELGARD I think it should be clearly stated: the Medical Bureau and the International Committee will only be concerned with whether or not the cure is inexplicable, not if it's a miracle.

ASSOCIATED PRESS Is there a difference?

MONSIGNOR DELGARD Bishop Caines said earlier that the cure must be medically inexplicable in the present state of science. The Committee will decide upon that aspect, not whether the cures had a religious or mystical connotation. What is considered medically inexplicable today might be perfectly logical a few years hence. It is the bishop and his advisors who must examine the spiritual aspects of the cures and decide if divine intervention is the cause of the recoveries.

The Bureau and the International Committee have to satisfy themselves on the following points:

Was the cure sudden, unexpected and without convalescence?

Is it complete?

Is it lasting? That, ladies and gentlemen, means a certain amount of time – say three or four years – must elapse before the cure can be confirmed.

How serious was the illness?

Was it due to a specific disease? Infirmity due to a mental disorder, for instance, would rule out any acceptance of a miracle cure.

Had the illness been objectively proved by tests, X-rays, or biopsies?

And was the medical treatment previously given responsible in any way, even if in part only, for the cure?

These are the criteria on which the Bureau and the International Committee must be satisfied. There are others, more technical, but I think those I've listed will give you the general idea.

PSYCHIC NEWS Can you tell us, Monsignor Delgard, just what is your involvement in this matter?

BISHOP CAINES Perhaps I should answer that. At the time of the first cure – when, in fact, Alice Pagett was able to hear and talk again after seven years of being unable to do so – an enormous amount of public interest was created. I felt then that Father Hagan would need some support and guidance in dealing with the crowds who would inevitably descend upon St Joseph's.

PSYCHIC NEWS But you've been involved in certain cases of unusual phenomena in the past, Monsignor Delgard?

MONSIGNOR DELGARD Yes, that's correct.

PSYCHIC NEWS Would you describe them as paranormal?

MONSIGNOR DELGARD (*Pause.*) They could be termed as such, I suppose.

PSYCHIC NEWS In fact, haven't you performed several exorcisms?

MONSIGNOR DELGARD Yes.

PSYCHIC NEWS Did you and do you now suspect that Alice Pagett might be possessed?

(*Laughter.*)

MONSIGNOR DELGARD By the Devil?

(*Laughter.*)

PSYCHIC NEWS	Or evil spirits.
MONSIGNOR DELGARD	I would think that's most unlikely. The child seems well-balanced enough to me.
PSYCHIC NEWS	Then why—
BISHOP CAINES	I've already explained why Monsignor Delgard was temporarily appointed to St Joseph's. While it's true to say he has investigated many strange incidents over the years for the Church and has made a study of psychic phenomena, Monsignor Delgard's role usually has been – if I might use the term – devil's advocate rather than devil seeker.

(*Laughter.*)

You see, the Catholic Church often has to undertake the examination of unusual incidents on behalf of concerned parishioners and clergy. We live in a peculiar world, you know, where human logic is not always applicable to certain events. Monsignor Delgard looks at both aspects of such happenings – natural and unnatural – and usually manages to provide the correct balance. At St Joseph's we have circumstances that are, without doubt, unnatural, so it's perfectly sensible to ask for the assistance and advice of someone who has had experience in such matters, and who can also provide a more material assistance in dealing with the public interest. The fact that Monsignor Delgard has performed exorcisms is quite irrelevant in this case.

May we have another question?

DAILY TELEGRAPH It's rumoured that Alice Pagett's illness could have been psychosomatic. Is it true?

BISHOP CAINES That's for the medical authorities and the Bureau to decide. But, of course, it's doubtful that all five of the other illnesses were due to psychosomatic causes.

LE MONDE What is the Catholic Church's opinion on faith healing?

BISHOP CAINES Jesus Christ was the greatest faith healer of all time.

(*Laughter.*)

GAZETTE (Kent) I have a question for Father Hagan. Some years ago you were assistant priest near Maidstone.

FATHER HAGAN (*Pause.*) Yes, in a place called Hollingbourne.

GAZETTE (Kent) You weren't there for very long, were you, Father?

FATHER HAGAN About six months, I think.

GAZETTE (Kent) You left rather suddenly. Could I ask the reason why?

FATHER HAGAN (*Pause.*) As assistant priest I went where I was needed most. Often the need was urgent and my departure from one parish to another could be abrupt.

GAZETTE (Kent) There was no other reason, then, for you to leave Hollingbourne, apart from being required elsewhere?

FATHER HAGAN As far as I can remember the parish priest of St Mark's in Lewes had fallen ill and assistance was badly needed.

GAZETTE (Kent) No other reason?

BISHOP CAINES Father Hagan has answered your question. May we move on to the next?

DAILY TELEGRAPH	Could this whole business of the miracle cures be a hoax?
BISHOP CAINES	A rather elaborate one, don't you think? And for what purpose?
DAILY TELEGRAPH	Isn't Banfield liable to make a considerable amount of money from tourism?
BISHOP CAINES	Yes, I suppose it's conceivable. The village is already the focus of world attention and I suppose sightseers will flock to St Joseph's even before the results of our investigations are made known. But unless you believe that all the children and the one adult involved in these cures are swindlers and liars – not to mention marvellous actors – (*Laughter.*) – then I hardly think your suggestion has any merit. And, of course, the children's parents and their general practitioners would also have to be involved in the fraud.
L'ADIGE	Alice Pagett claims to have seen a vision of the Madonna. Can you comment on this, please?
BISHOP CAINES	Not at this time.
NEW YORK TIMES	Did anyone else see anything? Father Hagan, you were present on two occasions when the child claimed she saw the Virgin Mary – did you see nothing at all?
FATHER HAGAN	I . . . no, no, I can't say that I did.
NEW YORK TIMES	But did you sense anything strange going on?
FATHER HAGAN	There was certainly atmosphere, yes, a highly charged atmosphere, but I can't account for it.

OBSERVER Surely it would have had something to do with the mood of the crowd, wouldn't it?

FATHER HAGAN Yes, I suppose so.

OBSERVER Sorry, Father, I didn't catch that.

FATHER HAGAN I said I suppose so. Certainly on the last occasion. Several of the other children present seemed entranced in the same way that Alice was, but they could remember nothing when questioned later.

DAILY MIRROR What steps are the Church taking to ensure the situation isn't exploited?

BISHOP CAINES Exploited?

DAILY MIRROR Commercially exploited.

BISHOP CAINES I believe we dealt with that in a previous question. There is very little the Church can to do prevent local traders and businessmen from, shall we say, taking full advantage of the situation. But that is hardly our province and we can only hope that proper restraint and discretion is used.

MORNING STAR But won't the Catholic Church itself exploit the situation?

BISHOP CAINES Why should we do that?

MORNING STAR For publicity.

BISHOP CAINES I hardly think God needs publicity. (*Laughter.*)

STANDARD But it wouldn't harm the Church.

BISHOP CAINES On the contrary, such publicity could be most damaging. Many churchgoers might have their illusions shattered if what they believe to be genuine miracles performed at St Joseph's are later proved by the medical authorities to be nothing of the

	sort. That is one of the reasons the Catholic Church is extremely cautious in such matters.
ASSOCIATED PRESS	Almost to the extent that miracles are harder to prove to the Church than to the layman?
BISHOP CAINES	Yes, in most cases that's true. In fact, the Medical Bureau at Lourdes dismisses nearly all Lourdes cures as non-miraculous. I believe there have been only sixty or so miraculous cures officially recognized at Lourdes since 1858.
OBSERVER	Many people claim they saw Alice levitate last Sunday. Could I ask Father Hagan and Monsignor Delgard if it really did happen?
MONSIGNOR DELGARD	I can't be sure. I wasn't as close to Alice as some of the others. To be perfectly honest, I have no clear recollection.
OBSERVER	Father Hagan?
	(*Silence.*)
MONSIGNOR DELGARD	Father Hagan and I were standing together, so we both had the same view. I don't . . .
FATHER HAGAN	I think Alice did levitate.
	(*Disordered questioning.*)
ECHO DE LA BOURSE	You actually witnessed this?
FATHER HAGAN	I can only say I think that's what happened. The grass in the field is long – perhaps she was merely standing on tiptoe. I just can't be sure.
OBSERVER	But other witnesses say her feet actually left the ground.
FATHER HAGAN	It's possible. I can't be sure, though.
	(*General conversation.*)

STANDARD If it is proved that the cures were miraculous and that Alice Pagett really saw the, er, Virgin Mary, will the girl be proclaimed a saint?

BISHOP CAINES How do you prove such a thing? And before someone can be considered for canonization they have to be dead for some time.

(*Laughter.*)

BRIGHTON EVENING COURIER Why is Alice Pagett being kept hidden away?

BISHOP CAINES Ah, it's Mr Fenn, isn't it? Well, Alice isn't being kept 'hidden away' as you put it. Judging by the amount of media people surrounding the Our Lady of Sion convent in Banfield I certainly wouldn't have said her whereabouts are secret.

Alice is resting. She has been through an extraordinary experience and, as you can imagine, is quite exhausted both physically and emotionally. She needs peace and quiet – her own doctor is adamant that she receives just that. And, of course, she's there with the full agreement of her parents. Alice is a delicate child, and until recently, classed as an invalid. She has to be treated with great care.

BRIGHTON EVENING COURIER Is she undergoing medical tests?

BISHOP CAINES Yes, very stringent tests.

BRIGHTON EVENING COURIER And interrogation by the Church authorities?

BISHOP CAINES Interrogation is far too strong a word. Obviously she is being questioned, but I

	promise you she is under no pressure. I think her only danger at the moment is that she might be smothered by kindness. (*Laughter.*)
BRIGHTON EVENING COURIER	How long will Alice be kept at the convent?
BISHOP CAINES	She is under no detention order, Mr Fenn. She is at perfect liberty to leave when her parents want her to and when her doctor thinks it will be in her own interest.
CATHOLIC HERALD	Has Alice had any more visions since last Sunday?
BISHOP CAINES	She hasn't spoken of any.
DAILY MAIL	Will she attend Mass this Sunday? At St Joseph's, I mean.
MONSIGNOR DELGARD	(*Pause.*) Alice has expressed a desire to. We must consider the consequence to herself, however. We're rather worried that with all the publicity these, er, incidents have been given, St Joseph's will be swamped with sightseers – and obviously the media itself. As Bishop Caines has just said, Alice is a fragile child and the continued excitement might be too much for her. She has to be protected.
INTERNATIONAL HERALD TRIBUNE	But she'll have to face the public sooner or later.
BISHOP CAINES	That's true, but I suppose that at this stage the medical team studying her case, her own doctor and the Church, would rather it were later. However, nothing yet has been decided regarding this coming Sunday.
BRIGHTON EVENING COURIER	But Alice does want to go to Mass this Sunday?

BISHOP CAINES Alice is somewhat confused at the moment. I think that's quite understandable.

BRIGHTON EVENING COURIER But she does want to?

BISHOP CAINES As the monsignor said, she has expressed a desire to.

BRIGHTON EVENING COURIER So it's a strong possibility?

BISHOP CAINES I believe I've already answered that question.

(*Disordered questioning.*)

BISHOP CAINES I'm afraid we must bring this Press conference to a close, gentlemen. Thank you for your questions and I hope we've been able to clarify a few points. I'm sorry, no more questions. Our schedule is tight and we now have television and radio interviews to do. Thank you for your time, ladies and gentlemen.

(*Press conference ends.*)

Wilkes

'If thy mother only knew,
Her heart would surely break in two.'

The Brothers Grimm, *The Goose-girl*

He couldn't sleep.

His hair itched, the sheets on the narrow bed felt soiled, stiff and unwashed. He wasn't hungry, he wasn't thirsty; he certainly wasn't tired. It was his own fault for staying in bed most of the day. He should have gone to the Job Centre, but what the fuck? They would only have offered him some poxy job waiting on tables like his last one, or digging bloody holes in roads, or working some machine in a factory. Or worse, Community fucking Service! Sod em! He'd have to blag the old lady for money tomorrow. Christ, how he hated going back there! *Look at you! Why don't you get your hair cut? You'll never get a decent job like that. And look at your clothes. When was the last time that shirt was ironed? And can't you at least polish your shoes?*

Worst of all: *When was the last time you went to church? What would your poor father say if he were still alive?*

Shit on her! If he didn't need the bread he would never go back.

He turned in the bed, a crease in his vest irritating his skin. He stared out the window into the dark night. Christ, if only he could get a bird up here; that would warm him up, all right! They didn't want to know, though. If you didn't have money, then they just weren't interested. If you were a nobody you were bloody nobody! He turned again and thumped the lumps from the pillow with an angry fist. He'd had a guy up there once, but that hadn't been too good. The jerking off was okay, but all that fucking kissing had made him want to puke.

He stared at the ceiling and pulled the end of the vest over his bare stomach.

It was all a big bucket of shit. You fell into it and the bastards wouldn't let you climb out. You just went round and round in the slime until you had to eat it to stop drowning. And then it poisoned you and killed you dead anyway.

But at least *they* had kicked back! Those three had swallowed the shit and spewed it right back into the onlookers' faces. *They* had found a way, and that was all it took.

He grinned in the darkness. Yeah, they had found a way.

He yanked back the covers and padded over to the wardrobe in stockinged feet. Standing on tiptoe, he reached up to the top of the wardrobe and found the box he was looking for. He brought it down, then took a small key from his jacket hanging over the back of the room's only chair.

Climbing back into the bed he inserted the key and opened the lid. He took a dark object out and pressed it to his cheek, smiling in the darkness. He placed the open box on the floor and covered himself.

Lying there in the darkness, he pushed the object beneath the bedclothes so that its cold metal lay between his inner thighs. He sighed as he felt himself grow hard.

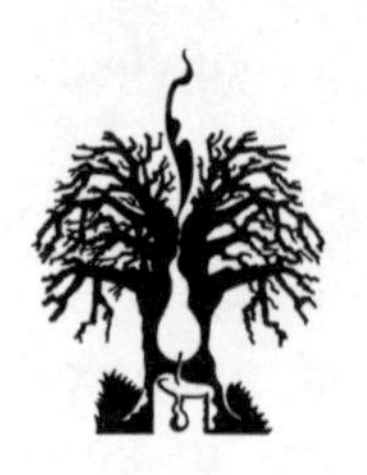

19

Here lies the Devil – ask no other name.
Well – but you mean Lord – ? Hush! we mean the same.

Samuel Taylor Coleridge, 'On a Lord'

Fenn yawned and checked his watch at the same time. 7.45. Jesus, so this was what the dawn was like.

Another car was approaching him from the opposite direction and he gave the driver a tired wave as though they were both members of the same exclusive club. The other driver looked at him as if he were mad. Fenn hummed a tuneless tune, only the fact that he was tone deaf making the noise bearable to himself.

He glanced at the South Downs to his left; the clouds were heavy over them, soft woolly bottoms scraping against the hilltops. It was going to be another cold, overcast day, the kind that dragged at the keenest optimism, muffled the most ardent enthusiasm. The kind of day to stay in bed until positive night-time darkness over-rode the negative dullness.

The houses on either side of the road were few and far between, mostly big and set back with high hedges or walls protecting them from unsolicited attention. The road was normally quite busy as one of the main routes from the coast to the larger Sussex towns, scything through country villages like wire through cheese; but on a chilly damp Sunday morning – a chilly, damp, *early* Sunday morning – birds and rabbits were a more common sight than motorists.

Fenn's humming droned to a stop when he saw the outskirts of Banfield ahead and the dregs of tiredness evaporated as if hoovered from his head. He grinned, ready to enjoy the special privilege he had been allowed and to forget about the warm bed he had just left. It was regrettable that Sue's naked body had not been in that bed (even though it would have been even harder to leave), but they were still not the close lovers that they had been. When they had slept together just three nights before, Fenn had imagined their relationship would be back on the same footing and had been disappointed to find on the following morning her new aloofness had only suffered a slight relapse. While not as cold as before, and certainly not as contemptuous, she had made it plain that she needed more time to think. She loved him, of that there was no doubt, but the confusion was still there and their love-making had not cleared it. Okay, it's down to you, Sue. You know my number.

Fenn was angry and frustrated at her change of moods, particularly at a time when things were happening for him, when he shouldn't have had such distractions. He cursed himself for not being able to cut her from his mind. Christ, he was buying his ticket to Fleet Street and she acted as though he had forged the money! The invitation for that Sunday morning was an indication of just how far he had advanced in prestige in a matter of a few short weeks. Only he and five other reporters shared the privilege, his colleagues chosen from the cream to represent the media world. So maybe he was over-rating his own importance a little, but the position he now found himself in was no mean thing.

He eased off the accelerator as he entered the speed restricted zone. The road swung sharply to the right, joined by another minor road from the left, the round white bump of a tiny 'mickey mouse' roundabout helping (or hindering) the merger. The Convent of Our Lady of Sion was almost opposite, just to the left, and Fenn brought his Mini to a halt, checking that the roundabout was clear. From his position he could see the upper windows of the large cream-coloured house and for one brief moment thought he caught a small pale face peering down at him. Then it was gone and he wasn't sure that it had been there.

A lone policeman stood outside the gates, his panda parked half on the kerb further down the road. To one side was a group of reporters, damp and miserable looking. They eyed Fenn's car suspiciously as he drove over the circle in the road. Fenn pulled into a nearby empty garage forecourt and parked. The garage was closed and, as it was Sunday, he guessed it wouldn't be open at all that day. He left the car and walked back to the convent.

The journalists and cameramen, pasty-faced, shoulders hunched, feet stamping the pavement, made ready to receive him into their midst, any newcomer welcome to break the monotony of their cold vigil.

'Morning, hacks,' he said, grinning and winking as he strode past them. He ignored their muttered replies as he walked up to the gates. The policeman on duty raised a hand.

'I'm Fenn, *Brighton Courier*.'

The uniformed man produced a folded piece of paper from his tunic pocket and quickly scanned the list of names.

'Okay, in you go.' The policeman pushed open one half of the gates just enough for Fenn to slip through. He chuckled at the indignant voices and groans of the other reporters.

Across the courtyard and at the top of three broad steps

was a black door, open and somehow forbidding. Fenn crossed the yard and took the first two steps in one. He stepped into a dark hallway and a hooded shape loomed up from the shadows.

'You are Mr . . .?' the nun asked.

'Gerry Fenn,' he told her, his heart skipping just a little, either from the leap up the stairs or her sudden appearance. '*Brighton Evening Courier.*'

'Ah, yes. Mr Fenn. Shall I take your coat?'

He slipped off his raincoat and handed it to her. 'There's no money in the pockets,' he said.

She looked at him, startled, then returned his smile. 'If you'd like to go through, you'll find nearly everyone has arrived.' She pointed to a door near the end of the hallway.

He thanked her and walked down the hall, his steps sharp against the shiny bare floorboards. The room beyond the door was large and on a sunny day would have been light and airy; today its natural brightness was muted grey. It was filled with people and hushed voices.

'Mr Fenn, glad you could come.'

He turned to find George Southworth approaching him.

'Glad I was invited,' Fenn responded.

'Your other colleagues have already arrived.'

'Oh?'

'A rather small selection of élite journalists. You're the sixth.'

Fenn enjoyed being among the 'élite'.

'*Associated Press, Washington Post, The Times* – that sort of thing. I'm sure you know them all.'

'Oh yeah, sure.' Fenn shook his head. 'I'm puzzled, Mr Southworth. Why me?'

Southworth smiled disarmingly and patted Fenn's arm. 'Mustn't be so modest, Mr Fenn. You've covered this story from the start. More than that, you brought it to the attention of the world. We could hardly have excluded you.'

'Hardly.'

'Quite. Would you like some tea?'

'No thanks.'

'I'm sure you'll appreciate our reluctance in allowing young Alice to attend Mass at St Joseph's this—'

'Your reluctance?'

'Well, to be honest, Bishop Caines' reluctance. And the doctors, of course – they feel the hullabaloo might prove too much for her. The cameras, the television, the crowds, people wanting to get near her, to touch her – that sort of thing.'

Fenn nodded. 'So you decided on a private service, without the fuss.'

'Precisely.'

'A lot of people are going to be disappointed.'

'I'm sure. Frankly, if I had had my way, I would have let Alice go to the church today as she wanted. But her well-being must come first.'

'She wanted to go to St Joseph's?'

'Apparently so.' Southworth lowered his voice. 'I heard she became quite upset when Reverend Mother told her she couldn't. Still, I'm sure it's for the best.'

'So you just invited certain members of the, er . . .' he scanned the room '. . . public and the media here.'

'Yes. My idea, actually. And the Bishop concurred. We're well aware, you see, that the public has to know what's going on. That's their right. This way, they'll see that Alice is being properly cared for.'

'And they'll know the Catholic Church isn't locking her away, and that she's not going through some modern-day Grand Inquisition.'

Southworth chuckled. 'That's very astute of you, Mr Fenn.

In fact, that was my argument to the churchmen. With the chosen few here, representatives of the people, as it were, and an excellent cross-section of the world media, public interest can be catered for without unnecessary but inevitable pandemonium.'

And without loss of maximum publicity, Fenn guessed. It seemed that Southworth (and Fenn was sure other local businessmen were involved) had to walk the tightrope between exploitation (and so risk the resulting criticism), and ensuring that Alice Pagett was sheltered from the public eye (and making sure they were seen to be doing so). He, Fenn, was necessary to the idea not because he was a brilliant journalist, but because as instigator of the story, his articles were followed more closely than any other reporter's. He was also 'local', therefore perhaps more in tune with local opinion. Well, don't knock it, Fenn. It made sense. And it had got him here today.

'In a moment,' Southworth was saying, 'I'll introduce you to a few people. Your colleagues are already well known to them, but I'm sure they will want to speak to you as the man who was "on the spot". Mass will begin at 8.30, so you'll have just . . .' he checked his watch '. . . just under half-an-hour to interview.'

'Will I get to talk to Alice?'

'We plan to have a brief question and answer session after Mass. Only twenty minutes, I'm afraid, and only if Alice feels up to it. I'm sure she will.' He moved closer to Fenn and said in a conspiratorial whisper: 'I'd like to invite you to dinner tomorrow evening. I think you'd be most interested in coming along.'

Fenn raised his eyebrows.

'I still haven't forgotten our little chat at the beginning of all this business, Mr Fenn. By the way, it's Gerry, isn't it? Do you mind if I call you that? It's far less formal. I think at the time you said the story would probably die out.'

Fenn grinned wryly. 'Someone once said that about Lennon and McCartney.'

'I think your opinion was very fair. But you remember my offer? Yes, well, I think you may have suspected my motives at that time. You can see now that the publicity machine is in motion of its own accord and needs absolutely no impetus from myself, or the parish council. It may need just a little steering from the inside, though, and I think you could be helpful in that respect.'

'I don't understand.'

We have enough confidence in you, having read all your articles in the *Courier*, to invite you to write the complete story of the Banfield Miracles.'

'For my newspaper?'

'For any newspaper you care to work for. Or for a book. We would make you privy to all council meetings and any other decisions, discussions and plans concerning this whole affair.'

Fenn's eyes gleamed. It was too good to be true. The *authorized* chronicler of the Banfield Miracles. Any newspaper editor would jump at serialization rights and any publisher would give his right arm (or his marketing manager's right arm) for the rights to the book. There had to be a snag. 'Why me?' he asked.

'I believe you asked that question before, or something like it. The answer's simple: because you were there at the beginning. You already have more inside knowledge than anyone else in this matter apart from the clergy. And even they – Father Hagan and Monsignor Delgard – were not there at the very beginning.'

'Would the priests be agreeable?'

'I've already broached the subject to Bishop Caines. He's interested but wary.'

'Oh?'

'He's pragmatic enough to realize the story has become almost exclusive to you. However, he is not altogether sure that, to use an old-fashioned phrase, your "intentions are honourable".'

'Are his?'

'I beg your pardon?'

'It doesn't matter.'

'That's the reason for my invitation to dine with us tomorrow evening.'

'Bishop Caines will be there?'

'Yes, along with Father Hagan and Monsignor Delgard. Our meeting initially is to talk about the development of a shrine at St Joseph's and Banfield's part in it. Bishop Caines is insistent that there should be full cooperation and liaison between the parish council and the Church.'

'It's moving things pretty fast for them, isn't it? I thought it took years for the Church to allow a shrine to be authorized.'

'Normally it would. Fortunately or unfortunately, whichever way you care to look at it, the pilgrims are going to come and nothing will stop them. The bishop wants to be prepared. Officially, the Church cannot declare St Joseph's a shrine, but that won't prevent the public from regarding it as such.'

'Do the two priests know I've been invited?'

'Yes. Bishop Caines, himself, told them.'

'And they agreed?'

'Reluctantly. I suppose you could say the Bishop gave them little choice. I hope, after all this, you are interested?'

'What do you think? Where and when?'

'My hotel, 8.30.'

'I'll be there.'

'Fine. Now, let me introduce you to a few people.'

Fenn spent the next twenty minutes talking to assorted 'guests', among them the local Tory MP, who was not himself a Catholic but professed a deep interest in all religions, several members of the clergy, whose titles he instantly forgot, certain leading members of the local community, the Reverend Mother of the convent and, most interestingly of all, the Apostolic Delegate to Great Britain and Gibraltar. Fenn understood that this clergyman was the official 'go-between' for the Catholic Church in Britain and the Vatican. A quietly-spoken, unassuming man, he seemed genuinely pleased to be introduced to Fenn, and gently led him to one side so that he could question him on the articles he had written and what he had personally witnessed. Soon the reporter began to feel like the interviewee, but he enjoyed the priest's frank questioning and the deference with which his answers were treated.

When the audience was over, for that was what it felt like, Fenn realized he had asked hardly any questions himself. He was puzzled by the priest's accent and one of the grey-garbed nuns who was flitting through the crowded room urging more tea or coffee on the assemblage provided the answer: The Most Reverend Pierre Melsak was from Belgium. Fenn accepted a coffee from the sister and wished he'd declined the ginger biscuit which resisted all attempts to be bitten. He left it on the saucer, his teeth groaning after the battle, and was sipping the lukewarm coffee when a husky voice said, 'Hi.'

He turned to see a dark-haired woman smiling at him; at least her lips were smiling – the eyes were too calculating to be easily happy.

'Shelbeck, *Washington Post*,' she told him.

'Yeah, somebody already pointed you out to me. How's Woodward?'

'Redford was better. You're Gerry Fenn, aren't you?'

He nodded.

'I liked your copy. Maybe we can get together later?'

'That'd be nice. What for?'

'Compare notes?' Her accent was pure New York.

'I'm ahead.'

'You could benefit.'

'How?'

'Financially, how else?' The smile had finally reached her eyes.

'Okay . . .'

The buzz of conversation stopped as sliding doors covering one side of the room were drawn back. Another room, white-walled and low-ceilinged, lay beyond. Fenn guessed it had once been a double-garage attached to the house that the Sisters of Our Lady of Sion had had converted into a small chapel. The altar was simple, no more than a rectangular table covered in a spotlessly white cloth on which stood a crucifix. Small benches stood before it, enough to accommodate the nuns who lived in the convent.

'If you would please take your places,' Bishop Caines told the select group, 'the Mass will begin in a few moments. I'm afraid there isn't room for everybody to sit, even though our kind sisters have volunteered to stand throughout the service, so could the male journalists please take a position at the back of the chapel.'

People began to move into the next room and Shelbeck winked at Fenn. 'I'll talk to you after the show,' she whispered. 'The name's Nancy, by the way.'

He watched her push her way into the chapel, heading for

a seat near the front. Her age could have been anywhere between thirty and forty, though he guessed it was at the higher end, say thirty-six or seven. She wore a sensible grey tweed suit, the kind native New Yorkers managed to make look business-like yet attractive. Her figure was slim and, from the back, her legs were good (which was the real test for legs). At a quick appraisal she was abrasive, brittle and more than a little shrewd, the kind of woman who could intimidate the more easily intimidated of the male species (which was most of them). She could prove interesting.

'Um, could we leave the front bench free for myself, Reverend Mother, Alice and Mr and Mrs Pagett?' Bishop Caines said, a beaming smile on his face. 'Monsignor Melsak, would you please join us at the front?'

The small Belgian priest did as requested and the bishop turned his attention back to the rest of the congregation. 'Alice will join us presently. The service will be kept short and she will be the first to take Communion. May I ask our friends from the media to refrain from asking any questions of the child when she enters the chapel. I promise you'll have the opportunity as soon as the Mass is finished. Only twenty minutes, of course, but you must remember she is under considerable strain.' He tried a disarming smile. 'I need hardly add that no pictures will be allowed and members of the Press have been invited on that understanding. So if any of you have cameras hidden about your person, please keep them that way – hidden and unused.'

Soft chuckles greeted his last remark and there were one or two embarrassed smiles among the Pressmen.

Everyone soon became settled and Fenn found himself standing to one side of the room at the back. He was above the congregation, for three steps led down from the general room into the chapel itself. He thought the drawn doors might be a good spot to lean against if the service wasn't as short as the bishop had declared. There was an air of expectancy, the same excitement present at St Joseph's on the previous Sunday. The nuns of the convent knelt around the side walls, heads bowed, rosaries entwined between fingers. The politician and some of the other dignitaries looked uncomfortable, not sure of the ceremony, anxious not to offend. He caught a glimpse of Nancy Shelbeck as she turned her head to study, and no doubt to make note of, her surroundings. Whispered conversation faded and the congregation settled into an uneasy silence.

Fenn turned as a door behind him opened. A man walked awkwardly into the room and Fenn quickly recognized him as Len Pagett, Alice's father. He wore an ill-fitting suit, one that had seen better days, its obviously recent dry clean giving it a short-term smartness. He looked with trepidation across the room into the chapel and Fenn could see resentment in his eyes. He stood back from the door, revealing the small figure of Alice. She emerged from the darkness of the hallway, a nervous, doe-like creature, her face pale, eyes wide and darting. She wore a pale blue dress and her blonde hair was tied back at one side with a white bow. Her father muttered something and she moved more quickly into the room. Her glance went immediately to the large patio windows overlooking the convent's garden and Fenn felt she was like a young caged animal, yearning to be on the outside, away from the smothering kindness of captivity.

Immediately behind came Molly Pagett, an uncertain smile on her face as she urged Alice onwards into the chapel. A nun was the last to enter; she turned to close the door, then stood with her back to it as though a guard.

All heads turned as Alice approached the steps; she

stopped for a moment to take in the scene before her. She seemed even younger than her eleven years, yet there was a subtle change in her features, a look that made her less of a child than before. Fenn could not define the change. Maybe it was in the eyes . . .

She turned towards him as though suddenly aware that he, in particular, was watching her. For a brief moment, something chilled him. Then it was gone, had passed, and he was only looking into the face of a small timid child. Something lingered with him, though, and it was a feeling he could not understand.

Alice stepped down into the chapel as Bishop Caines beckoned her forward. She genuflected before the altar, then disappeared from view as she sat with her parents on the front bench.

Once again, the door behind Fenn opened, the nun who had been standing in front of it quickly stepping to one side as the handle turned. Father Hagan entered, dressed in the bright robes of the Mass, followed by Monsignor Delgard, who wore his customary black garb. The first priest carried a covered chalice as he swept through the room into the chapel, his eyes downcast. Monsignor Delgard gave Fenn a brief nod of recognition as he passed.

Both men made their way to the altar and stood behind it, facing the congregation. Fenn assumed Delgard was there to assist Father Hagan in the absence of altar-servers. Again, the expression on another's face disturbed the reporter, for Hagan looked desperately tired and unwell. He placed the chalice on the altar and, even from where Fenn stood, his unsteadiness was evident. Still leaning forward over the altar, the priest's attention was taken by someone seated in the front row. Fenn knew that Father Hagan was staring into the face of Alice Pagett.

The priest became still for several seconds, then appeared to remember where he was and the service began.

Fenn was getting used to the Mass by now and was relieved it was to be a short one. Short though it was, he was soon looking around, totally unmoved by the service itself. Daylight, grey and depressing on such a morning, flooded the small chapel through a broad skylight, presumably built into the roof when the garage had been converted. The walls themselves were still of rough brick but painted gleaming white, and the floor was carpet-tiled. There were no windows, just a heavy, locked door leading out into the courtyard. The congregation, led by the nuns and the invited clergy, responded to the priest's intonations and Fenn tried to follow the proceedings in the Mass Book handed to him by the same sister who had served him coffee. He lost his place several times and eventually gave up. He found it difficult to understand the appeal of such a weekly ritual to someone like Sue, who was a level-headed, sensitive and capable woman. She was also pretty smart, certainly nobody's fool. So how come she was hooked on all this?

Something caught his eye. A sudden movement above. He looked towards the skylight and smiled. The shadowy form of a cat was moving across the slanted, frosted glass. It stopped and the ghostly head grew larger as the cat tried to peer through the unclear glass. It rested its front paws against the pane, head weaving from side to side as if frustrated. Its body appeared to stiffen, then it eased back down the slope and sat, only the shadow of its upper body visible.

Fenn and the other reporters knelt when the rest of the congregation knelt, stiffened to attention when those seated stood, and generally responded to the service in a superficial way. He realized it wasn't out of reverence, but more out of respect for the sweet-looking nuns who he felt might have been upset if the correct movements were not adhered to. A tiny bell rang and heads bowed. Fenn, kneeling uncomfortably, knew it was almost time for Holy Communion. He eased himself upright, sure that he wouldn't be noticed at this crucial point. The silence in the room was disconcerting. In a church, atmospherics, and general rustling of restless bodies, moaning children and muffled coughs were enough to combat any true silence, but here in the little chapel, even a rumbling stomach had no camouflage.

Father Hagan stood before the altar, the chalice and Communion wafer in his hand. His eyes were almost closed.

Fenn saw Bishop Caines lean over and whisper something to Alice. For a moment she did not move and he had to whisper again. She stood, her hair bright yellow, the white bow like a butterfly nestling in wheat. She looked frail, too small, and Fenn found himself concerned, caring about her. She had been through so much, this little squirt, and he wondered how she had remained so calm throughout.

She was looking at the priest, still not moving.

Her mother touched her arm, but Alice did not look at her. Eventually it was the Reverend Mother who rose and led Alice towards Father Hagan. The priest looked down at the little figure and his eyes widened. His hand was visibly trembling when he held the Host forward.

Fenn frowned, aware of the tension in the priest. My God, he thought, he's frightened. Something's scaring him bloody silly.

Alice's head tilted backwards slightly, as though she were offering her tongue to take the Communion wafer. The priest hesitated, then seemed to resolve something in his own mind. He placed the wafer on Alice's tongue.

Her head bowed and for a moment both she and the priest were still.

Then her small body began to shudder. Alice fell to her knees as the retching sound screeched from her. Vomit splattered onto the floor. Onto the shoes of the priest. Onto his white robes.

20

Then out has she ta'en a silver wand,
An' she's turned her three times roun' and roun';
She mutter'd sic words till my strength it fail'd,
An' I fell down senseless upon the groun'.

Anon, 'Alison Gross'

'Father, you've hardly touched your soup. Is there something wrong with it?'

The priest looked up, startled. 'I, uh, no, of course not. I'm afraid I'm just not very hungry.' Southworth looked relieved.

Bishop Caines laughed jovially. 'I swear you're wasting away before my eyes, Andrew. Come on, man, you must eat, especially if you're going to cope over the next few months.'

Father Hagan picked up his spoon once more and dipped it into the mushroom soup, his movements slow, distracted. Bishop Caines and Monsignor Delgard exchanged concerned glances.

'Are you still unwell?' Delgard asked quietly. The others on the table were watching the priest with interest. The man's decline in health had spanned the past few weeks, but the overnight change had been more dramatic.

Father Hagan sipped from the spoon. 'It's just a chill, I think,' he said unconvincingly.

'Would you like me to take you home?'

'No. Our discussion tonight is important.'

Bishop Caines dabbed at his lips with a serviette. 'Not important enough to keep you from a nice warm bed. I'm sure that's where you'd be better off, Andrew.'

'I'd rather stay.'

'So be it. But I insist you see a doctor tomorrow without fail.'

'There's no need—'

'Without fail,' the bishop repeated.

Father Hagan nodded, then laid down his spoon. He sat back in his chair, feeling strangely detached from his surroundings. Occasionally it was like viewing the scene through the wrong end of a telescope. Even the conversation sounded distant.

He looked across at the reporter who was sitting on the opposite side of the round dinner table, between the hotelier and Bishop Caines, and again he asked himself the silent question: why had they involved this man? Fenn wasn't a Catholic and didn't appear to have any sympathy at all towards the Catholic religion. Objectivity, Bishop Caines had said. They needed someone like Fenn, an agnostic, to write objectively on the Banfield Miracles, someone without bias who would be more credible because of it. He would report the untainted facts and, after all, that was all that was necessary here, for the facts alone would convince and perhaps convert.

Would the young reporter listen to him? Would he want to hear? And what could he, Hagan, really tell him? That he was afraid? Afraid of a child? Afraid of . . .? What? Nothing. There was nothing to fear. Nothing at all . . .

'. . . Alice is fine.' Bishop Caines was speaking. 'I'm afraid all the excitement yesterday was a little too much for her. Her own doctor gave her a thorough check-up and said there was nothing to worry over. She had a slight temperature, but that was all. A few more days of peace and quiet is all she needs.'

'I'm pleased to hear it,' Southworth said. 'She had us all worried yesterday. Mercifully it didn't happen up at St Joseph's in full view of the crowds. Very wise of you, if I may say so, Bishop, to keep the child at the convent.'

'Yes, much as I understand the need for people to see Alice, her own best interests must be considered.'

'Does that mean you won't let her return to the church for some time?' asked Fenn.

'Oh, no, no. It would be quite wrong to keep Alice from her beloved St Joseph's. She's known the church all her young life, Mr Fenn; it's a second home to her. In fact, you could say she was practically born there.'

'You mean she was baptized—'

'I think it would be wise to keep Alice away from St Joseph's permanently.'

The interruption surprised everyone sitting at the table. Bishop Caines studied his parish priest with evident impatience.

'Now, Andrew, you know that would be impossible. Reverend Mother tells me she has found the child weeping in her room because she misses the church so much. We can't keep her locked away forever.' He quickly looked at Fenn. 'Not that we are keeping her locked up, you understand. Alice is free to leave at any time her parents wish her to.'

'But she wants to leave,' Fenn said.

'Of course it's no fun for a little girl to be shut away in a convent, Mr Fenn. Naturally she would like to be seeing her friends, playing with them, carrying on with all the usual activities young children indulge in. And she will, before very long.'

'Don't let her come back to the church. Not yet.'

'Andrew, I cannot understand your attitude in this matter.' The soothing amiability had left the bishop's tone, although his words were still softly spoken. 'Just what is it that disturbs you about the girl?'

Fenn leaned forward, elbows on the table, interested in the priest's reply.

Father Hagan looked uncertainly around at the dinner guests. 'I . . . I'm not sure. It just . . . doesn't . . .'

'Come now, Father,' said Bishop Caines. 'I think it's time you shared your unwillingness to accept these rather wondrous events with us. Don't worry about our Mr Fenn here – we will have no secrets from the Press. If you have doubts, please voice them so that they can be discussed.'

The door opened and the head waiter unobtrusively entered the room. He quickly surveyed the dinner table, then nodded at someone just outside the door. A waitress hurried through and began to gather up the used dishes.

'Oh, I'm sorry, Father,' she said, about to take the priest's soup bowl.

'It's all right, I've finished.'

The dish was taken away. Nobody spoke until the waitress had left and the head waiter had closed the door, abruptly cutting off the noise from the public restaurant and bar below. Southworth had deemed it wise to hold the dinner in a private banqueting room on the first floor, away from the hotel's other guests, who that week were mainly visiting journalists.

'Andrew?' the bishop prompted.

'It's difficult, Bishop,' the priest said quietly.

'I beg your pardon?'

'I said it's difficult. Difficult to put my feelings into words.'

'Do try.' It was said kindly.

'Something . . . something is wrong. I can't say what it is, but something doesn't feel right. The church . . . St Joseph's . . . somehow seems . . . empty.'

'Empty? I don't understand.'

'I think I know what Father Hagan means,' said Monsignor Delgard. All eyes turned towards him. 'I've been concerned over the atmosphere inside St Joseph's for a few days now and I believe I understand what Father Hagan is trying to say.'

'Then perhaps you'd enlighten us,' said Bishop Caines.

'It seems to me the church has become spiritually devoid.'

'I'm very surprised at you, Monsignor,' the bishop said coldly. 'That remark could be regarded as sacrilegious. The House of God can never be spiritually devoid – it's impossible, contrary to all our beliefs to hold such a view.'

'A church is just a building made of stone, Bishop,' the monsignor replied calmly.

Bishop Caines' face reddened and Fenn hid his smile behind his wine glass.

'It might be better to confine our discussion tonight to the more, er, "material" aspects of the situation,' Southworth cut in. 'Don't you agree, Gerry?'

'Well, no. I—'

'Yes, you're absolutely right,' Bishop Caines said, not wishing to hold a theological debate now in front of the reporter who could so easily misinterpret everything. 'We can talk of this later.' He looked meaningfully at the two clergymen.

'As you wish,' Delgard responded stiffly.

Father Hagan opened his mouth to say more but, on seeing the stern expression on his bishop's face, he refrained.

Fenn was disappointed.

Southworth allowed no respite. 'One thing I'm sure the media will want, Bishop, is a statement on Alice's health at this present moment . . .'

'Haven't I already told you?' The bishop was still watching his two priests, but he turned to give Southworth a warm smile.

'Yes, but I meant her state of health generally. Yesterday was an exception.'

'Yes, that it was. A culmination of events, if you like. It had to catch up with the child sooner or later. The monsignor has the latest information from the medical team.'

'A medical report is generally private to the individual,' said Delgard. He nodded towards Fenn. 'Why should it be made public by the Press?'

'We have an understanding with Mr Fenn,' Southworth said.

Fenn looked at him in surprise. 'Now wait a minute. The only understanding that we have is that I'll write the truth.' Then he added, 'As I see it.'

'Naturally, Mr Fenn,' Bishop Caines assured him. 'We would not expect otherwise. However we would expect, er, discreet journalism.'

'Oh, I can be discreet. It's secrets I can't keep.'

He caught the glance that passed between the bishop and Southworth.

'Okay,' he said, raising a hand, 'I understand your dilemma. You want the story told without frills, without exaggeration, and truthfully. That's good, that's what I want to do. On the other hand, you want personal privacy respected and anything that could cause embarrassment smoothed over, if not scrubbed out.' He paused to take a breath. 'I'll go along with you on the first count. No exaggeration, no exploitation. As for personal privacy, I'm afraid that went out the window when Alice saw her first vision. Not just for her. For you. And for the whole of Banfield. On the third count – revealing anything that could cause embarrassment – well, you have to leave that to me.'

'I'm not sure that's good enough,' said the bishop.

'It'll have to be.' Fenn grinned. 'Look, I know Alice's father is a drunken old sot, but at this stage, I don't think it's essential to the story. It's not exactly a state secret, but I don't intend to make anything of it. Discretion, right?'

'Yes, Mr Fenn, but not much of a concession on your part.'

'True enough. But it's all I can offer.'

It was Southworth who saved the situation. 'Why don't we rely on that good old journalistic standby, "off the record"? That way you can be intimate with the situation as a whole, but professionally bound to keep certain items to yourself.'

It's either that, or be blown out entirely, Fenn told himself. 'Okay, so long as there aren't too many "off the records",' he said.

'Agreed, Bishop?' Southworth asked.

Bishop Caines was thoughtful. 'You understand, Mr Fenn, that we do not want to veil anything. The Church doesn't work that way.'

Oh no? Fenn said silently. Get the Pope to tell the world the third secret of Fatima. Or disclose all the Church's financial assets, exactly what companies and properties they're into. And any other items of world interest that the Catholic Church is keeping to itself.

'We want only the truth to be written,' Bishop Caines continued, 'but we do not wish any person to be harmed by it. If you take our view, then I'm sure there will be no problems between us. I'm sure there are many other journalists who would be only too pleased to understand.'

You wily old bastard. You know I can't refuse. 'All right.

But one proviso: if I really believe you're holding back on something that needs to be told – I mean, if I think it morally wrong not to publish – then I go ahead and do so.'

'Are you suggesting we would lie?'

'Not at all. But you might want to withhold information that doesn't suit the Church's image.'

'Then we'll let you be our conscience, Mr Fenn.'

'Okay.'

Southworth breathed a sigh of relief as Bishop Caines and the reporter relaxed in their chairs. 'You were going to tell us the medical team's findings to date,' he urged the monsignor.

'Their report is very detailed and extremely technical in parts, so I'll try to break it down as concisely and simply as possible. If you require the full text, Mr Fenn, I can obtain a copy for you.' He sipped his wine, then set it to one side. 'First let me deal with the findings on Alice's previous infirmity. There has been no physical change in the organs of her ears and throat, which consolidates the long-standing opinion that her handicap had psychological origins. There never had been any discernible damage to the auditory nerves, no apparent disorder to the ossicles, cochlea or eardrum of either ear. There may well have been some infection due to her illness seven years ago, but there were certainly no signs that it had lingered. There had been no hardenings or formation of bones in the inner ear, no inflammation of the membranes. Mastoiditis, otitis media – I'm sorry, that's middle ear infection – had been discounted long ago. As for her vocal cords, there was no damage or disease to the laryngeal nerve. Her condition was always thought to be a result of hysteria.'

'You're saying Alice was just suffering from prolonged hysteria all these years?' Fenn asked incredulously.

'It's not quite that simple, nor is it as unusual as your tone suggests. There may very well have been other infections present that were not detected by her family doctor when Alice suffered mumps at four years of age, infections that could have been the root cause of her condition. The doctor considered it to be a routine childhood illness and looked no further in the early stages. Tests came later when the disastrous consequences became evident. I should add that there is no criticism levelled at the GP in the medical report – at the moment we're dealing purely with conjecture.'

'Has the family doctor seen this report?' Fenn asked.

'No. And, of course, he would undoubtedly deny any suggestion of negligence on his part. But I would hate you to draw any hasty conclusions – this is partly theory now, just an attempt to offer reasons.'

'May I remind you of our discussion a short while ago,' Bishop Caines said, looking directly at the reporter. '"Discretion" was the favoured word, I believe.'

'Don't worry, I've no intention of getting into a lawsuit with an aggrieved general practitioner over something that couldn't possibly be proved after all these years. Anyway, the medical team could be entirely wrong.'

'Yes, they could well be,' said Monsignor Delgard. 'The point they are trying to make, however, is that the shock of being unable to hear or speak was sustained psychologically by Alice in her own mind. The more afraid she was of her handicap, the worse her mental block became. Medical records are full of similar case histories: fears growing into phobias, phobias into physical infirmity. The subconscious mind has its own peculiar logic. It took an altogether different kind of shock to break down the mental block Alice had imposed on herself. The vision – be it imaginary or real – released Alice from her self-inflicted illness.'

'You're saying categorically, then, that there was no miracle cure in Alice's case?' said Fenn.

'After seven years of silence she can speak, she can hear. Whether or not her disability was due to a mental or physical disorder, the result is still the same . . .'

. . . the church . . . the church . . . everything that happened to Alice was centred around the church . . .

Father Hagan put a soothing hand to his temple, pressing the thin flesh there, gently rubbing. The voices sounded distant again, somehow hollow, as if they were all in a vast cavern, the others far away on the other side. Or in a church . . . a vast, dark church. He was beginning to hate . . . the church.

No! The church was the House of God! No one could hate it! Especially not a priest . . .

'. . . general health?' Bishop Caines was speaking. 'How is she?'

'It can be summed up very simply and without any medical jargon,' Delgard replied. 'Alice is a perfectly normal, healthy child. A little tired perhaps, and somewhat withdrawn but that's to be expected after all she's been through. There is one small abnormality, however, but it's something she's had since she was a baby according to her own doctor.'

Fenn, wine glass halfway from the table to his lips, asked, 'What's that?'

Delgard hesitated, regarding the reporter warily. 'This has to be off the record. It's not very important, but it could cause the child some personal embarrassment. I promise you it has nothing to do with her cure.'

Fenn considered for no more than a second. 'I wouldn't want to hurt the kid.'

'Very well. Alice has a small growth on her body. It's on the left side of her body, a few inches below her heart.'

'A growth? Good Lord . . .' Bishop Caines began to say.

'Don't worry, it's nothing serious,' Delgard reassured them. 'It's what's known as a supernumerary nipple . . .'

. . .Supernumerary nipple . . . a third nipple . . . he knew something about that . . . had read something somewhere . . . oh God, what was it . . .?

'. . . nothing at all to worry about. It has increased a little in size since her doctor examined her last, but then her body is developing naturally. There's no reason to believe that it will grow any larger.' Monsignor Delgard sipped his wine once more. 'And there you have it. Alice Pagett appears to be healthy in every way, except for this slight, er, blemish.'

'That's very good news indeed,' asserted Bishop Caines. 'Thank you for your lucid report, Monsignor. Do you have any questions, Mr Fenn?'

At that point the door opened and two waitresses entered laden with dishes.

'Ah, our main course,' said Southworth. 'The hotel is rather busy tonight, gentlemen, hence the slight delay. A foretaste of the coming months, I believe,' he said, beaming happily. And hopefully, the coming years, he thought.

The conversation concerned itself with generalities as the food was served and Fenn found himself looking into the haunted eyes of Father Hagan. The priest averted his gaze and Fenn was puzzled. It was obvious that the priest was ill: there was a light sheen of perspiration on his sallow face, his eyes were dark and shadowy; there was something brittle in the movement of his long, delicate fingers. Bishop Caines should make the man take a rest. What was it they went into? Retreat. That's what he needed, a complete break away from all this. And the going was only going to get worse once the publicity machine was rolling. *That*, he understood from Southworth when he had spoken to him earlier that evening, was going to be one of the items on the agenda. Fenn smiled down at the medallions of veal in herb sauce placed before him and sipped his wine while waiting for the vegetables to be served.

He listened to Southworth as the hotelier tentatively broached the subject of publicity.

'I'm sure we all realize by now, Bishop, that we have a situation here that private entrepreneurs from all over the country will endeavour to make money from. I really do think it's time for us to seriously consider the setting up of an official publicity machine to monitor . . .'

'. . . somewhat premature . . .'

'. . . no, not at all. We must plan . . .'

'. . . Lourdes is not the best example to follow, George . . .'

. . . *I can't eat. The bishop shouldn't have insisted* . . .

'. . . hired for the papal visit to England in '82 . . .'

'. . . but, goodness, that organization took something like twenty per cent of profits . . .'

'. . . worth every penny . . .'

. . . *each night, the feeling gets worse* . . . *even with the monsignor nearby* . . . *the feeling of being alone* . . . *empty* . . . *yet there is something there!*

'. . . statues, T-shirts, records of the services . . .'

'Andrew, you must try to eat. It will do you good.'

'What? Yes, Bishop . . .'

'Entrecôte steak Roquefort is one of the chef's specialities, Father. I'm sure you'll enjoy it.'

'Of course . . .'

'. . . we cannot be seen . . .'

'. . . I understand your feelings, Bishop, but the Church has to keep a shrewd eye on the commercial world . . . as it has always done in the past . . .'

. . . *her eyes* . . . *why did she look at me in that way* . . . *why was the Host unacceptable to her* . . .?

'. . . findings from the Institute for the Works of Religion, the Vatican itself, Bishop . . .'

'. . . think not . . .'

'. . . bank itself . . . I'm sure they'd accept a modest collateral from the Roman Catholic Church . . . already spoken with the manager . . . member of the parish council . . .'

. . . meat . . . no taste . . . must eat, Bishop says must eat . . . her eyes . . . she knew . . . what are they saying . . .? Must stop them . . .

'. . . design a centre-piece, something like the one designed for the papal visit to Phoenix Park in Ireland . . . stunning simplicity . . .'

. . . can't swallow . . . the meat . . . can't swallow . . . oh, my God . . . it's growing . . . the meat is growing . . . in . . . my . . .

'Father!'

Delgard rose from his seat, the chair clattering backwards onto the floor. He reached for the choking priest, alarmed at the bluey-redness of the man's face, the wheezing breath squeezed from his open mouth.

Fenn ran round to the other side of the table. 'He's choking!' he cried. 'For Christ's sake, he's choking on something!'

. . . filling me . . . can't breathe . . . growing, growing . . .!

Father Hagan twisted in his chair, hands tearing at his throat. He tried to speak, tried to scream, but his words were blocked by the meat that was expanding in his gullet. He fell forward on the table, his wine glass tipping, cutlery jumping with the impact. His dinner plate crashed to the floor as his upper body straightened and fell back into his chair, a terrible, anguished rasping sound coming from his throat as he tried to suck in air.

'He's having a heart attack!' Bishop Caines cried. 'His heart is weak. Quickly, he must have his pills on him!'

'No, he's choking!' Fenn insisted. 'Get him forward so I can reach his back.'

Delgard held onto the squirming priest and Fenn brought his fist smashing down between the priest's shoulder blades. Father Hagan jerked with the force. Only a retching sound came from him. Fenn hit him again.

'It's no use, it won't shift!' said Delgard.

'I'll get an ambulance.' Southworth ran from the room, glad to be away from the priest's agony.

'It's a heart attack, I tell you,' said Bishop Caines.

'Okay, let's get him back and his mouth open.' Fenn reached for the priest's forehead and hauled him back into the chair. Monsignor Delgard cupped a hand beneath his colleague's chin and held his mouth open. The priest tried to twist away, the pain, the yearning to draw air into his starved lungs, unbearable.

Fenn looked into the open mouth, down into the darkness of the throat. 'There's something there, I can see it!'

He stuck his fingers into the priest's mouth, probing deep, desperate to reach the object lodged there. It took all his and Delgard's strength to keep Hagan from rolling to the floor.

'I can't reach it! Christ, I can't reach it!'

. . . hands . . . hands on me . . . can't . . . can't breathe . . . help me, God . . . eyes, her eyes . . .

His throat muscles were jerking spasmodically, but still the lump of meat would not dislodge. Instead it sank deeper. And grew larger inside him.

His body arched in a paroxysm of fear and pain and choking. He fell to the floor, taking the two men who were trying to save his life with him.

'Get his head down! Maybe we can dislodge it that way!' . . .

no good . . . it was too late . . . oh, God, the pain . . . in my chest . . . in my arms . . . oh, Jesus, they should be told . . .

'I've got it, I've got it! Hold him, I can . . .'

The priest screamed and the sound was just an agonized gurgling, a clogged scream of mortal dread. His body threshed wildly, his face took on a bluish tinge . . .

. . . *into Thy hands* . . .

. . . his eyes reflected the fear of approaching death . . .

. . . *I commend* . . .

. . . the noise from his throat was continuous, a wet, rattling sound . . .

. . . *my spirit* . . .

. . . that died just seconds after he died . . .

. . . *forgive me* . . .

21

> And did the Countenance Divine
> Shine forth upon our clouded hills?
> And was Jerusalem builded here
> Among these dark Satanic Mills?
>
> William Blake, 'Jerusalem'

Cold. Bloody balls-chilling cold.

Fenn locked the car door and pulled the lapels of his dark overcoat tight around his neck. Vapour from his mouth spread a small round mist over the side window as he stopped to insert the key into the lock. He straightened and looked towards the church.

For once the entrance to the grounds wasn't crowded with Pressmen. Probably yesterday's funeral had satiated their appetites for a while.

He trudged towards the gate, the earth verge beside the road, long since trampled of its grass, hard and brittle. Jagged ridges crumbled beneath his boots. A solitary figure watched him warily as he approached.

'Cold morning,' Fenn called out.

The man nodded.

'I'm Fenn, *Brighton Evening Courier*,' the reporter said when he reached the gate.

'I know you,' replied the man, a volunteer helper to St Joseph's, 'but I'd better see your Press card.'

Fenn fumbled for his wallet, his fingers already stiff with the chill. He flicked it open and produced his identity card. The man grunted, satisfied.

'I've come to see Monsignor Delgard.'

The man opened the gate. 'Yes, he left word.'

Fenn stepped through. 'Not so busy this morning.'

The man carefully closed the gate, then looked at the reporter. 'They'll show up later. Most are down at the convent.' He pulled out a handkerchief and blew his nose.

'I've just passed it. There's a few there, not many.'

'I suppose they had their fill yesterday. Leeches.' He stared at Fenn, no apology in his gaze.

'Did you know Father Hagan well?' the reporter asked, ignoring the slight.

'He was a good man. A good, hard-working man. This was all too much for him, I suppose, with his weak heart. We'll miss him.'

Fenn moved on leaving the man shaking his head, blowing his nose.

He went to the house and the door was opened by a young priest, one that the reporter either hadn't seen or hadn't noticed before. There were several at St Joseph's now, acting as clerks, secretaries – crowd controllers.

The priest smiled and said in a soft, Irish accent, 'Mr Fenn? Ah yes, Monsignor Delgard is at the church. Will I fetch him for you?'

'It's okay, I'll go over.'

Fenn turned away and the priest watched him walk towards St Joseph's for several moments before quietly closing the door.

The reporter shivered. There was a faint mist rising up

against the old building and swirling around the scattered green-stained headstones. He knew the freshly-dug plot was on the other side, a secluded place in the graveyard close to the boundary wall, and felt no desire to see it. Watching Father Hagan's coffin lowered into its frigid pit had disturbed him as much as when his parents, both dying within weeks of each other, one of cancer and the other, like the priest, of heart disease, were buried. It was as though the covering of earth were really the final and irrevocable consummation of life, the moment of death itself just the first phase. He had known others whose deaths were premature (didn't death always seem premature, even among the aged – not many were ever quite ready) but none had affected him in this way. It had been understandable with his mother and father, for they had died when he was still in his teens and their mutual parents/son affection had not had time to sour; but the priest had been almost a stranger, had even seemed to dislike Fenn. Perhaps it was because he had tried, and failed, to save the priest's life that he felt the loss so much. But then there was little he could have done anyway, for the post-mortem had revealed that Hagan had died of a heart attack; the meat he had swallowed may have started the priest's initial panic, but it was hardly big enough to have choked him. So why his own guilt which compounded the sense of loss? It was a question to which Fenn had no answer.

The church doors were closed and he twisted the heavy black metal ring to open one side. It was bitterly cold outside, but the church interior had a special chill to it. He closed the door and walked towards the altar, towards the black figure sitting near the front.

Monsignor Delgard did not turn around at the reporter's approach; his eyes studied the stained-glass window above the altar-piece, but his gaze was inwards.

Fenn sat next to the priest. 'Monsignor Delgard?'

The priest continued to stare. 'What is happening here?' he said, and the words were not directed at the reporter.

'Sorry, what was that?'

The priest blinked and said, 'I don't understand what is happening to this church, Mr Fenn. I don't understand why Father Hagan died, why he was so afraid.'

'Was he afraid?'

'Oh yes. He was in mortal fear.'

'He was ill.'

'Yes, he was ill. But something more. Something else took his strength.'

'I'm not following you.'

The priest sighed and lowered his face. He turned to the reporter. 'Do you believe in God, Mr Fenn?' he asked.

Fenn was surprised at the question and a little embarrassed by it. 'I think so. I'm not sure. Guess I haven't given it enough thought.'

'Everybody gives it enough thought, Mr Fenn. Are you reluctant to offend me because I'm a priest?'

'No, it isn't that. I'm really not sure, that's all. I can't believe in this great Father-figure in the sky, if that's what you mean.'

'There's no need to. In fact, it would be rather naïve to think of Him as such. Let me ask you this, then: are you afraid *not* to believe?'

'I suppose most people are.'

'But you?'

'Count me in with the crowd.'

'Do you fear death because of past transgressions?'

'No. I just hope when I get up there, He'll accept my apology. Look, what's all this got to do with Father Hagan?'

The monsignor returned his gaze to the altar. 'He was a devout priest, a truly good man; yet he was afraid of dying.'

'Maybe he had secrets you didn't know of.'

'Yes, we all have our secret shames. They're usually trivial; important – shameful – only to ourselves. Strangely, I heard Father Hagan's confession just the night before he died and I know he had nothing to fear.'

Fenn shrugged. 'Just death alone is enough. It's a big leap and no guarantee of a soft landing. Or any landing at all. It doesn't matter how strong your beliefs are, how deeply religious you may be, there's no guarantee been given, right?'

'Not quite true, Mr Fenn, but I take your point.'

'So when it came to it, Father Hagan was no different from the rest of us – scared of the pain and a little apprehensive of the Great Moment of Truth.'

'Father Hagan was afraid of what he would leave behind.'

Fenn looked puzzled.

'He was afraid of what was happening to his church.' The big priest turned to face the reporter once again, leaning one elbow on the backrest of the bench, his long fingers clasped together. 'You know, he hardly slept at all after the first so-called miracle. For some reason he no longer felt secure in his own church grounds.'

'I noticed his appearance was getting worse each time I saw him; I put it down to general ill-health, though.'

'You met him for the first time when you found the child in the field, didn't you?'

'Yeah. And he didn't look the picture of health then. But like I say, he grew worse each time I saw him. I thought it was all the pressure that'd been laid on him.'

'He was undergoing great mental stress long before that, I'm afraid. During my stay here we had lengthy discussions about St Joseph's, the child, Alice Pagett, and her visions. And about Father Hagan himself. He was a troubled man.'

'Did his, er, assignment in Hollingbourne have anything to do with his troubles?'

Delgard's features sharpened. 'Who told you of that?'

'Nobody. I just remembered the uncomfortable silence at the Press conference when a reporter from that area asked him about it. What was the problem, or is it still a big secret?'

The priest sighed. 'With your tenacity I'm sure you would find out sooner or later. It's all in the past and really not very important.'

'So if it isn't, tell me.'

'On the understanding it will go no further?'

'Absolutely.'

Delgard was satisfied. If he refused to tell, Fenn would be even more interested and would dig around until he raked up something; this way he was sworn to secrecy because of their 'off the record' agreement a few nights before.

'Father Hagan was young, a novice, when he was sent to Hollingbourne,' he began. 'He was uncertain of himself, but hard-working, eager to learn. And he was vulnerable.' Delgard fell silent and Fenn grew impatient.

'Are you trying to tell me he had an affair with one of the parishioners?'

'Not exactly. Not exactly an affair and not with one of his parishioners.' Delgard shook his head sadly. 'He ... he formed an attachment towards his senior priest.'

'Oh, Jes—'

'There was no sexual involvement, let me make that quite clear. If that had been the case, then neither one would still be in the priesthood.'

'Then why—?'

'Rumours spread. A small place where things are noticed.

Affection – deep affection – couldn't go unnoticed. It came to the attention of the bishop of that particular diocese and he quickly stepped in, fortunately before the situation could develop.'

'Forgive me for asking, but just how do you know it hadn't?'

'Both priests would have confessed the moment they were confronted.'

'You've got a high opinion of human character.'

'They wouldn't have lied.'

'So Father Hagan was assigned elsewhere.'

'Yes. The other priest – his name isn't important – left the parish some time later. I know what happened had tortured Father Hagan throughout his ecclesiastical career, and I also know such temptation was never succumbed to again. He buried himself in work and prayer.'

'But the guilt was always there?'

'He was a sensitive man. I don't believe he ever purged himself of the guilt.'

'That's something your religion dotes on, isn't it?' It was difficult to keep the rancour from his voice.

'An unkind remark, Mr Fenn, and not true. However, a debate on the theosophical ideals of the Roman Catholic Church would be rather pointless at this moment. Let's confine ourselves to the topic of Father Hagan and his fears for this church.'

'That's something that's been puzzling me since the night he died. He said there was something wrong with St Joseph's and you seemed to be in agreement.'

'Look around you, Mr Fenn. Does it seem dark in here to you?'

'Well . . . yeah. But it's misty outside, the light's pretty poor.'

'Now close your eyes, tell me what you feel.'

Fenn closed his eyes.

'What do you feel?'

'Stupid.'

'Don't. Just think of the church, think of where you are.'

He didn't like it. He didn't like having his eyes closed inside the church.

'No!'

His eyes snapped open and he looked at the priest in surprise. 'I'm sorry,' he said. 'I don't know what made me shout.' He shivered. 'I . . . I don't know what happened.'

'Did you feel an atmosphere?' Delgard prodded gently.

'No, I felt nothing.' He frowned. 'Christ, that was it! I felt nothing. It's empty in here. I don't mean it's empty of people . . . but what was it you said the other night? Something about the church being spiritually devoid . . .'

'That's exactly what I said. You felt it too.'

'I . . . I don't know. It's cold, and it's creepy, let's face it. But there's something creepy about any empty church.'

'Not to a man of the cloth. A priest finds only tranquillity in an empty church, a place to pray, to meditate. There is no such peace here, just a sense of desolation.' Delgard shifted from his position, sliding forward to the edge of his seat and resting his clasped hands over the seat in front. Fenn studied the man's profile, the high-bridged nose, the firm chin, the deep furrows on his brow. Only one heavy-lidded eye was visible from that angle and there was a sadness in its gaze, a weariness reflected from within. When the priest spoke again, his voice was strong, deep, but the inner sorrow was somehow contained in its timbre.

'If Alice truly had a Visitation, then the presence of the Holy Spirit would be overwhelming inside this place.'

'You said yourself a church is just a building made of stone,' Fenn said.

'I meant that it was a physical container that could be drained of its contents just like any other container. Bishop Caines should have understood that. This church has been drained.'

'I don't get it. How can you tell?'

'You only have to feel. Just as you did a few moments ago. Father Hagan had been going through the same trauma for many weeks, only his perception was greater, his feelings stronger. You noticed yourself how he was changing physically, how his vitality was being sapped.'

'The man was ill. His heart . . .'

'No. His life-force was being drained just as the spiritual essence of his church was being drained. I should have been aware sooner, I should have realized what was happening when he told me of his doubts. He didn't believe the cures were miraculous, Mr Fenn. Nor did he believe Alice saw the Blessed Virgin. At first he wasn't sure. Alice had always been such a good child, an innocent who liked nothing better than to help her mother in her work at St Joseph's. He'd known her since she was a baby—'

'Before she was struck deaf and dumb?'

'Oh yes. He arrived in the parish just before she was born. He watched her grow, gave her her First Communion, encouraged her to play with the other children despite the disability. Yet, towards the end . . . these last few weeks . . . he was afraid of her.'

'Afraid of an eleven-year-old kid?'

'You were there at the convent last Sunday.'

'Sure. She was sick.'

'Before that. The way Father Hagan looked at her.'

'You're right, he was scared. With everything that's happened since, I'd forgotten. He looked terrified.' Fenn tapped thoughtfully on the bench. 'But he was cracking up,' he said. 'Sorry, Monsignor Delgard, I don't mean to be disrespectful to him. But you know yourself his hinges were loosening. He was just about ready to fall apart.'

'That may be so, but for good reason. The stress he was suffering would have been too much for any man.'

'You mean the publicity—'

'I mean nothing of the sort. That was only part of it. I'm talking of the mental anguish he was going through, knowing his church was being raped, knowing a child was being used—'

'Hey, wait a minute. This is all getting a little far-fetched, isn't it?'

The priest smiled, but it was a grim smile. 'Yes, Mr Fenn. Yes, you would think so, and I can't say that I blame you. You're a born cynic and I think it's probably the cynics who suffer least in this world.' He regarded the reporter with eyes that held pity in them. 'Or perhaps they suffer most, who can say?'

Fenn swung round in the seat, facing the altar, away from the priest's gaze.

'It's your very cynicism that may help in this matter, Mr Fenn,' he heard Delgard say.

He slowly turned his head to look at the priest again.

'You're not a great believer in anything, are you?' Delgard said. 'You've no deep religious beliefs, you have no family, no wife—'

'How do you know that? You don't know anything about me.'

'Oh, but I do. I've had a long discussion about you with Miss Gates, you see.'

'Sue? She wouldn't . . .' His words trailed off as the priest nodded.

'Susan is a regular visitor to the church nowadays. I'm afraid she's very confused about you at the moment, Mr Fenn.'

'Yeah, I'd noticed. But why should she tell you about me?'

'Because I asked.' Delgard's voice became brisk. 'I need your help. I found out as much as possible about you – firstly, because of the association you now have with the Church under Bishop Caines' edict, and secondly, because I think you may be able to help in other ways.'

'You're losing me again.'

'Your employer tells me you're a good journalist. A troublesome one, but basically sound. Apparently you have an enquiring mind or, as your news editor puts it, a snooper's nose. He wasn't very complimentary about other aspects of your character, unfortunately, but that does not concern me greatly.'

'I can imagine what he said.'

'Good. So you and I are both aware of your faults.'

'I didn't—'

'It was Susan who told me you had a clinical, open mind towards most things, especially where your work was concerned. I must admit, having read your first article on Alice and St Joseph's, I thought you rather too emotional, hardly objective at all. But she explained that to me, in fact made me realize just how objective you could be. It was somewhat perverse, but I suppose I should respect your opportunism in some way. You didn't *believe* in what you wrote, although you wanted your readers to believe. You very skillfully sensationalized the story without giving any clear credence to what happened. It's only on second reading and with some knowledge of the author that one can detect the deliberate ambiguity of your statement. That was your objectivity: you wrote a crude, yet on the surface, sincere piece of journalism to promote your own interests. In other words, you wanted a scoop. And that you surely got.'

'Maybe you're giving me more credit than I deserve. That's if you are giving me credit . . . I'm kinda confused.'

'You have a sharp mind, Mr Fenn. And that's what I want. I need your objectivity also.'

'Can you get to the point of all this?'

'The fact that you're cynical about the Church could mean you're also cynical about its opposite. It could give you an advantage.'

'Over what?'

'Over the evil that's surrounding us now.'

Fenn grinned. 'Oh yeah?'

'You see, if you don't believe, then you won't be so afraid. Evil is a parasite that breeds on people's beliefs.'

'I thought it bred on ignorance.'

'It's often the ignorant who have unreasonable beliefs. But yours is not that kind of ignorance. You would believe something if it was proved conclusively to you and, furthermore, you would seek that proof; the ignorant would not. And that's what I want you to do, Mr Fenn. I want you to seek.'

Fenn tucked his hands into his overcoat pocket. He wasn't sure if it was the conversation or the church itself that made him feel so cold 'Just what is it you want me to seek, Monsignor Delgard?'

'I want you to find out about this church.'

Fenn looked at him in surprise. 'Surely that'd be easier for you to do.'

'Objectivity, Mr Fenn, and practicality. I shall be too busy in the next few months organizing St Joseph's itself, preparing for pilgrims, supervising the building work that will have to be carried out. As for objectivity, I'm too ensconced in the dreadful atmosphere of this place, too involved with the tragedy of Father Hagan, to see anything in a pure, objective light. More than that, I want you to find out about the village. It needs a researcher's eye, someone who can dig deep, find answers. You've already reached an agreement with Bishop Caines and George Southworth; this would merely be part of that work. All I ask is that you look for something more, something that could have happened here in the past.'

'Like what?'

'I don't know. That's for you to find out.'

Fenn shrugged. 'Okay. As you say, it would be part of the job anyway.'

'And one more thing: I want you to find out more about Alice Pagett. And her parents. There's something missing and I've no idea what it is. I only know we must find out.'

'I think you may be coming a little unhinged yourself, Monsignor.'

Delgard studied him coldly for a moment, then said, 'That's good. I want you to think that way. But before you leave, I want to show you something.' He rose from the bench and Fenn quickly followed suit, stepping into the aisle so the priest could get through.

Delgard genuflected before the altar, then walked towards the right-hand side of the church. He turned back towards Fenn when he was below the statue of Our Lady.

'Would you please come here?' he said.

Fenn, hands still tucked into his pockets, followed. He looked curiously into the face of the tall priest who indicated the statue with a nod of his head. 'Father Hagan told me Alice loves this statue, that she used to spend long periods sitting before it. You could say it was almost an obsession. If her visions were merely the hallucinations of a disturbed mind, it's not improbable that they would take the form of something she was fascinated by. Take a good look at the statue.'

He remembered studying the statue just two weeks before, on the Sunday of the miracles. He had noticed a flaw then, the faintest crack running from beneath the chin down one side of the neck.

Now the effigy was a mass of black lines, a crazy network of thin jagged veins that covered almost every inch of white stone. Cracks running from the corners of the Madonna's lips gave her a grotesque smile, an obscene leer. Even her sightless eyes were cruelly scarred.

Instead of a finely sculptured and compassionate image of the Madonna, it seemed that a hideously wrinkled harridan stared down upon the two men, her ravaged palms a mocking gesture of supplication.

Fenn stepped away, as if fearing the stone figure might reach down and touch him.

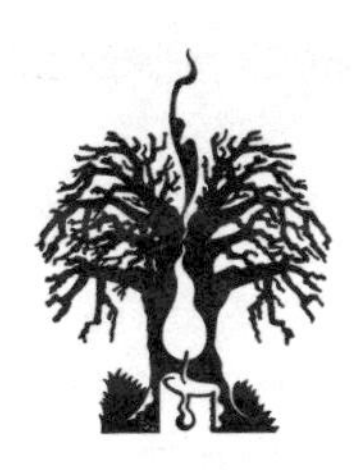

22

Dame, dame! the watch is set:
Quickly come, we are all met.
From the lakes and from the fens,
From the rocks and from the dens,
From the woods and from the caves,
From the churchyards, from the graves,
From the dungeon, from the tree,
That they die on, here are we!
    Comes she not yet?
    Strike another heat!

Ben Jonson, 'Three Witches' Charms'

He walked down the gravel path towards the gate. Overhead the branches of the leafless trees joined, forming a web-like canopy. Thin, winter-brittle branches snapped against each other, the cold breeze that shifted the mist causing their movement. His footsteps were unnaturally loud, as they had been inside the church, but now there was no echo, no hollow sound to reflect the emptiness of the sanctum. It was dark beneath the trees, almost as dark as inside the church.

The whole business was crazy! Bloody stupid crazy! What was Delgard trying to pin on the kid? An eleven-year-old, for Christ's sake! How the hell could she cause any harm? And why should she? Was he implying she was in some way responsible for Hagan's death? She hadn't even been there!

He stopped for a moment, breathing fiercely.

Delgard was becoming as neurotic – as paranoid – as Father Hagan! He just couldn't be serious! He had almost begun to believe the priest. Christ, he was nearly as crazy as the two of them!

He continued walking, shoving his hands deep into his overcoat pockets.

But the statue. What the fuck had happened to the statue? A flaw in the stone? Huh! That was a new one! Running cracks like ladders in tights. Maybe someone had been secretly pounding away at it. No way. It would have been chipped. The statue had scared him somehow . . . repulsive! Jesus, Delgard was to blame. He was the one making him jittery.

He jumped when something stepped out of the shadows.

'All finished, Mr Fenn?'

'Jes – . You gave me a fright.'

The man chuckled as he opened the gate for the reporter. 'Sorry about that. I was just keeping out of the breeze. Bit chilly.'

'Yeah.' Fenn stepped through the gate, glad to be outside the church grounds.

'Hey, Fenn,' a familiar husky voice called out. He turned to see the journalist from the *Washington Post* approaching. 'What gives?' she said. 'You look white as a ghost.'

'It's the weather,' he replied, heading for his car.

'Funny. I usually get a red nose.' She kept pace with him.

There were one or two cameramen loitering by the side of the road, but they lost interest when they saw it was only a fellow-journalist who had emerged from St Joseph's.

'I saw you drive past me in the village,' the woman at his

side told him. 'Figured you were on your way up here. How about a lift back to the hotel?'

He opened the car door, then straightened. 'It's Nancy, isn't it?'

'Yup. Shelbeck. We met last Sunday.'

He nodded. 'Jump in.'

With no further heeding, she ran round to the other side of the car. Fenn climbed in and opened the passenger door. She joined him inside and smiled her thanks.

'You're right,' he said. 'You do get a red nose.' He started the engine.

She waited until he had pulled out into the road, reversed back, then headed the Mini in the direction of the village, before asking, 'How come you get into St Joseph's when nobody else can?'

'You could have got in through the field next door.'

'You wanna bet? They've got a couple of priests posted out there.'

He took a quick glance at her. Even though her nose was red, she was an attractive woman. He noticed she had green eyes.

'So you were going to tell me?' she said.

'Tell you what?'

'Why you were allowed in.'

'The Pope's my uncle.'

'Come on, Fenn, give.'

'You could say I'm there by, er, papal appointment. I've been officially authorized to write the story of St Joseph's and the Holy Miracles.'

'Shit, how did you manage that?'

'They know an ace when they see one.'

'Forgive me for saying so, but you don't seem so happy about it. Money not too good?'

He laughed humourlessly. 'D'you know, I forgot to mention money.'

'How remiss. I'm sure you'll make it in other ways, though.'

'I'll do my best.'

'As a matter of fact, that's what I wanted to talk to you about. Remember I mentioned it last Sunday.'

'You said something about comparing notes.'

'Uh huh. Look, why don't we stop and have a drink?'

'At this time of the morning?'

'It's gone ten. Nearly half-past, actually. Your country pubs open early here. Come on, you look as if you need a snort.'

'You don't know how right you are,' he said, shaking his head.

They had almost reached the edge of Banfield where the first of the village's two public houses stood. He indicated left and pulled into its courtyard. There were several other vehicles already parked even at that early hour, but he knew many of the locals used the pubs as coffee shops that early in the morning, as they did the Crown Hotel further along the High Street.

The White Hart had just one L-shaped bar; polished brasses and hunting horns adorned the walls, and the heavy beams set in the low ceiling gave the interior a feeling of ancient solidity. A freshly-lit fire blazed in the huge inglenook fireplace. There were no more than a dozen people drinking, some of whom were vaguely familiar to Fenn. He recognized them as Pressmen.

'What d'you want to drink?' he asked the *Washington Post* reporter.

'No, let me. It was my invitation.'

Fenn acquiesced. 'Make mine a Scotch, no ice, no water.'

He found a seat by a window while she ordered the drinks

from a tall, bearded and bespectacled barman, and settled into it with a silent sigh. Jesus, his legs felt weak. The statue . . . it was hard to clear the hideous image from his mind. How could something like that happen? He could understand the stonework cracking into such a fine network over the years – and it would take a good many years for such results – but to reach that state in just under two weeks? It was impossible! And what was Delgard insinuating? What was—?

'I got you a double. You could use it.'

He stared blankly at the woman, then at the glass she was offering.

'Thanks,' he said, taking the whisky and drinking half in one gulp.

'I was right,' she observed. She sat next to him and sipped her drink from a half-pint glass.

'Bitter?' he asked in surprise.

'Sure. I like to try your beer. Want to tell me what's on your mind?'

Fenn studied her closely, taking in more than he had on their first meeting. Her dark hair had a reddish tinge to it, not one that came from a bottle, though (at least, not obviously so). It was still difficult to determine her age, for she was one of those women who could be either younger than she looked or older, but never guessed exactly. Her eyes, which were alert, watchful, said older – maybe approaching forty – but her skin, which was pale and smooth, and her lips, which were not full but were well defined, said younger. Her nose was a little too straight to make her pretty, but it gave her an appearance of attractive strength. She had removed her topcoat and her figure was trim, if not particularly shapely, beneath the roll-topped sweater and straight-legged trousers. He had noticed the high-heeled boots she wore earlier and they were of thin burgundy leather, stylishly cut.

'I feel as though I'm under a microscope,' she said.

'I was just thinking,' he said. 'You fit the image.'

'Hmn?'

'The hard-bitten New York reporter-lady.'

'Thanks. You must have a way with women.'

He laughed. 'Sorry, I didn't mean that nastily. As a matter of fact, it was a kind of compliment.'

'Yeah? I'd hate to hear your snipes.' She sipped her bitter again, then reached inside her bag for cigarettes. She offered him one first and he shook his head. She lit her own with a slim Dunhill lighter. 'What's the problem, Fenn?' she said, blowing blue smoke across the small table.

'My name's Gerry,' he said evenly.

She smiled. 'I think I prefer Fenn.'

He returned her smile, beginning to enjoy her company. 'I think I do too.'

'Is it the death of the priest, this Father Hagan, that's upsetting you? I understand you were actually there when he had his heart attack.'

He nodded. 'The post-mortem said it was a heart attack, but I was sure he was choking. I tried to save him.' He took another long swallow of Scotch. 'I'm certain I saw the meat in his throat. Christ, I even tried to yank it out.'

'But the coroner would have known if it was asphyxiation.'

'Maybe it was both, I don't know. Maybe he just imagined he was choking. The priest was in a pretty hysterical state towards the end.'

'That's likely when your heart is seizing up.'

'No, I didn't mean then. He was in a highly-strung state for weeks before.'

She was thoughtful for a moment. 'I noticed there was something peculiar about him that Sunday at the convent. Are you saying, in your sweet way, that he was bananas?'

'No . . . just, well, neurotic. He was upset by what was happening at the church.'

'But that had to be fantastic for any priest. He actually witnessed the miracles himself. What was it he didn't like? The publicity?'

Fenn realized he was saying too much. As a reporter himself, he should have known better. He quickly changed the subject. 'Have you got a deal to offer me?'

She raised her eyebrows. 'Where's your British reserve? Okay, to business. How'd you like to form a partnership with me in this little enterprise. We work together, you supply the information, I write the story for my paper, I get you a fat fee. I also get you your name alongside mine.'

'Are you kidding? Why the hell do I need you?'

'Because I'm a better writer.'

He put his empty glass down. 'I need another drink.'

'At this hour of the morning? Hey, wait a minute, don't get sore. Look, you're good, but I hate to say it – you're provincial. Come on, don't get up, just listen. You haven't had the experience of working on a National yet. I know, I've checked. You haven't the experience of working under a good editor, I mean, someone who's going to kick your butt 'til you get it right, someone who's going to *show* you how to get it right—'

'My butt's been kicked plenty of times,' he said in weak defence.

'Yeah, but there's different ways to kick different asses. All I'm saying is that you haven't had the right guidance yet. Sure, you're good to a degree, and okay, you're going to get a lot of offers; but I can make whatever you do with this thing better. Believe me, much, much better. And if you want to get down to figures—'

Fenn was no longer paying attention. He was looking

towards the door, which had just opened. A figure stood there, staring around the pub as if looking for someone. Two men immediately rose from their seats at the bar and hurried towards the man.

'That's Len Pagett,' Fenn said, more to himself than to the woman.

'Pagett? Oh, yeah, Alice's father.'

Fenn was already out of his seat, quickly making towards the three men, who were now shaking hands. Nancy Shelbeck soon followed.

'Mr Pagett?' Fenn said, barging into the group and offering an outstretched hand. 'You've met me before. I'm Gerry Fenn. *Brighton Evening Courier.*'

One of the other men quickly stepped in between Fenn and Pagett. 'On your bike, Fenn,' the man said, his voice almost a snarl. 'Mr Pagett's ours. We've made an arrangement.'

'Who're you?' Fenn asked, but he had already guessed. He now recognized one of the men as a reporter from one of the heavies.

'He's signing an exclusive contract with the *Express*,' the other man, who was just as belligerent, told him. 'And that means he doesn't talk to any other papers.'

'Don't be bloody silly. You can't—'

'Piss off.' A hand shoved him, and the first man took Pagett by the arm. 'Let's go somewhere quiet, Mr Pagett, where we can talk. We've got the contract ready for you.'

Pagett looked confused. 'Can't I have a drink first?'

'We've got plenty where we're going,' the first reporter assured him. 'It's not far.' He guided him towards the door.

The few other journalists in the bar who had been taking a sneaky morning nip (purely to keep out the cold for when they took up their vigils outside the church and the convent) were converging on the shuffling group.

'What's going on, Fenn?' Nancy asked when she reached his side.

'These bastards have done a deal with Alice's father. They won't let him talk to anyone.'

The second *Express* reporter blocked the doorway. 'That's right, he belongs to us now.'

'Wait a minute,' the New Yorker said. 'Has he signed any agreement yet?'

'That's none of your business.'

Fenn smiled thinly. 'I just heard you say you had the contract ready. That means he hasn't signed.'

The *Express* reporter wasted no more time with words. He whipped open the door and sped through, slamming it hard behind him.

'What's going on here?' The tall, bearded barman blinked through his glasses as the crowd barged through the doorway in pursuit. He welcomed the business, but wasn't too keen on the rowdiness of the journalists.

Outside in the carpark, a silver-grey Capri was revving up its engine and the *Express* reporter was running towards it. He pulled open the passenger door as the car moved off and jumped in.

Fenn and those who had followed him from the pub had to step back to avoid being hit.

'Where're they taking Pagett?' Nancy Shelbeck yelled.

'Probably to some nearby hotel. They'll keep him locked away for a few days where no one can find him.'

'That can't be legal.'

'It is if he agrees to it.' Fenn broke away, heading for his Mini. He climbed in, thankful that he hadn't locked the doors.

Through the windscreen he saw the other journalists scurrying for their own vehicles. The Capri was disappearing into the High Street. His passenger door swung open as he started the engine.

'This is ridiculous,' Nancy said, and she was laughing. 'It's like the goddam Keystone Cops!'

Fenn didn't have time to enjoy the humour, nor to tell her to get out of his car. He shoved it into first and roared across the carpark, swinging left into the High Street, barely looking to see if the coast was clear. He was in luck: the Capri carrying Len Pagett and the two journalists had been forced to stop at a zebra crossing while two old ladies, lost in conversation, ambled across.

He slapped the steering wheel in triumph. 'Got the bastards! They won't lose me now.'

Nancy laughed aloud. 'I don't believe this!'

Tyres burnt the road as the Capri screeched off. Heads turned as Fenn pushed his foot down and followed suit.

'Take it easy, Fenn. It isn't worth getting killed for!'

Both cars roared down the High Street as others, driven by the slower journalists, began to emerge from the carpark. Vehicles were parked on both sides of the road, making its centre a narrow channel and forcing the two cars to slow down when they met others coming from the opposite direction. Fenn was aware that it would be tougher to keep up once they were through the village and out on the open road, but he had an advantage: he knew the roads. He guessed they were heading for Brighton, using one of the many hotels there as a hideaway, and cursed them (although he didn't blame them) for their opportunism. Somehow, because of his involvement, he felt proprietor of this story and that the other newspapers were infringing on his territory. From what he had learned of Len Pagett, and from what he had surmised of the man himself, he wasn't surprised he had sold out to 'cheque-book journalism'. No one had to be famous any more to make money from selling their own personal story; they just had to know somebody who was.

The Capri was fifty yards ahead, approaching the end of the village. Fenn could see the road junction in the distance, the small roundabout, the garage next to it, the convent. Clear of parked vehicles, he increased his speed, desperate to keep up with the Capri, guessing it would turn left at the roundabout, keeping to the main road rather than carrying straight on into the minor one. The High Street was busy with shoppers, many of whom shook their heads in disgust at the racing cars, perhaps resigning themselves to the advance symptoms of what their once peaceful village was about to become.

Next to him, Shelbeck bit into her lip, amused by the chase but a little alarmed also.

They were nearing the roundabout. Shoppers were hurrying in and out of a grocery shop on the left, bags full, purses not so full. A huge yellow and green tanker stood in the garage forecourt on the right, shedding its load into the tanks beneath the pumps. Fresh virgin cars gleamed in the large showroom windows by the side of the service bay. A green, single-decker bus negotiated the tiny roundabout, rolling over the white-painted bump in the road as it headed into the village. The driver was accelerating as his bus straightened up.

The Capri barely slowed as it approached the roundabout.

Fenn did not know why he glanced ahead at the cream walls of the convent; the compulsion was just there.

He saw the small white face at the window, blackness behind giving it prominence. Instinctively he knew it was Alice. Watching the High Street. Looking at the cars.

Too late he saw the car in front weaving from side to side as though the driver had no control. He was almost upon it. Nancy was screaming. He was trying to turn the wheel, trying to avoid crashing into the erratic Capri. But the wheel had no say in what direction the vehicle took. It moved in its own wild direction.

He jabbed hard on the footbrake, but it was too hard, too panicked. The wheels locked, the car skidded.

The green bus, horrified faces peering from its windows like a row of peas in a split pod, turned to avoid the wildly-spinning Capri, but there was only one direction the driver could take. Into the garage forecourt. Where the tanker was emptying its contents.

The Capri smashed into the front corner of the bus, its bonnet buckling instantly, its engine rising up and shearing through its own windscreen into the screaming faces of the two men in front. The bus driver went forward with the impact, through the large front glass of his cab, hurtling beneath the tanker a split second before his bus hit it. Mercifully he was dead before he could realize what was going to happen.

As the long tube pumping fuel into the underground petrol tanks was sheared by screeching metal, sparks flew in all directions showering into the spilling volatile liquid.

Fenn saw the crash and cried out as his own car smashed through the showroom window. He was only vaguely aware of the blinding flash and the thunderous whoosh as the petrol tanker exploded.

23

'Your life is finished,' and he threw her down, dragged her into the room by her hair, struck off her head on the block and chopped her into pieces so that her blood streamed all over the floor. Then he threw her into the basin with all the others.

The Brothers Grimm, 'Fitcher's Bird'

Someone was shaking him. He groaned, but the effort to open his eyes was too much. His cheek rested against something hard.

A single voice began to filter through the cacophony of sounds, sounds which he wasn't sure were inside or outside his head. He groaned. Christ, his head hurt!

Tentatively he forced his eyes open, the effort exhausting, like trying to will himself awake from a nightmare. A face was nearby, a woman's face, someone he vaguely recognized.

'Fenn, are you all right?'

He wasn't ready to reply.

Hands reached around his shoulders and he was pulled off the steering wheel back into his seat. He felt his jaw clutched and his head shaken. He opened his eyes again and this time it was hardlly any effort at all. There was something wrong with Nancy's face, but he couldn't figure what. It was smeared red; thick cherry juice, dark red ink. No, blood. Her face was bleeding. He struggled to sit upright.

'Thank God,' he heard her say.

'What happened?' he managed to gasp, and it all flooded into his head before she replied. The careering Capri, the green bus, the petrol tanker – oh Jesus, all those people. His mind snapped into instant attention.

The Mini's windscreen was a spider's silver web of shattered glass, but through the side windows he could see the gleaming bodywork of that year's models. Yet there was a darkness out there that puzzled him until he realized it was swirling black smoke. A figure rushed by the window, arms waving, shouting incoherently. Fenn turned to the woman next to him.

'You okay? Your face . . .'

'It's okay. I hit the windscreen when we went through the showroom window.' She put a hand to her forehead and brought it away smeared with blood. 'It doesn't hurt; I think it's just a gash.' She clutched his arm. 'We've got to get out of here, Fenn. The tanker . . . the tanker out there exploded. The whole place is going up in flames . . .'

He pushed open the driver's door and the heat hit him immediately, even though the car showroom was partially shielded by a side wall. The smoke was growing thicker by the second and he began to cough as the acrid fumes poured into his nose and throat.

'Come on, quick!' he urged her.

'My door's stuck! It's jammed up against a car you hit!'

He pushed his own door open as far as it would go, denting the side panel of the new Rover standing next to the crashed Mini. He jumped out, then reached back inside to help her across. Nancy came scuttling through, almost throwing herself into the open. Fenn held her steady and quickly took in his surroundings.

Not much was left of the showroom window his car had smashed through; huge, lethal-looking shards of glass hung from the top like transparent stalactites. Smoke poured through the opening, filling the area with its choking denseness, and fire was already spreading across the width of the broken window. Flames filled the glass doorway by the side of the window and this suddenly exploded inwards with the heat. Fenn realized burning petrol must have spread all over the garage forecourt and was attacking anything flammable.

He pulled Nancy back, closing the door of the Mini so they could squeeze through the cars towards the rear of the showroom. 'Keep low!' he yelled at her. 'Try to keep under the smoke!'

To the rear of the display area was a glass partitioned office and he quickly ascertained that there was no back exit from it. The office was empty of people, the figure he had seen rushing by moments before obviously the salesman or manager who had occupied the room. Nancy doubled over, her body wracked by choking coughs.

Holding her tightly, giving her support, Fenn looked around for some other means of escape. He thanked God when he saw the door to his left.

Nancy almost collapsed to her knees when he tried to drag her towards the door. He allowed her to sag for a few moments, kneeling beside her, waiting for her coughing spasm to ease. Her eyes were streaming tears and her face was now a red mask from smeared blood.

'There's a way out, just over there!' he shouted over the rumbling, burning sound and the splintering of glass, the cracking of burning wood.

'Okay,' she gasped, at last controlling the seizure. 'I'll be okay! Just get me out of here!'

Fenn half-lifted her to her feet and she leaned against him as they made for the door. Such was their momentum that they stumbled against it and Fenn pushed out a hand to cushion the impact. He quickly pulled his hand away. The wood was scorching hot.

He pulled Nancy to one side, his back against the wall beside the doorframe. She looked at him questioningly, but all he said was, 'Keep back!'

Crouching, he reached for the door handle. It, too, was hot and he ignored the pain as he gave it a twist and flicked the door open.

Nancy screamed as flames roared through, bursting into the showroom as though exhaled from the jaws of a dragon. They both fell back to escape the intense heat and lay panting on the floor in a tangled heap as the fire withdrew to lap around the edges of the opening. Within seconds the door itself was blazing.

They rose and staggered away, collapsing against the bonnet of a Maxi. Both were retching now, their vision blurred by smoke-caused tears. Fenn tore off his overcoat and pulled it over their heads as they lay half-across the bonnet.

'We'll have to go out the front way – through the window!' he yelled.

'It's too hot there! We'll never make it!'

'We've got no choice! There's no other way!'

But by now, even that choice was not open to them.

They raised their heads from the overcoat and stared in disbelief at the wide showroom windows. The broken one, the window Fenn's Mini had smashed through, was totally filled with yellow-red churning flames, tongues of fire licking inwards to scorch the ceiling. A thick column of concrete separated it from the adjacent window, where the glass was already beginning to crack with the heat. The fire had spread across at least half its surface, the ground outside molten hot as the petrol gushed forth and flowed burning across the concourse outside.

'Oh my God, we're trapped,' Nancy moaned.

Fenn looked around wildly. There had to be another way out! The ceiling, a skylight. Through the billowing smoke he could tell the ceiling was solid as he realized there were offices above, not a roof. A stairway then, there had to be a way up. No stairway. It had to be through the doorway behind him, which was now no more than an opening into the furnace beyond. The fire was moving in, greedily pouncing on the hard plastic tiles of the showroom, creating fumes that were more choking and more lethal than the smoke above.

The display windows were the only way out.

He pulled the reporter upright and bent close to her ear. 'We're going out the front way!'

She shook her head. 'We'll never make it!'

Fenn wiped his sleeve across his eyes, then reached for a handkerchief, spreading it across his mouth and nose. He tugged at her roll-neck sweater, unfolding the material at the neck so it covered her lower face. Yanking her off the bonnet and holding the overcoat before them as a shield, he led her towards the front of the showroom in a stumbling run. He left her crouched between his own Mini and the Rover parked next to it and raced towards the still unbroken window. He ducked as a long jagged crack appeared in the glass and a sound like a gunshot rang out. For one long, dreadful moment he thought the window would shatter inwards to flail his body with shards of dagger-like glass, but the huge panes held. He went forward again, one arm holding his coat out to protect himself from the terrible heat. The display windows were the type that slid back into each other, depending on which side the salesman wanted to drive a car through, and Fenn went to the far corner, to the side that had been furthest from the fire; only now the scene outside was almost obliterated by the spreading flames.

He pulled at the handle and cried out as the red hot metal burned his fingers. Using the material of the overcoat to protect his hands, he tried again, but to no avail: the window was either locked, or the metal frame had swollen with the heat, jamming it solid within its housing. He swore, more of a scream of frustration than a curse.

The heat and fear of the glass exploding inwards forced him back. He returned to his companion who was slumped against the door of the Rover.

'It's no good! The window won't open!'

She looked at him fearfully, then yelled, 'Shit!' She grabbed his lapel and pulled him down to her. 'Can't you break the goddam window?'

'Even if I could the fire out there would roast . . .' He broke off. 'Prick!' he called himself.

He shoved her away from the car door and swung it open, groaning with disappointment when he discovered there were no keys in the ignition. Quickly he stood, then rolled over the Rover's bonnet to the Marina standing next to it. He yanked open the door and was once again thwarted: no keys. He went back over the bonnet and landed next to the woman.

'The keys must be in the office!' he shouted. 'You wait here!'

Then he was running back, crouching low behind a car as he passed the open doorway where the fire raged, noticing the floor around it was now blazing. Coughing and spluttering into the handkerchief, Fenn reached the rear office. He hurriedly pulled open drawers, spilling their contents onto the floor in his haste. No keys, no keys, no bloody keys! He looked around wildly, desperately. Where the fuck . . .? He groaned aloud when he saw the hooks in a cork notice board on the wall; labelled keys were hanging from each hook. He rushed to them, examined the labels, found two tagged 'Rover'. Taking both sets he dashed back into the showroom.

The suffocating heat hit once more and he knew that soon the whole area would be in flames. His breathing was laboured, drawn in in short, sharp gasps. The oxygen was being eaten by the heat and what remained was smoke-filled. He was staggering by the time he reached the woman.

He climbed into the Rover, Nancy crouching at the open door beside him. 'There won't be any gas in it!' she shouted.

'Course there bloody will! How d'you think they get them in here?' He jabbed in the first key, praying it would be the right one. It was. The engine roared into life. 'Jump in the back and keep down!' he screamed at her over the noise.

Without further bidding, she slammed his door shut, opened the one behind, and leapt in. The car was moving forward before she had slumped into the back seat. She tucked in her legs just as the Rover's momentum swung the passenger door shut.

Tyres screeched against the plastic floor as he stuck his foot down hard on the accelerator. The car zoomed towards the window and Fenn raised his arm to protect his face, hoping nothing solid was just beyond the flames outside.

Nancy screamed as the Rover burst through the huge panes of glass.

Shards flew back at the windscreen but it withstood their onslaught. The car was engulfed by the fire and Fenn kept his foot down, holding the steering wheel straight, expecting the vehicle to explode into flames at any moment.

It could have been little more than two seconds before they broke free of the fire, but for both of them it seemed like an eternity. The smell, the heat – the fear – was overpowering, and the sight of blinding, twisting flames all around was a nightmare that they would never forget. Self-preservation rather than coolness kept Fenn's foot down.

He yelled in triumph as they emerged from the inferno, the cry turning into one of panic as he saw the stationary car immediately in his path. He swung the wheel hard to his right and the Rover went into a curving skid, smashing sideways on into the other vehicle. His body bounced off the driver's door to be thrown across the passenger seat. Crushed metal made fierce rending sounds and the car jerked violently as its engine cut out. One of Fenn's hands was still on the steering wheel and he used it to pull himself upright. Without thinking he switched off the ignition.

He drew in deep mouthfuls of air, the burning stench still present but not to the same overwhelming degree. His eyes widened as he stared at the carnage before him.

Balls of flame were rolling upwards into the smoke-filled air, their very brightness, let alone the heat, stinging his eyes. The tanker itself was completely engulfed in fire, only brief glimpses of its shape visible as the flames shifted and weaved; most of the garage forecourt was alight, the burning liquid still spreading, still greedily devouring anything in its path. The car showroom was totally hidden behind a blazing wall, the top part of the building, where the offices were, already scorched black. There were faces at the open windows, terrified, screaming faces, with eyes that beseeched the people below to help them, *please, please help!*

The very ground shimmered with the heat and there were people crawling, dragging themselves away from the devastation. The green bus was imbedded in the side of the petrol tanker, half its length a mass of flames; most of the windows were shattered and there were still some passengers left, those who had not been instantly burned to death or made incapable of moving by the initial blast, struggling through the flames, bodies cut by remaining glass fragments, flesh seared by the intense heat. The silver-grey Capri was several yards away from the two burning vehicles as though it had rebounded on impact, but there were flames all around, licking at the metal body, melting the glass of its windows.

Fenn blinked his eyes against the glare. Had he seen something move in the back of the car?

Everywhere there were people running, staggering away from the destruction, but one or two moving towards it as if fascinated by the danger, the mayhem. Those who were paralysed by fear crouched against walls, or cowered behind cars.

A face was suddenly next to his, a tear-streaked, blood-smeared image that for a moment, through shock, he failed to recognize.

'You did it, Fenn!' Nancy shouted, her voice cracked and almost tearful. Her arm went around his neck and she pressed her cheek against his in a hug that made him wince. It also helped bring him to his senses. He pulled himself free and reached for the doorhandle. 'We've got to get away!' he shouted back at her. 'There'll be other petrol tanks below ground that the fire hasn't touched yet! When the heat reaches them . . .' He left the sentence unfinished, but Nancy understood the implication.

The dry, scorched air hit them like a blast from an open furnace as they emerged from the car and both put up their arms to protect themselves. It was difficult to breathe, for the atmosphere was filled with choking fumes. Fenn turned his head away from the scene in a reflex action and immediately wished he hadn't.

The village grocery was to his left and its huge, plate-glass windows had shattered inwards. Bodies of women who had been thrown against the windows by the blast lay scattered among the wreckage inside, tins and packaged goods littered around them like fallen pieces of masonry. Some lay still, others squirmed in pain. He wondered why the legs of one woman failed to move in conjunction with her twisting torso, then realized they had been almost severed at the thighs by the shattered glass. Another woman, young, and who would have been pretty were her face not contorted in agony, sat upright before the window, back resting against the wall below the frame, her hands clutching a wide rent in her throat, desperately trying to squeeze the sides together to prevent her life's blood from gushing out. Red liquid began to pump between her fingers as he watched.

The noise, the confusion – the screams for help – battered against his reeling brain. He put a hand against the Rover to steady himself and the metal was hot.

A hand tugged at his shoulder and Nancy was shouting, 'Fenn, there's someone moving in the other car!'

He turned, shielding his eyes, looking over at the burning wrecks. She was right, and he had been right a moment or two before: there was someone moving in the back of the Capri, a pair of hands beating at the rear window.

'Oh Christ, it's Pagett.' It came out as a low moan, for the knowledge struck a new fear into Fenn. Nancy was staring at him and he knew what she was going to say.

'You've got to help him!'

'It's no good! I'll never get near it!'

'You can't just let him burn!'

'What can I do?' He was shouting at her, almost screaming. What the hell did she want of him?

'Something! Just do something!'

'There's a woman over there!' He pointed desperately towards the supermarket window. 'She's bleeding to death!'

'I'll take care of her!' Nancy pushed him roughly away from the Rover. 'Please try, Fenn!' she pleaded.

'So much for Women's fucking Lib!' he yelled at her, then was running towards the fire, angry at her and shit-scared for himself.

As he drew closer to the burning vehicles, an even more intense wall of heat hit him, forcing him to whip off his jacket and hold it in front of him. He thought he could smell singeing material. Fenn moved in, feeling stifled, his skin dry and hot. Breathing was difficult, walking was agony. Not just his legs felt on fire, but so did his lungs. He lowered the guard just enough to steal a glance at the Capri.

Pagett's face was pressed against the rear window, his features flattened, the palms of his hands white against the glass. He was trying to push himself through the tailgate which was obviously locked, his mouth open to suck in scant oxygen, his eyes bulging with terror.

Fenn was forced to bring his jacket back up over his head, but even that made little difference. He felt hot air rushing round him, then he was in darkness as heavy black smoke swilled down to cover the forecourt in a dense fume-filled fog. Even the winter wind was playing its part in the havoc.

He stumbled, his eyes streaming tears, his lungs heaving as they expelled the poisonous smoke. He fell and his back was scorched as he rolled over on the ground, exposing it to the worst of the heat. The skin of his face and hands felt incredibly tight as if it were shrivelling in on itself. He had to get away. It was no use. He couldn't get any closer. He would be roasted alive if he tried.

He pushed himself back, digging his heels against the concrete, using an elbow that was quickly rubbed raw to gain momentum. The jacket was held before him to protect his face, but it was smouldering fiercely as though about to burst into flames. After a few feet he raised himself to one knee and risked another look at the burning Capri. What he saw was so horrific he forgot about his own searing pain.

He only caught brief glimpses through patches of swirling smoke and at first he could not understand what was happening. A strange, unclear shape was emerging from the back window of the Capri. It seemed to be blurred as though its form were distorted by Fenn's own tears. He blinked his eyes and realized they were already dry from the scorching heat. Then he understood.

Pagett was pushing his way out of the car, but the glass had not broken. It was melting, clinging to his face and hands like thick, viscous liquid, burning and moulding itself into his flesh, becoming a part of him. Pagett had become a writhing, ill-formed monster, a human larva prematurely struggling free from its shiny, clinging chrysalis, demented in his agony and that madness driving him on. His head twisted and his eyes were looking towards Fenn, but they saw nothing for the liquid glass had already burned its way through to the retinas. Part of his face and nose was still flattened, moulded into that shape and transfixed by the sticky covering. As he slowly, twistingly, emerged, the glass stretched, becoming thin, beginning to tear. A gaping rent appeared near his neck and shoulder, and smouldering smoke from his clothes mingled with steam from his body. He was screaming, but the sound was muted by the soft transparent screen covering his mouth.

It wasn't just the heat that made Fenn cover his eyes.

He tried to rise, but was too giddy and too weak to gain his feet. He began to crawl away, choking and sobbing as he did so. He had to get away from the horrible, dying creature in the car.

It was too much; the heat was drowning him. His hands gave way beneath him and he rolled onto his back.

Pagett was ablaze now. His arms thrashed in the air, one hand banging against the Capri's boot as though in frustrated anger. His hair burned and the glass on his face was running down his skin in red-glowing rivulets into the flames from his clothes. He fell forward and was still moving, climbing from the window, an automated, charcoaled figure that had no reason, no clear driving force any more, just movement caused by pain.

The petrol tank of the Capri exploded and the hideous sight was no more.

The fresh wave of torrid air flattened Fenn and he quickly rolled onto one side, pushing with his legs in a frantic pedalling motion, expecting to burst into flames himself. There were others around him, those who had leapt from the bus windows, those who had been caught walking near the garage, those who had come too near the fire to help others. All were crawling or staggering away, all trying to reach some safe point where the heat could not touch them, where they could breathe fresh, moist air. But the fire was not diminishing. It had found fresh sustenance, more material to burn, more inflammable liquid to reinforce its energy. Vehicles within the garage itself began to explode; cans of oil and petrol flared into incandescent balls of fire. The heat in the remaining tanks below ground was building up to the point where combustion was inevitable.

Fenn cursed himself for not having run away, for not

ducking into cover until the danger was over. He pushed feebly against the ground.

The cold air hit him and seemed to close every pore on his body. The heat was gone from his skin, the stinging from his eyes. He raised his shoulders from the ground, turned over onto one elbow to see what was happening, looking back at the flames, not believing what he saw.

Smoke swirled down and across the scene, forced by the wind, obscuring everything one moment, lifting to reveal all the next. The flames were dying. They seemed to be shrinking, becoming small patches of fire, losing their strength by the second. Wavering. Disappearing. The wrecked vehicles were just burnt-out, smouldering shells, the petrol station a blackened, smoking ruin.

And through the swirling smoke came a tiny figure, a small girl with blonde hair who walked slowly, unafraid, through the carnage. Her yellow dress was ruffled by the wind as she held out her hands, and what was left of the flames cooled and died completely.

Part Three

Come, hearken then, ere voice of dread,
With bitter tidings laden,
Shall summon to unwelcome bed
A melancholy maiden!
We are but older children, dear,
Who fret to find our bedtime near.

Lewis Carroll,
Through the Looking Glass

24

And like a ravenous beast which sees
The hunter's icy eye,
So did this wretch in wrath confess
Sweet Jesu's mastery.

Walter de la Mare, 'The Ogre'

Television broadcast from ITN, all regions, early Sunday evening:

'. . . the once peaceful village of Banfield in West Sussex today. Thousands gathered at the Roman Catholic Church of St Joseph's, hoping to catch a glimpse of Alice Pagett, the eleven-year-old schoolgirl who has been proclaimed a miracle worker. There was a two-mile-long queue of cars and coaches from both directions into the village and extra police had to be called in from the surrounding area to control the crowds. For an on-the-spot report we go over now to Hugh Sinclaire, who has been at the church since this morning . . .

HUGH SINCLAIRE: The scenes here today have been quite extraordinary. People began to gather outside St Joseph's in the early morning hours – devout Catholics, many, but others who were just sightseers, curious to catch a glimpse of this little girl who, it's claimed, can perform miracles. And perhaps they expected to see more miracles today.

Alice Pagett came to world attention just a few weeks . . .'

Television broadcast from BBC1, late Sunday evening:

'. . . cured five people who were suffering from various illnesses. Three were said by the medical profession to be incurable. Alice herself was deaf and dumb until – she claims – she saw a vision of the Immaculate Conception. Although there has been much scepticism over her claim, particularly from the Catholic Church itself, the fact that she and five others have been cured cannot be denied.

It's estimated that at least two thousand people went to St Joseph's this morning and that the numbers doubled throughout the day. Trevor Greaves is still in the village of Banfield tonight . . .

TREVOR GREAVES: Although the crowds have thinned considerably, there is still a vigil being kept around the old church of St Joseph's tonight. It's as though the crowds were waiting for the same apparition that Alice Pagett alleges to have seen. Earlier today the atmosphere among the many pilgrims could only have been described as electric. There was no mass hysteria – something the authorities feared among such a gathering – but there was much fainting, much weeping and much praying.

When Alice arrived for the Sunday service at 9.20 this morning accompanied by her mother and a bodyguard of priests and policemen, she found it difficult to get anywhere near the church, let alone inside. The Mass was delayed for forty-five minutes as her protectors struggled to get near this diminutive child, pale-faced and dressed in white, obviously distressed by the loss of her father, so tragically killed last Thursday . . .'

Radio broadcast from LBC, after midnight:

'. . . further interest in Alice Pagett was aroused only last Thursday when eyewitnesses say she quelled a fire which threatened to devastate a large part of Banfield village. The fire was started when a car in which Alice's own father was passenger collided with a bus and a petrol tanker. The fire was spreading, fuelled by escaping petrol from the damaged tanker. The tanker itself had been refilling tanks beneath a garage's pumps, and the danger was that the fuel below would ignite too, when Alice appeared and, eyewitnesses say, put out the fire. Ironically, Pagett was killed before his daughter arrived on the scene.

How Alice Pagett could have stopped the fire nobody knows, but those who were there claim that the flames just seemed to extinguish themselves as soon as she appeared. Accident and Fire Prevention officers who have made a thorough examination of the wreckage maintain there is no logical explanation for the incident. There was little rain that day, although it was bitterly cold. Apart from the initial explosion when the petrol tanker was hit, there were no others big enough to have "blown out" the fire. The investigation officers found half-burnt timber which should have been totally charred had the fire followed a natural course, and petrol still awash on the ground which had not burned. Only small, scattered and relatively harmless fires were still alight when the local fire brigade arrived. A fuller report is expected within the next day or so but, for the moment, the experts are saying very little.

Yesterday I spoke with people who had travelled from all over the country to St Joseph's in Banfield, many of whom were infirm themselves, or had brought along sick relatives or friends to the place they now consider to be a holy shrine . . .'

Extracts from interviews on Today, *BBC Radio 4, UK, early Monday morning:*

'. . . we couldn't get near the place. Somebody said the girl was there, but we didn't see her . . .'

'. . . yes, we were inside the church. There weren't supposed to be cameras in there, but there were, going off all the time. The priests couldn't control the newsmen, so I suppose they gave up in the end . . .'

'. . . she's a saint. I saw her. She looks like an angel. I suffer from chronic arthritis, but as soon as I saw her I felt better. It's her, I know it's her. She did it, no question . . .'

'. . . well, we got into the field by the side of the church. We weren't supposed to be there, the priests were trying to turn people back, but there were too many, you know? I carried my sister, I wanted to get her inside the church. She's crippled. We couldn't get anywhere near, though. Even the graveyard was swamped with people . . .'

'. . . oh, no, I'm not a Catholic. No, I just wanted to see what all the fuss was about. I saw her in the car going up to the church, but that was all. Just a flash as she went by. Still it was a day out, the kids enjoyed it . . .'

'. . . the village is chock-a-block. I couldn't even get out of my shop doorway earlier for people. Business was good. As a newsagent I was open 'til lunchtime. Had to close up long before, though – ran out of stock. I think the other traders were upset. Couldn't open up, you see, not licensed to. All the same, business should be good for the rest of the week . . .'

'. . . I camped out all night. Myself and a few hundred others. We all wanted to get into the Sunday service. I managed to, me and the wife. Yes, we saw Alice. She's got an aura about her, you know, like a saint . . .'

'. . . she's a holy child, you can tell just by looking at her. She smiled, even though she must have been dreadfully unhappy over her father. I'm sure she smiled directly at me. I felt her love go right through me, it seemed to fill every part . . .'

'. . . I'm still blind . . .'

Extracts from interviews on World at One*, BBC Radio 4, UK, Monday lunchtime:*

'. . . people were pushing, shoving. A girl in front of me fainted. It was terrible. Just like the Beatles all over again . . .'

'. . . everyone felt peaceful, everyone was serene. It was wonderful, like a wave of love flowing over us all . . .'

'. . . somebody stood on my foot. I think a toe's broken . . .'

'. . . we didn't want to leave. We just wanted to stay there and pray. Even though we didn't get inside the church we could feel the Holy Spirit's presence . . .'

'. . . I brought my father down from Scotland. The journey was terrible for him – he's got cancer. We only caught a glimpse of Alice, but father says he feels better, better than he has for months . . .'

'. . . everyone – well, nearly everyone – in the home

wanted to come. They insisted. As it's a private nursing home, they paid for the trip. Three coaches in all. Only those who didn't want to come and those too ill to be moved were left behind . . .'

'. . . she was only tiny, but somehow, somehow she stood above us all. She seemed to shine with an inner radiance . . .'

'. . . we were packed solid lunchtime and the evening trade is just as bad – just as good, I should say. Look around, you can see for yourself. I hear all the pubs in the area are just as busy . . .'

'. . . perhaps people will now understand there is only one true faith. Alice is showing them the way . . .'

Standard, *Tuesday, late edition:*

MIRACLE GIRL'S FATHER BURIED

The funeral of Leonard William Pagett, father of Alice Pagett, the proclaimed 'Miracle Worker of Banfield', was held today. He was not a Roman Catholic and so was buried in a public graveyard just on the outskirts of the village. Pagett, 47, was killed in a car crash on Thursday of last week. His widow, Molly Pagett, 44, was visibly distressed, not just over the tragic loss of her husband, but over the hordes of onlookers and Pressmen who besieged the cemetery. Alice stood silently by the graveside, seemingly oblivious to the crowds and obviously shocked by the second tragedy in her short life, within a week – a few days before her father's death, her parish priest, Father Andrew Hagan, to whom she was very close, died of a heart attack . . .

Transcript of interview on Nationwide, *BBC1, all regions, Tuesday, early evening:*

Q: Surely, Canon Burnes, after what happened last week, the Catholic Church cannot deny there is something rather extraordinary about the child?

A: I wasn't there, so I can't verify what took place.

Q: Yes, but there were many witnesses who say Alice Pagett stopped the fire. Some even say she walked through the flames.

A: The reports are confusing, to say the least. Different witnesses claim to have seen different things. Some say she appeared to walk through the flames while others say the flames died out as she approached them. And there are a few who say that Alice didn't appear until the fire was almost extinguished.

Q: Nevertheless, she does seem to have an extraordinary effect, wouldn't you say?

A: It would be hard to deny.

Q: And has the Church now reached any conclusions over the miracles Alice performed?

A: The 'alleged' miracles. They are still under investigation.

Q: Well, do you think the Church is the correct body to carry out such an investigation?

A: I'm sorry, I don't follow.

A: Perhaps parapsychologists should be looking into the matter. Or at least there should be one or two included on your committee of inquiry.

A: We have several members of the medical profession—

Q: That's hardly the same.

A: Our findings will be open to scrutiny from any recognized scientific institution that may be interested.

Q: But not to parapsychologists?

A: We would not wish to exclude any respectable organization. For the moment, however, we prefer to deal with the matter on a more rational basis.

Q: Why do you think there were no more miracles last Sunday?

A: I haven't acknowledged that there have been any miracles at any time. Unfortunately, the media is creating a huge burden for this poor child. It's they who are creating this image of a thaumaturge.

Q: A thaumaturge?

A: A miracle worker. People have come to expect it of her.

Q: Indeed, it seems St Joseph's has become a holy shrine to many. But that's hardly the fault of the media – we can only report on events that have happened.

A: And speculate.

Q: It's certainly a matter for speculation. How will you cope with the thousands that are bound to visit the church after all this publicity? I gather there was a near-riot on Sunday.

A: That's nonsense. The crowd was very well behaved, even though many must have been disappointed that they didn't actually see Alice.

Q: Are you expecting a larger gathering this Sunday? And if so, will you be better prepared this time?

A: I think I must emphasize to the public that it would be quite pointless to travel to St Joseph's. There really will be nothing to see.

Q: But it's true that there is construction work in progress at this very moment.

A: Yes, yes, that is true. Although we are asking the public to stay away, we must be ready for any contingency.

Q: Then you are preparing for – forgive me – a siege?

A: I hope not a siege. But yes, we are making preparations for a large number of visitors, although we are doing our utmost to discourage them from coming.

Q: Thank for you answering my question. Can you tell us the kind of, uh, preparations you're making?

A: We're simply constructing an altar-piece in the field adjacent to St Joseph's—

Q: Where Alice claims to have seen the Blessed Virgin?

A: Er, yes. Seating for as many as possible will be arranged around a central altar, but I'm afraid many will have to stand and endure the muddiness of the field itself. The Sunday service will take place there instead of inside the church.

Q: And one last question, Canon Burnes: will Alice Pagett attend Mass this Sunday?

A: That I can't say.

Conversation between building contractor and Monsignor Delgard, Wednesday morning:

'Does the tree stay, Monsignor? Shall we cut it down?'

'No. You mustn't destroy anything in this field. You have the plans. Build the platform around the tree.'

Telephone conversation between Frank Aitken, Editor of the Brighton Evening Courier, *and Head Office, London, Wednesday morning:*

AITKEN: 'I don't know where the hell Fenn is. He rang in last Friday, said he'd been burned slightly in the fire at Banfield the day before. Yeah, he saw the whole bloody thing – he was there, for Chrissakes! No, I don't know why he didn't bring in the story. I told you that last week. He said he had some leave coming, so he'd decided to take it. Bloody minded? Sure it is. You want me to fire him? I'll do it gladly. You don't want me to fire him? Didn't think you would. No, I've tried his home. No reply. I even sent someone round there. No one home. No, not since Friday. Hospitals? He wasn't that badly burned, but yeah, we checked. He's just disappeared, gone, vanished. Maybe he's moonlighting on an offer he couldn't refuse. Sure I raised his salary, soon as the story got big. I guess it wasn't enough. Christ, I've had to instruct our switchboard to politely tell all our "friends" in the business trying to contact him to go to hell. No, Fenn didn't say how long, but I'll break his bloody legs when I see him. No, Mr Winters, I won't break his bloody legs when I see him. Yes, sir, I'll kiss his arse. Thank you. I'll let you know soon as I hear.'

Extract from LBC interview, Brian Hayes Phone-In, London area, Thursday morning, with T. D. Radley, Professor of Eastern Religions and Ethics, University of Oxford:

'. . . of course, western religions emphasize God's uniqueness and regard him as a supernatural Being. Miracles can be worked by Him alone, although mere mortals may entreat Him by prayer to perform them on their behalf. Usually this is done through the personages of saints or mystics. Now, the eastern religions generally dismiss miracles altogether and this is because they tend not to draw the same distinction between God and mankind. To them, such happenings are all part of the total reality and obey a kind of cosmic law. But, of course, that cosmic law is outside the material order. Although the – let's call them miracles, then – are exceptions to *our* laws of logic, our nature, if you like, their source is from Beyond and of course, the logic of Beyond is not of our understanding, but nevertheless logical in itself . . .'

Extract from article in the Guardian, *Thursday morning, VISIONARY, FRAUD, OR SELF-DELUDED by Nicola Hynek, author of* Bernadette Soubirous: The Facts Behind The Fallacy *(Hodder & Stoughton, 1968):*

. . . in his book *Vraies et Fausses dans L'Église,* Dom Bernard Billet gives a complete list of Marian visions reported to have taken place around the world between March 1928 and June 1975. There were 232 in all, two of which were in England (Stockport, 1947 and Newcastle, 1954) . . .

From the Universe, *Friday:*

BISHOPS TO DISCUSS BANFIELD MIRACLE GIRL

The curious events surrounding the 11-year-old schoolgirl, Alice Pagett, will be discussed by cardinals and bishops in Rome next month. With unprecedented swiftness the Holy See has decided the conference must take place before completion of the Church Committee's special inquiry. It is thought that there is some apprehension over the hysteria being caused by the girl's claim to have received a Visitation, and her alleged ability to perform miracles.

Several high-ranking members of the clergy have stressed the urgency for such a conference, among them the controversial Cardinal Lupecci, prefect of the Congregation for Doctrine, who issued a statement yesterday in Rome: 'In an age where religious values are under constant attack, the Roman Catholic Church must take a firm lead in maintaining, or restoring, the beliefs of its followers. The Church must constantly seek divine guidance, and will ignore any sign or portent from God at its own peril. To disregard the latter, or to fail to determine whether or not they are genuinely God-sent, would be to put the Holy Church, itself, at risk.'

Extract from Psychic News *leader, Friday, IS IT REALLY EVOLUTION?:*

. . . many prominent geneticists believe that we have now developed the biological capacity to carry ourselves forward to the next level of evolutionary achievement, and that Alice Pagett is merely a forerunner, an advance representation of that progress. Their contention is that genetically conditioned educability, which has always been mankind's most consistently favoured quality in the process of natural selection, is now our most effective biological adaptation to our culture.

In a rapidly changing environment where cultures can adapt within a generation, whereas biological changes require thousands of years, man's psychic senses are developing in a rapidly proportionate degree, conferring upon us such mental powers as witnessed in Banfield over the past few weeks. It should be clearly stated that Alice Pagett is not exceptional, or will not be thought to be so within the next generation or two. There have been thousands of other authenticated cases of mental phenomena involving psychokinesis, paradiagnostics, psychophotography, psychometry; and, of course, faith healing and levitation have been with us through the centuries. Her experiences have been cunningly presented in a religious context, which those disillusioned with the overwhelming materialistic aspects of today's society and the spiritually deflating discoveries of modern-day science have clung to . . .

Extract from conversation heard in The Punch Tavern, Fleet Street, Friday, early evening:

'. . . it's all a load of shit . . .'

25

'I thought you were a ghost or a dream,' he said. 'You can't bite a ghost or a dream, and if you scream they don't care.'

Frances Hodgson Burnett, *The Secret Garden*

It was paper. Rough-edged, yellow parchment, the leaves filled with faded script. They were everywhere, floating in the air, scattered on the floor, filling his vision, everywhere, everywhere . . .

It's okay, he told himself. I'm dreaming. I can stop this. I only have to wake.

But the ancient pages were beginning to curl, the edges beginning to smoulder. Brown stains caused by small flames crept inwards.

Wake up.

It was dark in there. Tomb dark. But the flames were growing higher, throwing light, casting dancing shadows. He turned, fell. Smooth stone bruised his knees. He reached out and his hand touched rough-grained wood. He pulled himself up, half-sitting on the bench that he had grabbed. In the flickering light he saw other benches, plain wood, functional, no elaboration. He saw the altar and he shuddered.

Wake up, Fenn!

The flames grew larger, snatching at the old manuscripts in bursts of fire. The church was St Joseph's . . . yet, it wasn't St Joseph's. It was somehow different . . . smaller . . . newer . . . but older . . .

He had to get out! He had to wake up! He was conscious of the dream, so he had to be awake! But the flames were beginning to burn him and the smoke was filling his head. His outstretched foot was being singed.

He pushed himself erect and the fire rose with him. He backed away towards the altar and, as he did so, he looked down at the burning paper. One sheet lay at his feet, as yet untouched by the flames, although it was beginning to curl inwards. There were no lines of ancient script on its surface, just one word, written boldly, without embellishment. It said:

MARY

And the letters were being eaten by the flames and he saw that all around the other sheets of parchment bore the same inscription and these, too, were burning and the flames were ecstatic with their consummation.

Wake up!

But he couldn't because he knew he wasn't dreaming. He looked beyond the flames, down the aisle of the church that was St Joseph's yet wasn't, towards the door that was slowly opening. His skin was beginning to blister with the heat, but he could not move; he was locked into his fear. He knew he was burning, but he could only stare at the small white figure that had stepped through the door, watch her as she approached, her face passive, her eyes closed. She walked through the flames and they did not harm her.

And now her lips were smiling and her eyes were smiling. And she was looking at him and it wasn't Alice, it was—

'FOR CHRIST'S SAKE, FENN, WAKE UP!'

He wasn't sure if he screamed in the dream, or screamed when he awoke. A face was peering down at him, long, dark hair resting over naked shoulders.

'Jesus, Fenn, I thought I'd never wake you. Sorry for the shock, but I don't believe in letting people sleep out their nightmares.'

'Sue?'

'Oh, shit, you're terrific.' Nancy rolled away from him and reached for cigarettes lying on the bedside table.

Fenn blinked his eyes and focused on the ceiling, the dream fading rapidly. He turned his head apprehensively towards the sudden flare as a match was lit. 'Hi, Nancy,' he said.

She blew a stream of smoke as she shook out the match. 'Yeah, hi,' she said moodily.

Fenn's body felt sticky with perspiration and his bladder ached. He sat up and rubbed a hand over his neck and then his face. The stubble on his chin made a scratching sound. Lifting the covers, he swung his legs out onto the floor, then sat for a moment on the edge of the bed. He squeezed his eyelids tight and opened them again.

'Excuse me,' he said, almost to himself, then stumbled off into the bathroom.

Nancy puffed on the cigarette while she waited for him to return, the bedside lamp bathing her naked arms and breasts in a soft glow. What the hell was wrong with him? This was the second time that week she'd had to pull him out of a nightmare. Had the fire in Banfield frightened him that much? And what the hell had he been doing all that week, disappearing during the day, not letting her know where he was going, turning up late each night, half-drunk? She had let him move into her rented Brighton apartment because he wanted to get away from other newsmen – particularly from his own newspaper – to work on something special, something to do with the miracles in Banfield; but he wasn't letting her in on the act. Sure, he was paying his way, but she had hoped they would be sharing the project by now. When she mentioned teamwork, he would just shake his head and say, 'Not yet, babe.' She was being used and that was all wrong; she should be using him.

The toilet flushed and after a few seconds he appeared in the doorway, scratching at an itch just below his armpit. She sighed and flicked ash into the ashtray beside the bed. He flopped down next to her and groaned.

'Want to tell me about it?' she asked, no softness in her voice.

'Uh?'

'Your dream? Was it the same as before?'

He raised himself on his elbows and studied his pillow. 'It was something to do with fire again, I know that. It's a bit fuzzy now. Oh yeah, there were lots of manuscripts—'

'Manuscripts?'

He realized his mistake. She was staring curiously at him, the cigarette poised a few inches from her lips. Fenn cleared his throat, wishing his head could be cleared as easily. His mouth felt like something rancid had curled up inside and he silently cursed the demon booze. He made a quick decision, aware that Nancy was the kind of woman who would allow herself to be left out in the cold for only so long before snapping. He was sure she tried his briefcase every night (a case with a combination lock that he'd bought for the specific purpose of keeping snoopers out) when he was asleep, wondering what he had been up to during the day and just what was so precious that it had to be kept locked away. Well, the truth was, after a week of tedious research, there *was* nothing precious to be locked away. It was time to come clean with her, an easy decision because there was nothing to give away.

He sat up, resting his back against the headboard, pulling the covers over his naked stomach and legs. 'Do you want to get my briefcase?'

'Oh, you mean your portable wall safe?' she replied, confirming his suspicions.

Nancy jumped out of bed without further bidding and padded over to the briefcase leaning against a compact working desk. The apartment was really a holiday studio/flat, one of the countless off-season empty apartments that winter months bestowed upon the seaside resort, and ideal for the likes of Nancy whose stay in the country was to be fairly brief, but too long to make a hotel financially viable.

She came back to the bed and he winced as she dumped the case on his belly. She squashed out the cigarette and jumped in beside him, the pointed brown nipples of her small breasts as eager as the expression on her face. 'I knew you'd level with me sooner or later,' she said, smiling.

He grunted, working the dials of the briefcase locks with his thumbs. When the six-digit combination showed, he flicked back the locks and opened the lid. The inside of the case brimmed with pencil-scribbled notes.

Nancy reached in and took out a handful, turning back to the light with them. 'What the hell is this, Fenn?' She saw dates, names, short notes.

'That's the fruits of one week's solid research. And partly the cause of the nightmares.'

'How d'you mean?' she asked, sifting through the notes and reaching for more.

'When I was a student, I worked one summer in a restaurant. In a fairly high-class tearoom, to be exact; you know, the kind matrons and aunts go to for afternoon tea and scones. It was a busy place and the work was pretty new to me. In the first couple of weeks, all I could dream of at night was silver teapots and scalded fingers. This week I've been dreaming of old parchment papers. Tonight – and the other night – a little extra was thrown in.'

'But what's it all for? You writing the history of Banfield?'

'Not quite. I'm looking into it, though. You know the Church is paying me to write about the Banfield miracles—'

'That doesn't mean you can't write for us as well.'

'We've been through all that, Nancy. It doesn't exclude me from writing for anybody, but for now, I want to get the whole story straight in my own head.'

'You've been acting kinda strange since the fire.' She touched the discoloration on his forehead; the swelling was gone but the mark was still ugly. 'You sure the damage wasn't permanent?'

He took her hand away. 'You want to listen or not? I needed to get the whole historical background on Banfield—'

'Come on, Fenn. I don't buy that. You could get all the background from the local library. That's what I did, and so did the other reporters.'

'I wanted some in-depth material.'

'Okay, treat me like a hick, I'll go along with you for now.'

He sighed in exasperation. 'Just listen, will you?'

'Sure.'

'The local library was the first place I went to. It doesn't have too much – just a book written by a guy who used to be the vicar to the village in the thirties, and a couple of volumes on the history of Sussex.'

'Yeah, no meat.'

'So I went to the village hall, the public records office. The Parish Clerk was helpful, but their records only went back to the 1960s. From there I went to the county records office in Chichester and that's where I've spent the past week. I think the archivist who helped me is sick of the sight of me by now. I've been through every piece of paper on Banfield from the eighth century onwards – not that I understood much of the earlier stuff. Most of it was either illegible or written in Latin. Even the later scripts were difficult, all those "f"s instead of "s"s, you know the kind of thing.'

'What were you digging for?'

He looked away. 'I can't tell you.'

'Why not? What's the big secret?'

'There is no big secret.'

'Then why are you in such a state?'

He turned to her once more. 'What?'

'Have you seen how you look?' She brushed her hand roughly against his chin. 'Aren't you aware of how you've been acting? Getting back here each evening juiced up, keeping your goddam papers locked away like they were state secrets, your nightmares, mumbling in your sleep – screwing me like you were a goddam zombie!'

'You don't like my technique?'

'Shaddup! What d'you think when we're in the sack, that you're just paying your dues on the use of this pad? What the hell d'you think I am?'

He put a hand to her shoulder, but she slapped it away. 'I thought maybe we could get together on this thing,' she said angrily. 'I've stood back and let you get on, waiting for the time you'd open up to me. Just now you could've, but you chose different. Okay, my friend, since we have no deal, it's time for you to scoot.'

'Hey, there's no need—'

'Get out!'

'It's ... it's ...' he scrabbled for his wristwatch lying beneath his pillow '... it's after three ...'

'Tough shit! Get moving.'

'I can improve my style,' he said, brushing his palm against her nipple.

'I'm not kidding, Fenn. Out!'

His hand slid beneath the covers and around her waist. 'I'll shave.'

She pushed against his chest. 'Get lost.'

He gently ran his hand down her thigh.

She punched his shoulder. 'I mean it, you fucker.'

He rolled on top of her and her legs clamped tight together.

'You think,' she hissed, 'you're suddenly a hot lover? You think I'm going to swoon away, you little shit?'

He slumped against her, defeated, then rolled over onto his back and stared at the ceiling. 'Jesus,' he breathed, 'you're rough.'

Nancy sat up and looked down at him. 'I'm rough and I mean it. You've used me, Fenn, and given me nothing in return—'

'Okay, okay, you're right.'

'I guess it's your style, using people, situations. But not with this lady.'

'Aren't you the same, Nancy?' he said quietly. 'Aren't you the same kind of animal?'

She hesitated. 'Sure, it takes one to know one. That's why I'm wise to you. That's why I know I'm not getting anywhere—'

'Hold it. I said you're right and maybe I'm beginning to feel guilty. I've felt strange this week, almost ... well, almost obsessed with this kid Alice. Ever since the fire, ever since she came through those flames ...'

Nancy was silent, fuming still, and he looked at her as though seeking an answer. Her body was thin, her breasts not as firm as they probably once had been, faint lines around her neck betraying the passing years. The hardness in her face was softened by the dim light, but the fierceness in her eyes could not be muted. Even when she was younger he felt sure she had never been classed as beautiful, yet she had the attractiveness that any woman would envy, that would make most men want her (maybe just for one night, perhaps two – she would prove too hard to handle for much longer).

'I was there, too, you know,' she said, disturbed by his gaze. 'Alice didn't have the same effect on me.'

Fenn lifted himself up on one elbow so that his face was closer to hers. 'Tell me what effect she did have on you.'

'Wha – ? Hey, you're sneaking out of this, you're changing the subject.'

'No, tell me. I promise I'll come straight with you after you tell me.'

She looked at him doubtfully, then shrugged. 'What the hell do I have to lose?' She thought for a few seconds, thinking back to the Thursday of the fire. 'Okay. She had absolutely no effect on me at all. Nothing. Zilch. I didn't believe what was happening and I still don't.'

'But you saw it.'

'Yep. And I still don't believe it.'

'That's crazy.'

'Sure. I saw her arrive on the scene, I saw the fire die out. But something in here . . .' she tapped her temple '. . . won't, or can't, put the two together.'

He shook his head. 'And how about Alice herself? Do you have any feelings about her?'

'She's just a kid. A skinny, undersized kid. Quite pretty, but nothing special.'

'A lot of people say she has a radiance about her, a kind of holiness.'

'Maybe to some she has; not to me, though. In fact, if I have to be perfectly honest, she leaves me a little cold.'

'Why?'

'Well, I guess it's because she doesn't seem to sparkle like other kids. I know she's been through a lot, but there's something . . . I don't know . . . something flat about her. It's as if her emotions are locked away somewhere deep inside. She was obviously upset by the death of her father, but I didn't see her shed a tear at his funeral. Maybe she cried herself out in private.'

He sank back down in the bed. 'Lately I've had the same feeling about her. When I first saw her, the very first night I chased her into the field, she was just a scared, vulnerable little girl. Now . . . now she seems different. She probably saved me getting badly burned last week, yet I can't seem to find any gratitude towards her. And . . . oh, Christ, I remember now! I saw her just before the car crashed! I'm sure it was her.' He was sitting up again, arms over his raised knees. 'She was standing in the window of the convent, watching. Just before the cars went . . . out . . . of . . . control . . .'

'What are you saying, Fenn?'

'The cars. Don't you remember? The Capri in front went out of control, then so did mine. The steering just went.'

'I don't remember. I thought the Capri went into a skid and you tried to avoid it.'

'That's what I thought – until now. It just came back to me, Nancy. I couldn't control the bloody car. And she was watching all the time.'

'I don't get you. What the hell are you trying to say? That she was responsible?'

He nodded slowly. 'Maybe that's exactly what I'm saying.'

'You're insane.' She reached for her cigarettes again, lit one.

'If she can control a fire she can interfere with a car's steering.'

Nancy opened her mouth to speak, then just shook her head.

'Strange things have been happening around her,' Fenn insisted.

'Shit, that's an understatement. But there could be other factors involved, psychological reasons for these so-called miracles. And besides, her father died in that fire. The kid wouldn't have had anything to do with that.'

He rubbed a thumb across his lower lip. 'No,' he said slowly. 'No, of course not.' He became lost in his own thoughts.

Nancy ran a hand up his back towards his shoulder. 'You were going to level with me.'

Fenn relaxed against the headboard and Nancy withdrew her hand, letting it rest on his thigh.

'Simply, it's this,' Fenn said. 'Monsignor Delgard is seriously concerned over what's happening at the church—'

'That's hardly surprising.'

'Let me finish. He feels something wrong is going on there—'

'With all those miracles? He should be jumping for joy.'

'Perhaps he should be, but he isn't. He's worried about Father Hagan's death—'

'That was a plain old coronary.'

'Will you shut up and listen. He's also worried about the atmosphere of the church. He feels it's – to put it in his own words – "spiritually devoid".'

'What does *that* mean?'

'I suppose it means the sanctity has disappeared.'

'You can't be serious. You're not trying to tell me the place is possessed by demons?' She gave a short laugh.

'No. St Joseph's is empty. There's nothing there at all. Father Hagan felt the same before he died.'

'Hey, I can't write this kind of junk.'

'For Christ's sake, I don't want you to write about it! I'm telling you in confidence, because you wanted to know. You've baled me out this week, you've helped me stay away from the scavengers so I could get on with all this. I'm returning the favour by letting you know what I'm up to, but I don't want it broadcast to the bloody nation!'

'Don't worry, that won't happen. My chief would bury me. Now if you're saying there's some kind of fraud going on, then I'm with you all the way.'

'Yeah, maybe it is all some elaborate fraud, who knows?'

'Why go into this, uh, "spiritually devoid" shit, then? You're spoiling the chance of a good story, Fenn, probably the biggest that'll ever come your way, by going off on that tack.'

'It's hard to explain, but I feel there's something wrong, too.'

'You're a cynic. It's natural for you.'

'Thanks, but I mean *deeply* wrong. Like you, I think there's something strange about Alice.'

'I only said she didn't have much personality.'

'You implied more.'

'All right, you and the priest think something wicked this way comes. So what's the point of all this research? Where's it going to get you?'

'Probably nowhere, but I might uncover something in the church's history that could shed some light.'

'You mean root out some dark secret from St Joseph's past. Fenn, I don't believe this of you. I thought your flat feet were firmly on the ground and your grubby little fingers always ready to grab the golden egg. I'm not knocking you. From me it's a compliment, it's how I operate myself. But now you're beginning to disappoint.'

'Monsignor Delgard sees me the same way – that's why he hired me.'

'Oh yeah, that makes sense.'

'It does in a crazy way. He wanted someone to look at the whole business coolly and logically, someone who wasn't wrapped up in religion and someone who would scoff at bad vibrations.'

'Until a few moments ago I would have said he'd chosen the right boy. Now I'm not so sure.'

Fenn sighed and his body sank lower against the headboard. A smile slowly formed on his lips. 'Yeah,' he said, 'could be I was getting carried away. The crash, the fire – maybe it just scared the shit out of me, enough to make me think too much, anyway. I could have panicked and imagined the car's steering had gone. There may have been oil on the road – that would account for the other car losing control. Anyway . . .' he emptied the suitcase full of notes onto the floor '. . . I found nothing nasty in the history of Banfield or St Joseph's. Nothing, at least, that hasn't happened in every other village, town or city in England over the past few hundred years. I guess it should be a relief.'

Nancy looked down at the scattered paper. 'D'you mind if I go through your notes sometime?'

'Help yourself, there's nothing there that'll interest you.'

She settled down closer to him and her hand moved towards his inner thigh. 'What about us, Fenn?'

'Us?'

'Working together.'

'I thought you wanted me to leave.'

'That was before. Now you've told me what you've been up to.'

'There wasn't much to tell, was there?'

'No, but at least you confided in me. What about our deal?'

'I'm working for the Church, Nancy.'

'Come on, Fenn. You're working for yourself – you're *using* the Church. It's a way of being right up there in front and getting all the inside information you need. Whatever they're paying you, you'll make treble, probably quadruple, from other sources when your job for the Church is done. Isn't that why you accepted in the first place?'

His smile was slow to surface, and when it did it was strained. After a while, he said, 'I won't work with you, Nancy, but I'll pass on information, try to get you a ringside seat for any special occasions, and generally help in any way I can.'

'Up to a point, right?'

'Yeah, up to a point.'

She groaned, giving up the fight. 'I guess it's gonna have to do. I think you're a fool, though – I could have improved anything you wrote, given it style. I mean it, I could have. And I could have gotten you a good deal from the *Post*.'

He reached over and kissed her neck, the pressure of her hand having some effect. 'When do you have to get back to the States?' he asked.

'Soon as I figure I've got all I'm going to get on this miracle thing. I can't stay forever, that's for sure. Maybe a coupla weeks; unless, of course, even bigger things break.'

'It's hard to imagine anything more mind-blowing happening.' He wondered, though. Just a few weeks ago he had been saying the whole affair would fizzle out and Banfield would sink back into anonymity once more. For his own personal motives, he didn't want that to happen, but some small instinct which became elusive when he tried to focus upon it warned him that it might have been for the best.

Nancy nuzzled her cheek against his forehead. 'What I'm saying, Fenn, is if you're going to help me, it's gotta be soon. No keeping it to yourself. Okay?'

'Sure,' he agreed, not believing himself. He'd help her but, as he had already said, up to a point. Newsmen were generally selfish creatures where their work was concerned and he was no exception to the rule. Her hand had moved upwards and her fingers began to close around his stiffening penis. For the first time that week (and much to his own relief) his desire became much more than just the need to fulfil a bodily function. He squirmed when her movement gained a pleasurable rhythm.

He kissed her lips, turning towards her to press close, but she did not relinquish her possession, nor break the rhythm. Her palm, her fingers, were soft, knowing just the right pressure, knowing when to tighten, when to release. His kiss became hard, his lips moist. She bit down on his lower lip, gently, just enough to excite and not enough to hurt. Her tongue sought his and his whole body became tensed, the area of excitement spreading from his loins to his arms, his thighs, the muscles of his buttocks, his nipples. His own fingers slid over her hips, reaching for her breasts, caressing them, each one in turn, pressing and pulling at the erect nipples, flattening his hand to encompass every part, squeezing hard one moment, fondling tenderly the next.

She could feel his passion and it was unlike any of the other times during the week. It was as if he had finally roused himself from a semi-drugged state. She smiled inwardly. Or she had roused him from that state.

Nancy pushed him onto his back, using her shoulder to do so, not wanting to release him yet. She kept her fingers there, stroking, moving the soft skin against its rigid core in a steady motion, occasionally increasing the pace to heighten his excitement, then slowing the movement before it became too late for them both.

His hand slid down to her stomach, the muscles there quivering, then tightening, at his touch, but she pushed it away when it sought to reach lower. She raised herself to her knees, releasing his penis so that her hand could explore more of his body. Both hands felt their way across his stomach, moving upwards in small circular motions, gently kneading his skin, the pressure spread with open palms and outstretched fingers. She ran them across his chest, spending a little time around his nipples, bending to kiss, to suck, to make them wet, gently blowing on them before moving onwards, her hands smoothing themselves over his shoulders, around his neck, touching the backs of his ears with her thumbs.

He was smiling and she kissed his smile, shifting her body so that it was over him. She stretched herself down, resting her body against his, their skin touching and moulding together in a fusion that was comforting as well as exquisite, as though the pores of their flesh were opening themselves to each other, drinking in each other's juices. Nancy writhed against his hard body, her own pleasure beginning to rise, feeling the sensation deep between her thighs, the moisture there beginning to flow. Her legs opened, her thighs spreading around him. His penis was against her stomach and he shifted his hips so that it moved against her. She took his hands that were clasped around the small of her back and pulled his arms upward, fingers curling through his, holding tight, pushing his hands over his head, pressing them into the pillow, pinning his body down with her own. She moved herself upwards so that her opening rested against his testicles, the risen root of her own pleasure pressing hard against the swollen base of his rod. She moaned as she squirmed and he used his body to give her more pleasure.

She brought up her knees as the sensation grew, but still crouched over him, still pinned his arms back. She stroked her vagina, so moist, so alive, along the length of his penis, then down again, her whole body shivering with its sensuality. She moved upwards again until his tip touched hers, and there she lingered, bringing on her own excitement, the tremor quickly becoming unbearable, but too good to release.

Her fingers untwined from his and reached down. She raised her body, touched his penis more firmly against herself, one hand pushing his protective skin down and up in the coaxing, teasing – exhilarating – movement of moments before; she teased herself with him, allowing his body only partial entry, using him to titillate the outer lips of her vagina.

He groaned, pushing himself upwards, but she went with him, a deep-throated chuckle that was almost a moan escaping her. She allowed him more, her own wetness making the entry smooth, no pain involved, only pleasure. Inner muscles tightened, closing around him, holding him there, her hand still fondling the rest of him, touching between his legs, curling around his testicles and gently squeezing. Her hips moved in a circular motion and his hands clutched at her thighs, spreading around them, reaching upwards, along her body, touching her breasts, holding them together, releasing them, running back down, touching the top of her opening with his thumb, teasing her, but pleasing her as she teased and pleased him.

It was too much for her. She sank lower and he rose into her, every part of his erection surrounded by warmth, by wetness, by muscles that sucked at the juices within him, drawing them out, skilful contractions that needed little movement from the rest of their bodies.

They were both covered in a light sheen of perspiration, Nancy's hair hanging limply over her forehead. Her eyes were half-closed, the pupils rolled upwards, and her lips were parted just enough to show her teeth, her smile almost a grimace of agony.

Fenn looked at her and the sight increased his own sensations. He moved against her, but she controlled everything; the final pleasure would not be his until she was ready, until her own climax was ready to be fuelled. And that would be soon.

She gasped, the sound almost a tiny scream. Her whole body was moving now, pushing him into her, as much as she could take, which was all. He helped her movements, hands around her hips. He lifted her from the bed, his heels digging into the sheets, and she moaned sharply, wanting more, more. Her hands closed around his sides and pulled him upwards.

He felt the juices deep within begin their turmoil, erupting, pressure building for the moment they would break free.

She felt the change in him, the even stronger stiffening, his whole body becoming more forceful, more rigid, more intense. And she was ready for it. The tumult inside was ready to explode.

Her body tightened as though every sinew, every nerve, had drawn itself inwards. She could no longer draw in breath and her heart was straining with the exertion, its pace matching the rhythm of her own movements. And then the peak was reached and she was floating and soaring, reaching one great height and then another, the climax not just a single, exquisite burst, but a series of senses-reeling eruptions, the first two or three expanding in her mind so that it touched all of her, making each nerve part of the whiteness, part of her mind, its intensity diminishing slowly, leaving her panting, sensuously drained.

Her shoulders slumped forward, her arms bent, barely supporting her, long dark hair hanging down into his face. She gave a low, smiling sigh as the pleasure ebbed away until it was replaced by a deep satisfaction.

She slowly pulled herself free and lay down beside him, his fluid seeping from her to rest on her inner thigh. 'That was better,' she sighed.

'You did all the work,' he told her, wiping clinging strands of hair away from her damp brow.

'Yeah, but your cooperation this time helped.'

They were silent for a while, their bodies relaxing, their thoughts beginning to drift. Nancy heard Fenn's breathing become deeper, more regular, and she knew he was sleeping. She carefully eased herself from his arms and went to the bathroom, walking lightly, not wanting to disturb him. She washed herself and put on a bathrobe, then poured herself a glass of cold milk in the kitchen. Returning to the bedroom she gathered up Fenn's fallen notes, taking them through to the lounge and placing them on the room's sofa. She switched on a lamp, then went back into the bedroom to retrieve her cigarettes.

Nancy settled down on the sofa, lit a cigarette, shuffled the notes into three neat piles beside her, and began to read.

26

There was a little girl, and she wore a little curl
Right down the middle of her forehead
When she was good, she was very, very good,
But when she was bad, she was horrid.

Anon, 'Jemima'

Monsignor Delgard's stride had lost much of its briskness and his tall figure was more stooped than usual. The High Street was dark and quiet, the two public houses not having yet regurgitated their Saturday night trade onto the pavements; his footsteps sounded harsh and lonely along the concrete. Not many shop windows were lit, the lights from the few lamp-posts along the roadside feeble, creating shadows that were more menacing than natural darkness. It was bitterly cold again, no significant change in climate noticed as the borderline between February and March fast approached. The priest hugged the lapels of his overcoat tight around his neck, wondering if it was more than just age that allowed the night chill to penetrate his bones. He shuddered, feeling cold fingertips touch his nerves.

He could see the lights of the convent ahead, his eyes, beneath their heavy lids, usually keen, still having a clear vision that only disturbed thoughts or aching temples could sometimes blur. His head ached, the cool air no panacea, and his thoughts, too, were disturbed. The lights of the convent shone like a beacon, as though guiding him towards a friendly refuge, a place of Retreat, away from the brooding church. But was it a false refuge? What did he fear within its sanctuary? He shrugged off the doubts. There was only a child safely lodged within those walls, a frightened, bewildered child. But perhaps a child that was being used . . .

Delgard had encountered the phenomenon termed as 'possession' many times in the past, had helped victims conquer the evil inside themselves, had helped their minds break free of schizophrenic emotions which chained and tormented. In later years, the effort of such psychological battles had been almost too much for his drained body, his mind (or soul) taking longer each time to recuperate. But then it took broken bones longer to heal as age crept into them. He suddenly turned his head as though a disembodied finger had tapped his shoulder.

An empty street. The sightseers had left for the day and the reporters and cameramen had retired for the night, eager for tomorrow, Sunday, a day of labour. He looked towards the convent once more, his pace becoming faster, refusing to accept he was fleeing from a frightening uncertainty behind to a disturbing uncertainty ahead.

He passed the burned-out shell of the garage and thought of Gerry Fenn. Delgard had received one agitated phone call from the reporter the day after the terrible accident, telling him what had happened, what Fenn had witnessed, then . . . nothing. The reporter had disappeared, informing no one, not even his editor, not even Susan Gates, of where he could be reached, what he was up to. Delgard was concerned for the reporter; had he led the man into something he could not comprehend and so could not regard with the respect (and fear) it demanded? The man was no fool and his very cynicism afforded him some protection. But only up to a point. Beyond that point he was as vulnerable as anybody else. Delgard breathed in the frosty air and expelled a white mist as if it were an escaping soul.

The panda car was parked half on the kerb outside the convent and the policeman inside watched the tall priest as he approached the gate. Headlights dazzled Delgard, freezing him in their glare like a paralysed rabbit.

'Sorry,' a voice said from the window. 'It's Monsignor Delgard, isn't it?' The headlights died, leaving the priest sightless for a few moments. He heard a car door open and could just make out a dark shape as the policeman approached him. 'Didn't expect any visitors this time of night,' the voice said. The convent gate was pushed open and the policeman stood to one side to let the priest through.

'Thank you,' Delgard said as he entered the courtyard. 'No journalists tonight?'

The policeman chuckled. 'No chance. It's Saturday. They're either in the local pubs getting stoned or tucked up in bed waiting for the big day tomorrow. The former mostly, I'd say, knowing that crew.'

Delgard nodded and crossed the courtyard, mounting the three steps to the main door as the gate scraped closed behind him. He rang the doorbell and waited.

It seemed like a long time before the door was opened, the coldness reaching into him with deliberate intensity, punishing him because he dared to be still when only movement could keep the chill at bay. The nun peered out at him, her face barely discernible because of the light behind, her attitude cautious.

'Oh, Monsignor,' she said with relief. The door swung wide.

'Reverend Mother is expecting me,' he told her, stepping into the hallway.

'Yes, of course. Let me show you into—'

'I'm glad you could come, Monsignor Delgard,' said a voice from the other end of the hallway. Mother Marie-Claire, the Reverend Mother of the convent as well as Head Mistress of the convent school, walked towards them, the silver cross she wore outside her grey tunic briefly flashing as it caught the light from overhead. She was a small woman, thin, and vulnerable in the way most nuns, even the more robust, seemed to be. Light-framed spectacles perched on a narrow nose and her unplucked eyebrows gave her a severity that Delgard knew was not in her nature. Her hands were clasped low before her as they always seemed to be; it was as if she were constantly praying, and he thought that that probably was the case. She stopped before him and he could see her anxiety behind the thin lenses.

'I'm sorry I'm so late, Reverend Mother,' he said. 'There was much to do in preparation for tomorrow.'

'I understand, Monsignor. It was good of you to come at this hour.'

'Is she in her room?'

'Yes, but not sleeping. She appears desperate to see you.'

'Then she knew I would come?'

Mother Marie-Claire nodded. 'May I offer you something hot to drink before you see her? You must be frozen.'

'No, thank you. I'm all right. I think I'll go straight up.'

'You wouldn't rather see her down here? In my study, perhaps?'

Delgard smiled. 'No, she may feel inclined to speak more

freely in the privacy of her own room, temporary though it may be.'

'As you wish, Monsignor. I'll take you up.'

He raised a hand. 'I know where her room is, Reverend Mother. Please don't trouble yourself.' He made for the stairs, unbuttoning his overcoat as he went and handing it to the sister who had opened the door.

'Monsignor?'

He paused and turned back to the nun.

'Do you think it wise to allow Alice to attend Mass tomorrow?'

'It's what she wishes, Reverend Mother. She insists upon it.'

'She's just a child . . .' The nun let the words trail off.

'One who must be treated with great care,' Delgard said kindly.

'But the crowds. So many . . .'

'We cannot keep her locked away. The public would believe some sinister motive, I'm afraid.'

'But for her own good.'

'How upset she gets when we try to keep her away from the church. I'm of the same mind as you, Reverend Mother, but this matter is not entirely in my hands.'

'Surely Bishop Caines—'

'No, it isn't just the bishop who wishes Alice's exposure to the public. None of these decisions are made by one man any more. Please, don't concern yourself for her safety; she'll be well protected.'

'It's her peace of mind I'm concerned with, Monsignor.' There was no criticism, nor harshness, in her tone, just a caring sadness.

'We all are, Reverend Mother. I promise you, we all are.'

He began to climb the stairs, his footsteps slow, almost as though he were reluctant to reach the upper floor.

Mother Marie-Claire unconsciously fingered the silver cross dangling from the chain around her neck, then walked back towards the tiny chapel beyond the hallway where she had been deep in prayer before the priest arrived. The nun who had opened the door to Monsignor Delgard now locked it and followed her superior down the hallway, stopping on the way to hang the priest's overcoat on a coathook beneath the stairs. She glanced up at the tall, ascending figure before it disappeared into the gloom of the upper level, then returned to her duties in the convent's kitchen.

Delgard paused at the top of the stairs, allowing his eyes to adjust to the poor light. There were doorways on either side of the corridor, each one a nun's private, sparse cell. The room he sought was halfway down, to his right. He wondered why it was so urgent for her to see him that night and told himself he would soon know. He walked towards the door and tapped lightly on it.

There was no sound for a moment or two, but then a voice said: 'Who's there?'

'It's Monsignor Delgard,' he replied, his voice soft, not wanting to disturb those sleeping.

The door opened almost immediately and the pale, tired face of Molly Pagett was peering out at him. 'Thank you so much for coming,' she said, and there was a tremor to her voice.

'Mother Marie-Claire said you needed—'

'Yes, yes, I needed to see you. I'm sorry you've had to come out so late. Please come in.'

The room contained a single cot bed, a sink, a hard-backed, uncomfortable-looking chair, a tiny wardrobe, and no other comforts, except a black crucifix on the wall. After the gloom of the corridor, the single ceiling light was harsh, ugly. Molly Pagett sat on the edge of the bed, her hands clasped together in her lap, and Delgard took the chair from its position by the wall, placing it near to her. He sat, allowing himself a small groan of pleasure, pretending his bones ached more than they actually did, knowing she had some fear of him and wanting to appear less daunting.

'I'm afraid the cold weather stiffens these old joints of mine,' he told her, smiling.

She returned the smile, but it was short-lived, nervous.

He felt too tired for preamble, yet felt her need to be put at ease. 'How are they treating you here at the convent, Molly? Not very comfortable by the looks of it.'

She looked down at her hands and he saw they were clenched tight. 'They're very good to us here, Father . . . I'm sorry, Monsignor.'

He reached forward and patted her troubled hands, his own large hand covering hers completely. 'It's all right. There's no real difference between a monsignor and a priest; one's just a fancier title, that's all. You look tired, Molly. Haven't you been sleeping?'

'Not very well, Monsignor.'

'Well, that's understandable; you've been through so much. Hasn't your doctor prescribed something for you? Something to relax you, help you sleep.'

'Yes, yes, he gave me some pills. I don't like to take them, though.'

'I'm sure they wouldn't do you any harm. Your doctor would only give you something if he thought it was for the best.'

'No, it's not that,' she said quickly. 'It's Alice, you see. She might need me in the night. She might call out.'

'I'm sure one of the nuns would tend to her.'

'She'd want her mother. If she woke up in the middle of the night, she'd be frightened. She'd want her mother . . .'

He saw the tears beginning to well in her eyes before she bowed her head.

'Don't upset yourself, Molly,' he said kindly. 'I know there's a huge burden on you at the moment, but I promise you it will ease. The loss of your dear husband, this strange thing that's happening to Alice . . .'

She looked up and her eyes were shining through the unshed tears, an inner glory that she could not, nor tried to, conceal. 'It's a wonderful, holy thing, Monsignor. Leonard . . . Leonard . . . he couldn't understand it, couldn't appreciate what's happening to my Alice. He didn't believe in God, Monsignor, so it had no meaning for him.'

He was shocked by the distaste in her voice when she spoke of her late husband.

'He just thought he could make money out of it, did you know that, Monsignor?' She shook her head as though disbelieving her own statement. 'He wanted to make money out of my little girl.'

'I'm sure he was as concerned for her welfare as you are, Molly. I don't think he would have exploited her.'

'You didn't know him the way I did. He hated everything that was happening at first, scolded her, as if it were her fault. He didn't want us in this convent, didn't want us surrounded by these good sisters. Then he realized little Alice could make him money. Everybody else was cashing in, he said, so why shouldn't he, her own father? He was going to tell everything to the newspapers, to the highest bidder, everything about Alice, everything about me and him. He was wicked, Monsignor, wicked!'

'Please calm yourself, Molly.' His voice had become firm,

but was still low. 'You've been through too much, you don't know what you're saying.'

'I'm so sorry, I didn't mean . . .' Her body rocked back and forth on the bed and now the tears fell onto her lap.

'Would you like me to fetch you some tea, some water?'

She shook her head and continued to look down, her rocking motion slowly becoming more steady.

Delgard was annoyed at himself for allowing her to become upset, the exact reverse of his intentions, but the outburst had been so sudden, so unexpected. He decided there was little point in attempting to redeem the situation. 'Why did you want to see me, Molly? Was it about Alice?'

Her body seemed to hunch into itself and she did not answer immediately. Finally she pulled a crumpled handkerchief from the sleeve of her woolly cardigan and dabbed at her eyes before looking up. 'It's more to do with me and Len,' she said, her voice unsteady.

He leaned forward in the chair. 'What is it that's troubling you?'

'I . . . I never even told Father Hagan. In all those years I never confessed to him. Now it's too late.'

'You can make your confession to me, Molly. You know whatever you tell me will be between ourselves and God.'

'I was always too ashamed to tell him, Monsignor.'

'I'm sure Father Hagan would have understood. He wouldn't have judged you, Molly.'

'I just couldn't . . .' A shudder went through her, but she seemed to make an effort to gain control.

'What couldn't you tell your parish priest?' Delgard quietly urged.

She would not look at him and her words faltered as she spoke. 'He . . . Father Hagan knew I was pregnant when he married Len and me. I told him that, I confessed that . . .'

Delgard remained silent, his own large hands clasped together.

'But I didn't tell him everything.' The words came in a rush, and none followed.

'What did you omit to tell your priest?' Delgard was forced to ask. 'You know there can be no complete forgiveness if you have not confessed everything.'

Molly gave a small moan. 'I know, I know, but I couldn't say it, I couldn't tell him!'

'You can tell me now, Molly. There's no need to punish yourself further.'

She sniffed and raised her head slightly, but her eyes were still downcast. 'It's . . . it's just that the field . . . the field next to St Joseph's . . . it's become sacred ground, Monsignor. It's a holy shrine.'

Delgard waited patiently.

'Len . . . Leonard used to wait for me outside the church before we were married. He wouldn't come inside, said he didn't feel right there. I didn't realize then just how much he hated religion. Perhaps I would never've married him if I'd known.' She dabbed at her damp cheeks with the handkerchief. 'I used to work for the church even in those days, Monsignor. I loved the place, just as . . . just as Alice loves it. And Len . . . he'd wait for me, like I said.'

She took a deep breath, as though resigning herself to the confession. 'One day he was there, just beyond the wall, watching me – I was collecting the dead flowers from the graves. He called me over. We'd been going out together for a couple of months by then, but . . . but nothing had really happened between us. You know what I mean, nothing . . . nothing *really* serious . . .'

Delgard nodded slowly.

'But that day . . . that day, I don't know what got into us both. It was evening – dusk really – and it was in the summer. Warm, the end of a fine day. We kissed across the wall, sure no one could see us. And then he lifted me over. He was so . . . so strong, so demanding. And I couldn't resist, Monsignor, I couldn't help myself.' Her breasts rose and fell almost in a panting movement, as if the memory of her passion was still alive inside her. She flushed red, embarrassed by her own emotions. 'We lay down by the side of the wall, in that field, in that sacred ground, and we made love. I don't know what possessed me! I'd never gone that far with anyone before, please believe me, but that day I was helpless, I was swept away. We both were. It was as though we were different people, almost strangers to each other. There didn't even seem to be any love involved, just . . . just passion, just lust! Oh God, can I ever be forgiven?'

His hunched shoulders seemed even more pronounced as he spoke. 'Of course you are forgiven. You've been foolish to hold onto this unreasonable guilt all these years. If you feel you need Absolution, I—'

'Alice was conceived in that field, Monsignor, don't you see? And now there's a shrine to the Blessed Virgin . . .'

He suddenly felt nauseous. But it was ridiculous! Such a sin so long ago had no bearing on what was happening today! Yet his head reeled with the notion. He fought to conceal his dismay. 'You . . . you confessed your sin to Father Hagan all those years ago.'

'He was new to the parish. I was too timid to tell him where it had happened, so near the church and all.'

'That wasn't important.'

'But it was on sacred ground.'

'No, Molly, it was beyond the church boundary. And even

now, even now a service is to be held in the field tomorrow, the land hasn't been consecrated. There is no need for your confession.' He searched for the right words, needing to be sure, but aware of her distress. There was no delicate way to ask, though. 'Why . . . why are you so sure Alice was conceived there? Were there no other occasions—'

'No, no, Monsignor. It was just that time. I felt so ashamed afterwards, so very ashamed. And I was pregnant, I knew almost right away. Don't ask me how I knew – I just did. I never allowed Leonard to touch me after that, not till after we were married. But I was happy to be pregnant. I wanted my child. Despite our sin. I felt my baby was a gift from God. And she was, she is, don't you see? I wasn't young, Monsignor, I could have remained a spinster.' She gave a choked laugh. 'I'd almost resigned myself to that. Spinster of the parish! Perhaps that's why I devoted so much time to the church. It had become my life. But God gave me something for myself, something to cherish in the way I cherished the church. But that can't be right, can it, Monsignor? My sin shouldn't have provided such a gift, should it? God doesn't reward sinners.'

Delgard sighed inwardly, saddened by the woman's confusion, depressed by his own. If only there were simple answers. A priest had to conceal his own doubts, his own confusions; he had to appear strong in his beliefs, convinced that God's way was always right, never allowing the perplexity of those ways to infringe on his own faith. How to reassure this woman when her question pricked his own uncertainty? And when her words caused a peculiar revulsion within him. The revelation could have no special significance, yet why did it distress him so?

'You were blessed with a child,' Delgard found himself saying, 'and for that you must be grateful. You need not look beyond that.' It was inadequate, but what more could he have said? 'Don't concern yourself with what happened all those years ago. You raised a fine child in the ways of the Church, as God knew you would. Be content, Molly, look no further. God can reward now for what will come to pass later.'

She smiled, tears still sparkling in her eyes. 'I think I can understand what you're saying, Monsignor. Yes, Alice is a very special gift; He chose me to be the mother of . . . of . . .'

'Hush now. The miracles have still not been proven. You must not be so convinced, not yet.'

Her smile broadened, telling him *she* was sure, *she* knew. Her face clouded for an instant. 'Then . . . then there was no desecration of hallowed ground?'

'How could there be? It was more than eleven years ago, long before the field was thought of . . .' he paused '. . . as sacred. Your sin was one of passion, not irreverence, and for that you've already been forgiven.'

A weight seemed to have been lifted from her. 'Thank you, Monsignor. I'm sorry if you think I'm foolish.'

He patted her hands. 'Not foolish, Molly. Recent events have put concerns into your mind that are not so important as you may think. I can only urge you to put such worries behind you; the coming weeks, months, will impose their own new burdens. Would you like to say a short prayer with me?'

'A penance?'

'No, not a penance. I told you that the sin you spoke of has long since been forgiven. Let's both pray for strength to sustain us in whatever the future may bring.'

Delgard bowed his head and for a few quiet minutes they prayed together. He made the Sign of the Cross before her, then rose to his feet. She smiled up at him, and he could see there was still ill-concealed anxiety in her eyes. 'Thank you, Monsignor,' she said.

'Peace be with you.' He turned back to her before opening the door, not sure what prompted the question. 'Is there anything you'd like to tell me about Alice?'

Molly looked startled. 'Alice? What do you mean, Monsignor?'

He stared at her for several seconds before turning away again. 'It doesn't matter, Molly.' He opened the door. 'But if you ever need to speak to me, if anything at all about your daughter gives you cause for concern, please don't hesitate to tell me.' He closed the door behind him and stood in the dark hallway for several moments, collecting his thoughts. Alice, conceived in the field where she now saw the visions! It could have no meaning. Surely it could have no meaning? Her illness, when she had been struck deaf and dumb – had she been in the field then? No, no, that had nothing to do with it. It had just been a perverse legacy from a child's normal illness. There could not possibly be any connection. Why the unease in his mind? Why did what Molly Pagett had just revealed trouble him so? His fingers went to his brow, moving to a point below, between his eyes, squeezing the bone there to relieve the pain. He had never been so unsure. In all the days of his ecclesiastical career he had never been quite as uncertain as now. Perhaps the sudden death of Father Hagan had unsettled him more than he knew. He began to walk quietly down the corridor towards the stairs, still careful not to wake those sleeping beyond the doors on either side. Father Hagan had seemed so—

He stopped abruptly, a rush of blood causing his heart to beat rapidly. A dark shadow moved from the other shadows towards him.

'Who—?'

'It's me, Monsignor Delgard, Mother Marie-Claire. I'm sorry if I alarmed you.'

Delgard let his breath go. 'Reverend Mother, a man of my years shouldn't be subjected to such frights.' He endeavoured to keep his voice light. 'A tired old heart doesn't enjoy the shock.'

'Forgive me, but I want you to hear something.' Her words were whispered.

'What is it, Reverend Mother?' he asked, immediately concerned.

She drew him back along the corridor. 'Every night since Alice has been with us I, or one of the sisters, have stopped by her room to see if she is sleeping soundly. On two separate occasions I've heard her voice beyond the door. Sister Theodore has also heard her.'

'Is Alice having difficulty in sleeping? Many children talk to themselves when they're alone.'

'Oh no, Monsignor, she has no problem in sleeping. In fact, I would say the child sleeps too much and too often. However, the doctor thinks it's just as well considering the stress she's under.'

'You mean she's talking in her sleep?' His voice was too loud and he adjusted it as he said, 'It's nothing to be alarmed over, Reverend Mother. It's just a symptom of the turmoil she is going through. The loss of her father—'

'It's the words she says that concern me, Monsignor. They're . . . strange, unchildlike.'

Intrigued, Delgard moved closer to the door beyond which he knew Alice slept. 'What kind of words?' he whispered. 'What does she say?'

'Hear them yourself, Monsignor.' The nun turned the handle quietly and slowly opened the door a few inches. They listened. Delgard looked at Mother Marie-Claire quizzically and, although she could not see his face in the gloom, she sensed his puzzlement. 'She was speaking just a few moments –' Her voice broke off when they heard the murmurs from the bed. The nun pushed the door open further and slipped through, Delgard following close behind. A night-light on a small table standing against the wall threw a dim glow around the sparse room, revealing the small, white-sheeted bed, the bundle lying beneath the covers. The figure stirred and the priest and the nun held their breath.

'O, do not deny me, sweet . . .'

Delgard tensed. It was Alice's voice, soft-spoken, mumbled almost, but there was a difference to it. He strained to hear the words.

'. . . let thy passion fill me . . .'

The voice was heavily accented, the vowels broadened, almost coarse.

'. . . mad, exceeding mad . . .'

Almost unintelligible, sometimes too soft to hear, sometimes too . . . too strange to comprehend.

'. . . have used me unmannerly . . .'

It wasn't a foreign accent, but one of an English county that he could not quite place. West Country, yet not quite. Too thick, too heavy . . . She said a name, but Delgard did not catch it.

'. . . passion that flails my body . . .'

He made as if to move towards the bed and felt his arm held lightly by Mother Marie-Claire. 'Best not to disturb her, Monsignor Delgard,' the nun whispered.

He hesitated, wanting to hear more. But Alice's voice had deteriorated into a droning mumble, the words slurred and joined almost into one continuous sound. Even as he watched, she seemed to drift off into a deeper sleep and soon there were no more words, just a regular deep breathing.

The nun beckoned him to follow her from the room and, reluctantly, he did so. She closed the door quietly. 'What manner of speech is that, Reverend Mother?' Delgard asked, remembering to keep his voice low. 'Is it the same each time?'

'It seems to be, Monsignor,' she replied. 'Please come with me – there is something more I'd like to show you.'

Delgard glanced once more at the door before following the dark shape down the corridor. As they descended the stairs, the nun said, 'It's hard to understand what it is she is saying. At first I thought it might be an impediment of speech working subconsciously in her sleep. All those years of deafness – it would have to have had some effect.'

'No, I'm sure that would be impossible. If the situation were reversed, if she spoke with an impediment while conscious and perfectly when asleep, there might be some sense to it. Not this way, though.'

'I agree, Monsignor. It was just a silly first thought, and quickly dismissed. Besides, I believe the words are well-formed, though strange to our ears.'

'Are they a dialect?'

'I believe them to be so, but one I can't place.'

'Nor me. Cornish, perhaps, but not quite.'

'No, not quite. Unfortunately, Alice talks in her sleep only in brief snatches, never enough to identify the source of her accent, or the meaning of her words.'

They reached the bottom of the stairs and Mother Marie-Claire crossed the hallway and opened the door to her private study. She indicated a chair for the priest to sit in. 'May I offer you a hot drink now, Monsignor Delgard?'

He shook his head. 'No, no. Perhaps in a moment. You said you had something to show me.'

She turned away and went to a chest of drawers. Before opening the top drawer, she said, 'Alice has been forced to spend a lot of time alone in her room. Perhaps too much time for one so young. There isn't much the convent can provide to keep her occupied, but she appears to enjoy working with paints and crayons.' She opened the drawer and drew out a folder. 'I've kept her discarded work since she's been with us.'

She returned to her desk and laid the folder on the top. 'Her fascination is for one subject alone.'

'Ah yes,' Delgard said, leaning forward. 'Father Hagan showed me some of her pictures before he died. Her mother had allowed him to take them from the house. They were all of one person, a person we surmised to be the Blessed Virgin.'

'Yes, Monsignor, that's right. Alice has no real skill as an artist, but she has a certain ... enthusiasm for her subject. To the point of obsession I would say.'

'The child worships Mary.' He allowed himself a smile. 'I think that's obvious to all. I think her devotion may ...'

'Devotion? Is that what you think, Monsignor?' Mother Marie-Claire opened the folder and held the first sheet towards him. He took it and the sheet trembled in his grip.

'It can't ...'

'The same figure throughout, Monsignor.' The nun spread other sheets of paper from the folder on the table. All bore the same crude workmanship, the same garish colours, the same broad, slashing strokes of the paintbrush.

Even the painted-in obscenities were the same, although an erect phallus in one might be different in size and colour from the next, the shape of the breasts different in shape from another, the grinning red mouth more distorted than the one next to it.

27

Their belief in the Magic was an abiding thing.

Frances Hodgson Burnett, *The Secret Garden*

Ben scooted along the rows of benches, Indiana Jones fleeing from hundreds – no, *thousands* – of screaming Arabs, ready to turn and whip swords from the hands of any who got too close, his imaginary bull-whip settled comfortably over his left shoulder and no weight at all. Up one row, down the next, slipping once on the damp grass, but up in a flash, pausing only to gun down the seven-foot-tall, black-clothed assassin brandishing a long curved sword, laughing at his scream of surprise, speeding on in his race to find the Lost Ark before the dirty Nazis got to it and used its power to win the world. Indiana Jones was better than Han Solo (even if it was the same man) and Han Solo was better than Luke Skywalker. Run, out of breath, mustn't stop, mustn't catch me, out of breath, got to keep going, mustn't – somebody's foot!

He sprawled on the ground and hands reached down to pick him up. It hadn't hurt, just jarred his knee. He rubbed at the earth on his jeans and a voice said, 'Careful, son, you're going to hurt yourself if you tear around like that.'

He said nothing, remembering he was still Indy, a man of

few words. The hands released him and with one bound he was free.

The field was fast filling up with people, the benches nearer to the scaffolded centre-piece – not those specially roped off for particular Church and non-Church dignitaries, nor those reserved for certain religious associations – becoming more and more full, the crowd spreading outwards like a blossoming flower. It was still early, two hours before the Mass was due to begin, but already the people were pushing through the newly constructed entrance gate to the field, eager to find a seat near the altar, many wanting just to see the Miracle Girl, others wanting to be close so that her holiness would wash over them, fearful that it wouldn't stretch too far back.

The sun was just a dull glow in the hazy sky and there was a harshness in the air that was particularly unkind to the invalids in the crowd. The buzz of conversation, of excitement, and of a certain fear, increased as the numbers swelled; the well-organized stewards, ushers, the young priests called in to help marshal the expected huge congregation, could not help but feel a trembling of their own senses as the intoxicating atmosphere spread. Voices were hushed, reverential, as though the gathering were inside a cathedral, only their multiplicity giving them an overall loudness. Wheelchairs, their passage through the field not easy because the soft earth had been churned up by too many feet, were already beginning to obstruct the aisles and the ushers made mental notes that an area would have to be sectioned off for such invalids on future occasions.

Ben ran on, this time careful to avoid booby-trap feet, keeping to the less occupied benches, an eight-year old enjoying his game, oblivious to the gathering tension, lost in the excitement of his own mind's creation. A truck-load of dirty Nazis was tearing down on him and he rolled over the bench to his right, shooting the driver in the face as he went by. Then he was up again, running on, fearless and to be feared. He was dimly aware that the game would have to end soon, that his mother had made him promise to return to the church before the field became too full. If she wasn't there, she would be in the priest's house. It wasn't too full yet, there were plenty of empty benches, plenty of dark, Arab alleyways, plenty of—

The man had just entered that particular row and Ben's hurtling body caught him momentarily off-balance, knocking him onto the bench on which he was about to sit. He held the boy's shoulders to steady him and Ben, startled and breathless, looked up into his face. The man cringed inside when he saw the boy's eyes widen in shock, his mouth drop open, his body become rigid. The man could only smile to reassure him, but even that made his physical mask more grotesque.

He released his grip and the boy slowly shrank away, never taking his eyes off the man's ulcerated mouth and nose, the terrible disfigurement of facial tuberculosis. He lifted the silk scarf, dislodged when the boy had cannoned into him, to his face again, the mask natural enough on such a cold day. He shouldn't have been here, not with this terrible affliction; people were afraid of him, friends, so-called loved ones, afraid his disease was contagious. In the old days *lupus vulgaris* was known as 'dog's muzzle' and the description was appropriate; sometimes they treated him warily, like a crazy dog, afraid he would bite them and they would become as he. The skin disease was rare, but that gave him no feeling of distinction, just a sense of hopelessness, a feeling of impotent fury that he should be chosen to bear the hideous brand which, for him, no antibiotics could clear. One last hope. Today, one last hope. If not, if he could never again feel another's lips against his, never look into another's eyes without seeing the barely-hidden revulsion therein – never hold a child without feeling their muscles tense to run away – then there was no point to it all, no reason to go on. What was so precious about life that you felt obliged to live it? Better cold, senseless oblivion than a scorned existence. He watched the boy run from him and tried to retain the numbness in his mind, his only barrier against the seeping self-pity.

Ben ran on, afraid now of this big field, these people pouring in, all strangers, all suddenly a threat. Time to find Mummy; Indiana Jones had faded without final credits.

'You'll have to move on. Nowhere to park here.'

'Press.' Fenn leaned across and flashed his card at the constable.

'Yeah, you and eight thousand others. Keep moving.'

Fenn forced his car into the slow-moving traffic. 'Bloody carnival day again,' he muttered.

'What?' Nancy asked.

'It's amazing how many'll turn up for a free show, isn't it?'

'I think a lot of them have stronger motives for coming than that, Fenn.'

'Maybe.'

They were nearing the drive to the priest's house and Fenn saw even that was blocked with vehicles, presumably those of visiting clergy and helpers. He swore. 'I should have cleared it with Delgard to get parking space. I'm supposed to be "official".'

'I guess we should have gotten here earlier.' Nancy studied the shuffling people, the queue spilling into the road, police and stewards at various points endeavouring to keep some kind of order, preventing the thoroughfare itself from being swamped. The coach in front of Fenn's hired car came to a halt and he reluctantly eased his foot down on the brake pedal. Nancy poked her head out the window on her side to see what was causing the hold-up.

'There's an ambulance up ahead – by the entrance to the field, I think,' she told him. 'Yeah, it's unloading. Jesus, coupla stretcher cases.'

'Doesn't surprise me. They'll be bringing their dead along next.'

Nancy rummaged in her bag for cigarettes. 'I'm not sure why you're still so cynical,' she said as she lit up. 'You gotta face it, there's been results.'

'I know, but look, look over there.' He indicated to the opposite side of the road where makeshift stalls were set up on the grass verge. Through the gaps in the crowds around the stalls they could see small statues and holy trinkets hung from wire frames, while flimsy posters of the Virgin Mother, the Virgin and the Christ-baby, the Virgin at the Crucifixion, hung limply from long strings tied to the branches of trees behind the stalls. They caught a glimpse of a poster of the Pope in a cowboy hat, another blurred one of him being shot. The traders looked sullen, even though business appeared to be brisk. A Mr Whippy van looked busiest of all, and Fenn wondered if Madonna ice-lollies were on sale.

'I'm surprised your police allow it.'

'Probably too busy keeping the crowds under control to worry about unlicensed traders,' Fenn replied, moving the car on again as the coach in front advanced.

'Looks like nobody's getting into St Joseph's today,' Nancy said as they approached the church gate.

He saw the policemen moving the queue along past the

locked gate, patiently explaining to the more insistent that the service was to take place in the field today, not the church. 'They don't look too happy about it.'

'I'm not surprised – it's goddamned cold outside.'

'It's not going to do some of those invalids much good.' Fenn shook his head. 'I can't understand their doctors allowing it.'

'You can't stop human nature, Fenn. If they think they're going to get cured, nothing'll keep them away. How would you feel, say, if you had an incurable disease, or a terminal illness? Wouldn't you take one last desperate chance, even if you thought the possibility of being cured was a thousand – or even a million – to one?'

He shrugged. 'Who knows?'

'You'd have nothing to lose.'

'Except to feel pretty stupid.'

'What's stupid against a chance to live again?'

He remained silent, accepting the point. Then he said, 'There's the entrance to the field. Look, it's jammed solid.'

They could now see that the queue converged on the gate from both directions, forming an untidy mass at the entrance.

'If only I were selling tickets,' Fenn muttered.

They drove on, the journey slow, cars, vans and coaches now parked bumper to bumper along the roadside, only the immediate area around the church and field entrance kept clear by the police. 'You want to jump out here while I find somewhere to park?' Fenn suggested.

'You're going to see Delgard, aren't you?'

He nodded.

'Then I'll stick with you.'

'Suit yourself.'

'Like glue.'

'Okay.'

Ahead, he saw the driver of a coach parked half on the grass verge having a heated argument with a policeman. Guessing what the dispute was over, Fenn swung in towards the vehicle's rear tyre and stopped. Angry blasts from horns behind greeted the manoeuvre as other drivers were forced to swing around and squeeze through the gap between his hired Fiesta and approaching traffic.

'What the hell are you doing, Fenn?'

'The road isn't wide enough for coach parking so the driver's being moved on now that his passengers are unloaded.'

'It doesn't look like he's moving to me.'

'He will be.'

Fenn was right. With a last gesture of disgust the driver disappeared back inside and the coach throttled into life. He pulled out into the traffic without signalling and without waiting for space. Fenn whipped in quickly, two cars behind following his strategy. 'There you go,' he said triumphantly as he pulled on the handbrake.

They left the car and began the walk back to St Joseph's, keeping to the opposite side of the road from the shuffling queue. 'There's gotta be thousands upon thousands here today,' Nancy remarked, pulling her scarf around her throat to keep out the cold.

'There were thousands last week.'

'Yeah, but not this many. Even the Pope couldn't haul in these kind of numbers.'

Soon they were forced into the roadway to avoid the people clustered around the traders' stalls. They stopped for a closer inspection of the wares. 'Unbelievable,' Fenn said, shaking his head and smiling at the same time. 'Look, over there.' He pointed. 'Flasks containing Holy Soil from the field of the Madonna. Jesus wept!'

Nancy picked up a small dome-shaped transparent container filled with water in which an ill-defined plastic version of Mary stood. She shook it and snowflakes almost obliterated the image.

Fenn shook his head again in amused dismay when he saw a seven-inch shrine, again made of plastic, small red candles in holders on either side of an inset photograph of Alice which had obviously hastily replaced another kind of holy picture. The black and white shot had been reproduced from a newspaper, for the blow-up revealed the fine printed dots to a crude degree.

Nancy pointed out a white-painted grotto whose lights flashed on intermittently to reveal a Madonna and what could only have been Bernadette of Lourdes.

They watched as a pilgrim picked up a tiny doll which bore the faintest resemblance to Alice Pagett, and a mechanical parody of a child's voice said, 'Hail Mary, full of grace, the Lord is . . .'

'I don't believe it,' Fenn said. 'How can they manufacture these things so fast?'

'They call it enterprise,' Nancy said, not amused by any of the trivia on display. 'They're just quick and simple adaptations of junk that's been selling for years. I'll bet under some of those labels saying "Alice, the Miracle Worker" or "Our Lady of Banfield" you'll find others referring to something totally different.'

They moved on, passing medallions of all shapes and sizes, crucifixes plain and gaudy, chinaware, handbags, even umbrellas, somehow alluding to the fact that they were all touched by holiness. They were approached by a man selling postcards of Sussex villages, Banfield itself not among them. Fenn declined the offer to buy with a bemused wave of his hand.

They crossed the road when they were opposite the gate leading to St Joseph's, dodging between the slow-moving cars and plunging into the queue. The policeman they had spotted earlier directing the crowd barred their way.

Fenn took out his Press card. 'Monsignor Delgard is expecting me.'

The policeman turned towards a steward who was lurking beyond the entrance. 'D'you know anything about a Mr Gerald Fenn?'

The small man, who had spoken with Fenn on a previous occasion, nodded his head. 'He's okay, you can let him through.'

The gate swung open and Nancy made as if to follow her companion.

'Sorry, miss, Mr Fenn only.'

'But I'm with him.' Nancy opened her bag and took out her card. 'Look, I'm Press too.'

'Miss, er, Shelbeck?' The policeman had scrutinized the card and turned towards the other man again.

'No, don't know anything about her.'

'Sorry, miss, you'll have to use the other entrance further down. Only authorized persons allowed through here.'

'But I told you, I'm with *him*.' She pointed at Fenn who was trying not to grin.

'I'd like to oblige you, miss, but I'm afraid I can't.'

'Fenn, will you speak to this guy?'

'Sorry, Nancy. I guess orders is orders.'

'You bastard! You knew this would happen.'

Fenn held out his hands in mock denial. 'How could I?'

Nancy's mouth became a straight line across her face. 'Now, look, officer, I'm from the *Washington Post*. I'm here to cover this—'

'I'm sure you are,' came the polite but firm reply, 'but if

you'll just join the queue. You can go straight to the front, just show your Press card.'

'But—' She saw there was no point in arguing. 'I'll see you later,' she snapped at Fenn before shoving her way back into the crowd.

Fenn passed through the gate, the grin broad on his face. It slowly faded as he walked along the shadowed path towards the church. He felt uncomfortable, as though the old building itself were watching him, the black open doorway waiting to devour his soul. If there was such a thing as a soul. He wasn't sure (he'd reached no definite conclusions – and how could anyone?), but he thought he believed in the 'spark' of life, an essence inside which gave man his drive, generating energy as well as thoughts, through chemically derived impulses. A tiny pilot light, if you like, that was necessary to set everything else in motion. So what was God? A bigger spark? Were his and all the others just offshoots from the big one? Or was God everything the different religions wanted Him to be? And did it really matter? Not to Fenn. And maybe not even to God.

But the church puzzled him. There was a coldness to it that seemed to be more noticeable each time he visited – unless he, himself, was absorbing the fears of first Hagan, and now Delgard. 'Spiritually devoid' was a strange expression to anyone who had no particular beliefs in that direction, so why did it seem so apt to him? He had been disappointed that his week's research had uncovered no deep mysteries or scurrilous activities surrounding St Joseph's or the village, but only because it would have provided an interesting, perhaps intriguing, storyline. Yet had he been that cynical when he had first undertaken the research, or was it just rationalization after discovering no hidden skeletons? He remembered that his attack on the archives had been almost obsessive. The fire, the deaths of the priest and Alice's father, the strangeness of Alice herself, and the veiled insinuations of Monsignor Delgard had instilled doubts and suspicions in his own mind, had kindled a peculiar fear within himself, one that he had not understood and could not ignore. Perhaps the week of relentless research had purged the fear from him, the multitude of mundane historical facts and dates overwhelming the real purpose of his searches.

He stood outside the worn building and gazed up at the small tower. Its origins dated from way back – no one was sure just how far back its history went – and he wondered at how much the ancient stones must have witnessed, how times had changed beneath its spire, those changes escalating with each passing century. It had stood, or parts of it had stood, from pre-mediaeval England to the era of microchips and space rockets, through sorcery and superstition into the age of the realist. If the church were human, if stone and mortar were flesh and blood, the window its eyes, the altar its brain, how would it absorb those vast changes, what effect would they have on its living being? And would its spiritual aura survive the debasing onslaught of materialism? Or would the wisdom-giving years pass on a new perception that far surpassed the achievements of scientific knowledge?

He shook himself. Jesus, Fenn, a philosopher yet. It was just a pile of stones standing before him, with no feelings, no brain, and no soul. Man-made, stamped and packaged by the Roman Catholic Church. End of profound philosophical contemplation. Footsteps made him turn sharply.

'Can I help you?' It was a different priest to the young Irishman that Fenn had spoken to in the church house more than a week before.

'Ah, yeah. My name's Fenn. I'm looking for Monsignor Delgard.'

'Oh yes, Mr Fenn, I've heard all about you. I've just left the Monsignor up at the presbytery.'

'Thanks.' The reporter turned in that direction.

'He's rather busy now, preparing for Mass.'

'I won't take up much of his time,' Fenn replied over his shoulder.

The priest went into the church.

As he walked, Fenn could see the gathering in the field just beyond the graveyard. He paused and squinted his eyes, looking towards the distant oak tree, noticing with interest the platform built before it, the raised altar. 'Showtime,' he muttered and went on.

He knocked on the door of the presbytery, then rang the doorbell too, his usual method of announcing his arrival when given two options, and raised his eyebrows in surprise when Sue answered.

'Hi,' he said.

'Hello, Gerry.'

'You on the team now?'

'Just helping. So much is going on.' She stood aside so that he could enter. 'Did you want to see Monsignor Delgard?' Sue asked, then added pointlessly, 'Of course you did.'

'It's good to see you.' And it was, even though she looked tired, dark shadows under her eyes, hair not as springy and vibrant as usual. 'You been losing sleep, Sue?'

'What?' She brushed a wisp of hair away from her face and looked away as though embarrassed. 'Oh, no, no, I'm fine,' she said with false lightness. 'Working too hard, I suppose.'

He moved closer. 'Doing two jobs: the radio station and the church.'

'St Joseph's doesn't take up too much time, not really.'

'What do you do here?'

'It's not just me, there's a few women from the village who

come in to help. We clean the church, the house. Buy food in for the Monsignor – he's terribly busy, you know. This morning I've been answering the phone for him – it seems to have been ringing non-stop.'

'And answering the door?'

'Yes, that too.'

'Is Ben with you?'

'He's around somewhere, in the field, I think. I tried to call you lots of times this – last – week.' She looked at him with concern.

He smiled, pleased that she had. 'I got snowed under. Thought I needed to keep away from people for a while.'

'You weren't at the *Courier*.'

'No, I was doing some digging for Monsignor Delgard. Sorry you couldn't reach me, but then I didn't think you wanted to.'

'After the accident last week, the fire? You didn't think I'd care? I heard you were involved, heard it from others.' Her eyes glistened softly.

'Oh, Chri . . .! I really am sorry, Sue, but you know you've been kinda funny towards me. I didn't even know if you wanted to see me again.' He reached out and put a hand on her arm.

She looked down and was about to say something when the phone, nearby in the hallway, rang. 'I'll have to get that.' She turned away from him and picked up the receiver. 'Oh, Bishop. Yes, did you want the monsignor? No, I haven't been out there myself for a while, but one of the priests told me it's getting very crowded . . .'

Delgard emerged from a door just off the hallway. He smiled and gave a small wave when he saw Fenn. Sue handed him the receiver and whispered, 'It's Bishop Caines, wants to know how everything's going.'

Delgard nodded and took the phone. Sue came back to Fenn. 'It's pretty hectic just now,' she said, speaking quietly so that the priest would not be interrupted.

'Can I see you later?' Fenn asked, feeling slightly ridiculous having to ask.

'Do you really want to?'

'What kind of question is that?'

'Where were you last week? I mean, where did you stay?'

The lie came easily. Only he decided not to tell it. 'We'll talk about it later.' He was surprised himself that he had not immediately told her he had stayed in a Chichester hotel, near to John Dene House where the historical records of Sussex were kept.

'You're not keeping something from me?'

He decided honesty couldn't run too deep. 'Nothing,' he replied.

Delgard had replaced the receiver and was coming towards them. 'Gerry, I'm certainly glad to see you again. I thought perhaps I'd frightened you away.'

Sue looked at the priest sharply, but said nothing.

'You don't know how much you got me to chew off,' Fenn said. 'I haven't crammed so much since I left school.' He added as an afterthought, 'Although I didn't cram too much then.'

'You can tell me on the way over to the church. I have to get into my vestments for the Mass.'

'You're taking it?'

'I seem to have inherited a parish, at least temporarily. Susan, will you look after Alice and her mother while we go to the vestry?'

'Alice is here? In the house?' Fenn's voice rose in surprise.

'I thought it best we install her in here early. That way she won't have to fight her way through all the people who have come to see her. We'll just go through the churchyard into the field.'

'Seems like a good idea. Could I see her?'

'I really must make ready for the service now and I'm anxious to hear what you've uncovered. I'd rather you came over to the church with me.'

'Sure. Maybe later?'

The priest did not answer, but glanced at his watch and said to Sue, 'Bishop Caines is on his way from Worthing, he should be here in twenty minutes or so, unless the traffic holds him up. Will you wait here with Alice and the Reverend Mother until he arrives, then take them to their places five minutes before Mass begins?'

She nodded.

'I think the bishop may arrive with an entourage.'

'I'll take care of them, Monsignor.'

He smiled his thanks and led Fenn outside. As they walked back towards the church, he said, 'You look tired, Gerry.'

'You know, I was just about to say the same thing to you. And so does Sue. I think she's taken on too much.'

'Perhaps we all have.' He turned his head to study the reporter's face. 'She's a good woman, very able, very sincere. She told me her faith had wandered for a while, but now it seems to have returned with a renewed vigour.'

'Because of Alice?'

'They say the true miracle of Lourdes is not the sick that are cured, but the replenishing, the strengthening, and even the beginning, of faith for the pilgrims.'

'Sue appears to have caught the bug.'

The priest laughed. 'I think that's an appropriate description. It is rather like catching a bug, although there are no ill-effects, just good ones.'

'That's a matter of opinion.'

'Ah yes, I understand your relationship is under some stress. But do you really blame Susan for that, Gerry?'

'Not entirely.'

Delgard thought it best to leave the subject alone; there were far more important issues to concern himself with at that time. Fenn was an impulsive, and certainly selfish, young man. Some aspects of his scepticism were healthy and clearly intrinsic in the profession he'd chosen, while others were somewhat destructive. He had an air of ruthlessness about him, although it was often disguised beneath an apparent nonchalant attitude; yet Delgard suspected the reporter was a compassionate man, again that sensitivity concealed beneath an indifferent exterior. It was the priest's understanding of the human character through years of listening, delving, consoling, that allowed his harsh assessment – not judgement – of Fenn to be tempered by more kindly impressions. The man was complex but ultimately likeable, someone whose faults could irritate but could be soon forgotten.

'Have you discovered anything of interest, Gerry?' Delgard asked.

Fenn took a deep breath. 'Nothing that relates to our – your – particular problem. I'll type out my notes for you in some kind of order giving correct dates and names, but I can give you a brief rundown now.'

They had reached the church door and Fenn shivered when they entered the gloomy interior. 'It's cold.'

'Yes,' was all the priest said.

The church was empty, the priest that Fenn had passed earlier either in the vestry or having left to join the congregation in the field.

'Let's sit here.' Delgard pointed to a bench.

'I thought you were in a hurry.'

'There's time to talk. Please proceed.'

They sat, Fenn on one bench, Delgard in front, his body twisted to face the reporter, his back to the altar.

'Okay, here goes,' Fenn said, taking out a notebook from his pocket. 'I'm afraid this place isn't famous for much. I'll amend that: it isn't famous for anything. It gets its first official mention as far back as 770 AD when the Saxons had a castle nearby at Stretham. The Lord of the Manor was granted a charter by Osmund, the King of the West Saxons, to assign fifteen hides of land to endow the church in Banefelde. Presumably it was this one, St Joseph's, since there's no record of any other churches existing at that time. The village seems to have had a variation in spelling over the years, by the way. Banefelde, Banedryll, Banefeld without the "e" on the end; Banfield got to be the final handle.

'Before the coming of the Saxons, prehistoric men had a track right across the county, east to west, and it went right through the settlement which eventually became this village. You've got to remember this part of the country was nearly all forest-land; the settlement was probably just a clearing in the forest.

'Its second earliest official mention was in the Domesday Survey in 1085 when William wanted to know just how much the kingdoms were worth and who exactly was in them. Not much seems to have happened since. A little excitement around Reformation time and the Civil War in the following century. Sixty-two villagers died of the plague in the seventeenth century. Not much of any importance until it became a staging post on the London to Brighton turnpike in the eighteenth. Oh yeah, that's when it got its own workhouse, too, for the parish destitutes. The villagers also got their own railway line around 1880 and kept it until the cuts a hundred years later. It could be the line will be re-established with all the attention Banfield's getting now.

'A few familiar names keep cropping up over the years, some going right back to the thirteenth and fourteenth centuries. Southworth's one of them. Two others, Backshield and Oswold, are with him on the parish council today. There's a Smythe who gets several mentions, Breedehame, Woolgar, Adams and a Charles Dunning who seems to have been of some note. He was knighted in the time of Henry VIII. Most were independent landowners or farmers. There was conflict between some of the families during the Civil War – some supported Charles I, others hung in with Cromwell. Knowing village feuds, they probably resent each other to this day. A few of the villagers have been involved in smuggling. I suppose it was an open road from the coast with plenty of places to hide along the way. That was about all the skulduggery that went on, or at least was recorded.' He smiled at the priest.

Delgard waited for him to continue and frowned when he didn't. 'That's it?' he asked in surprise.

'That's the bones of it. You'll get the details in my typed notes. Sorry I couldn't provide you with murders, pagan sacrifices or witch-burning, but they're just not there.'

'It's something of an anticlimax.'

'Especially when you've been through just about everything written on the place since Saxon times. Dead-ends are never fun.'

'The church itself. There must be more on the church.'

'There is. Not much though. In England, Sussex was one of the last pagan strongholds. It was cut off from the north by forests, on the east and west by marshes, and the south by sea. Augustine and his Christian followers from Rome got short shrift from the natives at that time. It took a bishop called Wilfred, who was driven onto the Sussex coast by rough seas, to make the breakthrough. He was appalled by the barbarism and resolved to come back and convert the savages. He did, twenty years later, and got his way. The story goes that Banfield, or Banefelde as it was known, was one of the last settlements to hold out. The interesting thing is that the first Christian church – and we can only assume it was St Joseph's – was built over the pagans' place of worship. And their burial grounds.'

There was an iciness in Delgard's stare that was a reflection of inner thoughts and not directed at Fenn. He said, 'That's probably not significant; many churches have been built over pagan altars as a firm and symbolic rebuttal of what previously took place. And burial grounds have always been sacred in the minds of men, Christian or pagan.'

'Sure. It's just a statement of fact from me, not an insinuation.'

The priest nodded. 'Please go on.'

'The first curate to get a mention here was . . .' he consulted his notebook '. . . a John Fletcher. That was in 1205. The church records, by the way, only go back as far as 1565, and they deal solely with marriages and deaths. I got the information on Fletcher from a book on the village.'

'Are you sure?'

'Yeah. But I discovered something else that I'll get to in a minute. As I said before, Banfield was particularly resistant to Bishop Wilfred and his followers when they began converting the Sussex people. A lot of blood was spilt. Once the church was established, though, there were no more problems – at least, none that have been recorded. Some trouble with Charles II – the minister here was a Royalist and was involved in sneaking the king across the Downs to the coast where he took a boat to France. Cromwell had the priest executed. Apart from that, the clergy have kept a low profile in Banfield; no scandals, no misuse of church funds, and no anarchy.

'But the records only date to the late sixteenth century.

We don't know how this church was affected with the spreading of Lutheranism in England. Those were troubled times for Catholics.

'The Reformation brought change and problems to all the churches in this country, but I couldn't find anything specific to St Joseph's. One or two dignitaries in the area got into heavy trouble when they wouldn't swear allegiance to Henry VIII as head of the English Church, but most decided to go along with the idea for the sake of peace. Besides, many were benefiting from the transformation; Henry was selling off the lands available with the dissolution of the monasteries, and the gentry were the recipients.'

Something was nagging at the back of Delgard's mind, a teasing, darting thought that dissolved like a disturbed dream each time he tried to focus on it.

'There were opposing factions in Banfield,' Fenn continued, 'and the controversy was probably used to continue feuds that had been going on for some time. Anyhow, there are no church records touching that period in the archives. And that leads to the matter I mentioned earlier.'

Delgard leaned towards the reporter, as though hearing his confession.

'Is there an old chest somewhere in the church?' Fenn asked.

The priest looked at him in surprise.

'An old chest made of thick elm or oak?' Fenn went on. 'It's held together by bands of Sussex iron. And, oh yeah, it has three locks.'

The priest shook his head slowly. 'I don't know of any such chest. I haven't seen it.'

'Could it be stored away somewhere?'

'There's only the vestry and the crypt. I'm sure it isn't in either.'

'In the house? The attic?'

'What size is it?'

'I'm not sure. Something like five feet by two. It's ancient, dates back to the fourteenth century.'

'No, it's not in the presbytery. Why is it important?'

'Because that's where old documents, church valuables, books and records were kept. I found mention of it in the archives. Henry VIII ordered that every church had a strong coffer, paid for by the parish, in which records were to be kept. That was in fifteen-something-or-other but, according to the archives, Banfield already had its own chest dating back two centuries before. We may be able to find more about St Joseph's from it.'

It was important. Somehow Delgard knew the chest was important. It tied up with the elusive thought he had had moments before. 'I can check the crypt later, after Mass.'

'I can do it now.'

Delgard hesitated, looked at his watch, and said, 'Very well. Come with me into the vestry and I'll give you the key; the entrance to the crypt is outside.'

He rose, a tall, dark-clothed man, his eyes in shadows. Fenn, still sitting, looked up at him and remembered how indomitable the priest had appeared when he had first laid eyes on him; now some of that strength seemed to have waned as though Delgard were drawing into himself, his vibrancy not gone but diminished. Although the change was barely discernible, Fenn was sure it wasn't just in his own imagination.

'Is something wrong?' the priest asked.

Fenn pulled himself together. 'Uh, no, just thinking. Let's get the key.'

As they walked towards the vestry, footsteps unnaturally loud in the empty church, Fenn glanced over at the statue of the Madonna. There was no whiteness left to it.

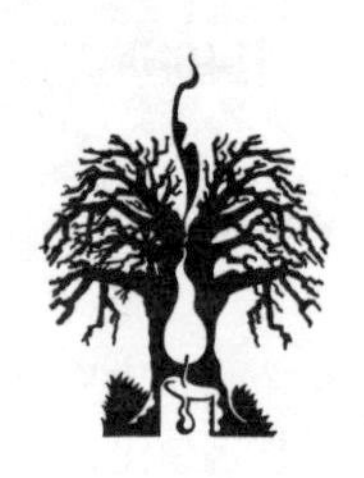

28

> Then a child's puzzled voice was clearly heard. 'He's got nothing on!'
>
> Hans Christian Andersen,
> 'The Emperor's New Clothes'

Ben jiggled his buttocks on the hard wooden bench, one cheek to the other, hands jammed beneath his legs. His mother sat beside him, eyes closed, oblivious to the noise around her.

Ben was over his earlier fright, having seen a lot more worse sights than the man with the funny face: men with no legs, children with heads too big and silly wobbly eyes, women with lumps and bumps and jelly limbs; and nervous eyes peering out of rag bundles in wheelchairs.

'I'm cold, Mummy,' he complained.

'Hush,' Sue told him. 'Mass'll be starting soon.' She looked around, amazed at the vast numbers. Here and there banners waved above the sea of pink faces, proclaiming districts and religious associations. Many in the row she sat in wore small badges denoting the wearers as pilgrims to Lourdes. A smart young man directly behind her bore a plastic identity card boasting that he was Anthony Roberts of St Peter's Tours.

Others around him sported different coloured badges than those on her bench. A leaflet lay in the churned earth at her feet, discarded with some disgust by a pilgrim further along who had received it from a young girl as he had entered the grounds; it asked for contributions towards the followers of the Rev Sun Myung Moon in order that the Unification Church might become an important economic force. A muddy heelmark had sullied the moon-face of the man beaming from the leaflet, reducing the image to that of a soiled oriental Mr Happy. A contingent of white-robed figures sitting a few rows back had puzzled her at first, their bright ribbons and cloaks unfamiliar to any ecclesiastical order that she knew of, until the woman sitting next to her had noticed her gaze and given her a nudge. 'They're just a lay society,' the pilgrim had confided. 'Knights of the Holy Sepulchre they call themselves. We often see them at Lourdes.'

She and Ben were fortunate enough to be seated close to the recently erected altar-piece, its platform raised five feet above the ground so that all the congregation could witness the ceremony; a young priest, acting as usher and who knew Sue as a voluntary helper, had made the pilgrims shuffle along the bench until there was room for her and her son. The only reserved area was the benches in front of her and that was now filled with a mixture of clergy, nuns and 'civilians', some of whom in the latter group she recognized. The man called Southworth was one and she could see him chatting and laughing quietly with Bishop Caines, giving the impression that they were waiting for an open-air concert to begin rather than a holy service.

Across the centre aisle from her a wide area had been left clear for stretchers and wheelchairs; members of the St John's Ambulance Brigade, crisply-dressed young women who were obviously private nurses, and relatives of the invalids, sat on benches directly behind them. The Press had been given no special privileges, apart from being allowed early entry, and most had managed to find places near the front where they grouped together, some with notebooks poised, others who had seen it all before (though nothing quite like this, they had to admit) passing wry comments and wondering if it would be sacrilege to smoke. Cameramen were squeezed onto ends of benches, and many squatted on the grass in the central aisle, having already been moved back from directly beneath the altar. Television cameras had not been allowed inside the grounds, but cranes leered over the tall hedge along the roadside, zoom-lenses focused on the twisted oak tree and the simply decorated rostrum before it.

From certain sections of the congregation voices raised in gentle hymn could be heard; the chanting drone of prayers came from other groups.

Sue was tense and she sensed the people around her felt the same. If anything, the excitement that Sunday was at a higher pitch than on the previous week. The expectancy had somehow increased. Even Ben's eyes were shining, his usual boredom with just 'hanging around' not voiced, nor even hinted at. He was cold, but she felt his shivering was more akin to hers than to the chill; it was pure exhilaration, a feeling shared with everyone present. There was a sudden hush, and then a low, wondrous moan rippled through the crowd. Alice had been seen emerging through a newly-created opening in the church's boundary wall.

Molly Pagett held her daughter's hand and the Reverend Mother from the convent led the way to the seats in front of the altar. There was white apprehension on Molly's face, yet Alice was expressionless, her gaze only on the tree, not once looking at the crowds who watched her with reverent awe. Total silence descended.

Ben jumped to his feet, anxious to see what the grown-ups could see, but was too small to get a clear look over the heads and shoulders in front. Before his mother could stop him he clambered onto the bench. He saw Alice and was unimpressed.

Fenn descended the short flight of steps, careful not to slip on the moss-slimed surfaces, and inserted the long key into the door's rusted lock. Surprisingly, the key turned easily. He pushed open the door and stood there for a few seconds, allowing his eyes to become accustomed to the gloom inside, remembering the old TV programme he used to watch as a very young kid. 'Inner Sanctum' it had been called, and the credits each week always began with an old crypt door slowly swinging open, the creaking sound classically drawn out. He'd had bad dreams about that door and the unknown thing that lay beyond, but morning had always brushed the memory aside like a hand sweeping back a drape. Only now it was morning and this wasn't a dream. A damp, musty smell lurched out to greet him.

He smiled at his own nervousness. Delgard had assured him that St Joseph's no longer kept its dead below stairs.

His hand groped around the wall just inside the door, feeling for the light switch, He found it, clicked it down.

'Wonderful,' he muttered. The poor light barely reached the chamber's four walls.

He moved in and felt a fresh – no, a dank – coldness creeping under his skin. Something scuttled away into some dark recess. Cardboard boxes littered the floor. An old table with heavy Michelin legs and battered surface stood in the centre, a wooden, paint-blotched ladder leaning like an inebriate against it. Other grey shapes loitered just beyond the circle of light.

Fenn looked around, hoping to find the chest without searching. A low, squarish object covered by a dust sheet caught his eye and he cautiously headed towards it. The floor was uneven and his shoes became wet as he walked through puddles that had formed in the dips. He squatted and reached towards the mildewy cover.

Monsignor Delgard turned to the congregation, his large hands resting on either side of the lectern, eyes looking into the expanse of expectant faces rather than the missal before him. He drew in a sharp breath, his stooped shoulders almost straightening.

Dear God, there are thousands, *thousands.*

Why have they come here? What do they want of the child?

His heart grieved for the sick among them, the cripples and invalids who regarded him with shining eyes, with lips that were parted, smiles of anticipation lightening their haunted features. Oh dear Lord, please help them in their faith; don't let disappointment taint it. What happened before with the child cannot be repeated, they must realize that. Let today be the end of all this! Show them there are no miracles here.

The two microphones skilfully fitted into the lectern whined disconcertingly for a few moments.

A small breeze licked at the pages of the missal.

The emotions of the congregation seemed to sweep over him in euphoric waves and his head felt light with its directed energy. Flushed faces spread out before him, pink pebbles on an undulating beach, reaching back, beyond the point where there were no more benches, the change in level resembling a tide-caused step, stretching to the entrance of the field, the high hedges that bordered the road a green, containing sea wall. It's madness, he told himself. A foolish delusion in which the Catholic Church should take no part. Bishop Caines was smiling encouragingly below him. Southworth had his head turned, watching the crowds. There were many other priests out there, their presence giving credence to the deception. But no, there was no deception! Alice Pagett was a sincere child! There could be no deep, grievous sin on her young soul. Perhaps it was he, the priest, who was in sin with this doubt, this refusal to accept that which he himself had witnessed. Perhaps he lacked the humility to believe that a child could evoke such spiritual power. Perhaps . . .

He raised his hands to shoulder level, palms outwards, and began the service. Alice was watching him intently, her eyes staring yet somehow glazed, expressionless, looking right through him . . . looking . . . looking not at him . . . but at the tree . . .

The cover felt clammy to his touch and Fenn had to force himself to grip the material and pull it away. A wooden box lay beneath and tiny black things fled across its surface from the exposing light. He knew immediately that it wasn't the chest he sought – it was too small and not ancient enough – but decided to open it anyway; the relevant documents might well have been transferred to it some time in the past. There was no lock; he lifted the lid.

Swirling dust particles caused him to sneeze and he looked down at the old books and papers with watery eyes. The lid fell backwards as he reached inside and grabbed a book. It was a well-worn Parish Mass Book, the words inside in Latin. Dead. Defunct. Only to be used by religious diehards since the Vatican had decided that modern-day native language was flavour-of-the-month. The book beneath was the same, the one below the one beneath also the same; the box was full of them. The papers were yellowing hymn sheets, nothing more. He closed the lid, disappointed. That would have been too easy.

Fenn stood and, hands on hips, scanned the underground chamber once more. Christ, it was cold! He moved to the centre, the light bulb, with its heavy metal shade, just six inches above his head and casting black shadows beneath his brow and nose. Two insects flickered around the light, unknowingly seeking death in their personal sun.

How many ancient bones were beneath this floor? Fenn wondered. Pagan bones, heathen remains. Did their spirits linger when their bodies were done? He realized he was spooking himself unnecessarily and mentally kicked his own shin. Get on with it, Fenn, and then get out!

He followed his own advice and strode over to a pile of boxes behind a stack of chairs in one corner of the crypt, whistling tunelessly as he began pulling at them. A quick look-through should suffice, no need to examine anything too closely, it was an old chest he was after, quite big, too big to hide itself away easily. A discarded radiator, disturbed by his searching, began to slither down the wall it had been leaning against; it crashed to the floor with a thunderous clang, the noise echoing off the damp stone walls.

Fenn froze, shoulders hunched, until the reverberations died away. Sorry, he apologized to the ghosts, then continued looking.

He went over to the grey shapes that had been silently watching throughout. They stood like stunted spectres, and he winced at their disfigurements as he drew close. There were four of them and two still had some faded colour left in their chipped plaster clothes; the other two had begun life as white, but now were almost as black as the darkness around them. You've got a pal upstairs who'll be joining you soon, he silently told them, thinking of the crazy-paved Madonna. The nearest was a noseless/chinless Christ, who appeared to be holding something in one curled arm; its other arm was broken off at the elbow. Fenn bent slightly, curious to see what was the strange looking object he held. 'Nice,' he murmured when he discovered it was a stone heart with a little cross protruding from the top like a faded strawberry stalk.

The statue behind was taller, its surface discoloured and grimy. This one was presumably a sculpture of Jesus too, although, without a head and just part of a beard above a ravaged neck, it was hard to tell. The next was as small as the first and its form was slightly bent, the man depicted carrying a child on his shoulders. The staff was missing and both faces, the child's and the bearer's, had been mutilated, but Fenn easily guessed it was St Christopher and the Christ-boy.

He turned quickly towards the light as it dimmed momentarily. 'Don't you bloody dare,' he snapped. It grew bright instantly.

Fenn returned his attention to the damaged statues. There was something familiar about the one at the very back. He narrowed his eyes, wishing the light were stronger; the metal lampshade cutting out half its beam didn't help much either. Squeezing past the first statue, he peered between the two blocking his way. The face that stared back sightlessly was the same as the face upstairs in the church. It was Mary and she looked serene.

He frowned in puzzlement. From across the chamber, this

figure had looked in as bad shape as the others, soiled, cracked and parts missing; it must just have been the poor light throwing deceptive shadows, for no mutilations or grime were evident that close. He tried to get nearer; there was something about the blind staring eyes . . .

Resting one hand on the headless statue to his right, he leaned forward. The white face was smiling. And he had the uncanny feeling that the eyes could see him. His other hand touched the St Christopher and the child-burdened figure wobbled dangerously. He steadied the statue and eased his body closer to the shadowy Virgin. It had to be a trick of the light: the smile on the stone lips seemed to have broadened. He blinked. They seemed to have parted, too.

There was a numbness in his mind as though pain freezer had been sprayed onto certain brain cells. The pupil-less eyes were mesmerizing. Fenn's breathing was shallow, but he hardly noticed. He had to get closer, had to touch the statue, had to touch those parted lips.

The light was dimming. Or did it appear to be, because he could only focus on those moist lips, those piercing eyes? There was a faint sputtering noise behind, but he barely registered the sound or noticed the flicker.

He was only a foot, perhaps just inches away, and he could get no further; the other two statues held him in check. He stretched forward, craning his neck towards the soft lips, the two guardians beginning to tilt.

He could not move any nearer, but just before the light disappeared, the statue of Mary moved towards him.

PRIEST My brothers and sisters,
to prepare ourselves to celebrate the sacred mysteries
let us call to mind our sins.

The wind stirred headscarves and banners and ruffled the hair on uncovered heads. People coughed above the silence. Somewhere a baby howled.

PRIEST	Lord, we have sinned against you: Lord have mercy.
RESPONSE	Lord, have mercy.

On top of a crane overlooking the field, a cameraman looked quizzically at his machine.

'Hey, what's going on down there?' he shouted, heedless of the Mass in progress. 'The power's fluctuating. Do something before the whole thing's messed up!'

PRIEST	Lord, show us your mercy and love.
RESPONSE	And grant us your salvation.

A press cameraman quietly cursed the motor on his Nikon. 'What a bloody time to pack up.' He didn't notice that several of his colleagues were having the same problem.

PRIEST	May almighty God have mercy on us, forgive us our sins, and bring us to everlasting life.
RESPONSE	Amen.

A woman reporter who had been quietly talking into her micro-cassette recorder shook it impatiently when the cogs slowly stopped turning. 'Fuck,' she cursed, keeping her voice low, and smacking the machine against the palm of her hand.

PRIEST	Lord, have mercy.
RESPONSE	Lord, have mercy.
PRIEST	Christ, have mercy.
RESPONSE	Christ, have mercy.
PRIEST	Lord, have—

Monsignor Delgard clapped his hands to his ears as the microphones shrieked violently, then went dead.

Through half-closed eyes he saw Alice rise from the bench and come towards him.

The statues on either side of Fenn crashed to the floor and he fell with them. He cried out, suddenly aware he was in total darkness, the smashing of stone joining the cry. Something crushed his fingers, but the pain was hardly felt. A heavy weight fell on his shoulders, bearing him down, stunning him with the blow. Instinctively he tried to roll away and something to his right prevented him. He thrashed out, terribly afraid, remembering the Madonna statue, how it had moved, how it had wanted him . . . the desire in her eyes . . .

'No!' he shouted, his voice ringing around the corrupt-smelling chamber, and the sound increased his panic. He kicked out, pushed, shoved, heaved. The statue was unreasonably heavy, pressing hard against him. He managed to half-turn and his hand grasped at the cold stone. It was wet with slime and his fingers slid along its surface; at points his hand ran into what could only have been lichen but which felt like soft, rotting flesh.

He could almost feel hot, fetid breath warming his skin.

Fenn managed to pass an arm beneath the cumbersome weight and roared as he pushed. The statue slowly slithered off his body; a grating noise as it hit the floor. He turned, elbows beneath him, gasping in the foul air, his chest heaving. He had to get out, the very darkness was closing in! Reason told him the cellar was filled with dead, inanimate things; imagination insisted they could move, could breathe, could see. Could touch.

His feet slipped in wetness as he scrabbled to rise. He

blinked against the blackness, afraid he would be smothered by it. The doorway, there was grey daylight coming from the doorway. He had to reach it.

He began to crawl, over dead, mutilated figures, through the sticky puddles formed on the uneven floor like stagnant underground lakes, knocking aside boxes, anything that got in his way, trying to gain his feet but still too unsteady, desperate to reach the light, desperate to get away from cold, lifeless fingers that stretched towards him from the darkness . . .

Only the light could return those fingers to stone. But now there was a shadow in that grey rectangle of open doorway, a mass of blackness that devoured the light as it moved closer to Fenn. As it reached out to him.

There were no more sounds from the crowd; no more coughs, no more children wailing, no more mumbled prayers. It was as if the thousands present were holding their breath as one. Even though only those nearest the raised platform could see what was happening, some mass-consciousness sent the tension eddying around the congregation like widening ripples on a disturbed pond. They held their breath and looked towards the centre-piece.

Then a hushed coalescent 'aaaah' escaped them as the tiny figure of the child mounted the steps to the altar. Wonder and excitement brimmed in their eyes. The television cameramen, on top of their cranes, could only groan with frustration at the untimely breakdown of their generator, none of them aware that their rivals were experiencing the same problem. A policeman outside the gate, and oblivious to what was taking place inside, could only frown at the static from his hand-radio as he tried to call in reinforcements. The crowds were fast becoming uncontrollable as they tried to push their way through the jammed entrance to the field.

Delgard felt his legs trembling as the rapturous little face approached him up the steps. She was so tiny and so frail, and her eyes saw something that was visible to no one else. Alice passed him and his body drained of vitality as though she were a strange spiritual magnet attracting energy. He swayed and had to reach for the lectern to steady himself. The oak tree rose up behind the altar, a black twisted giant, a looming creature that seemed to beckon the child.

Alice's eyes half-closed when she stood before the tree, white slits only showing between the lids. Her face slowly tilted upwards as if she were looking into the upper branches and a smile drew back over white teeth. Her yellow hair fell low between her shoulders and her hands rose away from her sides, ready to embrace. Her breathing came in short, sharp gasps, quickening so that her chest moved rapidly, gradually slowing, becoming even, deep, steady. Stopping.

The air shimmered around her and the clouds seemed blacker overhead. But then the sun broke through and the field, the altar, the tree, were bathed in a pure light.

Alice slowly turned to face her spellbound audience, her small body trembling, shivering with some inner ecstasy which the onlookers could feel growing within themselves.

Alice suddenly gasped as though an invisible blade had pricked her flesh; the smile remained, though, and became even more serene. And now the crowd gasped as she began to rise into the air.

'Fenn, what the hell is the matter with you?'

He stopped struggling, stopped trying to kick himself away

from the figure stooping over him. His mind began to clear, although the panic still remained. 'Who . . . who is it?' he asked, voice shaking.

'Who the shit do you think it is, you idiot? It's me, Nancy.' She reached down for him again and this time her hand wasn't slapped away.

'Nancy?'

'Yeah, remember? The *friend* you unloaded at the church gate.'

He scrabbled to his feet and she had to hold him back as he tried to break for the door.

'Take it easy,' she snapped. 'There's a lot of junk lying around here – you'll break your goddam neck.' Nancy kept her arm through his, restraining him as they made for the open door. The last few steps were too much for him; he tore himself loose and rushed through. She found him leaning against the church wall outside, a stream of saliva running from his mouth as though he had just been retching.

She gave him a few more moments to recover, then said, 'You gonna tell me what happened down there?'

His shoulders heaved as he tried to regain his breath.

'I was on the other side of the wall,' Nancy said, concerned at his condition. 'I just caught a glimpse of you through the graveyard going down the steps to the door back there. It took me a little time to sneak over without the holy mafia stopping me.' Her voice softened. 'What happened, Fenn? You look as though you've seen the proverbial ghost.'

He let out a long sigh and turned to her. His eyes were watery. He said breathlessly, 'I . . . I . . . think I may have.'

Nancy chuckled and, now that he was outside in the day-light, in the open air, it seemed almost ridiculous to himself. Only *he* had been there; *he* had seen it. 'There . . . there was a figure . . .'

'You mean a statue. I heard the crash when you knocked it over, only it sounded like more than one.'

'There were four of them. But one . . . one at the back, the one of Mary wasn't. It wasn't a statue. It moved.'

'Hey, Fenn, are you serious? You just bumped into it and it toppled. I saw you from the doorway scrabbling around like a maniac. Why were you stumbling around in the dark anyway?'

'There was a light. It must have blown.'

'Yeah, scaring you to death when it did. That must have been when you tripped and knocked over the statues.' She chuckled again. 'Nice going.'

He shook his head; it all seemed so unreal.

'What were you looking for?' Her eyes were sharp, the amusement gone.

'Uh? Oh, a chest, an old chest we thought might be down there. It could have some early church records inside.'

'Let's go back and see if we can find it.'

She turned away and Fenn grabbed her arm. 'No, it's not there, I would have seen it.'

'Sure you're not just chicken?'

'I would have seen it!'

'Okay, okay, I believe you. Look, the service has already started, so let's get over there before we miss too much. You never know, it might just be another miracle day.' She took his hand and pulled him away from the wall. 'You're shaking,' she said in surprise, stopping to face him squarely. 'Jesus, you were really frightened.'

'I'll be okay in a minute.' But would he be okay when it was time to close his eyes and sleep?

'Sure.' Nancy touched fingertips to his cheek. 'Take it easy for a moment. We'll take a slow walk to the field.' She led him away from the church, away from the black hole in its side that was the crypt. Every so often, she sneaked a look at his face and frowned. She could understand his fright, his crashing around down there in the dark; it had scared *her*, for Chrissakes, just hearing the racket! Tripping through the graveyard with its crusty old tombs and toppling slabs had made her uneasy even though it was broad daylight. The little mountains of earth scattered around didn't lighten the atmosphere, either. By the time she'd reached the steps leading down into what looked like a murky pit, she was more than a little edgy! It was only because she thought Fenn had fallen and hurt himself that she had ventured inside. Still, scary or not, he was panicked to a ridiculous degree. Strange, he hadn't seemed the type to be scared of bogeymen.

Something felt wrong as they neared the recently-created gap in the low boundary wall, and Nancy couldn't quite figure just what. Fenn was too preoccupied with his own thoughts to notice. It dawned on her slowly as they drew nearer to the field. It was the silence. In a nine or ten acre plot crammed full with people, there was total, blanket silence.

She came to a halt and Fenn looked up in surprise. He, too, finally noticed the absence of sound. When they looked towards the raised altar they understood.

Monsignor Delgard sank to his knees, one hand still grasping the top of the lectern. Those watching, those who could tear their eyes off the child hovering five feet in the air, would have thought it was a gesture of homage and not just a sapping weakness in the priest's limbs. The altar-servers, who had been kneeling just moments before, were now half-sitting, half-lying on the platform, arms and elbows outstretched to support them.

Delgard's eyes felt misted; it was like watching the girl

through a fine veil. He wiped his free hand across his brow, his arm leaden with its own weight, and told himself that what he saw was impossible. He wasn't dreaming though, she was there above him, her face still tilted towards the sky, her arms slightly outstretched, the breeze ruffling her skirt. His lips moved in silent prayer.

One by one, the momentum gathering, people began to slip from their mats onto their knees, their action one of worship and not involuntary. Soon it was like a vast moving wave as the reaction spread, the shuffling sound curiously muted. There were tears on the faces of many, smiling adoration on the faces of others; some had to close their eyes against the glare that emanated from the girl, while others only saw a tiny, still form that appeared to glimmer and fade in their vision. All were humbled by the miracle child.

Delgard tried to rise and the strength just wasn't there. He watched open-mouthed as Alice bowed her head and her eyes, her gloriously blue eyes, opened fully. She smiled. And slowly, singularly, many of those who had been lying on stretchers on the ground or who had sat helplessly in wheelchairs raised themselves to stagger and leap towards the altar. They gathered there, supporting each other, faces looking upwards, their eyes beseeching, a growing cluster of shattered, shrivelled bodies. Quiet, throaty murmurs came from them as they praised the child and the Madonna for what they felt was happening to them.

There was a sudden cry as a man with a hideously swollen and marked face pushed his way through the throng of invalids and collapsed on the steps leading up to the altar.

He stretched out a wavering arm and implored, 'Help me! Help meeeeee . . .' the sound dying in a high-pitched moan. His uplifted hand shot to his face and he screamed; when he took his hand away, bubbles of pus were bursting from his cheeks, mouth and chin.

Only Ben, who could see clearly, for he stood while others knelt, could not understand what was happening.

29

'How do you?' she chirped. 'I'm so glad it isn't yesterday, aren't you?'

Eleanor H. Porter, *Pollyanna*

Riordan carefully closed the door to the cowshed, not wanting to disturb the creatures inside; they were tetchy enough already. He crossed the yard, making for the back door of the farmhouse, lights from the windows guiding him towards the warmth within. He shook his head and mumbled something under his breath. Times were hard enough without livestock playing up. He stopped for a moment, listening, coldness clamping tightly around him like a blood-pressure cuff around an arm. That bloody dog was howling again like a banshee in the night. It was the usual mutt, old Fairman's, starting it all off. His own, Biddy, would be next, then the Rixbys' in the house further down the road. Three nights they'd been at it and there wasn't even a full moon for them to be making a fuss of! As if on cue, his labrador, Biddy, began to whine and then to howl from inside the house.

Mebbe it was that floodlight they kept on all night in the field yonder. It looked eerie enough, the way it lit up that blasted oak; mebbe Fairman's animal could see the glare from its kennel, the light being unfamiliar en'all. Riordan had never liked the tree when he had owned the field it stood in, although he had never understood why – it was just ugly, he supposed – but the field was only used for grazing so the oak was doing no harm, wasn't worth bothering with. Still, the land belonged to the Church now, and a nice price they'd paid for it. Why they thought a dead oak was special just because a little girl was doing some peculiar things in front of it, he couldn't fathom. But it was a bloody nuisance having it lit up like that, scaring the dogs.

He heard his wife cursing Biddy inside the house, shouting for the animal to keep quiet. Some chance once she'd started.

And it was a bloody nuisance having all those people clomping through the field on Sundays! That's what his cattle were afeared of; they kept well away from that area, cowering at the far side of their own field as if they thought the crowd might harm them, rolling their eyes at him when he came to herd them in, trembling as though there was thunder in the air.

He stood in the middle of his yard looking back past the covered silage pit and machinery store, studying the beam of light cutting through the indigo blue sky two fields away. Somehow it made even him feel uncomfortable. It was a silvery intruder, unfamiliar and unwelcome, disturbing the stability of the country night. He looked up at the stars, the sky clear, no clouds to smother the shimmering clusters; yet there was thunder in the air, an electricity that made his senses tingle. It was unearthly and he didn't like it, not one little bit. When dogs howled at night it was usually a forewarning of death; tonight, standing there alone in the yard, coldness and darkness embracing him like sisters of oppression, he felt the howling was a warning of something more. Much more.

Oh bloody hell, not more trouble! He studiously finished filling the pint glass, ignoring the raucous voices from the other end of the bar for the moment. He took the money for the round, rang it up, then casually sauntered towards the source of trouble, sighing wearily when he saw it was three locals who were causing the disturbance.

He was a big man, though not a rough one, and his mere arrival on the scene of trouble was usually enough to pacify even the most belligerent of customers. He'd had to make his presence felt twice the night before, and once (unfortunately to no avail) the night before that. While he appreciated the extra trade all the publicity had brought in, the aggravation that came with it wasn't so welcome. The White Hart had always been a peaceful pub – at least, relatively so – and he intended to keep it that way.

'All right, lads, keep it down now.'

They regarded him resentfully but, he thought, respectfully. The glass that whistled past his head had no respect at at. He could only stare after the three figures, stunned, as they pushed their way through the crowded bar and disappeared outside, an obscenity their goodnight bidding.

All conversation had ceased when the glass shattered against the optics behind the bar, and now the customers stood watching the tall barman, as surprised as he. A barmaid rushed forward to mop up the spilt beer and pick up the broken glass; the barman could only shake his head in bewilderment.

'What's got into everybody?' he said and his customers could only shake their heads in sympathy. Conversation returned, a trickle breaking into a flood, and the barman turned his back on the bar and poured himself a double Scotch, breaking his own rule never to drink before ten o'clock. Those three are barred, he told himself sullenly. He had never known them to cause trouble before, but he was sure as hell they would never cause trouble in there again. What was Banfield coming to? It had been alive, buoyant, over the past few weeks, but the mood seemed to be changing. At night there seemed to be a heaviness hanging over the village, like in summer when broody black clouds lay low and threatening; yet the air outside was oddly crisp and there were no clouds.

He gulped the Scotch, pulling a face, but grateful for the sudden rush of warmth.

'You promised, you bastard!'

Tucker put up a stubby hand as if to soothe her temper, his eyes staying on the road ahead.

'It's early days yet, Paula,' he said placatingly. 'I don't know if the plans are going to go through yet.'

'You know, you bastard. Everything's going through now! Everything!'

'No, no, we have to wait for the District Council to give the go-ahead and you know how slow they are. And even if they granted planning permission, it'd take another year to have a supermarket built, maybe more.'

'You said you were going to buy out a couple of shops in the High Street and knock them into one.'

'I would have, but no one's selling now there's likely to be a boom on.' That wasn't true, for he'd put in tentative offers for two shops side-by-side, the owners ageing and fearful of extra trade rather than eager for it. No point in mentioning it to Paula until the sale was a certainty. What a pain in the bloody arse she was becoming!

'Even so, even if you build a new supermarket, why can't you say yes to me running the old one? At least I'll know where I stand.'

'Paula, there's a lot more to running—'

'You promised!'

The XJS swerved as she punched his arm.

'For fuck's sake, Paula, what's wrong with you? You'll have us off the road.'

He squealed as she lunged for the wheel. 'Paula!' Pushing her back with one hand and steering the car with the other, he silently cursed the day he had got involved with her. He'd misjudged Paula, he realized. She was dumb, but she was conniving, too. The Jaguar slowed down and he pulled off the main highway into a side road. He stopped the car, switched off the engine and lights. 'Now look, pet—' he began to say.

'You don't care about me! You just want me for one thing!'

True enough, he thought. 'Don't be daft. You know how much I think of you.'

'You don't care! What have you ever given me?'

'There were those earrings at Christmas—'

'Bastard! You don't even know what I'm talking about.'

Although the car was stationary, his hands still gripped the wheel and his eyes still watched the road ahead. A frantic bird or bat fluttered darkly across the windscreen. His grip stiffened and his words came out through tight lips. 'Just tell me what you *are* talking about, Paula.'

'I'm talking about my life! Me! My future! I've helped you – your business and *you*. I've worked for you night and day, never complained . . .'

His eyes rolled upwards.

'. . . always been there when you needed me. I've always

been available, for business or pleasure. I've given up so much for you.'

'What are you bloody talking about? I've given you a bloody good job, I've given you presents, I've taken you out—'

'To a sodding motel! That's just about your mark! And you give better presents to your wife! I've seen her parading round the village in her stinking fur coat and jewellery!'

'You want a fur coat, I'll give you a fur coat!'

'I don't want a fucking fur coat! I want something more!'

'Just tell me what!'

'I want the supermarket!'

There was an astonished silence in the car for a few moments. Then he said disbelievingly, 'You want the supermarket.'

She turned her head away.

'You want the bloody supermarket?' His voice had risen several octaves. 'You're fucking mad!'

'I don't want all of it, just part. I want to be a partner.' Her voice had sunk several octaves.

Tucker was just as incredulous. 'And how d'you suppose I'd explain that away to Marcia?'

'You could tell her you need a partner for business.'

'Need a partner? You? You must be fucking joking!' He tried to laugh, but it came out as a dry, rasping sound in his throat. 'You're a good screw, Paula, and not bad with figures and ordering stock. But running a business – actually running a business – and being a partner? I love your snatch, darling, but I don't worship it. You can take a running fucking jump!'

She was on him, scratching, clawing, punching, grabbing his hair, spitting on him, screaming at him. Tucker tried to grab her wrists, but her arms flailed at him viciously, hysterically.

'Paula!'

The car was rocking with her strength.

'Paula!'

'I'll tell her, you bastard! I'll tell her everything! You're not treating me like a piece of dirt! She's going to know everything, you bastard!'

'Paula!'

His hands found her throat and the fit was snug, pleasing. He squeezed.

'You bastard, I'm going to—'

Oh, that was good! That was keeping her quiet! Her neck was soft, mushy. He could feel the beginnings of an erection. Yes, that *was* good!

'You . . . you . . .'

It was dark, but he could see the whiteness of her eyes, and he could smell her fear. Try to blackmail him, would she? Thought I was that stupid, did she? Stupid of her, fat slug of a cow! Muscles in her neck were trying to resist the pressure and that felt good too; he wanted it to take time.

Her hands were on his chest, squeezing the fat there, and even that wasn't unpleasant. In fact it was rather nice.

He could see her tongue beginning to protrude from the whiteness of her face, like a beak hatching from an eggshell. Now a funny sound was coming from her, a whining, gurgling noise. That's better, you bitch, that's better than all those nasty, blackmailing words. That was a much sweeter sound. He increased the pressure. Funny how small a neck can become when you squeeze hard enough. Probably one hand could go round it at the death . . .

. . . at the death . . .

Oh my God, what am I doing?

'Paula!'

He released her throat and she fell away like a rag doll.

'Paula, I'm sorry, I'm sorry . . .'

Her eyes were staring at him and there were still gurgling noises coming from her.

He leaned towards her. 'I didn't mean . . .'

She cried out, but the sound was still strange, as though still squeezed from a flattened aperture. He touched her arm and she flinched violently. What had he been trying to do, what had come over him?

He tried to touch her again and this time she thrashed out wildly. Tucker jumped back, fingernails raking his cheek before he was out of reach. She was scrabbling around, searching for the door-lock. She found it, pushed the door open, the light exposing rounded buttocks as she tumbled from the car. She lay in the road, the squealing sounds still coming from her and he reached over the automatic column shift, his own eyes now wide with fear.

'Paula!' he said yet again.

She was on her knees, tights torn by rough concrete. She staggered to her feet, was running, stumbling, gasping for breath.

'Paula!' he called after her. 'Don't tell anyone . . .'

She was gone, swallowed by the night, and he sat there for a long time afterwards, door closed, in his own cocoon of darkness, wondering what had come over him, why he had tried to strangle her. It just wasn't like him.

Southworth closed the accounts book, a smile of satisfaction twisting his lips. He flexed his narrow shoulders and placed his elbows on the desk, steepled fingers resting against his chin. Then his smile broadened and he relaxed back into the chair.

Everything was going well, marvellously well. Banfield had

changed almost overnight, the merchants flushed with new trade as tourists poured in, the pubs and restaurants packed tight each day and night. And his hotel had been overbooked since the miracles had begun. Morale in the village was high, the excitement sending waves of adrenalin coursing through its inhabitants, bringing them alert again, the sluggish burden of decline thrown off. All this achieved in just under two months, an incredible escalation of events, miraculous in that context alone.

In the coming months, when the clerics had stopped their predictable dithering and the shrine had become truly established, trade would increase tenfold, for pilgrims would journey from all over the world to see the scene of the Visitation. Southworth was already negotiating with the village's only travel agent, a small concern whose revenue had been slowly sinking with the country's economy, to form a new partnership. 'St Joseph's Tours' was to be the title of their joint venture, Southworth himself supplying the capital (his credit was particularly good with the bank these days) to buy a fleet of coaches which would cover the British Isles, the agent's connections abroad helping to form alliances with other, foreign, travel companies. Such a partnership, apart from the obvious financial gain in the tourist business itself, would prove extremely beneficial to his own hotel trade.

Soon work would begin on a new hotel, one that was more modern, easier to run and geared for a fast turnover. There were other properties, also, that he secretly owned in Banfield, shops that he had acquired cheaply over the years when their owners had given up trying to make a decent living in the lacklustre village, bought by him under a company name, his solicitor handling all negotiations so that no one else knew who the true purchaser was, not even – *especially* not even – his fellow members of the parish council. The tenants he leased the properties out to would have something of a shock when their rents were doubled, probably trebled, within the next few months. They could hardly appeal, not with the way business would be booming, and if they refused to pay, well then, there would be plenty of others eager to move in. And their rents would be even higher.

Southworth rose from the desk and walked to the drinks cabinet. He reached for the sherry bottle, then changed his mind and took out the brandy. The brandy glass chimed pleasantly as the bottle touched its lip. He sipped slowly, pleased with himself, pleased he had been the first to see the opportunity and seize upon it.

Father Hagan had been a problem, the bishop much more susceptible to Southworth's persuasion; but then Bishop Caines had his own private ambitions. Of course, Southworth regretted the priest's untimely death, but it had meant the removal of what could have proved to be a minor stumbling block. Yet would he really have? Bishop Caines, a shrewd politician as well as a respected man of the cloth, would surely have stepped in and gently eased the doubting priest from the situation. In fact, in his many private discussions with Southworth, the bishop had hinted that Father Hagan might soon need a long rest, the fuss much too draining for a man of such ill-health. Monsignor Delgard, a priest who had much experience of what might be termed as 'phenomena', would have acted as both investigator and overseer. Southworth knew the bishop had no other choice but to send in a man with such unique qualifications and he wondered how skilfully he had balanced his briefing to Delgard. Scepticism well to the fore, no doubt, but with enough receptiveness for a message from God to keep Delgard's mind open. And now nobody, *nobody* could deny the miracles.

On Sunday, before thousands and thousands (*eight to ten*

thousand, it had been estimated, had travelled to St Joseph's, most of whom had not been able to get into the field for the service) more miracles had been performed. None could yet be confirmed, of course, for they could have just been temporary improvements, the sufferers deluded by their own hysteria: the boy whose condition was known as postencephalitic dementia (brain damage caused by a virus infection) could just be experiencing a brief spell of normality; the young girl whose asthma was an almost constant companion and whose attacks could send her close to death, might find it returned within a week or two; the man whose multiple sclerosis confined him to a wheelchair might find that nerve tissues had not been impossibly regenerated and he would soon need his wheelchair again. There were others, many others, some trivial, some literally deadly serious, the victims claiming they 'felt better' or that they felt 'uplifted'. There was one case, though, that was indisputable.

A certain man had come alone to the field next to St Joseph's, a man who, through shame, had kept his face hidden from the crowd. His lower jaw, lips and nose had been infested with open sores and scabs, much of the flesh eaten away. Lupus was the medical term for the condition; tuberculosis of the face. Standing below Alice, whose small body had risen into the air (there were those among the vast congregation who swore they had *not* seen her rise, but these were far away, some near the back, and their view would have been impaired), the man's face had suddenly begun to blister, the scabs falling away and the sores closing upon themselves. His face had healed in full view of all those present, for he had turned to the crowd so that they could witness the miracle. By the end of the service (completed with such incredible emotion, the child taking her place back among the congregation, her face white, skin taut) the deep pits in the man's flesh were being covered by rapidly-growing skin. The most cynical of men could not repudiate what had physically happened in front of thousands.

Even Monsignor Delgard could not reject such an astounding thing.

Southworth returned to his desk, taking the brandy with him. He sat, his mind alive with the new prospects that the Miracle Girl had opened up for him. That was *his* miracle: the revitalization of his own expectations. The Southworth name would not sink with Banfield into the mire of obscurity but, like the village, would again become a name to be noted, would enhance its centuries-old heritage. The village would grow, and he, his name, his wealth, would grow with it.

He raised the glass to lips and wondered why an awful instinctive fear had begun to nag at these happy thoughts.

The priest rose wearily from his kneeling position by the bed, his compline, the last prayer of the day, completed. His knee-joints cracked with the effort and he stretched his stiff back, feeling old, spent. He turned and sat on the edge of the bed, too tired for the moment to go through the before-bed toiletries. A hand that trembled slightly brushed against his forehead as if it could wipe away the weariness. There had not been many times in his life that he had felt this depleted; usually it had followed particularly wearing exorcisms – rare occasions but not as rare as some people might think – and times when he had witnessed the world at its most dreadful – Biafra, Bangladesh, Ethiopia. At the age of twenty-one he had helped in the aftermath of Nagasaki, and perhaps that was worst of all; the nuclear weapon exemplified man at his most potent and most loathsome. It was at those times that his spiritual being had sagged, then plummeted to despairing depths awash with hopelessness; but the human spirit had a buoyancy of its own. On each occasion, though, the upward journey took longer, the years and events making the burden more cumbersome. But why the spiritual fatigue now?

Father Hagan had not needed to speak of it before he died; it was evident in his appearance, the weariness of his soul reflected in his lustreless eyes. Why was this depression hovering over the church, over the house? Why, when the sick were being miraculously cured, when a dramatic religious interest, perhaps even revival, was spreading throughout the country and, it was reported, throughout the world, was he so afraid? The Episcopal Council had convened that very day to question Alice further and the child had remained calmly resolute in her conviction that she had conversed with Mary. Why the miracles? they had asked. And why did the Mother of God choose to appear to her, a mere child? What had Alice done to receive such grace? And what was the purpose of the Visitations? Alice had just one answer to all the questions: the Lady would reveal the purpose in time; now was too soon to know.

It was an unsatisfactory reply.

The bishops had been divided, some believing the child really had received a divine vision, others claiming there was no evidence at all that the visions had been divine. It was still too early for the cures to be claimed miraculous and, as for the levitation, it was an illusion that could be seen in theatres all over the world. When it was argued that Alice could not possibly have used trickery in front of so many people and in such an open setting, it was counter-argued that Indian fakirs also performed such feats in similar circumstances with the use of mass hypnosis. To strengthen their claim, those churchmen who were 'anti', stressed that not everyone present had seen Alice levitate, and furthermore, not one television or still camera had recorded the phenomenon. It seemed their mechanisms had been mysteriously interfered with; only blank film had emerged. That in itself, those 'pro' claimed, was evidence of paranormal influences at work. Quite, the others scoffed, but that did not deem it holy. The debate had gone on late into the evening with no conclusions drawn. The bishops would reconvene tomorrow, in London, and the inquiry would continue until some kind of official proclamation could be given to an impatient world, although it would be a carefully-worded avoidance of any specific acknowledgement by the Church.

Delgard was puzzled by the failure of the cameras and the lectern microphones, wondering if it was linked in some way with his own sapping of energy that Sunday. He had fallen to his knees with the weakness that had come over him and those in near proximity had done the same, although they might now claim they were merely paying homage. Could there be some strange parasitical force at work which drained energy from the body and power from man-made machinery? It didn't seem possible; but then, neither had levitation nor miracle cures. Yet levitation and miracle cures were not unknown. The Catholic Church had its own levitators such as St Thomas Aquinas, St Teresa of Avila, St John of the Cross, and St Joseph of Cupertino, as well as many blessed with the miracle of stigmatism, the appearance of bleeding wounds on the hands, feet and side, resembling the wounds of Christ on the Cross. Some even bled from the head as if a crown of thorns had been placed there. And miracle cures had become almost religious lore. As well as that, perhaps the most stunning miracle of all had been at Fatima, in Portugal, when nearly seventy thousand onlookers had witnessed the sun spiral in the sky and descend towards the earth. Mass hallucination? Was that the explanation for Fatima and for what had happened in England on that Sunday? It was a logical man's reasoning, a scientist's smug answer. But even so, what had caused the hallucination? Alice was just a child.

Delgard walked to the window and gazed out into the night sky. He could see the bright floodlight in the field beyond, accentuating the twisted form of the oak tree. Its visibility disturbed him; he would rather it were hidden by the darkness. Vandals – perhaps just worshippers who cherished what the tree represented, in the same way that the Church cherished the wood of the Cross – had begun to strip the bark, wanting the aged wood for souvenirs or their own personal sacred relic, and now the tree had to be guarded, the light itself acting as a deterrent. The tree dominated the field as it had never before.

He drew the curtains together, the sight somehow distasteful to him; but when he was undressed and in bed, his eyes unable to close against the shadows around him, the light still glowed through the material, reminding him the tree was still there, a sinister sentinel. Waiting.

Alice's head twisted from side to side, slamming into the pillow with a force that would have stunned had it connected with anything solid. Her lips moved constantly and her pale body was damp with perspiration, even though the room was winter cold. The words she whispered, anguished, tormented, were said in a voice which scarcely resembled that of an eleven-year-old child.

The bedclothes lay loose and rumpled around her ankles, and her thin legs were stretched and trembling.

'*. . . aye good Thomas, fill me with thy seed . . .*'

Her pelvis jerked spasmodically, her cotton nightdress thrown high upon her chest.

'... *so dear in heart, of such good strength* ...'

Her small chest sank and heaved with her dream.

'... *disperse thyself into me* ...'

She moaned, a long, howling moan, but there was an ecstasy in the sigh that followed. For a moment, her body became still and her eyelids fluttered but did not open. She moaned again and this time the sound was languid.

'... *more filling than e'er it was* ...'

The moaning became deep breaths of pleasure, sighs that exalted the joy to her senses. Something small and black moved against her white stomach.

Outside, in the hallway leading to the nuns' cells, a dark-clad figure stood listening, breath held, tensed fingers on the door handle.

'... *allay their tongues, my priest* ...'

Alice's eyes snapped open, but her body had not woken from the dream.

'... *cursed Mary* ... *cursed MARY* ...'

The nun's eyes widened in shock, her grip tightening on the door handle.

'... *CURSED MARY* ...'

Alice's body stretched upwards, her heels and shoulders digging into the bed. The black creature on her stomach was almost dislodged and the girl cried out in pain as sharp needles pierced her tender flesh. But she did not wake.

She fell back to the bed and lay still, no longer making any sound.

The nun, Mother Marie-Claire, Reverend Mother of the convent, one hand unconsciously clutching the crucifix that lay against her chest, pushed the door open slowly, quietly, as if afraid for herself. The beam of light from the hallway broadened as the door opened wider, the nun's shadow an elongated spectre on the room's floor. Coldness flew out at her and it was unnatural, almost painful.

She moved in, footsteps slow and soft. 'Alice?' she whispered, reluctant to wake the child but not sure if she slept. There was no reply from Alice, but another sound came to the nun's ears, a strange yet not unfamiliar noise. It was vaguely repellent, a sucking sound. The nun's forehead creased into a puzzled frown. She approached the bed and looked down at the near-naked form lying there.

Saw the small, bristling shape hunched on the child's stomach.

Raised the crucifix to her lips in horror when she discovered it was a cat.

Felt nauseous when she realized it was suckling at Alice's third nipple.

30

Look out! Look out, boys! Clear the track!
The witches are here! They've all come back!
They hanged them high – No use! No use!
What cares a witch for the hangman's noose?
They buried them deep, but they wouldn't lie still,
For cats and witches are hard to kill;
They swore they shouldn't and wouldn't die –
Books said they did, but they lie! they lie!

Oliver Wendell Holmes, 'Look Out Boys'

The two men emerged from the crypt into the daylight, the shorter one leading, bounding up the stone steps as if relieved to be away from the musty chamber. Fenn stood in the graveyard, hands in his topcoat pockets, and waited for the priest to join him.

Delgard's progress was slower, his legs moving as though they were tied with weights, his shoulders more hunched than usual. Fenn was concerned for the priest: his pallor and demeanour were similar to Father Hagan's before he had died.

The priest reached him and they walked through the gravestones towards the boundary wall.

'That's that, then,' the reporter said, deliberately scuffing the top off a molehill as they passed. 'No chest, no information on the church's history.'

They had searched through the underground chamber with a fine toothcomb, Fenn's nerves jangling every moment they were down there, only the tall priest's presence keeping him from running out into the open. The light bulb had been working, even though Fenn had insisted it had blown the previous Sunday; nevertheless, both men were armed with torches just in case the power failed again.

'That may not be so.' Delgard's voice was heavy, his eyes focused on the ground before him. 'The chest wouldn't have been lost, not if it contained documents referring to St Joseph's earliest days. It must be elsewhere.'

Fenn shrugged. 'It could have been stolen or destroyed.'

'Possibly.'

'Well, where else can we look?'

They had reached the wall and both men looked towards the centre-piece in the field.

'That tree gives me the shudders, d'you know that?' Fenn said, not waiting for a reply to his previous question.

Monsignor Delgard smiled grimly. 'I can appreciate your feeling.'

'You too, huh? It's hard to reconcile it with a place of worship.'

'You think this ground is sacred?' the priest asked, nodding towards the field.

'You're the priest: shouldn't you be telling me it's so?'

The priest gave no answer.

Workmen in the field were carrying in benches, the rows of seating spreading outward, as yet barely covering half the field. Refinements to the centre-piece were in progress, the makeshift altar of the previous Sunday replaced by a large and more ornamental carved-wood version; close by was a small uncovered credence table. Posts which would eventually carry banners were being put up along the aisles and a low rail had been erected around the raised platform for the congregation to kneel at while the priest or priests administered Communion. The activity gave a normality to the scene which belied the extraordinary events that had taken place there just a few days before.

Delgard thought of Molly Pagett and the irony of the less-than-immaculate conception that had happened here. His conversation with Mother Marie-Claire earlier that morning made him wonder just what the illicit coupling nearly twelve years before had spawned.

'I feel it's vital that we locate the church chest, Gerry,' he said, his hands resting on the cold stone of the wall.

'I'm not so sure; what could it tell us? It's probably filled with old Mass books and hymn sheets, like the box in the crypt.' His flesh seemed to tighten around his bones when he thought of the underground chamber.

'No, I'm sure it's important.'

'How can you be? I think we're clutching at straws.'

'It's just a feeling – a very strong feeling. The other records you found go back to the late sixteenth century; why not before that, why should it begin there?'

'Who knows? Maybe that was the first time they thought of keeping any documentation.'

'No, the idea of keeping records goes way beyond that period. It could be that they've been purposely hidden.'

'I think you're guessing. I can't believe—'

'Still disbelieving, Gerry? Last Sunday you believed a statue of the Virgin Mary – a white unblemished statue – moved towards you. You said its lips and eyes were alive, that they even tried to seduce you. And today? What do you believe today?'

'I don't know what happened!'

'But a few moments ago in the crypt. There was no such statue, just a broken and old stone carving, almost unrecognizable as the Virgin, lying behind three other equally disfigured statues.'

'I fell against it, knocked it over.'

'The breaks were grimy with age, not fresh at all. And there was no face on the Virgin.' Delgard's voice was reasoning, no hint of criticism in it. 'Can't you believe something happened there that you cannot logically explain?'

It was Fenn's turn to remain silent. Eventually he said, 'What makes you so certain the answer's in past records?'

'I'm not sure, not at all. But the Reverend Mother of the convent came to me this morning. I'm afraid she was a little agitated.' That was an understatement: the nun had been frantic with worry. 'Alice has been speaking in her sleep again. Last night, Mother Marie-Claire listened outside her door as I had just a few days ago. She couldn't catch much of what Alice said, but it was in the same form as we had both heard before. She recalled some of the words, one or two of the phrases. "Fill me with thy seed" was one, "Allay their tongues" was another. Mother Marie-Claire also heard the word "priest".'

'Old language. Sounds like Shakespeare.'

'That's precisely what it is. It was the peculiar accent that puzzled me before; it made Alice's words sound garbled, nonsensical. Today I remembered a new treatment of Shakespeare's plays at the National I saw several years ago. I should say an "old" treatment; all the actors spoke in Elizabethan English, but not just using Elizabethan dialogue. An authority on the subject had tutored them in the accent used at that time. It was quite different, not just in form, to the language we speak today. It was the same language used by Alice as she slept.'

'She was quoting Shakespeare in her sleep?'

Delgard smiled patiently. 'She was speaking the language of that period, possibly before that time, in its correct idiom.'

Fenn raised his eyebrows. 'You can't be sure of that.'

'I'm not. However it gives us a basis to work from. How can a child of Alice's years – and remember, one who has been profoundly deaf for most of those years – know of a language she has never heard or probably even read before?'

'What are you getting at? Possession? Demonic possession? Speaking in tongues?'

'I wish it were that simple. Perhaps we could call it retrogression.'

'You mean reliving a past life? I thought Catholics didn't go in for reincarnation.'

'Nobody has ever proved that retrogression has anything to do with reincarnation. Who knows how much race memory is retained within our genes?'

Fenn turned to sit on the wall, his hands still tucked deep into his pockets. A light drizzle had started while they were talking. 'No wonder you're anxious to see what records are in that old chest. You know, a coupla weeks back I would have laughed at all this. Now all I can manage is a half-hearted chuckle.'

'There's more, Gerry. Something else I should have remembered before.' The priest squeezed his temples with thumb and fingers of one hand as if trying to press away a headache. 'The night Father Hagan died, the night we had dinner at the Crown Hotel.'

Fenn nodded, urging Delgard on.

'Remember I was talking of Alice's general state of health

at that time? I said she was fine except for feeling tired and being a little withdrawn.'

'Yeah, I remember.'

'I also said the doctors had noticed a small growth in her side, beneath her heart.'

'You said it was a – what was it? – an extra nipple of some kind, nothing to worry about.'

'A supernumerary. I happened to be watching Father Hagan when I mentioned that and noticed he became even more agitated than he had been earlier during the evening. It slipped my mind because of the tragedy that followed. I think it struck a chord somewhere in him, something that was in the back of his mind and which he could not bring to the fore. I was a fool not to have known myself.'

'Forgive my impatience, Monsignor, but I'm getting wet. Are you going to tell me what it is you've remembered?'

Delgard pushed himself away from the wall and looked back towards the church. The light rain had created small speckles of dew on his face. 'Reverend Mother told me she had found a cat in Alice's room last night. It was resting on her sleeping body and it was drinking from her.'

Fenn's head, kept tucked in against the drizzle, snapped up. 'What the hell are you talking about?'

'The cat was suckling at Alice's supernumerary nipple.'

Fenn's face crinkled in disgust. 'She was sure? She actually saw it?'

'Oh yes, Mother Marie-Claire was certain. When she told me I realized what I had previously forgotten.' He looked away from the church and directly at the tree in the field beyond the wall. 'I remembered the ancient folklore concerning witches. It was generally believed that such women bore a mark on their bodies. It could be a blue or red spot, the flesh sunken, hollow; it was known as the Devil's Mark.

Naturally enough, in such superstitious times, scars, moles, warts, or any natural excrescences on the body of a suspected witch could be given diabolical significance, but there was another protuberance or swelling which established the guilt of any person bearing the deformity beyond question.'

'The supernumerary nipple?'

Delgard nodded, his eyes still on the tree. He asked. 'Do you know what is meant by a witch's familiar?'

'I'm not sure. Isn't it something to do with a guide from the spirit world?'

'Not exactly. You're thinking of a spiritualist's familiar, a spirit who helps the medium contact souls on the other side. A witch's familiar is alleged to be a gift from the Devil, a spirit-beast which helped in divination and magic. Usually it was a small animal, anything from a weasel, rabbit, dog, toad, or even a mole.'

'But more often a cat, right? I've read the fairy stories.'

'Don't dismiss such stories out-of-hand; they're often based on folklore passed down through the centuries and can contain some element of truth. The point is this: such spirit-beasts were sent on mischievous and often malicious errands by the witch and rewarded with drops of the witch's own blood. Or they were fed from the witch's supernumerary nipple.'

The reporter was too stunned to scoff. 'You're talking about witchcraft, here, now, in the twentieth century?'

Delgard smiled thinly and finally tore his eyes away from the oak. 'It's by no means unusual nowadays; there are many witches' covens throughout the British Isles. But I believe I'm speaking of something much more. You associated witchcraft with fairy tales. What if such myths were based on a reality, something which the people of that time could not understand, could only perceive in terms of sorcery? Witchcraft would have been something they could not understand, but could accept. We laugh at such ideas today because it's comfortable for us to do so, and our scientific technology precludes such notions.'

'You're losing me. Are you saying little Alice Pagett is a witch, or that she's not? Or that she's the reincarnation of some ancient sorceress?'

'I'm saying none of those things. But I think we must delve into the past for some link with what is happening here today. This force must emanate from somewhere.'

'What force is that?'

'The force of evil. Can't you feel it around us? You, yourself, experienced it last Sunday in the crypt. The same force weakened, then destroyed, Father Hagan.' He did not add that he felt that same pressure bearing down on himself.

'There's nothing evil about the miracles,' Fenn said.

'That,' Delgard replied, 'we do not yet know. We don't know where or what all this is leading to. We must keep searching, Gerry. We must find clues. We have to find the answer before it's too late, while there's still a chance to combat this force.'

Fenn let out a long sigh. 'You better tell me where else I can look for the chest,' he said.

Fenn was a dumbhead. He should have seen the connection. Maybe all the research he had been doing had addled his brain. Guess it was easy to be objective when all the work had been done and you only had to read through the notes. But still, she could be wrong: it might not be here at all.

Nancy stood before the heavy-looking door inside the porch, its wood painted and marked with time, wondering if it would be locked. She twisted the metal handle and her eyes glinted with satisfaction when it turned and the door opened easily. No reason for it to be locked in such an isolated place.

It was when Fenn had told her that the old church chest he was looking for wasn't at St Joseph's that she realized the possibility. If he hadn't played so cagey with her, she'd have told him. That's what you get, Fenn, for trying to cut me out.

She pushed the door open wider and stepped in from the porch. The light inside was dull, diffused by the thick, leaded windows.

The chest dated back to the fourteenth or fifteenth century and must have disappeared some time during the sixteenth, for that was as far back as the records Fenn had found went. That had been her clue.

The door made a low growling noise as she closed it, a muffled thump disturbing the stillness inside when it shut completely. Nancy looked around the miniature church, loving its quaintness, impressed by its tradition. A leaden font stood before her, the dark, letter-ornamented metal speaking of another time, a different era. Nearly all the pews were boxed in, the panels chest-height, narrow doors allowing entry. Whole families probably sat in each one, Nancy assumed, cut off from their neighbours, enclosed in their own small islands of worship. The wood panelling was stripped of any varnish, its bareness somehow complementing the character of the chapel itself. No more than thirty to forty feet away, at the head of the narrow aisle, was the tiny altar.

So this was where the lord of the manor came to pray, Nancy mused. Cute.

She moved around the font into the chapel and at once gave a small cry of triumph. There it was. It had to be the one!

The chest stood against a wall to her right, immediately below a large polished-wood board, the names of all the clerics who had served the church from 1158 to the present day inscribed on its surface in gold. She stared at the long, low chest, scarcely believing her eyes, but almost certain it was the one Fenn had been searching for. It matched the description in his notes perfectly: made from planks of thick elm or oak, bound together with metal bands, the wood battered and marked, an indication of its antiquity; and there were three unusual looking padlocks on its facing side.

Nancy squatted beside it, still smiling in triumph, and handled all three locks. 'Great!' she said aloud. 'Now all I need is the goddam keys.'

She pushed herself erect and looked around. Where would the priest be? He obviously wouldn't be resident, there was no house, only the large mansion some distance away. The board in front of her said that the priest since 1976 was a Father Patrick Conroy of Storrington. Ah, that was it. The priest obviously bussed in from the neighbouring parish to run the show here. She would have to go to the town or village of Storrington to locate him. But then, would he allow her access to the chest? Probably – no, definitely – not. Fenn might get permission, though with his church connections. Shit, she would have to tell him.

Unless.

Unless the keys were kept in the church. Improbable, but worth a look. Maybe in the vestry.

She strode down the aisle towards the front of the nave, her footsteps brisk. Shadows of light passed across the high windows, heavy, low clouds moving by outside. The sound of wind whistling through a gap somewhere in the church roof. A small scratching sound, a mouse working at wood somewhere in the shadows.

Her footsteps faltered as some subliminal change in her awareness told her she was not alone in the church.

She stopped for a moment and listened. The scratching

had stopped as though the mouse also knew there was an extra presence nearby. The clouds outside thickened, the light diminishing.

Her footsteps were slower, more cautious, when she moved on. She peered over the tops of the high box pews, almost expecting to find someone praying in one. To her right, by the side of the altar she could see the closed vestry door. To her left was a corner, the interior flanking out in that direction possibly to form a side chapel. Yet the unvarnished wood panelling indicated it had to be another pew, this one set apart from the rest. This would be where the lord of the manor sat with his family, she reasoned.

No sound came from that direction, but apprehension stabbed at her chest like a thin, sharp icicle.

Get a hold of yourself, asshole. There could be someone there, but why not? It *was* a church, for Chrissake! She coughed, loudly, hoping for some reaction if there was somebody praying in there. A shuffling of knees, or a returned cough would do. Anything to show that whoever it was wasn't skulking. There was no other sound.

It would be stupid to leave, Nancy told herself. Stupid and childish. She walked on, her footsteps deliberately loud on the stone floor.

The first thing she saw when she drew level with the chest-high partition was a picture on the far wall. It was a painting of the Madonna and Child in the style of Perugino, and it hung above a fireplace. The recess, in fact, was a small room, obviously built for the comfort of the squire and his family from the huge Tudor manor house which shared the estate with the tiny church. She moved closer. The door in the panelling was open.

A figure sat on one of the benches inside, a small, dark-clad figure.

Nancy almost whistled with relief when she saw it was a nun.

But the habit was strange. It wasn't the two-toned grey she had seen the nuns in the village wearing, and the skirt was longer. The black hood was pulled forward, well over the face.

She was sitting sideways to Nancy, her back hunched over, hands hidden deep within her lap, the loose black material flowing around her.

'Excuse me,' Nancy said quietly, tentatively, standing in the doorway of the pew, one hand on top of the panelling, fingers curled around it.

The nun did not move.

'I . . . I'm sorry to bother . . .' Nancy's words trailed away. There was something wrong. Oh God, there was something wrong. She moved as if to back away, not knowing why she was afraid, only aware that she was irrationally, inexplicably, in mortal dread of this thing sitting there; but her limbs would not react, would not take her away from the dark, hidden figure.

Her legs sagged and a small trickle of urine dampened her inner thighs as the nun slowly turned to face her.

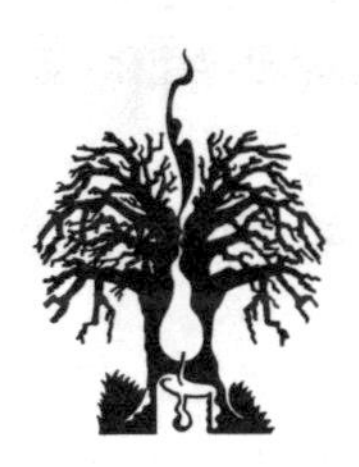

31

'Who knocks?' 'I, who was beautiful,
    Beyond all dreams to restore.
I, from the roots of the dark thorn am hither.
    And knock on the door.'

Walter de la Mare, 'The Ghost'

Rain spattered against the windscreen as Fenn drove through the tall iron gates. He slowed the car, expecting to be challenged, but there was no one on duty. Must be out of season, he explained to himself. The estate was probably closed to the public until the spring. He picked up speed, ignoring the sign indicating that 10 mph was the approved pace.

Outside the clouds were low and dark, overloaded with rain, the speckles on the windows just the appetizer for what was soon to come. Trees rushed by on either side, their barren branches like petrified arms thrown out in alarm. A flicker of movement to the left caught his eye and abruptly he was braking as a deer bounded across the narrow road. He watched it disappear into the trees, a fleeting light-brown spectre, and envied its skittish grace. It was gone from view within seconds, swallowed up by the stark arboreal sanctuary.

The hired car resumed its journey, slowing again when it reached an open gate, rattling its way across the deer grid. He frowned at the dullness in the air, the dismal weather making the late afternoon seem like evening. Winter in England could be bearable if only it didn't drag itself through eight or nine months of the year. The road curved, emerging from the trees to be confronted by a sweeping panorama of lush fields, the misty South Downs in the distance a rolling backdrop merging into the grey puffy sky.

The drive dipped easily, then separated, the main arm going onwards towards the grey-stone manor house, the other, narrower, arm branching off to the left, towards a levelled compound behind a group of elms, a non-obtrusive carpark for sightseers to the estate. Beyond the carpark, no more than a quarter of a mile away, stood a small church.

Stapley Park, Barham. The big Tudor house was Stapley Manor. The little twelfth-century church was St Peter's.

Fenn silently swore at himself for being such a jerk; he really should have made the connection. It was all laid out for him, all there in the notes he'd taken from the archives. The trouble was he'd become too swamped in the history to give full attention to details that had not seemed relevant. Well, it didn't matter that much now; he was pretty sure the chest in the little church was the one he had been searching for. Earlier that day, after leaving Delgard, and on the monsignor's advice, he had gone to the cathedral at Arundel hoping to find further documents concerning St Joseph's, and it was there that he had learned of St Peter's at Stapley, and of Stapley Manor itself.

The Catholic Church had owned the Stapley Estate, in whose ground St Peter's stood, before being dispossessed of such lands and properties at the time of the Reformation in England.

In 1540, with the Dissolution of the Monasteries, when the lands and properties of the Church were being 'legally' acquired by the Crown, Henry VIII granted the manor house at Stapley and its entire estate to Richard Staffon, a mercer of London. He lived there with his family until the counter-Reformation under the new Catholic queen began its short-lived but fearsome reign of terror. Staffon was fortunate: he and his family were driven into exile with many fellow Protestants, whereas almost three hundred others were burnt at the stake as heretics.

By devious means, the estate was passed on to Sir John Woolgar as a reward for his loyalty to the Catholic Church in Henry's time. Woolgar was a wealthy Sussex businessman whose only son was the priest at St Joseph's in Banfield.

Fenn had stopped the car and was surveying the panorama, allowing the information to assemble itself in his mind. He had learned of the connection between Stapley Manor and Banfield from his research into the Sussex records, the warden at Arundel merely prompting the recall; the further information concerning the Reformation had been added by the priest he had just left at Storrington.

This priest, a Father Conroy, as well as serving his own parish at Storrington, also served weekly Mass at St Peter's in Stapley Park; apparently it was a duty handed down to each new priest to that particular parish. He had confirmed that there was, indeed, a large ancient chest in St Peter's, the description matching Fenn's, and a phone call to Monsignor Delgard (for whom Father Conroy had undisguised respect) gave him the authority to hand over the keys to the reporter. Fenn also gained permission to take away any documents he might find useful, provided he made a complete list, signed it, and allowed Conroy to examine those he had taken. The priest would have accompanied him to St Peter's himself, but various duties dictated otherwise. That suited Fenn fine: he preferred to snoop alone.

The priest had filled in other details concerning the Stapley Park Estate and St Peter's. There had originally been a small village around the church, but it had become regarded as a source of infection after a mysterious plague had broken out in the early 1400s killing off most of the villagers; subsequently, the houses around the church had been destroyed. Much alteration and restoration had taken place over the years, each new lord of the manor contributing financially to the work, whether they were Catholic or not, for, like the mansion itself, St Peter's was of historic importance and an attraction for the many tourists who flocked to the estate during the summer months. Father Conroy recalled reading somewhere that the chest had been taken to St Peter's from Banfield in token acknowledgement of a stained-glass window that Sir John Woolgar had donated to St Joseph's.

A crow landed in the roadway, twenty yards ahead of the car, and seemed to challenge its further progress. It was a breed of bird Fenn found hard to admire; too big, too black. He allowed the car to move slowly forward, the tyres crunching against the gravel road. The bird calmly walked to the side and watched Fenn with one eye as he drove past.

The vehicle gained momentum as the road dipped. Herds of black-backed deer, settled in the grass beneath trees, gazed on with stiff-necked curiosity as he approached, the stags among them, antlers high and menacing, glaring as if daring him to come closer. He drove into the branch-off, making for the empty grass carpark, and the deer in that area rose as one to move away, their flight unhurried, cautious but unafraid.

The grass in the compound was cut short, the parking areas neatly marked by straight, narrow lines of soil, unobtrusive and neatly patterned. Bullocks in a field nearby bawled at him, the sound echoing around the trees, as if they, too, did not welcome his presence.

Fenn grabbed a hold-all from the passenger seat and pushed open the door. The wind tore into him as he stepped from the car; it swept over the Downs from the sea, carrying with it a damp chill and an unrestrained force. Pulling his coat-collar tight around his neck and blinking against the wind-driven rain, he set off for the church, the strap of the hold-all over one shoulder.

A long, straight path led from the carpark to the mediaeval church; to the right, about a quarter of a mile away, stood the daunting manor house, an impressive structure of Tudor design, yet curiously empty-looking, lifeless. Indeed, it probably was at that time, for Fenn had learned earlier that the owner had died some years before and his family only stayed at the house for certain months of the year, preferring sunnier climates in the winter months.

As he trod the narrow path, the church loomed up like an image framed in a slow-moving zoom lens, and he began to feel very lonely and very isolated. Like the manor house in the distance, St Peter's was constructed of grey stone, green-stained with age; one section of the roof was covered with large moss-covered slates, the rest with red tiles; the windows were leaded, the glass thick and smoothly rippled as though each pane had been placed in its frame still hot and melting. He saw now how oddly-shaped the building was and could imagine the various segments being added at various times through the centuries, each portion reflecting its own period. The path led past the church, presumably to where the entrance had to be, for he could see no doors as he approached. The expanse he had just crossed had been bare; now there were trees, mostly oak, around the church, and the wind rustled through the empty branches, an urgent, rushing sound that increased his sense of isolation. Small branches broke away and scuttled in the air before reaching the earth; stouter branches lay scattered, victims of previous, stronger gusts, resembling twisted human limbs. The horizon, just above the distant Downs, now glowed silver in a strip that was held level by the dark, laden clouds above. The contrast between broody clouds and condensed sky was startling.

Fenn stepped off the path into rough grass to get near one of the church windows and, cupping a hand between brow and glass, peered in. There was an unappealing gloom inside and he could just make out the empty pews enclosed by wood panelling. At first glance it reminded him of a holy cattleshed. He took his hand away and twisted his neck, nose almost pressed against the glass, in an effort to see more. There were other windows opposite that threw little light into the interior, but he could just make out the shape of a font and more enclosed benches nearby. A movement caught his eye and it was so sudden that he drew back a few inches. Then he realized, the blood vessels in his throat seeming to constrict, that the action was not inside the church, but was a reflection in the glass.

He turned quickly and saw there was nothing there. Just a swaying branch.

Creepy, he told himself. Creepy, creepy, creepy.

Hoisting the hold-all back onto his shoulder, he rejoined the path and headed for the front of the church. When he reached the corner the wind tore into him with fresh force, driving the rain into his face like ice pellets. A square tower rose above him, too short and stubby to be majestic, reaching no more than forty feet into the air, its rampart top almost as grey as the clouds above it. A matt, rust-coloured door stood beneath the tower, the shade drab and unimaginative, paying no dues to the history it guarded. An unlocked iron gate protected the door, only inches away from the wood surface like some early misconceived idea of double glazing.

Before entering the church, Fenn took a walk to the other side. Beyond a flint wall was a small graveyard, the gravestones crammed in as though the corpses had been buried standing up. Here and there were more spacious plots and some headstones that appeared to have been regularly scrubbed clean; there were also one or two rotting wooden crosses laid in the grass, marking the resting places of those who could not afford better. Opposite the church was a two-strutted fence, beyond that, waist-high undergrowth, beyond that – nothing, it seemed. The land obviously dropped steeply away into a small valley, woodland rising up on the other side towards the slopes of the Downs.

Fenn turned back to the doorway, his hair flat and wet against his forehead. He opened the iron gate, then the heavy door, and stepped into the church, glad to be away from the hostile weather. The door closed behind him and the wind outside became just a muted breathing.

As in all churches he had visited, which wasn't many, he felt uncomfortable and intrusive, as though his presence showed a lack of respect rather than a mark of it. The interior was certainly unusual with its enclosed pews, low barrel ceiling, and tiny altar. A raised pulpit stood near the altar, behind it a door he assumed led to the vestry. Would the chest be in there? The priest at Storrington had omitted to say.

Then he saw it, no more than five feet away to his right. His eyes lit up and he smiled ruefully. You better be worth it, you bugger, he said to himself, remembering the experience of searching the crypt at St Joseph's. Above it was a plaque of highly-polished wood, names and dates inscribed on its surface. He took a closer look, realizing it was a list of clerics who had served at St Peter's. He found one that was familiar:

REV. THOMAS WOOLGAR 1525–1560

Thomas would be Sir John's son, the priest from Banfield. Presumably he arrived after his father had been granted the estate, so if he had died in 1560, the service had been only for a few years. He quickly worked out the priest's age at the time of death: thirty-five; young by today's standards, but reasonable for that period.

Rain lashed at the windows with a new intensity, beating at the thick glass as though demanding entry.

Fenn rummaged in his pocket for the keys that would open the three locks. He hesitated before inserting the first one. Maybe this is crazy, he told himself. How could something that had happened – *if* anything significant happened – over four hundred years ago have any relevance to what was happening at St Joseph's today? Just because a kid used an old, outdated language in her sleep and had a blemish on her body that used to be thought of as a witch-sign, it didn't mean the answer lay somewhere in history. Was Delgard truly convinced of it, or was he just desperate? Alice, the Miracle Worker, was a modern-day phenomenon; why should the past play any part?

The wind outside became louder as it battered against the old church walls; a fresh squall of rain threw itself at the windows like thousands of tiny shrapnel pieces.

A noise somewhere near the front of the church made Fenn turn his head.

He straightened, uneasy.

The noise came again.

'Someone there?' he called out.

No reply and no more noise. Just the wind and rain outside.

He walked to the centre of the aisle and waited. The sound again. A small scraping sound.

Could be anything, he reassured himself. A mouse, a trapped bird. Then why was he so sure that there was someone else in the church? He felt he was being watched and automatically his eyes went to the pulpit. It was empty.

The sound again. Someone or something near the front of the church.

'Hey, come on, who's there?' he called out with forced bravado.

He began to walk towards the altar, refraining from whistling a happy tune, eyes searching left to right at every pew he passed. All were empty, but the last one disappeared around a corner, the building jutting out in that direction. He was certain that was where the sound had come from. He reached the corner and stopped, for some reason reluctant to go further. He had the distinct feeling that he really did not want to see whatever was lurking there. The noise came again, louder this time, startling him.

He took several quick paces forward and peered over the enclosure.

Empty.

Fenn breathed a sigh of relief.

It was a strange room, a fireplace at the far end, a picture of the Virgin and Child hanging above the mantel. Cushioned benches stretched the full length on either side. He heard the sound again and saw the tree branch outside, buffeted by the wind, scraping at a window. He was too relieved to even smile at himself.

Going back to the chest, he knelt and turned the first key. When nothing happened he remembered the short metal rod

Father Conroy had given him. As instructed, he inserted it into a small hole at the side of the padlock, pressed a lever, then twisted the key again. The padlock came away in two parts.

He repeated the procedure twice more and laid the separate sections on the stone floor. His tongue flicked nervously across dry lips as he prepared to open the lid.

The porch door rattled as though someone were banging their fists against it. It was the wind, he told himself, just the wind.

The lid was heavy and at first resisted his efforts. Then it came slowly up, hinges groaning at the unfamiliar movement. Fenn swung the lid right back so that it rested against the wall behind. He looked down into its depths, a musty odour leaping out at him like a released animal.

Old vestments lay scattered on top, their colours faded, the material no longer springy soft. He pulled the clothing out, draping them over the side of the chest. Beneath lay sheaves of yellowed paper and various books, worn and wrinkled with age. He took the latter out one by one, quickly leafing through the pages, placing them on the floor when he discovered they did not date back far enough. He felt some of the various papers would have proved interesting to a historian, but to him they were useless. Next he drew out several loosely-bound books, the covers in hide of some sort, the paper inside thin and rough edged. He opened one and saw it was a form of ledger, an accounts book for St Peter's. In neat script it listed payments made to workmen for tasks carried out for the church. The first page gave the year: 1697. The other books dated back further, but none to the century he sought.

There were more scattered papers, several Latin Mass books, and then he found what he had been looking for.

There were three of them, each book roughly measuring twelve by eight inches; the covers were of stiff, yellow vellum, the inside leaves bound together by twisted vellum tackets, braided through hide strengthening pieces. The writing on the pages was forceful in style, each letter precisely angled, the ink brown and, unfortunately, very faded. Even more unfortunate was that it was all in Latin. But the date said 1556.

Eagerly he looked at the other two, and the dates ran in consecutive years. As he handled the third book, a sheaf of loose leaves fell from the back into the chest. He reached for one and noticed it was undated. The writing was in the same brown ink and although similar in style to the previous handwriting, it was scrawled, less tidy, the lettering spidery and undisciplined. It, too, was in Latin. Fenn gathered up the other scattered pages, quickly scanning them for a date, smiling when he found one.

The roof groaned loudly as the wind pounded on it; something broke away, probably a slate, and slid down, its fall muffled by the soft earth around the church. Fenn looked up anxiously and assured himself that the church had stood up to such battering for centuries and was unlikely to collapse around him now. Nevertheless, he quickly opened the hold-all and put the three vellum-covered documents inside, first placing the loose leaves in the back of the book they had fallen from.

The church door was rattling insanely and nothing could be seen through the windows, so fierce was the rain. He began stuffing the other books, sheets and vestments back into the chest, unwilling to search any further, the urge to be away from the church too great. He had the same sense of black oppression that he'd experienced in the crypt of St Joseph's. The lid closed with a heavy thump and Fenn stood, relieved that it was done. Back to the car now, away from this godawful place, with its tearing wind and dark, dark church . . . He hadn't noticed before just how dark it had become.

He stepped into the aisle, averting his eyes from the altar. The howling wind outside sounded like the wailing of lost souls. The door before him shook violently and something made him back away. The lift bar above the lock jiggled up and down as if some neurotic hand outside were playing with it. The wood trembled within its frame and he could sense the pressure behind it, the gale screeching for entry.

An awareness crept upon him with dank, scaly fingers. Something else, not just the wind, wanted to get into the church. *Something* wanted to reach him.

He was still backing away, his eyes on the agitated porch door, drawing closer to the altar, passing pews one by one, the partitions screens behind which things could hide. The pulpit came into the periphery of his vision, rising over him like a tensed predator. To his right was the strange segregated room, with its empty fireplace, its picture of the woman and the Christ-child, with its window, the branch tapping and scraping at the glass like a hand begging for admission . . . with its dark-clad figure sitting by the empty grate . . .

He stopped, his legs paralysed, his throat constricted.

The figure was hooded, the head crouched low over its knees. It began to straighten, to turn towards Fenn.

And the porch door burst open with a force that shook everything inside the church.

32

> There never more she walks her ways
>   by sun or moon or stars;
> she dwells below where neither days
>   nor any nights there are.
>
> J. R. R. Tolkien, 'Shadow-Bride'

Fenn was thrown backwards, more by shock than force. He stumbled, fell. The floor was hard against his back, but he felt no pain, only a jolting numbness.

The wind howled around the church, a banshee let loose, so that even the leaden font seemed to tremble against its wrath. Fenn's clothes were buffeted by the wind, his hair swept back, coat collar flapping against his cheek. He was forced to turn his head aside from the initial onslaught, his eyes squeezed tight against the blast. Rain was carried in, dampening the walls, the pews, an ally to the whirlwind. The roar of air was amplified by the tight confines of the stone building, assaulting his ears with its frenzied screaming.

Something was moving to his right, something black, small, rising from the seat in the side room, standing in the opening. Bending to touch him.

He dared not look. He sensed its presence, glimpsed the

dark shape only on the edge of his vision. He did not want to see.

Fenn scrambled to his knees, swayed there for a few moments, the circling wind rocking his body. He tried to rise, found his legs were not strong enough to support him, even though the gale was not as fierce, its force deflected by the walls into confused and separate currents. He began to move forward, dragging the hold-all along the floor with him, fearful of the storm bursting through the open doorway, but more fearful of the hooded figure that watched him.

He flinched as though he had been touched, but reason told him he was not within reach of the thing that stood there. It seemed that cruel fingers had raked his arm, leaving the flesh beneath his clothes torn and branded. The same sensation clawed at his cheek and he gasped, the pain searing, yet unreal. More heat – for that was what it felt like, raw, white heat against his skin – touched his outstretched hand and when he glanced down he saw the red weals already beginning to rise. His head was snapped upwards as though long fingers had tangled themselves in his hair and pulled. His body arched as jagged nails scored bloody tracks down his back.

Yet the figure was still beyond touching distance.

He staggered to his feet, fear lending him strength, and stumbled along the aisle, fighting the wind as a drowning man fights an undertow, forcing himself towards the grey light of the doorway, collapsing against a partition, clasping its ridge, pushing himself away, feeling malignant eyes on the back of his neck. He fell again, the wind shoving him with giant, unseen hands, knocking him to the floor.

The large wooden door swung on its hinges, banging into the wall, cracking the plastered stone. Outside, the driven rain had turned the landscape into a hazy, moving pattern of muted greens.

Fenn was still afraid to look back, not understanding where the dark-cloaked figure had come from, only knowing it was there, an unearthly presence that burned with malevolence. He crawled again and something tugged at his ankle. He screamed as the scorching grip tightened and dragged his leg backwards.

His hand reached for the corner of a pew, the other scrabbling at the cracks in the uneven floor. His heart felt it would come loose in his body, so wildly was it beating. He was shouting now, ranting at the thing that drew him back, tendons in his wrists high and rigid against the flesh as he struggled to pull himself free. Then he was kicking, frightened yet enraged, eyes blurred with the tears of his own anger and frustration. Kicking, kicking, his knees scraping raw against the stone, globules of blood collecting beneath the fingernails of the hand that scratched at the rough floor, kicking, kicking, eyes closed with the effort but mouth open to force out the shouts.

He was suddenly free, thrusting at empty air. He found himself moving forward once more, the wind still pressing against his shoulders, whipping his face with rain icicles. He was on his feet, staggering towards the door, still refusing to look over his shoulder, hot, corrupted breath warming the back of his neck. His footsteps slowed . . . slowed . . . slowed . . . the compulsion behind dragging at him, creating the nightmare of legs in quagmire . . . the childhood dreams of . . .

. . . the Frankenstein monster ploddingly catching up, arms outstretched to grab, huge club-foot boots shuddering the ground . . .

... the grinning Fe-Fi-Fo-Fum giant swinging his axe ...

... the slush-slurp of the Creature emerging from the Black Lagoon ...

... the dead son returning from the grave, thumping against the other side of the bolted door for his mother, who clasped the monkey's paw, to let him in ...

... the thing that was always waiting in the dark at the bottom of the cellar stairs ...

... the green-faced bogeyman tapping at the bedroom window in the middle of the night ...

... Norman Bates, dressed as Mother, behind the shower curtain ...

... the white shape at the foot of the bed, who would not let him wake from the nightmare until it had dissolved back into the night ...

... the hand that would coldly curl around his ankle should he let it slip from beneath the bedsheets ...

... all the nightmare companions of his childhood were gathered there behind him in the church, every late-night dread creeping up on him, their images the tentacles that bound him ...

And like a nightmare, it had to break when the terror became too much.

The release was like being blasted from a cannon. He burst through the doorway, skidding and falling heavily onto the path outside the church. He rolled over, resting on one elbow, and the rain beat against his upturned face with such force he was sure it would leave indentations on his face. The arched door loomed over him, the interior a murky cavern of gargoyles; the stunted tower rose above and for one brief moment he imagined he was looking down from the ramparts at his own prone figure lying on the path. He blinked his eyes against the rain and against the confusion.

He began to push himself away from the threatening doorway, using heels and elbows, his clothes and skin already soaked, the hold-all dragged across the path with him. Chill softness brushed his back as he slid into the rough grass. He stared back at the ancient church, his eyes wide and face deathly pale. His brain screamed at him to get up and run. As he pushed himself upright he saw a fleeting figure just on the other side of the perimeter fence.

It had risen from the sea of green like a swimmer breaking surface, and then it was running, pushing a path through the foliage, heading away from Fenn, away from the church.

The figure looked familiar, but his thinking was too haywire to allow recognition for a moment or two. When he finally realized who it was he was even more bewildered. Grabbing the hold-all and tucking it under his arm, he ran to the fence, used one hand to leap untidily over, and fell into the foliage on the other side. The figure had disappeared by the time he regained his feet.

A low gust tore across the undergrowth creating a sweeping ripple that reached him and made him unsteady.

'Nancy!' he called out, but the storm smothered any reply. He pushed through the foliage, gathering speed as he went, shouting her name. He wasn't just afraid for her; he needed her. He was frightened for himself.

Fenn ran on through the rain, the wind, almost blinded, recklessly crashing through the undergrowth. Then he was falling, slipping, tumbling over and over, rolling into an abyss he hadn't realized was there. Stalks and brambles snapped at his face and hands, and he thought the slide would never end, that the world would never re-stabilize itself. He came to a cushioned halt at the bottom of the slope and leaves closed over his eyes like mischievous hands.

He sat up and tried to shake the dizziness from his head.

The movement only made it worse and the world continued to tumble for long seconds after. When the spinning finally settled, he searched for her running figure. He was in a narrow valley, woodland rising up on the opposite side. A rough, earth roadway led through the valley, disappearing in the distance round a jutting slope. Directly in front, no more than two hundred yards away, was a barn, the likes of which he had never before seen. It was very old and obviously no longer used, such was its disrepair; immediately below a thatched roof supported by stout beams, were openings, the covered sides of the barn itself reaching only to a certain level. The wood was faded and weather-worn, the thatch still thick but dark with age.

Fenn knew she would be in there.

He got to his feet and picked up the bag. Then, hunching his shoulders against the pounding rain, he lurched towards the barn. The wind in the bottom of the dip was weakened, its rushing sound softened. He turned quickly to look back up the hill and saw that St Peter's was out of view, not even the tower showing above the false horizon; the foliage at the top of the slope swayed back and forth, bowed but resilient to the elements.

There was no door to the barn, just a vast opening running half the length of its side, a post from floor to roof dividing the entrance. From where he stood he could see the interior was crammed with old logs, wood planking, and some rusted machinery. He had no desire to enter, for it looked even darker and just as foreboding as the church. Only the whimpers above the noise of the muted wind urged him in.

He found her crouched behind a pile of wood at the back of the barn, her frightened sobbing guiding him to her. Her head was buried into her knees, arms clenched tightly around herself, and she shuddered violently when he touched her shoulder.

'Nancy, it's me, Gerry,' he said softly, but she would not look at him.

He knelt beside her and tried to take her in his arms; with an animal yelp she pushed against the side of the musty barn scrabbling to get away from him.

'For Christ's sake, Nancy, calm down. It's me.' He gently pulled her back to him and rocked her in his arms. 'It's me,' he kept telling her, his voice falsely soothing, for the hysteria was not far from his own mind.

It took some time before he could lift her head and force her to look at him. And when he did the expression in her eyes frightened him almost as much as the thing inside the church.

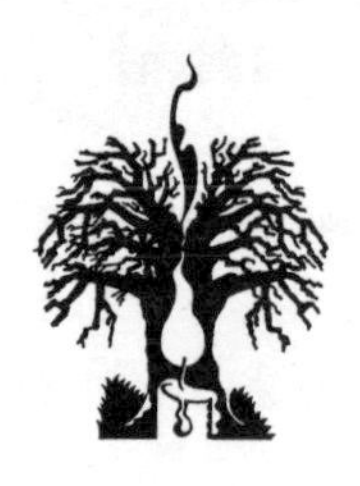

33

Wake all the dead! What ho! What ho!
How soundly they sleep whose pillows lie low,
They mind not poor lovers who walk above
On the decks of the world in storms of love.
    No whisper now, nor glance can pass
    Through wickets or through panes of glass;
For our windows and doors are shut and barred
Lie close in the church, and in the churchyard.
    In every grave make room, make room!
    The world's at an end, and we come, we come.

Sir William Davenant,
'Wake all the Dead! What Ho! What Ho!'

Delgard pushed the reading glasses up from the bridge of his nose and rubbed at the corners of his weary eyes. The reflection from the ultraviolet light cast a bluish-white tinge over his features, the stark, artificial glare ruthlessly exposing lines of fatigue. The faded papers lay spread on the table before him, parchment edges rough and flaky through time; to one side was a thick, heavily-bound book, an aid to the translation of the ancient but enduring language on the parchments. He clicked off the fluorescent tube, no longer needing its peculiar light to enhance the faded script, and quickly scribbled more notes onto his writing pad. Then he laid the pen down, held his spectacles with one hand and massaged his forehead with the other. His shoulders appeared even more hunched, his chest even more sunken.

When he took his hand away, his eyes were haunted, filled with disbelief. It couldn't be true, the papers had to be a madman's dream, the guilt-ridden imaginings of a man born nearly five hundred years before.

Delgard's mouth felt dry and he flicked his tongue uselessly across brittle lips. There was a tightness to his skin, a stiffness to his joints, the tension of the last few hours the cause. He craned his neck towards the reporter, who lay slumped in a nearby armchair, and imagined he could feel his own bones grind against one another as he turned. Fenn was fast asleep, exhaustion, and perhaps even boredom, stealing him from the late-night vigil with the priest.

He should rouse the reporter, tell him what he had learned, but for the moment Delgard felt a stronger need. A need to cleanse himself, to pray for spiritual strength and guidance. And to pray for the defiled soul of one who had perished centuries before.

Delgard rose and his large frame was unsteady. He had to rest his hands on the desk for several moments before he felt able to stand fully erect. The room settled around him once more, but his strength and vitality were still fading. He pushed back the chair and walked to the door, pausing to look back at Fenn before going through.

'Gerry,' he said, but not loudly enough.

The reporter slept on and it was hardly surprising; his mind was taking refuge from the terrors of the day. When Fenn had brought the old manuscripts to the priest's house earlier that evening his whole demeanour had been one of bewildered nervousness. A cynic who did not believe in ghosts believed – *knew* – he had now seen such an apparition. It had taken two hastily swallowed whiskies before he was calm enough to tell the story coherently.

Delgard regretted having let the reporter go to the church at Barham alone; he should have realized the danger sooner.

After the incident at St Peter's – an incident which Fenn had described in great detail, as though needing to rationalize it with the spoken word – he had found the American reporter, Nancy Shelbeck, hiding nearby. She had refused to be taken to a hospital where Fenn hoped she might be treated for the obvious shock she was in, and he had been too afraid to leave her alone in his or her own apartment. So he had taken her to Sue Gates, in whose flat she had fallen into a dazed sleep.

Sleep. The tiredness was upon him, too. It was as though the unseen presence, the presence that had emanated here, in these church grounds, was parasitical, taking its strength from the human psyche. The weakness he had felt at the onset of the miracles, the interference with electrically operated machinery, the strange atmosphere, the vibrancy in the air itself, all suggested a reaction was taking place, perhaps a sapping of existing energy to create a new form. And, he now felt sure, the catalyst, both physical and spiritual, was Alice Pagett.

He glanced back at the faded manuscript papers. The answer lay there, written in Latin, the ancient language common to priests since the Christian religion began. It was incredible, but then he had witnessed the unbelievable as reality many times before. The link, centuries old, was in those papers, the tortured, quirky handwriting giving evidence of the tormented, even demented, man who had written the shame-filled words. And that man had been a priest, a sixteenth-century cleric, who had sinned not just against his faith, but against humanity itself.

And what made the priest's iniquity even more unforgivable was that he had the gleamings of understanding in an age of superstition and ignorance. He had been aware of parapsychological forces, had been capable of differentiating them from misguided concepts of sorcery; yet he had encouraged and used his fellow-man's false perceptions for his own purposes and, in so doing, had invoked a far worse power against himself. The people of that time believed they had destroyed a witch under the authority and incitement of their ruler, a queen called Mary. *Mary Tudor.* But they had destroyed something more than a mythical invention: they had destroyed someone whose extraordinary mental powers could transcend her own death. And eventually, when certain psychical elements came together, could possibly recreate her own physical being.

Witchcraft, the name of *Mary*, the mental energy released by religious fervour: these were the strange, intrinsic ingredients. The latter-day priest who had sinned, the child who had been conceived in sin: these were the catalysts. And it was Alice who played the most important part in the metamorphosis, *for she had been created in the same field where the nun had been butchered then burnt to death almost five hundred years before.*

Delgard leaned against the door, incredible, insane theories rushing into his head.

Could a centuries-late metempsychosis, the migration of a soul at death into another body, have taken place? Had Alice been taken at the very spark of her existence? She had grown into a child guided by her mother, devoted to the church, worshipping the name of Mary, becoming severely handicapped at the age of four, an infirmity her doctors could not satisfactorily explain, to be inexplicably released from that disability seven years later. Miraculously. The cures to others had appeared miraculous, too. But were they really psychically induced?

He shook his head against the jumble of thoughts.

Alice had spoken in a tongue alien to her own, the voice mature, the words old-English, the content . . . disturbed, lustful. Had she been possessed? Or . . . or was she a reincarnation? As a Catholic priest, the idea should have had no validity to him, but it was a nagging thought he found impossible to push away.

Yet even this was quelled by the question that over-rode all others: what was the purpose of it all?

Foreboding dragged at him with such intensity that his body sagged and he was forced to cling to the door for support. The premonition of disaster was nothing new – the feeling of dread had been with him for weeks – but now he knew it was imminent. The brief insight was like a physical blow, striking at him and vanishing instantly, so that all he was left with was a feeling of total desolation, a distressing cognizance of . . . nothing. A void, absolute in its emptiness. It was the most frightening thing he had ever perceived.

The need to be on hallowed ground sent Delgard staggering from the room. He had to pray, had to seek spiritual guidance to combat the impending evil.

He threw open the front door and outside the night seemed as black as the void he had just briefly borne witness to.

A cold draught of air found its way down the hallway and into the open room where the reporter slept. Fenn changed position restlessly as the drop in temperature touched him, but he slumbered on, his dreams no refuge, merely extensions of the daytime nightmare. The corners of the faded papers on the small desk stirred with the chill breeze.

Sue glanced at her watch. Nearly eleven. What was taking Gerry so long? Was he going to leave Nancy Shelbeck here all night? He said he'd get back.

She stirred the coffee and took it from the kitchen into the lounge. The door to her bedroom was slightly ajar and she stopped to listen for a few seconds. Nancy's breathing seemed more regulated, deeper, the earlier disturbed panting having faded to small childlike whimpers before a more natural sleep had taken over. Sue went to the sofa and sat, placing the steaming mug of coffee on the coffee table before her. She sank into the soft cushions and closed her eyes.

Abruptly she opened them and stood up; she walked to the window and drew the curtains together. For some reason she had felt the night intrusive. She returned to the sofa and absently stirred the coffee.

What had happened to make them both so frightened? Earlier that evening Gerry had garbled something about finding the American at a church in Barham, in a state of shock, then pleaded with her to take care of the woman until he got back. He had hurried out, clutching his bag as if it contained his year's salary, telling her he had to see Monsignor Delgard, that he had something important to show him. What could have been so important? Why had he and this woman gone to the church at Barham in the first place? And what were they so afraid of?

Sue tapped at her chin in frustration. Why bring her here of all places? Was he so insensitive to the situation? It was obvious that something was going on between them. Yet Sue knew that Gerry's insensitivity was often a put-on, that he was fully aware of the emotions he aroused in others, that he preferred reaction to inertia. But this time there was a desperation in him that dismissed any notion of lovers' games; he needed Sue's help and that it involved another woman with whom he had a relationship had no relevance.

She sipped the coffee. Damn him! She had tried to fall out of love with him, had even tried to despise him for a while, but it had been no use. Her religion, the work at the church, the time spent with Ben, had all contrived to compensate, but the fulfilment had been short-lived and, if she were to be completely honest with herself, never entirely realized. She had found renewed spiritual awareness, but still it could not fill her emotional needs, could not replace or dispose of a different kind of love, the love of one person for another. At first, just weeks before, she had thought such physical love unnecessary; its traumas, the dependence on another (particularly when the other person wasn't so dependable), the jealousies, the *responsibility*, was a trial she would be better off without; but it had gradually dawned on her that to love and be loved on equal terms, with all its hang-ups, was essential. For her, anyway.

Sue frowned as she held the mug in both hands, her elbows resting on her knees. She had been trying to escape, thinking she had found another refuge, an alternative, only to discover that both were equally important. The realization had been there for the last few days, but it had taken their meeting earlier that evening for the fact to hit home. Perhaps it was his new vulnerability that had moved her. Or perhaps it was the thought that this other woman might mean something to him. The fear of losing had always been a prime motivator.

Just what was she to . . .

The scream caused her to spill the coffee over her hands. Quickly Sue slammed the mug onto the coffee table and ran for the bedroom. She fumbled for the light switch, flicked it on, and stared aghast at the woman who was trying to bury her head into the pillow. Sue went to the bed. 'It's okay, you're safe, there's nothing to worry – '

Nancy thrashed out, pushing her hands away.

'Nancy! Stop! You're all right now.' Sue's voice was firm as she tried to pull the American around to face her.

'Don't, don't . . .' Nancy's eyes were unfocused as she struggled away from Sue.

Sue grabbed her wrists as long nails tried to lash her face. 'Calm down, Nancy! It's me, Sue Gates. Don't you remember? Gerry brought you here.'

'Oh God, don't touch me!'

Sue pinned the frightened woman's arms to her chest and leaned heavily on her. 'Calm down. Nothing's going to harm you. You were dreaming.' She spoke steadily, repeating the words, and eventually, Nancy's struggles became weaker. Her eyes began to lose their glazed look and came to rest on Sue's face. 'Oh noooo!' Nancy moaned, and then she was weeping, her thin body wracked by the sobs.

'It's all right, Nancy. You're perfectly safe.'

Nancy threw her arms around Sue and clung to her as an upset child would cling to its mother. Sue soothed her, stroking her hair, feeling awkward, but compassionate enough not to pull away. Laughter drifted up from the street below, late-night revellers returning to their homes. The bedside clock ticked away the minutes.

It was some time before Nancy's sobs ceased and her hands relaxed their tight grip around her comforter's shoulders. Her body trembled as she mumbled something.

'What?' Sue pulled away slightly. 'I didn't hear you.'

Nancy drew in a shuddering breath. 'I need a drink,' she said.

'I think I've got some brandy. Or gin. Would you prefer that?'

'Anything.'

Sue left her and went into the kitchen, opening the larder where she kept her meagre supply of alcohol. She took out the squat bottle of brandy, then reached into another cupboard for a glass. On reflection, she brought down two glasses. Her nerves were jumpy too.

She took the two brandies into the bedroom and found the American sitting upright against the headboard. Her face was white, its paleness made grotesque by the streaks of running mascara. She was staring blankly at the wall opposite, her hands twisting the edge of the bedsheets into a crumpled roll.

Sue handed her one of the glasses which she grabbed with both hands. The amber liquid almost spilled over the sides as she raised the glass to her lips. Nancy drank and began to cough, holding the brandy away from her. Sue took the glass from her and waited for the choking to subside.

'Try it more slowly this time,' she said when Nancy reached out again. The reporter followed her advice and Sue sipped at her own drink.

'Th – thanks,' Nancy finally gasped. 'You don't . . . you don't have a cigarette, do you?'

'Sorry.'

'It's okay. There's some in my bag.'

'I'm afraid you didn't have a bag with you when Gerry brought you here. You must have left it in his car.'

'Oh shit, no. It's back there at the church, probably somewhere in the undergrowth.'

'What happened? Why did you leave it there?'

Nancy looked at Sue. 'Didn't Fenn tell you?'

'He didn't take time to. He said something about St Peter's at Barham, asked me to take care of you, then dashed out. What were you doing at the church?'

Nancy took a swallow of the brandy and leaned her head back against the wall, closing her eyes. 'I was searching for something. I assume he came looking for the same thing.' She told Sue about the chest and the historical records they had hoped to find inside. Her voice still shook with tension.

'That's what he must have had in his bag,' Sue said.

Nancy's head came away from the wall. 'He found them?'

'I think so. He said he had to take something to Monsignor Delgard.'

'Is that where he's gone – to Delgard, to St Joseph's?'

Sue nodded.

'I know this sounds odd,' Nancy said, clutching Sue's arm, 'but what did I tell him? I . . . I just can't remember anything after running from that goddamned church.'

'I don't know. You were in a state of shock.'

'Yeah, I must have been.' Her whole body shuddered. 'My God, I think I saw some kind of ghost.'

Sue looked at her in surprise. 'You don't look the type.'

'Uh-huh, that's what I thought. But something scared the shit out of me inside that church.' She closed her eyes once more, trying to relive the memory. Her eyes snapped open as the image came to her. 'Oh no,' she said, then wailed, 'Oh no!'

Sue shook her gently. 'Take it easy. Whatever it was, you're safe now.'

'Safe? That was a fucking dead thing I saw back there! How can you be safe from something like that?'

Sue was stunned. 'You must have imagined it. You couldn't possibly have – '

'Don't tell me that! I know what I saw!'

'Don't get upset again.'

'Upset? I got a right to get fucking upset. I'm telling you, I saw something that's never gonna leave me, something I'm never gonna forget.' The tears were flowing again and the brandy glass clattered against her teeth as she attempted to drink. Sue steadied her hand for her.

'Thanks,' Nancy said when she had managed to swallow more of the alcohol. 'I didn't mean to yell. It's just . . . you don't know what the hell it was like.'

'Do you want to tell me?'

'No, I don't want to tell you, I want to erase it from my mind. But I know I never will.'

'Please, it might help you.'

'Do I get another drink?'

'Take mine.' They exchanged glasses. It took two more sips – but at least they were just sips – for Nancy to speak again. Her words were slow, as though she were trying to control them, to rationalize them in her own mind.

'I was inside the church – St Peter's on the Stapley Estate. D'you know it?'

'I've heard of it. I've never been there.'

'Give it a miss. I'd found the chest – '

'You said you were looking for some historical records.'

'Right. Fenn said a certain part of St Joseph's history was missing. We tracked down the chest they might have been kept in. It was at St Peter's.'

'You went there together?'

'No, separately. Fenn didn't want me in on the deal. You know how he is.'

Sue said nothing.

'I'd found the chest – I was sure it was the right one. Then I heard – maybe I just felt – someone else in the church. I walked down towards the altar to take a look. There was someone sitting behind a kind of alcove, in a closed-in pew affair. It looked . . . it looked like a nun.'

She gulped back more brandy.

'Only it wasn't a nun,' she continued. 'It wasn't a nun . . .' Her voice trailed off.

'Tell me, Nancy,' Sue urged quietly.

'She was wearing one of those hooded cloak affairs, a habit of some kind, but not like those you see nowadays. It was old, I'm sure it was goddamned old. I couldn't see her face at first.' She was trembling again. 'But she . . . it . . . turned towards me. Oh God, oh God, that face!'

Sue could feel the bristling of her own hairs on the back of her neck, the sudden rising of goose-pimples down her spine and arms. 'Tell me,' she said again, horrified but peculiarly fascinated.

'It was just a charred, cindered mess. The eyes were black, just slits with burnt gristle poking through. The lips and nose had been scorched away, the teeth were just burned-out stumps. There was nothing left to it, no features, nothing human! And I could smell the burning, I could smell roasting flesh. And she began to move. She was dead but she began to move, to rise, to come towards me. She touched me! She touched my face with her burned stubble of a hand! And she tried to hold me there. She breathed onto my face! I could feel it, I could smell it! Her fingers, just withered stumps, touched my eyes! And she was laughing, oh God, she was laughing! *But she was still burning! Do you understand? She was still burning!*'

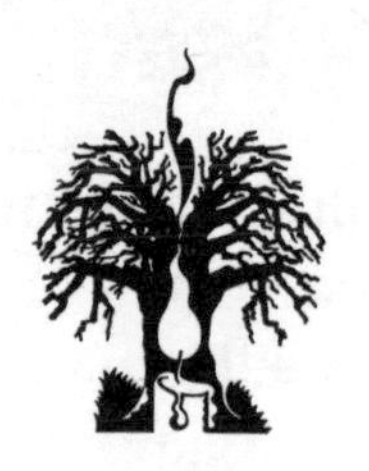

34

And sleep shall obey me,
And visit thee never,
And the curse shall be on thee
For ever and ever.

Robert Southey,
'Kehama's Curse'

When Fenn awoke he was shivering. He rubbed at his eyes, then peered around the room.

'Delgard?' he called out. The door was open, cold air sweeping into the room. He wearily pushed himself from the armchair and crossed the floor. Peering into the dark passageway, he called the priest's name again. There was no answer. Fenn noticed the front door was open. Had Delgard gone over to the church? He stepped back into the room and checked his watch. Jesus! Nearly one in the morning!

His eyes fell on the small writing desk and the scattered papers on its surface. With a final glance into the hall, he closed the door and went to the desk. He picked up a few sheets of the old parchment paper, realizing they were the same papers that had fallen from the vellum manuscript inside the church on the Stapley Estate. He studied them for a few seconds as though the words would translate themselves, then returned them to the desk. The top pages of Delgard's notebook were folded over as if the draught had disturbed them. He flicked them back and scanned the lines on the first page. He slowly sat, his eyes never leaving the words before him.

Leafing through the pages, he saw that the monsignor had translated most, if not all, of the ancient papers, adding and initialling his own notes as he went along. His tiredness quickly dispersed as he read Delgard's first note:

> (The script is unclear in parts, much of the writing almost illegible. The handwriting is erratic, scrawled, unlike the neat hand of the manuscript these papers were found in, even though author seems to be same. Translation will be as close to the original as possible, but own interpretation and meaning will have to be used to make sense of certain sections of text. Also, Latin is not correct in parts – may be due to disturbed mind of writer. D.)

Fenn picked up a single sheet of parchment once more and frowned at the scrawl. A disturbed mind, or a frightened one?

He looked over at the door and wondered if he should find Delgard. How long the priest had been gone, he had no way of knowing, but the translation must have taken hours judging by the amount of notes. Fenn was annoyed at himself for having fallen asleep. It was a strange time for Delgard to have gone into the church, but then he, Fenn, knew little of the lives of such men: perhaps it was normal for him to make his devotions at such a late hour. On the other hand, Delgard may have just gone out to check on the two young priests whose duty it was to keep an all-night vigil in the next-door field. With some of the crazy people around it would have made more sense to bring in Securicor but, he supposed, the Church had its own way of doing things.

It was still cold in the room, even though the door was now closed. He noticed the fire was low, almost out, the burnt logs charcoaled with patches of white ash breaking the blackness. He went to the fireplace and threw on two more logs, cinders briefly flaring as they landed. He rubbed his hands together to clear the wood-dust and willed the logs to ignite, the chill beginning to sink into his bones.

The wood sizzled as gas escaped and small flames began to lick at the underneath. He grunted with satisfaction and turned towards the desk. For some reason his eyes were drawn towards the window and at the long narrow gap between the curtains; he drew them tightly closed as if the night outside were a sinister voyeur. He sat once more and pulled Delgard's large notebook towards him. He began to read, and he was still cold.

Seventeenth Day of October in the year 1560

She is dead yet dwells not in the underworld. At night I see her before me, a vile thing from Hell that cannot rest, nor yet let me be, a rotting creature of the grave that once I cherished. But then, her beauty was unspoiled. Now sweet, Damnable, Elnor will not leave, not until she has me with her amongst her corrupted brood. 'Tis true I deserve such fate, for my Sins cry out and are not to be forgiven by Our God in Heaven. Mayhap my madness is an earthly Penance and this makes better choice than the Hell to which she draws me. But she has bid me, and she, my Elnor, will surely take me.

(Script impossible to read here and

My hand trembles for she is here! Her corpse's presence surrounds me and makes foul the air!

no meaning can be guessed at. D.)

My father, that noble Lord, forbids that I confess to my Bishop, for he sees only madness in my eyes and would mute my madman's utterings. Thus he keeps me prisoner in this mean Chapel where only the servants and landsmen bear witness to my decline. No longer am I a freeman, for I have fallen in his eyes and no blame to him for that. Yet how long must I hear his Chaucer jibe:

'That if gold rust, what then will iron do?
For if a Priest be foul in trust
No wonder that a common man should
rust!'

For all his scorn, still I know he understands not the depths of my Sin. Haste now! Though my brow be fevered and my hand trembles as if with ague, this must be set down that others may read of she whose vengeance is boundless nor leashed by earthly time. Give me strength, Dear Lord, and deny me not the courage to carry out this duty, that others shall know her vileness and be warned. My guilt lies open in these my words. You who read them dismiss them not as a madman's ravings. But keep close hold of the vision of Our Saviour that is within you, lest your Soul be tainted by this Confession.

(Scrawled lines at this point and many deletions. As if writer cannot put his thoughts on paper. D.)

I served long years at the Church of St Joseph's in Banefeld and there I knew joy. The village was my house, the villagers my trusting children. Disputes I settled and they had Faith in my Word for they believed it the Word of God. The womenfolk unburdened their worries upon my shoulders and I was pleased to give counsel to these simple people, for it gave purpose to my life and Grace to my Soul. The children had some small fear of me for my countenance is not pleasing. Yet fear of God's Servant on Earth is proper to the young. My Holiness was revered and the True Faith was kept in my Parish throughout all those troubled Heretical times.

(He refers to the Reformation and the Establishment of the Church of England during the reign of Henry VIII. D.)

No man betrayed my trust, though Evil entered my Soul and yet holds sway.

It was the Prioress who brought Elnor to me, unknowing that she did the Devil's work. Elnor, this Cursed Nun, was fair and gentle to look upon; a child, an innocent, whose treachery to God and Mankind I did not perceive. Blacker than jet was her Soul, her mind full of guile and her personage well-armed with deceit. Her mistress considered her spirited, but her own cheveril conscience could not perceive Elnor's subtle wickedness. She was to be of help in the Church, an aid much needed, for my duties were plenty. Then was I stirred by carnal desires, urgings of the flesh that could not be subdued, unholy dreams that betrayed my Chastity. And it was as though straightway she had Knowledge of my hidden Sinfulness, for her eyes saw clearly into my very Soul. Such was her Mystery. Too soon I knew that Elnor was as no other woman and that her Holy Vocation was but the aberration of a perverse mind. Yet it was her mind that first distracted me from my duties. My studies have encompassed astronomy, medicine, physics and even the

(As the son of a wealthy nobleman, his learning may well have ancient esoteric craft of alchemy; and of medicine and alchemy her knowledge was by far the greater.

I was soon to become fascinated by her Knowledge and thus captivated.

From the beginning, she was like no other Religious of my acquaintance; in truth, like no other woman. Elnor fulfilled her duties pleasingly well, but always there was the smile that held some veiled secret, the gaze that lingered too long on my own. I was soon Bewitched and was later to deem that term rightly used. In those first days I saw only guileless innocence, not the true self which made fool of me. We prayed together and her adoration inclined most towards the Blessed Mother of Christ, daughter of St Anna. There was at this time a sickness in the village, no plague this, but illness that sent many to their beds. Two children died yet these were frail from birth, so God was praised for His Mercy and for sending so skilled a mortal in the tending of the sick. For her powers of medicine were soon made manifest and even our physician, a pompous though well-meaning fellow, ventured his admiration. Two other young Holy Sisters joined us in our work. Novices these, whose names were Agnes and Rosemund, and they remained at the Church when the sickness was passed. It was said that a Divine Hand guided hers, that by gazing upon a man, be he reeve or hayward, she could tell if he were dry or cold, moist or hot. Thus would she administer her restorative

included such diverse subjects. But how could this nun know of such things? D.)

(A person's body was conceived of being composed of the four elements: Earth, Water, Air and Fire. Earth – cold and dry; Water – cold and moist; Air – hot and moist; Fire – hot and dry. Sickness was an imbalance of these. D.)

(Effigies. D.)

simples and cures. She also used images to be worn about the neck when the planets were favourably inclined; energies descended into the image with great benefit to the dependent. I had cause to scold Elnor for such practices, but she would smile and say it was Faith that offered the cure and nothing more. If I found this sacrilegious, I would keep my peace because of the deep interest it aroused in me. Such then was my initial Enchantment with Elnor that I did not consider to consult with the Prioress. It was when a mysterious malady struck down my own body that pending illfortune had its consummation. Elnor was sent by her Prioress to tend me and, in my delirium, I felt her hands upon my body, soothing my pains, bathing away fever's moisture; and kindling a desire that had been smouldering. Perchance it was her own potions which aroused my passion. Thus ensnared was I, and once so, became her willing captive. My abandonment was complete, my taste for her delights insatiable. I am too shamefaced to relate all that took place in our sinful fornication; suffice to say that our carnal acts plunged into bestiality of such low nature that I fear my Soul is perished, never more to be reborn in God's light.

(More incoherent writing here, much of it indecipherable. Although stated he will not detail his indecencies with his woman, it appears he has done so to a certain extent. Unclear whether it is guilt that has subconsciously made writing almost illegible, fear, or his own reawakened excitement.

As Elnor opened her flesh to me, so too did she open her mind. She spoke of things ancient and of matters not yet of this Earth. She spoke of voices that were from the dead, and of forces that rode the air like silent thunderstorms; forces perceived only by the

Much sacrilege and the use of holy objects seems to be involved. Names here and there, but can make no sense of them. D.)

Chosen. She likened these incorporeal powers to great unsighted tidal waves sought entry into the shallow world of men, Furies that if unleashed would destroy and recreate in their own image. I would ask her if it was the Devil's power she spoke of and she would mock me and tell me there was no greater power than the Will of Man. I cowered at such blasphemy and believed her to be a sorceress; but in the passage of time I learned that she was much more. To her, magic was but a product of the Will, and potions, poisons and transmuters the tools of alchemists and physicians, not of the sorceress. I was irrevocably lost in her; this wretched Nun dominated my existence. My frail body, so exquisitely scourged by her instruments, lived only to gratify itself with her pleasures. As well I sought her Knowledge; yet still am I mystified.

From whence does your Evil come? I would ask of her. And from where your Goodness? For still she cured the sick. Why do you venerate the Holy Name of the Sacred Virgin, yet blaspheme her presence by fornication before her Image? Why choose the righteous path of handmaiden of Christ when your secret deeds are not to His Way? And why have you made prisoner of this poor Soul? These questions I asked many times, but she answered them not until one year had gone by and, I think, until she was sure that the invisible chains which girdled my Will could not be loosed. She cured the sick that her name should be exalted as was the name of Mary; and she exalted Mary's name that she, Elnor, be as the Virgin Mother, an intermediary of power, though not yet fully tested. I am a Nun, Elnor told me, because I seek position over others, that I may be revered and obeyed. As Prioress, I shall gain that trust and 'tis you, sweet Thomas, who will help me in this, for has not your noble father great influence with the Church? As I write the Chapel goes colder, swift dissolving breath clouds fading to the page below. The wind shakes windows and doors, and Demons seek me out. Stay away Elnor! This ground is Sacred, its Sanctity inviolate. Still my fingers grow numb with the freeze and become brittle as if fit to snap. O God have Mercy on this miserable creature and allow my Chronicle to be written.

Methinks I hear a voice that calls my name from without. Would that it were the mewlings of some night animal, but I fear 'tis the voice of my dead mistress. The Chapel is dim and the lamp cannot light up the dark places. There is no peace for me here, nor will be until she is laid to rest. But who will do that deed? Not I, that I know.

In truth then I knew Elnor, but still could not resist her Will. She laughed at my words and scorned my horror. She spoke of poison for the Prioress: Orpiment or Realgar would be the insiduous assassin.

(Trisulphide of arsenic and

The poisoning would be slow that no suspicion would arise. The Prioress would suffer disulphide of arsenic. D.)

a long and wasting sickness and it would be seen that even the skilled and tender administrations of Sister Elnor would not prevent the aged Nun's death. O cunning Witch! Yet Witch you are not. No sorceress you, sweet, Damned Elnor; something more, something much more.

Too late I learned of these ambitions, poor debauched fool that I was. Weak, lecherous disciple of Sin! Help me God before my dying comes.

Yet so lost to her own lust was Elnor that her downfall was of her own doing. And Blessed be to Jesu for that. My people revered her for they considered her pure of heart and she had cured many an ailment. They brought to her gifts, some mere trinkets and others of value. The latter kind she stored secretly in the Crypt of St Joseph's lest the Prioress discover them, and those of little value she gave to the Priory. And all thought her most fair and generous.

The children flocked to Sister Elnor, this vile creature of depravity, adoring her, beseeching her Blessing, for they knew from their elders that here walked a Saint on Earth; and her black heart welcomed them, for they were as lambs to a wolf. What makes a Soul thus? There is no answer in this World, but lies in a place of darkness, where shadowed spirits conspire with devils to destroy Mankind's peace.

In Church she prayed long hours, her body prostrate before the altar, that all might witness her devotion. At night, when observers were none, then would she defile that same altar in practices that now cause sickness in my throat, for I was her willing accomplice. Still I know not what led me to this disgrace, what Spirit released this carnal lust in me. I reason that her Will governed mine, her thoughts controlled my own; but in my heart I know the Will had first to come from me. Her temptations were so cursedly sweet, the torture upon my body so cursedly glorious! Her child's face, her white flesh, that Devil's gateway between her thighs from which she bade me drink, these were too wondrous to forswear.

Yet I wander, my thoughts no longer gathered. My father, that steadfast patron of the Church, thinks me mad; and perhaps 'tis so. Still I have not the madman's escape into delirium and there is no comfort in my dreams.

But in the second year of my Knowledge of Elnor, suspicions were whispered abroad. My demeanour had changed. I had never been a robust man, but there was a weakness upon me, a stoop to my stature that was plain to see. My obsession with the young Nun would no longer be disguised. Worse yet was the disappearance of the children, lost over several months in the nearby forests, never to be seen again. Three children in all, whose names I have already set down.

(Set down? D.)

How these simple peasant children had believed in sweet Sister Elnor, and how I had

(The names must be those mentioned in the earlier unclear passage. The priest and the nun killed the children! D.)

to stifle their screams when her punishment was visited upon their small bodies. Dear God, there can be no forgiveness for my part in these foul deeds. I could not even pray over their hidden graves.

The Prioress had become weakened, her life's spirit ebbing more each day. Stealthy was her demise, for Elnor would not allow that any should say the hand of another played part in the old nun's death. Bolder became this Devil's Daughter and more demanding in her excesses. My endeavours were no longer sufficient for her lusts and less often could my tortures satiate her appetite. As well, it had become dangerous to take more children from the district. Her appetites were turned upon the two young novices who came daily to St Joseph's. One accepted her debasement willingly, for her heart was already lost to Elnor; the other submitted but fled shamefaced afterwards. This novice took her own life in remorse, but first Confessed her Mortal Sin to the ailing Prioress.

Outrage gave the Mother Superior a new-found strength. But so too was she cunning, for my father's coffers were ever open to the Church. His loyalty to our Holy Roman Pope had not wavered during the Heretical time of Henry's Lutherism, nor during the confused reign of the young Edward. Now my father was favoured by good Queen Mary and justly rewarded for his fortitude and loyalty. To have him as enemy would not have been wise for the Prioress, who had oft times benefited from his generosity.

This wise woman sent for me and, knowing all was lost, I threw myself on her mercy. The blame lay all with the vile temptress, Sister Elnor, whose magic potions had robbed me of my reason. I wept and scourged myself before the Prioress; I confessed my most grave and sinful fornication with Elnor and begged forgiveness. But I did not tell all, for I was afraid for my life.

Though she looked upon me with loathing in her eyes, the Prioress gave me her forgiveness. Elnor's Spirit was darkened by spectres who rejected the Christian Path. She was a child of Satan whose sorcery had overcome my Will. A mere mortal, I could offer scant resistance to the leeching of my strength and the magic potions she fed my body. I eagerly accepted these Judgements, well knowing they were my Salvation, willing to believe I was but helpless victim to Entrancement. That day we discussed the punishment of Sister Elnor.

The Prioress doubted not that Elnor was Witch and Profaner and, 'though I knew she was more, I readily agreed. Good Queen Mary had decreed that both Witch and Dissenter should be driven from her Realm and from this Mortal World. Rumour had it that two hundred and more Heretics had already been burnt at the stake, and the County of Sussex had played part in many of these burnings. I myself had witnessed two in

(Summoner: someone paid to bring

sinners to trial before an ecclesiastical court. D.)

nearby Lewes. The Summoner was sent for and I denounced Sister Elnor as Heretic and Witch. The Prioress was well pleased with this and seemed satisfied with my Contrition. When the Summoner had left us to make arrangements for Elnor's confinement, she bade me warn my congregation of the Nun's evil-doings lest more suffering ensued. There was a gleam to her eyes when she hinted that Elnor might lie too well at her trial, and my own person would be brought to book. I well knew that the truth would indeed bring this about, and I suspect the Prioress, my new found guardian, knew this too. I journied back to Banefeld with much haste, my brow as fevered as when the true fever had been upon me. I was mindful of my own safety and wished to protect the good name of my father. In the village I quickly told certain members of my Congregation of what the Prioress and I had discovered of Elnor, and word spread like flames in a forest fire. These good people were full of wrath, for to have their Faith abused and in such a manner was more than they could bear. Those whose children had been lost screamed for vengeance and their cry was taken up, along with sticks and cudgels, by their fellows. They hastened to the Church of St Joseph's, a vehement, threatening mob, and I followed, spurring them on, enlivened with their passion, for had I not been unwittingly Seduced into her Wickedness? There were children amongst us, those who had once revered this Holy Nun and who now despised her. So sudden was our descent upon the Church that Elnor was found by the altar, beneath the statue of Our Lord's blissful Mother, there embraced in the arms of the novice, Rosemund, who had so easily succumbed to her wiles. As had I. Elnor was dragged screaming from the Church, her protesting companion in desire thrown to one side. O how I cowered when Elnor's eyes met mine; it seemed poison-tipped daggers had plunged into my heart. She knew at once that I was her betrayer and such was the malevolence in her eyes that I fell to the ground. My flock believed me Spellbound and tore at her eyes with fingers and sticks. Even when she wailed piteously, sightlessly, they gave no mercy but flailed her for her witchcraft. She cried out that I, their spiritual leader, was partner to her iniquity, and I denied her charges most absolutely, bidding them pay no heed to the Heretic's lies, urging them to look for the Devil's Mark about her person, for secretly I knew that upon her body was a third nipple, an aberration that the ignorant believed to be a suckling breast for a witch's Familiar. They stripped her of her Nun's robes and found the Accursed Mark. Their rage all but consumed them. The menfolk beat her relentlessly, their women and children urging them on, until her naked body ran with blood. And all the while they beseeched her to Confess to witchcraft. But still she did not; curses were her only words. They pulled hair, greased with her own blood, from her body,

(Alice! D.) }

until she was an obscene, hairless figure; yet still she would not admit to sorcery. O the torture they inflicted upon her! And yet my pleas for the punishment to end were feeble and went unheard. They broke her limbs, these Christian men, and dragged her through the mire as the children and women stabbed at her with pointed sticks. I could not stop them and I no longer tried.

Elnor implored mercy but still did not Confess to the crime of which she was accused. So angered were they that they dragged her to a nearby ditch, the river too far for their seething passion. The water ran scarlet when they put her to the Test and her tortured body gave way at last to the agony. She Confessed to witchcraft, and such was my own fear and need for vengeance that I almost believed this to be true. May He that Harrowed Hell forgive me, but this I wanted to be true.

They carried Elnor to a young oak nearby and there they tied a rope about her neck and hoisted her aloft. Still she screamed, and those screams filled my head until I felt my skull must needs burst. And when they lit the fire beneath her naked, dangling feet, it seemed her agony consumed my own flesh. Those bloodfilled sockets, once the holders of the softest of eyes, stared at me through the mob each time her twisting body turned in my direction, and her broken lips poured Curses upon my head, and upon all those present, each man, woman and child, and their descendants. And she cursed the name of Mary. I knew not whether she meant Christ's Holy Mother, or our own Good Queen Mary, and I wonder if by then this demented creature knew herself. Even when the carpenter, a strong man this with no weak stomach, cut into her bowels and drew down her organs so that they sizzled and roasted upon the fire below, her Curses still filled our heads.

At her death I knew that this woman was indeed more than Witch, for the sky darkened and the ground trembled beneath our feet. Those that could, ran, whilst others cowered in the mud. I thought my Church nearby would topple, but its sturdy build held fast, though several stones fell. So afraid was this poor Mortal Soul that I believed I saw spectres rising from the graveyard. I know not what foul force from Hell had been released by Elnor's death. The very earth appeared to open beneath my feet and I stared into a Black Pit and there I saw the twisted creatures of the lower world, wretched Lost Souls, whose sins so foul were irredeemable, whose anguished moans rose up in torment to pervade the darkened landscape. What manner of creature she to invoke such horrors! Now fallen, crawling on my belly like a worm, I turned my head from this Hellish sight and looked upon the black-charred carcass of she who once had been my sweet, wicked mistress.

The rope from which she hung broke and its

gruesome burden dropped into the fire below where it did seethe and hiss until it was as charcoaled wood. I thought that I heard from this blackened thing one last howling screech, but this could only have been my own tortured imaginings for, in surety, there was nothing human left of that once fair body. It became as night, though day was not spent, darkness falling upon darkness, and I ran from that Infernal Place, the vile stench and inhuman cries rising from the Black Pit to assail my senses. I fled, unsteady on my feet, for the ground still shook, and beseeched the Lord Christ to save me from Satan's Anger. The Church Crypt was my refuge, my Sanctuary, and I covered my eyes against the demons that rose and beckoned me from their disturbed resting places. Three days I hid in that tomb of darkness, curled in the blackest corner, my head covered by coarse sacking, my eyes closed tight against the shadows. Mayhap the time spent in that lonely dungeon loosed my reason completely, for when my father's servants found me at last, no words of meaning came from my lips. They took me from there and my eyes were blinded by the light of day. It was well, for I had no desire to look upon that ravaged scene again. I was locked in a room in my father's house and physicians endeavoured to soothe my ramblings with medicines and kind words. When at last my ravings had calmed, my Bishop came and spoke quietly with me, my father at his side, a staunch rock of reality.

They told me that the people of Banefeld, the landsmen, their women folk, their children, would not speak of that Evil day but to say that Elnor had Confessed to witchcraft and the slaughter of three children, and had Cursed them in her dying breath. A thunderstorm had shaken the land and dark clouds had gathered low overhead, though no rain had fallen. But they did not tell of rising demons, nor black openings to Hell. I implored my father and the Bishop to believe me, but their reply was gentle admonishment: Elnor had poisoned my mind with her drugs and I had seen that which was not, had lived only in the realm of my own thoughts. At this I further ranted and two servants were summoned to strap me to my bed.

Weeks passed, though I know not how many, and in that time it was decided between my father and the Bishop that my health, by which they meant the condition of my mind, might be better served if I stayed away from St Joseph's and Banefeld. I suspect the hand of the Prioress was in this, for while she would not condemn me before my father, her Conscience would not allow my tainted person within her Province. Thus my days would be spent at the small Church of St Peter's, on my father's estate, where my babblings would be ignored by his servants and the tenants. I would serve as Pastor. Here I would stay safe, locked in my own cell of madness. Money was given to St Joseph's by my father for repairs to fallen stonework – ha! Struck by lightning they said, and a new stained glass window was set into the south wall. He brought to me several items from my old Parish, vestments and such like. The Church chest was also carried to St Peter's and I believe it was of this he was most mindful. Methinks private words had passed between my father and that wily Sister of the Cloth, the Prioress, for he seemed eager to obtain this chest in which were kept all records of St Joseph's and the Parish of Banefeld. He need not have been thus concerned, for I had not been foolish enough to set down my carnal acts with Sister Elnor, nor any statement which would speak foul of her. How he must have pored over these letters and scripts, searching for that which would bring down shame on the Woolgar crest, and how he must have sighed when none was found. How then would he view this paper that I now scribe for future reading, which will remain well-hid until God deigns it shall be found? Not well, I am sure.

Hark now! The door rattles once more, but already she is within. Her stench grows stronger and I will not look at the dark shadow that lingers at the edge of my vision. My body is stiff with cold and the quill with which I write scratches deep into the page. Yet my fear will not let me rest! I must finish this task quickly lest my courage fail and others be not warned! I have served my days here with diligence and with Godliness, knowing my Soul is forever Damned. After a while, many months to be sure, I learned to keep dread contained within me, giving vent only when alone to the anguish and remorse that tortured me. They thought me still mad and their gaze avoided mine. But no longer were they burdened with my rantings, my impassioned pleas against unseen forces. Once more our Holy Pope in Rome is denied now that Elizabeth has come to the throne, but that concerns me little, for I am left alone in peace here. In peace! What insanities I write! Yet would I gladly exchange persecution from our new Queen for the vile pursuance of this soul-less spirit. I have not seen the Prioress since I was ensconced here and she ignores the messages I send through my father's servants (it may be that he intercepts them). His reeve had told me that Sister Rosemund was cast out of the Priory after Elnor's death and took to living in the forests near the village. This may well be true; I care not. My pity is for myself alone. None is to spare for that unfortunate. Elnor breathes upon me and it is the fetid breath of Death! She wills me look into those bloodfilled eyes, to fall into her lover's embrace. A withered hand touches my shoulder and still I will not look! Not yet, dear Elnor. Not 'til this task be done, these words set down that others may learn. Doubt not these words, reader; denounce them not as the ravings of a madman, but pay them heed! Her Evil is not yet done and her maligned Spirit is not yet at rest.

The door is opened and the howling wind

enters the church. It shrieks at these papers, seeking to tear them from my hand. But I will resist. She shall not have them. They will be well kept, hidden away, and then shall I turn to my Elnor. And I shall embrace her as I have embraced her in dreams of late, for my desires are still of her. I see only her beauty, not this scarred, blackened creature who stands over me, whose lipless mouth stays close to my cheek, whose

Enough of this! She has me, for there are no lies between us now. I still fornicate with her in my thoughts and it is my Sinful lust that binds us forever. I leave this warning for those who seek it. She touches me and I am hers once more!

Guard your soul. With this script I may find some Redemption. Guard your Soul and Pray for one who is already lost.

(End of document. Beyond doubt Thomas Woolgar, priest of St Joseph's, Banfield, and latterly of St Peter's, Barham, son of Sir Henry Woolgar, is author. D).

Questions:

1. *Was* Thomas Woolgar insane?
2. What did he mean: Elnor more than just a witch?
3. Is curse coming true??
4. Father Hagan/Molly Pagett: catalysts?
5. IS ALICE ELNOR?!!!

D.

Fenn sat back in the chair, his eyes never leaving the papers. He let out a long sighed breath. Jesus Christ! Was it possible?

Were these words just the rantings of a madman, or were they the truth? Could this event, this terrible, misguided witch-burning that happened nearly five hundred years ago be the cause of everything that was happening at St Joseph's today? No, it *had* to be superstitious mumbo-jumbo! Witches were from fairy tales, folklore, legends that parents loved to tell their kids around a cheery fire on a dark night. But then Woolgar wasn't claiming that Elnor was a witch. In fact, he *disclaimed* it. But was the supernatural any more real than fairy tales or folklore? Even though he, Fenn, had witnessed events in Banfield that could only be called paranormal, his logical mind found it difficult to accept such a term as fact. But how could he dismiss what had happened to him that very day? There had been something in that church with him, something that threw out a malignant aura of evil. It had scared Nancy half to death and loosened his own bowels somewhat. So what the hell was it? The ghost of poor Sister Elnor?

'Aaah,' he said aloud in disgust. It just couldn't be. There were no such things. 'Keep telling yourself that, Fenn,' he muttered. He studied his hand and there were no weal marks on it, no demon marks on the skin. Yet there had been inside the church, for he had seen them appear. And there were no other marks on his body save where the foliage had lashed him during his tumble down the slope.

He wondered what Delgard's opinion would be. As a priest, the supernatural was part of his dogma, and the concept of life after death was the basis of his religion. But the manifestation of an evil woman's curse from another era? How would that grab him? If he believed in all this, maybe he'd gone over to the church to pray for help!

Fenn shook his head. It was all too incredible. And yet it was happening.

He pushed back the chair and stood, suddenly realizing how stiff and cold he was again. The fire had burned low once more. He reached for his topcoat and shrugged it on, pulling the zipper all the way up to the neck. Better find Delgard, talk it out with him. The priest was no fool despite his vocation; if he felt there was some relevance to the document, then there sure-as-hell was. And if that was the case, the problem would be what to do about it.

Fenn left the room, pulling the neck of his coat tight around his cheeks, not sure whether it was the coldness of the night that made him shiver, or the faded script lying on the desk top.

He closed the door and walked the length of the hallway, an icy draught greeting him from the doorway ahead. He stepped out into the night and automatically looked up at the sky: it was clear, as if freshly scrubbed of clouds by the winds of the day, its blueness deep, almost black, the star clusters sharp, vivid. There was a light showing dimly through the windows of the church and Fenn walked briskly along the path towards it. His pace quickened until he was almost running. There was something strange about St Joseph's, something he could not understand. It seemed totally black, darker than the night around it, no starlight reflected from the flint walls, no relief in its shape, no shades of grey. Unnaturally black, just a dim light glowing from its windows. He could feel his heart pounding and suddenly he did not want to reach the church; he wanted to turn away, to run from the grounds, away from this malevolent place. He felt as he had at St Peter's earlier in the day: afraid and bewildered.

But he knew Delgard would be in there, alone, unguarded, unaware of the transformation that had occurred. Fenn had to warn the priest, to get him away from there, for he suddenly understood that St Joseph's was no longer the house of God, but the sanctum of something unholy.

When he touched the door, it felt repellent to him, as though the wood, itself, were unclean. He was badly frightened, but he forced himself to push the door open.

35

> 'But I want my payment too,' said the witch, 'and it's not a small one either . . .'
>
> Hans Christian Andersen, 'The Little Mermaid'

Monsignor Delgard's wrists rested against the low altar rail and his head was bowed into his chest, his back arched into an unpleasant shape. His lips moved silently in litany, yet there was an immobility about his face, as though his features had been carved from grey stone. He had no idea of how long he had prayed at the altar in St Joseph's; an hour, perhaps less. His fear and confusion had not yet subsided, nor had any solutions to the imminent problem presented themselves. He had no doubts that the ancient words he had translated had been written in truth and he was equally sure that the curse was coming true. He believed that the power of the human mind had no limits on this earth, and neither did the human psyche. Elnor had possessed a power far beyond the knowledge or understanding of her fellow-men; she was of a breed that was rare, unique, a development in genetic terms that most men could barely perceive let alone strive to attain. She had had the ability to draw the wills of others, their energies, their beliefs, into a collective power that could transcend mere human forces. She had not cured the sick; they had cured themselves. Elnor's role had been one of psychic 'director'. That power was now acting through Alice and in a more potent way than in the nun's own lifetime. Had death, that entry into the spiritualistic world where no physical restrictions controlled the mind's energy, enabled her power to increase to this awesome degree? Something more had occurred to Delgard. He had reasoned that Father Hagan and Molly Pagett might have been the catalysts for unleashing these terrors: now he also wondered if it had taken Elnor's spirit this long to develop her strange powers in the 'other' world (what were a few centuries to infinity itself?). And it was this thought that frightened him most for, if Elnor really had returned, how strong would her psychical forces be, and to what purpose would she put them?

He felt inadequate and defenceless. How could he combat something he could not even fully comprehend? Through his bishop he must seek the help of those skilled in such matters, laymen some, while others were men of his own calling; perhaps together they could control this evil. But mostly, he would seek God's help, for only the omnific could truly vanquish such a creation.

A sharp sound made him raise his head. He looked around and the church interior was dim, the lights fading. He could see no one else in the church. His attention turned back to the crucifix on the altar and his heavy eyelids closed as he resumed his prayers. His joints felt brittle and once more, as it had frequently over the past few weeks, his body reminded him that age and weariness of mankind's ills were taking their inevitable toll. Perhaps, when all this was done, he would seek his own peace, a retreat into—

The sound again! A sharp, cracking noise. It had come from his right.

He looked over at the disfigured replica of the Virgin Mary and his lips moved, this time caused by an old man's trembling rather than prayer.

Delgard pushed himself upright, the effort seeming to take more than it should have. His footsteps were slow, almost a shuffle. He approached the statue and stood beneath it, looking up with curious eyes at the grotesquely cracked face. The Virgin Mother's hands were spread slightly outwards as if to welcome him, but her smile was no longer the tender expression of maternal love: the cracked stone had distorted it into a sinister leer.

His eyes widened as the once-beatific face seemed to change expression and he quickly realized that the cracks were deepening, running into longer jagged lines. Several pieces of stone dropped away, falling to the floor to crumble into dust. The smile became broader, malevolent. Its lower lip fell and it was as though the mouth had opened to silently laugh. The surface plaster began to move, currents moving through it, and Delgard tried to back away, but found himself transfixed, fascinated by the change in its structure.

He stared up into the statue's eyes and powdered dust slid from them so that they became hollow, empty.

His mouth opened in horror and he began to raise a trembling hand to protect himself, as if suddenly aware of what was going to happen.

Fenn stumbled into the church and immediately saw the tall priest at the far end, near the altar. Delgard was looking up at the statue of the Madonna, one hand half-raised.

And there was something else in the church. A small hooded figure, sitting in one of the pews just a few rows behind the priest.

The dark coldness that enveloped Fenn was now a familiar sensation. He felt his stomach muscles grip together and his hair stiffened. He tried to call out to the monsignor, but just a hissing sound escaped his lips. He began to move forward, but was already too late.

The statue exploded and thunder roared through the church. Thousands of stone pieces tore through Delgard's exposed body like metal shrapnel, lacerating his flesh, cutting through his face, chest, hands, groin, throwing him backwards so that he fell over the first bench into the next row, fragments that had found entry through his eyes already lodged deep in his brain, destroying cells so that the incredible pain was only momentary. His body, now unfeeling, twisted and twitched in the narrow confines between the benches, and one large torn hand raised itself as if pleading with something unseen. It gripped the back of the bench and tightened, closing around the wood in death's grip, a last contact with the material world.

Fenn ran towards the fallen priest. He stopped in the aisle, his hands on the backs of benches, looking down at the bloody, twisted figure, Delgard's face ripped open, his white collar stained crimson. He screamed Delgard's name, even though he knew the priest would not hear, nor ever hear again.

With eyes filled with enraged tears, he looked towards the small black-garbed figure. But there was nothing there. The church was empty. Apart from himself and the dead priest.

Wilkes

'But is there nothing I can do to get an immortal soul?' asked the little mermaid.

Hans Christian Andersen, 'The Little Mermaid'

He locked the box, testing the lid to make sure it was secure. Satisfied, he picked it up from the table and crossed the tiny room to the wardrobe, taking no more than three paces; stretching his body, he placed the box on top of the wardrobe, and shoved it hard so that it slid to the back out of sight. He presumed his snooping landlady had already discovered it, but saw no reason to re-arouse her curiosity by letting her eyes fall on it each time she inspected the room. He smiled, imagining what her reaction would be if she ever discovered its contents. But that was his secret. He was sure even his mother did not know it was missing; or, if she did, had not reported the loss to the police, for it was, after all, an illegal possession.

He sat on the narrow, single bed, brushing away the blond hair that fell over his eyes. The newspaper lay spread on the floor at his feet and once more he quickly scanned the article he had been reading. A local Sussex reporter had tried to discredit the little saint, had maintained that the priest had not been killed by a bomb planted by some fanatical anti-religious movement, had made himself a laughing-stock by denouncing all that had happened at Banfield as some crazy witch's curse!

He looked thoughtful, nodding his head several times as he read the article. A bishop, in turn, had denounced the reporter as a sensation-monger who was trying to make as much mileage out of the story for his own financial gain. Although the Church could not yet acknowledge the St Joseph's cures as miraculous, they could most certainly issue a firm rebuttal to the idea that they were the work of some ludicrous 'fairy-tale witch'.

He smiled.

Furthermore, the little saint had asked that a special service should be held for the murdered monsignor and the parish priest who had died earlier. She had told the Church authorities that the Lady of the Vision had asked for a candlelight procession through the village in memory of the good priest, and that a Revelation was to follow. The Church was to comply with her wishes, for it was felt that, while they did not expect to receive any such Revelation, the priests, one of whom had been a courageous victim of those who denied Christ's work here on earth, merited such a tribute.

He was not smiling now.

He lay back on the bed, his head and shoulders resting against the wall behind, his teeth chewing at a thumbnail that had already been bitten to the quick. Three faces, cut from old newspapers and Sellotaped to the wardrobe door, stared back at him. Pasted across the dot-printed photographs was the name of each man. Soon he would take the images down and put them back among the other newspaper articles he had kept in a scrapbook dedicated to them.

But for now he silently mouthed the three names, his faraway smile returning.

CHAPMAN
AGCA
HINCKLEY

36

> The Hag is astride
> This night for to ride;
> The Devil and she together:
> Through thick, and through thin,
> Now out, and then in,
> Though ne'er so foul be the weather.
>
> The storm will arise,
> And trouble the skies;
> This night, and more for the wonder,
> The ghost from the Tomb
> Affrighted shall come,
> Called out by the clap of the Thunder.
>
> Robert Herrick, 'The Hag'

It was madness. Sheer bloody madness.

Fenn brought the Mini to a halt and wound down the window. 'What's the hold-up?' he called out, gesturing towards the snarled traffic ahead.

The policeman, who was trying to bring some order to the chaos, strolled over, the slow walk a disguise for his agitation.

'You won't get through the village,' he said brusquely. 'Not for some time, at any rate.'

'What's the problem?'

'The High Street's chock-a-block. The procession starts from there.'

'It's only seven; I thought it didn't start 'til eight.'

'They've been arriving since six o'clock this morning and pouring in all day. God knows how many there are in the village by now, but it's a good few thousand, that's for sure.'

'Look, I'm from the *Courier*. I need to get through to the church.'

'Yeah, well we all have our problems, don't we?' The policeman scowled at the cars that had stopped behind Fenn's, several further back tooting their horns. His arm lifted towards them like a conductor's baton bidding silence. 'You could try the back roads. Go around through Flackstone; it'll get you nearer at least.'

Fenn immediately put the car in reverse and backed as far as he could go towards the vehicle behind. When he felt the gentle touch of bumpers he pushed into first and eased the wheel around. It took four backward/forward shuttles, even though he used the grass verges on either side of the road, but eventually he was pointed away from Banfield and heading into the dazzling lights of oncoming traffic.

He should have realized it would be this bad; the media had been full of the story over the last few days. Why hadn't the bloody fool of a bishop listened to him? Fenn banged the steering wheel with the flat of his hand, his anger boiling over.

He soon reached the sign pointing towards Flackstone and swung into the unlit country lane. It was a winding road, few houses on either side until he reached the hamlet itself; even here there were just one or two country cottages and flintstone houses set on a blind bend. To his left, he could see a strange glow in the sky and he knew it was from Banfield, the village lit up as it had never been before. He swore under his breath. And then aloud.

Fenn reached another main road shortly after and groaned when he saw the amount of traffic all headed in the same direction. He made a quick decision and pulled over onto the grass verge. He locked the car and started walking, knowing that the traffic moving slowly past him would soon be brought to a halt. It was at least a mile to the church, but walking was the only way to get there before everything, even pedestrians, came to a standstill.

Madness, he kept repeating to himself as a rhythm to his walking. They've all gone bloody crazy.

A strong white light shone high into the night, a beam that was separate from the diffused glowing of the village. It was the main searchlight of the shrine itself and it seemed to him like a siren beacon luring wayfarers to some devious destruction. The eerie whiteness made him shiver. There were heavy rolling clouds above, their fringes occasionally caught by silver moonlight, briefly accentuating their ragged and turbulent form.

The pilgrims he passed, in their coaches, mini-buses, cars – and even on motorbikes and bicycles – all seemed in good humour despite the long delays in any kind of forward movement. Hymns of praise came from many vehicles, the low intonations of prayer from others. Yet it soon became obvious that there were groups among them whose journey derived from curiosity only, those seeking thrills, the unusual, the inexplicable. And there were others who had made the trip because there was nothing much on telly.

Again, as Fenn drew nearer to St Joseph's, he felt the peculiar vibrancy in the air. It was akin to the atmosphere in London in the summer of '81, on the day of the Royal Wedding, or Pope John Paul's visit the following year. Yet the coming together of this conscious energy had a peculiar potency of its own, a heady surging of impulses that he knew would find its peak in the area around the shrine. He knew now that this was Alice's source of power, just as it had been Elnor's so many years before. He knew this as surely as if dead men had whispered the secret to him. The omnipotent mind-energy that transcended the physical, which allowed disabilities in the physical form to be overcome in those who would allow the scavenging of their own psyche. In those who *truly* believed. And that, he was convinced, was the gift of all faith healers: the ability to direct the psychic energies of others. The words of the wretched sixteenth-century priest had provided the key; the dream-whispers of latter-day priests who, like their early predecessor, no longer lived, had provided the answer. But Bishop Caines had not listened to Fenn. A sensationalist reporter's beleaguered dreams had meant nothing to the clergyman. Proof, Fenn, it was proof that was needed.

Where was the manuscript he spoke of?

Dust on the floor of the priest's house.

Where was the late monsignor's translation?

Dust on the floor of the priest's house.

Where, then, was the proof?

Dust, like the statue of the Virgin Mary inside the church.

Fenn's shoulders were stooped, his eyes pouched through nights of disturbed sleep. He had known when trying to convince the bishop that his intensity was near-demented and his words frantic, too emotive for Caines to regard him seriously; but in truth, he had felt a shade too close to insanity for his *own* liking. He had even less luck with Southworth, the businessman behind the scenes, whose greed had skilfully engineered the commercial aspect of the shrine. And no luck at all with the head of the Catholic Church in England.

It was hardly the eminent cardinal's fault, he knew, for Bishop Caines' warning of a lunatic reporter on the loose had preceded his own attempts to reach the Cardinal Archbishop. His alternative was to turn to his own profession and it, too, had shunned him. Even the *Courier*, still miffed that he had turned his back on the newspaper but desperate for his story anyway, had baulked at his revelation. They had compromised with an interview, a piece written by one of his own colleagues with the same scepticism he would have allowed himself just a few weeks before had he been the interviewer. It was a come-uppance that was hard to take; and yet he could see the ironic humour of the situation. The cynic was being paid for his past cynicism; the sensationalist was disbelieved because of his past sensationalism.

Fenn could almost smile at himself. Except it hurt when he tried.

A car's horn made him jump and he realized he had wandered into the path of a slow-moving vehicle. He kept to the side of the road, his breathing heavy now, but his pace faster than the traffic travelling alongside him.

He reached a T-junction and there was the church further down to his left. The main road was jammed with people and vehicles, the hubbub tremendous. There were more stalls than ever by the roadside, selling food, drinks and all kinds of trinkets, as well as the usual religious paraphernalia; the police were obviously having enough trouble coping with the crowds to deal with the flagrant infringement of trading laws.

He pushed his way into the shuffling mob, heading for the side entrance to the church, and it took a good twenty minutes to cover no more than five hundred yards. He reached the gate, now brightly lit, and attempted to push it open.

'One moment,' a voice said from inside.

He recognized the man whose whole life seemed to be devoted to guarding the church entrance. This time he was flanked by two priests and a constable.

'It's okay,' Fenn told him. 'It's me, Gerry Fenn. I think you know me by now.'

The man looked embarrassed. 'Yes I do, sir. But I'm afraid you can't use this entrance.'

'You're kidding.' Fenn showed his Press pass. 'I'm working for the Church on this.'

'Er, that's not what I've been informed. You'll have to use the other entrance.'

Fenn stared at him. 'I get it. *Persona non grata*, right? I must have really pissed off the bishop.'

'There is a special Press entrance now, Mr Fenn. It's just further along.'

'Yeah, I passed it. Looks like I'm no longer among the privileged.'

'I'm just following instructions.'

'Sure, forget it.' Fenn moved off, knowing there was no point in arguing.

He made his way back to the small entrance marked PRESS, which had been cut through the hedge surrounding the field, and was relieved when his pass got him through without further hitch; he wouldn't have been at all surprised if the ban had extended to all entrances, including the public one. He stopped just inside and his tired eyes widened.

Jesus, he thought, the beavers've been busy.

A network of benches all but covered the field like a carefully constructed spider's web, at its centre the spider itself. The twisted oak may have been inanimate but, to Fenn, it now had all the sinister predatory aspects of the creature he had likened it to. The altar-piece below the tree was more ornate than before, although there were no statues, no images of Christ and His Mother that would mean the Catholic Church was fully committed to the popular belief that this was hallowed ground. The religious authorities had been subtle: there were no extravagant displays of crucifixes, save for the solitary cross on the altar itself, but there were many such symbolisms woven in the cloths that covered certain sections on and around the main platform. The centrepiece itself had been broadened to allow for more seating above congregation level, with a deep-red canopy on either side to protect the worshippers from the more inclement weather; a special tiered section had been constructed to the left to contain, he guessed, a choir. Banners were rooted at intervals along the side aisles, their bright reds, greens and golds giving a rich, though dignified, cast to the vast arena. He noted PA systems at strategic points in the field so that no one should miss the words of the service. And the cameras were no longer confined to the outer limits, for platforms had been erected inside the boundary hedges where a congregational view could be taken of the proceedings.

The overall lighting was dim, enhancing the startling vividness of the centrepiece with its bank of floodlights and dramatic single searchlight, which gave the tree and its upper branches a peculiar flatness against the night sky. This central blaze of luminescence dominated the field, a focal point to which every worshipping mind would be drawn.

As he watched, two figures in white cassocks mounted the platform and began to light rows of tall devotional candles that had been placed behind the altar. The question struck him again, as it had repeatedly over the past few days: why had the Church acquiesced to Alice's strange request for a candlelight procession through the village of Banfield? She had told them that the Lady had asked for this to be done in memory of Father Hagan and Monsignor Delgard, and that a divine revelation was soon to come. Bishop Caines had been restrained in his announcement that a procession was to take place, playing his now-familiar public role of reluctant advocate. He had stressed that the ceremony was more in the way of a tribute to two fine priests, one of whom had been assassinated by what would appear to be an anti-religious fanatic's bomb, than compliance with the wishes of a young girl who may or may not have had a vision of the Sacred Virgin. But why had the bishop been so vehement in his attack on Fenn when the reporter had tried to persuade him that there was no goodness in what was happening, only evil? Ambition – for oneself, for one's cause – could be a great blinker to truth, and a formidable dismisser of argument – religions and ideals had succumbed to its influence throughout time – yet he had expected more of this Church representative. He, the unbeliever, wanted more from those who professed to believe. At any time, the disillusionment would have been bitter, but could have been accepted with a cynic's shrug; now it provoked a deeper resentment, a desperate anger whose root cause was fear.

He moved down the aisle as if attracted by the bright light, the soft layer of churned mud beneath his feet sucking weakly at each step.

The field was filling up fast and he vaguely wondered how so many people – those in the vehicles that he had passed, those who were to walk in the procession, and those still milling around the entrance, eager for a ringside seat – were to be accommodated. And where would they all run to?

'Fenn!'

He stopped and looked around.

'Over here.'

Nancy Shelbeck was rising from a bench in a section marked PRESS.

'I didn't expect to see you here,' Fenn said as she approached.

'I wouldn't have missed it.' There was an excitement in her eyes, although trepidation was just behind it.

'After what happened to you? Didn't it scare you off?'

'Sure, I got spooked. I still have to make a living though. Can you imagine what my chief would say if I flew back without a report on the main event?'

'The main event?'

'Can't you feel it? The tension? The air's thick with it. It's like everybody knows something big's gonna happen.'

Fenn's voice was low. 'Yeah, I can feel it.' He suddenly clasped her arm. 'Nancy, what did you see in the church the other day?'

They were jostled as people pushed by, eager for seats near the front.

'Didn't Sue tell you?'

'I haven't seen her since I took you to her flat. I've been pretty busy the last few days.'

'She tried to reach you – we both did. No reply to our phone calls, no one there when we went to your place. Just what have you been up to?'

'I've been trying to get this show called off. Now answer my question.'

She told him and was surprised he wasn't shocked. 'Is that what you saw, too, in St Peter's?' Nancy asked when she had finished.

'I guess so. To tell the truth, I didn't take too close a look. But it all fits.'

'Fits into what?'

'It's too complicated to explain now.' He looked around and was surprised to see just how full the field had become in the few moments he had been speaking to the American. 'Is Sue here?' he asked her.

'I saw her just a little while ago. She had her kid with her. They're somewhere near the front, I think.' She pulled his face around towards her. 'Hey, are you okay? You look kinda rough.'

He managed to smile. 'A couple of restless nights, a few bad dreams. I've got to find Sue and Ben.'

She held onto him. 'I had a long chat with Sue, Gerry; she knows about us.'

'It's not important.'

'Thanks.'

'I didn't mean it—'

'That's okay, I know what you mean. She wants you, schmucko, you know that? I think she's reached some kinda decision about you.'

'It's taken a long time.'

'It would have taken me longer. And then I think I'd have dumped you.'

'You trying to make me feel good again?'

'I figure it'd have been hard to live with you; we'd be a bad combination.'

He shrugged. 'I'm relieved I didn't ask you to.'

'I'm not saying I couldn't change my mind, you understand?'

He held her and kissed her cheek. 'Take care of yourself, Nancy.'

'I always do.' She returned his kiss, but on the lips.

Fenn broke away and she watched him disappear into the crowd. The tension showed in her face once again. She was frightened, badly frightened, and only her professionalism had brought her back here. She knew that she would never have returned to the other church, St Peter's, not for a million bucks or her own network chat show. For those around her, the atmosphere must have been vastly different; their faces revealed only shining expectancy, a willingness to believe that the Holy Virgin had blessed this field with her presence and that, if they wished it enough, she would appear again. Or, at least, the child would perform more miracles.

Nancy stood aside to let an old woman, assisted by a younger one, both bearing a vague resemblance to each other – mother and daughter perhaps – shuffle by. The reporter turned away, desperate for a cigarette but not sure it was proper in such a place, and made her way back to the Press section. To hell with it: Alice had given these people a new hope in a sick world where optimism was considered banal, trust in a higher goodness misguided. While it was true that the shrine had proved a rewarding commercial venture for opportunists, it had also succoured the faith of thousands – maybe even millions throughout the world. But the nagging doubt persisted: should the word have been *suckered*? Nancy sat in the reporters' bench and pulled her coat tight around her; the desire for a smoke took second place to her yearning for a stiff bourbon on the rocks.

Paula helped her mother down the aisle, hoping to get her as close to the altar-piece as possible. She had been told at the gate that spaces had been provided beneath the central platform only for the very sick, those brought on stretchers and in wheelchairs; those who could walk, whether assisted or not, had to take their place among the other members of the congregation. An arthritic hip and hypertension were not considered severe enough ailments, even as a combination, so her mother could be given no special treatment. Having seen the number of walking wounded that had turned up,

Paula was hardly surprised. God, it made a person feel ill just to look at them all.

'Not far to go, Mother,' she coaxed her burden. 'We're quite near the front row now.'

'What's all the bright lights?' came the querulous response. 'Hurts my eyes.'

'It's just the altar. They've lit it all up with floodlights and candles. It looks lovely.'

Her mother tutted. 'Can't we sit down now? I'm tired, dear.'

'Nearly there.'

'I want to see the girl.'

'She'll be here soon.'

'I've suffered enough.'

'Yes, Mother. But don't expect too much.'

'Why not? She's cured all them others; what's she got against me?'

'She doesn't even know you.'

'Did she know them others?'

Paula groaned inwardly. 'This'll do, Mother. We can sit on the end of this bench if this gentleman will kindly move up a bit.'

The gentleman seemed reluctant, but the squinty stare of Paula's mother encouraged him to do so.

The old lady groaned aloud as she sat, assuring those in close proximity of her disability. 'This cold weather isn't going to do my hip any good, is it? When's it all start, when's it all over?'

Paula was about to give an impatient reply when a familiar face caught her attention. Tucker was standing by a bench just a dozen or so rows ahead and he was calling to someone. Paula's eyes narrowed when she saw a plump hand tugging at his elbow, obviously urging him to sit down. She half-lifted herself from the seat to peer over the heads of those in front, and her eyes frosted when she recognized the bulky fur-coated shape next to Tucker. So the fat slug had brought the fat she-slug along with him. Dear, pampered Marcia. Trust her not to want to miss anything! Well maybe tonight she'd learn something new about the pig she was married to. A little confrontation between them, mistress and wife, might offer some compensation for the scare she, Paula, had suffered under Tucker's podgy hands! She hadn't been into the supermarket since – hadn't even sent in a sick note – and her boss was too much of a coward to ring and find out how she was. Well tonight, in front of Miss Piggy's ugly sister, she would tell him exactly how she was! Let's see how he coped with that.

Paula's mother was muttering something about the dampness from the ground creeping into her boots and the man beside her hadn't moved up far enough and she was being squashed and wasn't that Mrs Fenteman in front who never went to church except at Christmas and Easter and wasn't she carrying on with the man in the hardware shop?

Paula did not even look at her mother. She said slowly and evenly: 'Just . . . shut . . . up.'

Tucker ignored his wife's tugging and pushed his way past knees to reach the side. 'What are you doing here, Fenn?' he said loudly when he reached open space.

Fenn turned back and recognized the fat man. 'My job,' he said, ready to walk on.

'You're not working for the Church any more, I hear.'

'No, but I'm still working for the *Courier*.'

'You sure of that?' The question was accompanied by a sneering smile.

'Nobody's told me otherwise.'

'Well you're not very welcome here with all the lies you've been spreading.'

Fenn moved nearer to him. 'What're you talking about?'

'You know very well. George Southworth gave me a personal account.'

'Yeah, Southworth and the bishop must have had a good laugh between them.'

'We all did, Fenn. Pretty lunatic, wasn't it? Witchcraft, nuns coming back from the dead. Did you expect anyone to believe it?'

Fenn waved his hand towards the altar. 'Do you believe all this?'

'It makes more sense that what you've been saying lately.'

'Financial sense, don't you mean?'

'So some of us are making a nice profit. It's good for the village and good for the Church.'

'But particularly good for you and Southworth.'

'Not just us. There are plenty of others who're reaping the benefit.' Tucker's sneer became more pronounced. 'You haven't done so badly yourself, have you?'

The reporter could think of no adequate reply. He turned away, forcing himself to ignore the chuckle of derision from behind.

He drew nearer to the centrepiece, the bright lights causing his eyes to narrow. A broad section before the platform had been kept clear and stewards were directing stretcher bearers and those pushing wheelchairs into it. He stopped beneath a squat, scaffold tower where a cameraman was aiming his television camera into the invalid section. Fenn was jostled from behind and he reached out towards the metal scaffolding to keep his balance. He quickly withdrew his hand as a tiny static shock tingled his fingers. He frowned and, as an experiment, touched the metal frame of a passing wheelchair. Again, a tiny shock crackled at his fingers. He knew that every possible safety precaution would have been taken with all the electronic machinery in the field, particularly bearing in mind the damp soil that the insulated cables would be buried beneath. He looked up into the night sky, at the dark, thunderous clouds, now so low and menacing. A storm was in the air, its charge already in the atmosphere. Sudden feedback from several of the amplifiers spread around the field made the gathering congregation gasp and good-humouredly rub their ears, laughing and smiling at their neighbours.

Fenn could see no humour in it at all; in fact, the peculiarities in atmospherics increased his dread. He looked ahead at the tree, the twisting of its gnarled limbs accentuated in the glaring light, and remembered the first time, just a few weeks before (it seemed a lifetime), when patchy moonlight had exposed its grotesqueness, hovering over the kneeling child like a monstrous angel of death. The sight of the oak had frightened him then and it frightened him even more at this moment.

He eased his way through the long line of invalids until his path was blocked by a man wearing a steward's armband.

'Can't go through this section, sir,' he was told. 'Invalids only.'

'Who are those benches for?' Fenn asked, pointing at the rows behind the open space.

'They're reserved for special people. Can you move please; you're blocking the way.'

Fenn spotted Sue sitting on the end of one of the privileged benches, the small figure of Ben next to her. He produced his Press card. 'I just need to speak to someone in there – can I go through?'

'I'm afraid not. You reporters have got your own section back there.'

'Just two minutes, that's all I need.'

'You'll have me shot.'

'Two minutes. I promise. I'll come back then.'

The steward grunted. 'Make it quick, mate. I'll be watching you.'

Fenn was through before the man could change his mind.

'Sue!'

She spun round and he saw relief flush across her face. 'Where've you been, Gerry? My God, I've been so worried.'

She reached out for him and Fenn quickly kissed her cheek.

'Hi, Uncle Gerry,' Ben greeted him cheerfully.

'Hi, kiddo. Good to see you.' He tweaked the boy's nose as he squatted down by Sue. The rest of the bench was occupied by nuns from the convent and they looked down at him disapprovingly. He drew Sue close and kept his voice low.

'I want you to leave,' he said. 'Take Ben and get out.'

Sue shook her head, consternation in her eyes. 'But why? What's wrong, Gerry?'

'I don't know, Sue. I can only tell you something bad is going to happen. Something nasty. I just don't want you two around when it does.'

'You've got to tell me more than that.'

His grip tightened on her arm. 'All these things, Sue, these strange events, there's something evil behind them. Father Hagan's death, the fire in the village, these miracles. Alice isn't what she seems. She caused Monsignor Delgard's death . . .'

'There was an explosion . . .'

'She caused that explosion.'

'She's a child. She couldn't possibly—'

'Alice is more than just a child. Delgard knew; that's why he had to die.'

'It's impossible, Gerry.'

'For God's sake, all this is impossible!'

The nuns began to whisper among themselves, gesturing towards him. Several began to look around for a steward. He glanced at them and tried to keep his voice calm.

'Sue, please trust me.'

'Why didn't you come to me? Why didn't you ring?'

He shook his head. 'I just didn't have time. I've been too busy trying to stop this thing.'

'And I've been bloody frantic! I've been so worried . . .'

'Yeah, I know, I know.' His hand brushed her cheek.

'Nancy told me what had happened at Barham. That wasn't true, was it, Gerry? It couldn't have been.'

'It was true. She saw something there – we both did. It's all connected with the past; this whole business is the result of something that happened centuries ago.'

'How can I believe you? It just doesn't make any sense. You say something evil is happening, but look around you. Can't you see how good these people are, how much they believe in Alice? All the good she's done?'

He held both of her hands in his. 'We found an old Latin manuscript in the church on the Stapley Estate. Delgard translated it and found the answer. That's why he was killed, don't you see?'

'I don't see anything. Nothing you say makes sense.'

'Then just trust me, Sue.'

She raised her eyes slowly and looked deeply into his. 'Is there any reason why I should? Are you really that trustworthy?'

He knew what she was referring to and became silent. Then he said, 'If you love me, Sue, if you really love me, you'll do as I ask.'

She jerked her head away angrily. 'Why now? Why have you left it so late?'

'I told you: for the last couple of days I've been running around like a lunatic trying to get this whole thing stopped. I didn't get home till early this morning, and then I just slept and slept. And the dreams were clearer than ever.'

'What dreams?' she asked wearily, wanting to believe in him again, wanting to forget his opportunism, his unreliability, his infidelity, but telling herself she would be a fool to.

'The priests, Hagan and Delgard, spoke to me. I saw them in my sleep. They warned me about this place.'

'Oh, Gerry, can't you see you're deluding yourself? You've become so wrapped up in this thing that you don't know what you're doing, what you're saying.'

'Okay, so I'm going nuts. Humour me.'

'I can't leave . . .'

'Just this once, Sue. Just do as I ask.'

She studied him for long seconds, then grabbed Ben's hand. 'Come on, Ben, we're going home.'

Her son looked up at her in surprise and Fenn's head slumped with relief. He kissed her hands and when he lifted his head again his eyes were sparkling with unshed tears.

Fenn stood and pulled her up with him. It was at that very moment that a hush fell over the crowd. The voices became whispers, the whispers fading, the settling of a breeze. Everybody was listening intently.

Voices could be heard in the distance. Voices singing in praise of God and the Virgin Mary. The strangely haunting sound grew in strength as the procession from the village approached.

Fenn looked back at the oak and he closed his eyes as though in anguish. His lips moved in silent prayer.

37

But the old woman was only pretending to be friendly. She was really an evil witch.

The Brothers Grimm, 'Hansel and Gretel'

'Okay Camera 1, let's get a nice close-up. Slow zoom in on Alice. That's good. Keep it slow. We'll cut to 2 in a moment for the overall shot. Keep the CU coming, 2. Good, it's a good one of the girl – what's happening, 1? Picture's breaking up. Oh for Christ's sake, cut to 2. That's better, keep on that. What's happening, Camera 1? Where's the interference coming from? Okay, sort it out. Stay on 2. We'll cue Richard in five. Camera 3, that's good on Richard. Slow pull-back to show congregation in field as soon as he starts speaking. I want a good shot of the altar and that bloody tree in the background. Okay, Richard – 4 – 3 – 2 – Camera 3.'

'As the procession approaches the field, now called by many "The Field of the Holy Virgin", the lights around are dimmed. Soon, the procession will enter this, what has become, open-air temple, led by the Bishop of Arundel, the Right Reverend Bishop Caines, followed by priests, nuns and of course, little Alice Pagett herself. It seems that thousands have joined this holy march, many from the village of Banfield, while others have journeyed

from far and wide to be here today. Not all have held deeply religious beliefs before; indeed, when I spoke to many of them earlier in the day, they told me (static) *in this small Sussex vill – Banfield that has made – realize a deeper truth—'*

'What's happening with sound out there? John, we're losing Richard's voice. Keep talking, Richard, we're having problems, but still receiving.'

'Perhaps then, this vast gathering this evening is a symbolic gesture of people's faith in a world – turmoil (static) – (static) *prevails—'*

'Oh God, we're losing picture now!'

'. . . in memory (static) *priest who was cruelly struck down – Thursday by* (static) *explosion – the perpetrators of such* (static) *– knows, but—'*

'Jesus bloody Christ! Everything's gone!'

Fenn turned with the rest of the congregation as the leaders of the procession entered the field. Flashlights were popping from all points, casting strobe effects on the chanting leaders. Even from that distance he recognized Bishop Caines, who was flanked by robed priests on either side. The first candles were thick and high, held by young altar-servers, their small flames flickering with the breeze. The singing grew louder and the people already in the field joined in. Voices broke off as Alice entered and the worshippers and the curious alike rose to catch a glimpse of her. Fenn stood with them trying to peer over their heads. It was no use: all he could see were the raised candles and banners carried by the marchers. Sue stood by his side and Ben clambered onto the bench for a better view.

The emotions of the crowd seemed to swell like an ocean tide as the singing grew louder and the four lines of marchers drew deeper into the field, the bobbing candles a dazzling display of warm light. Fenn scanned the faces around him: even in the darkness he could see their eyes shining, their lips smiling in some deep-felt rapture. The same expression was on Sue's face. He touched her hand and flinched as another tiny spark snapped at him. Staring at his fingers, he thought: *The whole bloody field's alive.* He shook her gently, this time touching only the cloth of her coat.

'Sue,' he said quietly. 'We've got to leave *now*.'

She looked at him blankly, then turned away.

Ben stifled a yawn.

Fenn tugged at her arm once more.

'No, Gerry,' she said without turning, 'it's too wonderful.'

The head of the procession had reached the centrepiece and Bishop Caines was mounting the steps, smiling down at the invalids spread out on blankets and in wheelchairs below. Alice Pagett followed him, her mother close behind, hands clasped tight together, head bowed in prayer.

Voices all around rose in a crescendo of sound, the hymn soaring into the sky as if to push back the low, brooding clouds. Fenn thought he heard the rumble of distant thunder, but couldn't be certain. Bishop Caines took his seat by the side of the altar and beckoned Alice and her mother to sit next to him as priests and servers filed onto the platform. The benches in front of Fenn began to fill and many of the faces were familiar to him. Some were those cured by Alice in previous weeks, while others were local dignitaries and clergymen. He watched as Southworth took his place and saw the hotelier cast a long sweeping look around the congregation; his smile seemed to be one of satisfaction rather than blissful worship.

A movement on Fenn's bench caught his attention: one of the nuns had fainted and her companions were gently lifting her onto her seat. He felt Sue beside him sway and he held her steady. Others here and there in the congregation were silently collapsing, their neighbours catching them before they could harm themselves.

Fenn drew in a breath. Hysteria was in the air like a rampant germ hopping from person to person.

The hymn singing reached its height, the voices ecstatically unified in the repetitious refrain. He felt strange: there was a lightness in his head, an unsettling in his stomach. This time it was he who felt dizzy and he clutched at Sue. She almost fell, but instead they both sank to the bench.

Ben knelt on the seat and put his arms around his mother's shoulders, one outstretched hand brushing Fenn's cheek. Immediately, the dizziness left the reporter; it was as though the uncomfortable weakness had been discharged into the boy. Yet there were no visible signs of distress in Ben.

The hymn came to its end and the sudden quiet was almost stunning in its effect. The silence was soon broken as the congregation sat, but it returned once they had settled. There were no coughs, no whispers, no shuffling of bodies. Just a hushed, reverential quiet.

The young priest who was to take the service stepped forward to the lectern with its array of microphones. He raised his arms towards the congregation, then made the Sign of the Cross in the air.

'Peace be with you,' he said and the vast crowd responded as one. The priest spoke for a few moments of Father Hagan and Monsignor Delgard, dedicating the special Mass to the two late priests, paying homage to the exemplary work they had carried out in the name of the Holy Catholic Church. He was forced to stop several times when the microphones whined and hummed, and seemed relieved when the preliminaries had been completed. He nodded towards the choir, which had taken its position in the specially erected tiers, and a fresh hymn began.

Candles all around the field were lit, creating a myriad star cluster around an effulgence that resembled the sun.

In the village of Banfield, less than a mile away from the church of St Joseph's, an old man stumbled along the kerb-side. It had been a long walk for him, ten miles or more, but he was determined to reach the shrine before the service was over. Although walking had been his sole occupation for the past fifteen years – tramping the quieter roads of Southern England, surviving on the kindness of others, embittered by the non-caring of yet others – his feet were sore and blistered, his breathing laboured. Brighton was his base, for there were enough churches and charitable organizations in the seaside town to keep his belly fed and his body warm on the coldest of nights. Never too well fed, never too warm; enough to keep him alive, though. What had brought him to this level of existence was not important – not to him, anyway. At that moment, he was what he was; dwelling on the past would not make him or his circumstances different. On the other hand, dwelling on the future might do so.

The belief that he was not completely irredeemable had come to him only that morning when the word had spread along the reprobate grapevine, the efficient word-of-mouth communications system of his kind that never failed to report 'easy pickings'. He had been told of the little miracle girl, of the service that night where thousands were expected to turn up, people of good will who would not reject the entreaties of those less fortunate than themselves. But curiously, it was the miracles of this child that the old man was interested in, not the chance to beg from others.

He had knocked on the door of a priest, a man of God who knew him, who had always shown kindness without reprimand towards him. The priest had told him it was true, that there was a young girl in Banfield who had performed certain acts that could be described as miracles, and that tonight there was to be a candlelight procession through the village. The old man had resolved that he would be there, that he would see this child for himself. He knew, as any man who was dying instinctively knew, that his death was not far away; yet he did not want the miracle of further life. He craved salvation. One last chance to witness something that was beyond this mortal and despicable world. A chance to believe once again, a positive sign that atonement would not be in vain.

Like thousands of others who flocked to the shrine, he sought the means of his own redemption, a physical symbol of the immaterial. A living saint who disproved omnipotent evil.

But would he get there in time to see her?

He leaned against a shop window, a hand resting against the cold glass. The High Street of the village was dimly lit, but there was a beacon in the distance, a bright light that pierced the sky, striking out from a suffused glow around its base. He knew that this was his first glimpse of the shrine, a brightness in the night that called him to observe the greater goodness.

And as he leaned there against the window, gathering his strength, a new gleam in his rheumy old eyes, something touched his soul and passed on. Something cold. Something that produced a shudder in his brittle bones. Something that made him sink to his knees, leaving him bowed. Something whose destination was his own. Had been his own.

His head sank to the pavement and he wept. It was some

time before he crept into a dark doorway and curled up into a foetal position. He closed his eyes and waited.

The tall, bearded barman of the White Hart blinked glumly at his only customer. He sighed as he leaned on the bar. A bloody pint of mild and a packet of pork scratchings would last the old trouper all night. Two barmaids stood idly chatting at the far end of the bar, enjoying the quietness of the usually busy Sunday evening.

Still, the barman thought, the service can't go on all night. They'd be piling in here in an hour or so, desperate for a drink, and he certainly couldn't complain about the recent trade: his turnover had not just doubled – it had trebled! If he had had a bigger pub it would have quadrupled! The brewery could hardly refuse to put up the money for an extension at the back now. What a great little miracle worker that kid was.

He wiped the bar for the eleventh time with a damp cloth, then poured himself a bitter lemon. Cheers, he saluted the absent crowds. Don't stay away too long.

Lifting the bar-flap, he crossed the floor and retrieved two glasses left by earlier customers.

'Judy,' he called to one of the barmaids, placing the glasses on the counter. Let the lazy cow do something for her money, he thought. He turned and, hands in pockets, strolled to the door. Standing in the opening, one foot jammed against the door, he surveyed the High Street. Empty. Not a blessed soul where, less than an hour before, it had been packed with marchers. Banfield was like a ghost town, nearly all its residents gone to the shrine. The village was empty without them, all right, he thought, then chuckled at his own irrefutable logic.

The chuckle ceased and the smile froze as something cold passed by him. It was like standing in a chilly draught, except that it seemed to cling to his body, searching out hidden crevices, covering every part of him like cold water before being sucked away, journeying onwards to who-knew-what destination. The lights in the pub behind him seemed to flicker momentarily, then gain their normal brightness.

He looked down the road towards the church and saw the sudden breeze as a shadow creeping towards the light.

The tall man shivered and quickly went back inside. He resisted the urge to lock the door behind him.

To the north of St Joseph's, little more than a mile away, a motorist kicked at the deflated rear tyre of his Allegro. Nearly there and this had to happen, he complained bitterly to himself.

'Is it flat?' a woman's voice asked from the passenger window.

'Aye, it's a bloody flat. All the way from Manchester and we get a blow-out now. The place must be just down t'road.'

'Well you'd better just get crackin then. Our Annie's fallin asleep already.'

'Better that she is. It's been a long journey for her. I just hope it's worthwhile.'

'Our John travelled to Lourdes with cancer.'

'Yes, an a lot of bloody good it did im,' the woman's husband muttered quietly.

'What did you say, Larry?'

'I said he didn't last long afterwards, did he?'

'That's not the point; he made the effort.'

Aye, an it finished im off a lot bloody sooner, the man thought. 'Bring the flashlight out, will yuh?' he said aloud.

His wife rummaged around the glove compartment and found the torch.

'What's wrong, Mummy?' a voice came from the back seat.

'You just hush now, pet, and go back to sleep. We've got a puncture and your father's going t'fix it.'

'I'm thirsty.'

'I know. We'll be there soon, never fear.'

'Will I see Alice?'

'Course you will, pet. An she'll see you and make you better.'

'An I won't need sticks no more?'

'That's right, pet. You'll be runnin like t'others.'

Their daughter smiled and snuggled back down beneath the blanket. She pulled Tina Marie's plastic cheek close to her own and she was smiling as her eyes closed.

The wife left the car, guiding the flashlight towards her husband as he opened the boot and reached inside for the jack.

The errant wheel was off the ground when the light beam began to fade.

'Hold bloody light steady,' he told her.

'It's not me,' she replied testily. 'Batteries must be going.'

'Eh? They're fresh uns in.'

'Bulb, then.'

'Aye, appen. Get a bit closer, will yuh?'

She bent towards him and he searched for a spanner in the car's tool kit.

Suddenly she dropped the torch.

'Aw, flamin eck!' he groaned.

Her hand clasped his shoulder. 'Larry, did you feel that? Larry? Larry!' She could feel him trembling.

At last, he said, 'Aye, I felt it. It must have been the wind.'

'No, it wasn't the wind, Larry. It went straight through me. Right through me bones.'

His reply was slow in coming. 'It's gone,' he said, looking towards the glow in the sky just about a mile away.

'What was it?'

'I don't know, lass. But it felt like someone walking over me grave.'

From the car came the whimpers of their daughter.

In the Riordan farmhouse, on the land adjoining the field in which the night-time service was taking place, a dog yelped and ran helplessly around the kitchen. At the end of each circuit, Biddy would hurl herself at the door, desperate to get out into the open. Her owners had left her to guard the place – 'too many strange people wandering around the area because of that blessed shrine' – while they, themselves, took part in the Mass – 'better than going to the pictures' – and now the dog sensed the agitation from the cows in their stalls. Sensed and heard, for they were frantically kicking in an effort to break free, and their piteous bellowing was driving the dog into a frenzied fit.

Biddy scratched at the door, raking the paintwork with her claws, howling with the outside ululations, matching their pitch. Around the kitchen the dog ran, back to the door, jump, scratch, push, bark, yelp, howl, around the kitchen once more. Round and around, and round and—

The commotion had stopped. Had stopped more suddenly than it had started.

The dog stood in the centre of the darkened room, one ear cocked, head to one side. She listened. There were no more sounds. She sniffed the air. There were no strangers outside.

She began to whine.

Something was moving through the farmyard, quietly, stealthily, something that had no smell, that made no sound, that had no shape. The dog's tail dropped and her legs bent, her back bowed. Biddy whimpered. She whined. She shook. The dog crawled beneath the kitchen table.

And one eye watched the kitchen door, fearful of what was out there.

It crept through the night, unseen, intangible, a thing of no substance, which existed, but only in the deep corridors of the mind. Now it was drawn inwards, focusing towards a centre induced by a kindred power, slithering through the darkness like an eager reptile towards a helpless insect, guided by someone, something, that had transcended the natural.

It was sucked into the vortex to be absorbed and used.

But evil belongs to the individual and, as any one marching soldier can upset a platoon's rhythm, so individual evil can disrupt the purpose of the whole.

Wilkes

'I did it,' he said, reflecting. 'When ladies used to come to me in dreams, I said, "Pretty mother, pretty mother". But when at last she really came, I shot her.'

J. M. Barrie, *Peter Pan*

The third hymn was drawing to its close and he tucked his hands between his thighs so that those around him would not see how much they trembled. His head was bowed, lank yellow hair falling across his forehead, curling inwards and almost touching the tip of his nose. He stared into his lap and there was a shiny brightness to his eyes that was not akin to the brightness in the eyes of other worshippers. His vision was not focused on his own body; it was focused on the future. Pictures of his own destiny flashed before him: he saw his name written in large, black headlines, his face, smiling, flashed on screens all over the world, his life, his motive, discussed, dissected and wondered at by knowledgeable persons, by eminent persons, by . . . *everybody*!

He could hardly contain the shuddering expansion of his inner self, the blinding whiteness that pushed outwards against his chest. The sensation left him so weak he could hardly breathe.

He had travelled down the night before, sleeping rough inside a bus shelter near the village, feeling certain he would freeze to death with the cold, only the thought of what was to come sustaining him, giving him comfort. He had hardly slept, his brief dozes fitful and full of bad images.

He had been dismayed at the size of the gathering outside the church of St Joseph's next morning, thinking he would be first there, wanting to find a prime position on the benches inside the field. To his further dismay, no one was allowed into the shrine that early; work was still in progress to accommodate the expected crowds, and entrance would not be permitted until early evening. So he had queued with the rest of them, joking with his fellow pilgrims, playing the good guy, pretending interest in boring stories of their little lives, feigning devotion to the Church and all its works, secretly laughing at these insignificant fools who had no idea whom they were standing next to.

At last they were granted entry and he faced what he imagined might be the severest test. But, although bags and containers of any kind were glanced into for security purposes, no body searches were made; so the object tucked into his underpants and taped against his groin, and which caused a semi-erection whenever he was conscious of its weight (which was most of the time), was not found nor even suspected. Even if they had asked him to unbutton his old grey overcoat, the shirt he wore outside his trousers would have covered any unnatural (or unseemly) bulge around his fly area.

Although it was hours before the benches were filled and the procession started, he was not bored with the wait; too many visions screamed into his mind for that.

Like everybody else, he craned his neck to see the girl

when she arrived with the procession and, because he had chosen a seat right on the centre aisle, as near to the altar as possible, Alice passed within feet of him. The urge to do it there and then – no one could have stopped him – was almost overwhelming but he knew it would be better, more spectacular, to wait. He wanted them all to see.

And now the third hymn was almost over. He had watched her at the beginning of the service, had soon found he could not study her small, enraptured face for too long; her goodness, her divinity, seemed to spread outwards and it made him uncomfortable. The words of the Mass were just a mumble in the back of his chaotic thoughts and, although he stood when the congregation stood, knelt when they knelt, sat when they sat, he did it in automated fashion, a robot response to the activity around him. And all the while he kept his head bowed.

The smiling suddenly began to fade, taking a short while to die completely, for not everyone saw Alice rise to her feet and walk to the centre of the platform at the same time.

He looked up, puzzled by the interruption to the background wall of noise, and he saw the little girl in the middle of the stage, her face pointed upwards, her glazed eyes looking at something no one else could see. Behind her was the altar and, behind that, the brilliantly illuminated and grotesquely twisted oak tree.

The field was quiet, all eyes on the small figure in white, breaths held in excited anticipation. There was fear also in their expectancy, for the unknown always generates such emotion.

Alice lowered her head and looked down at the crowd, scanning the multitude of adoring, fearing faces. She smiled and to most it was enigmatic.

In the distance, thunder rumbled.

She spread her arms outwards and began to rise into the air.

He left the bench and nobody saw him unbutton his coat, lift his shirt and reach into his trousers, for everyone was transfixed by the small figure in white rising above them.

He strode down the aisle to the altar, the German Luger, the *Pistole '38*, a relic of the last big war when half the world had gone mad with bloodlust, held down by his side, barrel pointed towards the churned earth.

When he was directly below the platform and just a few feet away from the girl in white who hovered at least eighteen inches in the air, and before anyone could realize what he was about to do, Wilkes raised the gun and fired point-blank into Alice's young body.

He kept firing until the fifth of the Luger's eight bullets jammed between chamber and magazine.

38

> And it was only a moment before she opened her eyes, raised up the lid of the coffin, and sat up alive again.
>
> The Brothers Grimm, 'Little Snow White'

It was a scene from a nightmare, a sluggishly unfolding drama of horror.

Fenn saw but could not understand.

Alice had walked to the centre of the platform and the hymn had faltered, then died on the people's lips. Her face had been beatific – even *he*, knowing what he did – had been enchanted. She had looked skywards and then slowly down, scanning the crowd; and that was when he had shuddered. She had smiled. And it seemed that her eyes had found his. He saw her smile as a rictus grin, wide, malevolent and, somehow, greedy. It mocked him personally and sneered at the crowd generally.

Yet it was just a child's sweet smile.

The crowd was mesmerized and, to him, it was the fascination of a fear-paralysed rabbit staring into the deadly eyes of a snake.

Yet it was just a child standing there.

He felt weak once more, his vitality drawn from him and those around him, drawn into this malignant thing standing in a blaze of light.

Yet she was just a child too young to know evil.

The lights had flickered, dimmed, and then Alice was moving upwards, rising above them in a slow but steady ascent, her arms stretched outwards as though beseeching their love. Their trust.

The crowd moaned as if in rapture, and there were gasps and cries from different parts of the field. Fenn felt his throat constricting and dizziness invaded him once more. It was difficult to breathe, difficult to keep on his feet.

He was only vaguely conscious of the thin, blond person striding down the aisle towards the altar and did not understand when that person raised his arm and pointed something at the small figure floating above him.

He did not even hear the gunfire – at least, the four sharp reports did not register in his brain; but he saw the blood spurt from four points in Alice's chest, gushing out in separate fountains to fall back onto the whiteness of her dress, a crimson dye scattered on a field of snow.

There was shock, disbelief, and finally pain in her small face, before she fell to the platform to lie in a crumpled heap. The blood spread outwards, finding the edge of the platform, flowing over in two sickeningly plentiful streams.

There was no sound among the crowd. The pilgrims, the sightseers, the believers, the unbelievers, all stood in total, uncomprehending silence.

Until thunder roared directly overhead, and pandemonium erupted in the field.

*

Fenn caught Sue as she slumped against him.

The rush of noise was terrifying, a chaotic babble of screams and shouts that soon became a wailing lamentation, the anguish affecting groups, individuals, in different ways: many – men as well as women – were reduced to hysterics, while others merely wept quietly; some just stood in numbed silence, too shocked to do or say anything; the anguish of others quickly turned to rage, shouts of vilification against the assassin passing from person to person, joining in a vehement chant for revenge. There were yet others among them who had not seen the brutal act and who pulled at their neighbours, demanding to be told what had happened.

Ben was frightened and grabbed at his mother's limp body. Fenn put a protective arm around him while still holding Sue upright.

Figures broke from the mass to rush at the blond man who had shot Alice Pagett and who still held the German pistol at his side. He went down under a tumult of bodies and screamed as he was flailed by fists and feet. Sharp fingernails raked his face, a lower eyelid was pulled down and torn, bones in the bridge of his nose were crushed and he felt the crushed fragments pour from his nostrils with the blood. The gun was torn from his grasp and the fingers on that hand were caught awkwardly beneath someone's weight. The snapping sound was lost in the cries of the mob, but the sharpness of the pain could not be lost to his own consciousness.

He shrieked as his limbs were pulled and joints were stretched free of their sockets. His tears ran into his own blood as impossible, suffocating weight pushed against his chest. Something was giving way there and he could not quite reason what. The bones in his chest slowly caved in, pressing against his heart and lungs, restricting the pumping organ and squeezing life-giving air from the delicate sacs. It slowly dawned on him that perhaps he had made a mistake.

Nearby, a young girl who had come to the shrine to pay homage to the little miracle worker for the gift she had bestowed on her, stared at the still, blood-stained bundle before the altar. The girl's face suddenly twitched. One side of her mouth moved downwards, grotesquely twisting into a gargoyle's grimace. An eyelid flickered once, twice, and then would not stop. Her arm jerked, then shuddered; it began to move spasmodically. Then her leg joined in the unsightly and uncontrolled dance, the girl screamed and collapsed to the ground.

– As did the boy in another part of the field, who had come back to the shrine in adoration of the child called Alice, the living saint who had restored the use of his legs. Their strength was gone and he floundered between the benches, calling out in frustration, afraid to be a cripple once more –

– Elsewhere, a man's vision rapidly began to fade, the blaze of light in the middle of the field becoming a hazy cloud, the cataracts which the child had caused to clear returning with a speed that was unnatural and inexplicable – just as their disappearance had been. He cupped his hands to his face and slowly sat down on a bench, a low moaning sound coming from him—

– While in a different part of the field a young girl found once more that sounds emitted from her throat could not be formed into words and that her distressed mother did not understand her when she asked what was happening—

– And a boy in the crowd whose hands had begun to fill with ugly verrucas could only wail and beat his fists against the bench in front—

– A bench where, further along, a man felt his face exploding into open sores, his skin cracking like parched earth. He gasped, not just because the opening wounds hurt, but because he knew he was becoming a freak once more, a man wearing a dog's muzzle of hideous lacerations and dripping ulcers.

From all over the field came such moans and cries of piteous despair, for there were others who fell to the ground, others whose limbs became useless, others whose afflictions suddenly and cruelly returned to dominate their lives. They had thought, had prayed, that their cures were permanent, that Alice Pagett had granted them a new and lasting hope, a divine manifestation of God's caring that would not be erased with time. Now they were betrayed, lost. Defeated.

Fenn no longer felt weakened, and the dizziness had left him. His nerves were taut, tightened, so that his actions were swift, his senses aware. He huddled Sue and Ben close to him, protecting them from the confusion all around. Sue began to revive and her legs took her own weight.

'Gerry?' she said, still dazed.

'It's okay, Sue,' he replied, his head nestling hers. 'I'm here; so's Ben.'

'Is she . . . is she dead?'

He closed his eyes for a second. 'I think so. She must be.'

'Oh, Gerry, how could it happen?' She was sobbing. 'How could someone do that to her?'

Ben clutched at his mother, wanting to comfort her, upset but still not understanding everything that was happening. 'Let's go home, Mummy. I don't like it here any more. Please let's go home.'

Fenn looked over the sea of moving heads towards the altar. 'Christ,' he said, 'nobody's gone to her yet. They're all too shocked.' And he knew that they were all too afraid, even her own mother, to approach the inert body. Afraid, possibly, to discover that Alice really was dead.

'I've got to get up there,' he said.

Sue's grip tightened on him. 'No, Gerry. Let's just get away from here. There's nothing we can do.'

He looked down at her. 'I've got to make sure . . .' He could only shake his head. 'You wait here with Ben; you'll be okay.'

'Gerry, it's not safe. I can feel it's not safe.'

'Sit here.' He gently lowered her to the bench. 'Ben, keep hold of your mother; don't let go.' He knelt beside them both, oblivious to the chaos around them. 'Stay here and wait for me. Just don't move from this spot.'

She opened her mouth to protest, but he quickly kissed her forehead and then was gone, climbing over benches, pushing his way through the disoriented crowd.

Fenn found himself in the clearing before the platform, the ground littered with beseeching invalids, a battleground after the war had passed. To his right was a mob of shouting, tearing people, and he knew what lay beneath their stomping feet, sure that the man with the gun could no longer be alive. They had always been impotent over past publicity-blazed assassinations and assassination attempts, forced to contain their anger, their spite, against the perpetrators, frustrated in their grief, despising those who mocked and flaunted the very rules of civilization. But now the aggressor was within their reach, one of the Devil's legion lay beneath their feet; for once the people had the power to take revenge.

He kept clear of them, making for the stairs at the side of the platform. A man, visibly distressed and wearing a steward's armband, made a half-hearted attempt to bar his way, but the reporter easily brushed him aside. Fenn was almost at the top of the steps when he stopped.

Most of the altar-servers were weeping; some were on their knees praying, their faces wet with tears, while others could only rock their bodies to and fro, heads buried in their hands. The priest who had been conducting the service, ashen-faced, his lips moving in silent prayer, supported Molly Pagett; she was obviously in a state of extreme shock, for her eyes were wide, her mouth open and her movements stiff. Bishop Caines, in all his finery, had the same unsteady awkwardness, the blood drained from his face.

Fenn shared their grief and wondered if he had been wrong about her. It was impossible to believe that evil could exist in that tiny prone body, in a child that had brought so much happiness and renewed faith.

He climbed another step and the lights – even the candles – began to dim.

He fell to one knee, a hand dropping to the platform to steady himself. Giddiness struck him once again and he fought against nausea. He was faintly conscious of the lightning flash, followed by rolling thunder.

He shook his head and looked towards the group on the stage. Bishop Caines, the priest, and others around them, were sinking to their knees. Only Molly Pagett stood transfixed, one hand outstretched towards the bloodied bundle that had been her daughter.

The bundle that was beginning to stir, beginning to sit up. The daughter who had been shot four times and who was rising slowly to her feet.

The daughter whose face no longer resembled any earthly child's, who looked around with malevolent intent and smiled. And grinned. And chuckled.

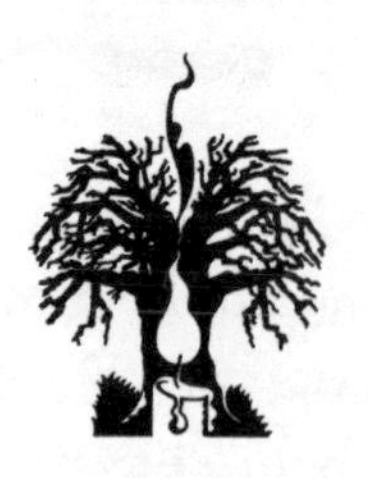

39

We spelled our loves until close of day.
I wished her good-night and walked away,
But she put out a tongue that was long and red
And swallowed me down like a crumb of bread.

Robert Graves, 'The Two Witches'

Fenn slumped against the steps, one elbow supporting his upper body, a hand still on the platform itself. He wanted to run; if not to run, then at least to slither down the steps and crawl away from this monstrosity that stood in the centre of the sanctified stage. But there was little strength in him. He could hardly move. He could only watch.

Her head was turning in his direction and every nerve in his body tensed; it seemed as though a deeply cold shock were running through him, paralysing his muscles, scraping the *inside* of his skin, working its way into his bloodstream so that even his life's fluid was almost frozen, moving slowly, nearly stopping. He tried to draw in breath, but his lungs would hardly stretch, would hardly expand to take in air.

Her eyes found him. But there were no eyes, just deep, black holes. Her flesh was burnt, charred, her body misshapen. Her head was at a strange angle, almost resting against one shoulder, and her neck was scarred, a tight restricting band of indented flesh cutting across her windpipe. Thick oozing blood still poured from the wounds in her body and the child's dress was no longer white: it was a red, blood-smeared rag. And then the hideous doll-like figure was smouldering, curls of smoke rising from the cloth and flesh. Her face began to blister, the skin began to tear. Her skin turned black.

And she was Alice once again.

Confused, lost, a small child who had experienced death's advent and could not understand why she did not lie dying.

'Alice, Alice!'

The girl turned, her eyes wide, afraid, to face her mother. 'Oh God,' Fenn moaned softly as he saw her features change once more.

Her voice was low, rasping. 'Rosemund.'

Molly Pagett, who had found strength to move towards her daughter, stopped and her mouth opened in a scream that tried to deny the sudden perception. 'No, no!' Molly fell, yet her eyes would not leave the little figure standing before her. 'No!' she screamed, 'I'm not Rosemund! Not her!'

The steps on which Fenn lay seemed to reverberate with the thunderclap, but the trembling did not stop. He clung to the wooden stairs as they shook, the agitation becoming more jarring, more violent.

An explosion to his left as a floodlight popped, sparks leaping outwards like dragon's breath. A fluctuation of light as other lamps dimmed, became bright, exploded. Cries of panic from the crowd as an earth tremor ran beneath their feet. The ruffling of his hair and clothes as a wind swept across the platform, bending the candle flames before extinguishing them. A crash as the crucifix on the altar fell to the carpeted boards.

Sue and Ben huddled together as panic-stricken people rushed by. The nuns, with whom they had shared the bench, were filing into the centre aisle, the vibrations from the ground causing them to lurch from side to side. They held onto each other as though they were a blind group being led to safety.

Others of the crowd were clambering across the benches, shoving their way through fellow worshippers who were too shocked to move, or who could not flee fast enough. Those who had brought along invalid relatives or friends struggled with them through the thronging mass, desperately trying to keep up with the human tide, falling with their charges when the merciless crush became too much, pleading for help, protecting their sick with their own bodies, disappearing under a welter of thrashing arms and legs.

The bench on which Sue and Ben clung to each other was toppled over and they found themselves on the shuddering ground, the narrow crevasse between fallen bench and the one behind affording them some protection against the frenzied mob. Sue pulled the boy close, a hand against his cheek, an arm around his shoulders, while he closed his eyes against the terror and tried to shut out the noise, the screams, the cries, the low rumbling that came from underground.

Television and film cameramen were leaping from their perches into the throng, their machines and the very platforms they were mounted on live with dangerous power, the current running through the technicians' bodies in swift waves, not strong enough to kill or maim, but enough to shock their systems rigid. Photographers, many who had steadfastly continued to shoot the bizarre scene on the central platform despite the panic around them, were forced to drop their instruments as the metal casing scorched their fingers.

The congregation which had come to worship, to idolize, to witness, fled towards the field's three exits, converging on these points to form their own human blockade. Many were squashed against the tall locked gates that had been erected at one side of the field, a wide entrance meant for lorries bringing in construction materials and film equipment, before the heavy lock gave way under the strain. As they burst open, those people pressed against them fell and others fell on top, and still more fell onto the scrambling heap.

Police at the central entrance gate tried to control the fleeing mobs, but were swept away with them. Children were held high by their parents and many suddenly felt themselves adrift on moving waves of heads and shoulders. The less fortunate slipped into the smallest openings to be drowned in the pulverizing human current. Those who managed to escape the field, bruised, battered and almost demented, fled into the road, many running towards the lights of the village, others just fleeing in all directions, into the darkness of opposite fields, along the road heading towards open country, dragging helpless companions with them, thanking God that they were safely away from the dreadful place, that ground they had thought to be hallowed, sacred. And they thanked God that the earth no longer shook beneath them.

The Press entrance was too narrow to take the deluge; it was totally blocked. The pile of crushed bodies grew higher as more and more people tried to scramble over and became entangled themselves in the mass of writhing bodies. Others were lacerated as they attempted to force themselves through the tough bramble hedges surrounding the field, the natural barrier acting as hundreds of barbed-wire coils.

Those who had been outside the shrine throughout the service – the stallholders, the police, the pilgrims and sightseers who had arrived too late to be allowed entry into the already overcrowded compound – could only stare aghast. They had heard the rumbling thunder overhead and had glanced anxiously at the troubled clouds, somehow aware that the atmosphere had changed, that there was danger close by. They could not explain the feeling and had looked at one another with uncertainty; something had seemed to pass through them, a frigid coldness, a nerve-tingling iciness, and their apprehension became an overt fear. Many of the stallholders had begun to pack away their goods, all good-natured bantering between them gone. Disappointed worshippers and tourists suddenly felt relieved that they had not gained access; they began to hurry back to their vehicles, not sure of their feelings, but wanting to be away from this place. Their anxiety increased when the engines of their cars, vans and mini-buses whined and refused to start. The police officials outside the grounds were alarmed and a uniformed sergeant tried to radio through to his chief inspector who was inside the field keeping an eye on proceedings. The sergeant received only static on the handset.

Despite their concern, nothing untoward had occurred until the third hymn was drawing to a close. There had been a long silence, then four unmistakable gunshots had rung out, followed by pandemonium. Even though they had heard the clamour from within, they did not realize the extent of the panic until the congregation had come pouring out, sweeping over the uniformed men who stood in their way.

But not everyone inside had tried to escape. Certain individuals fell to their knees and clasped their hands together in prayer, their eyes raised upwards to the turbulent skies; some were collected in groups, quavery voices raised in hymn, afraid but stalwart; others cowered on the shaking ground, clutching grass and mud as though afraid they would slide off the face of the earth. And yet others lay there never to move again, life pressed from them by the trampling feet.

Paula was pulling her gibbering mother to her feet, for they had both fallen in the initial rush. Bewildered, she looked around; everything was in gloom, confused, chaotic. She could hear singing above the cries for help, but it was faraway, remote. Brittle, claw-like fingers scratched at her throat and her mother's fear-struck, tremulous pleading filtered through to her. She pulled the feeble hands away and tried to see more clearly.

The only light came from the altar, the bright beacon still shining high into the sky, lighting the misshapen tree whose branches quivered and oscillated as though it were a living creature. There were silhouettes in front of the light, a black drama acted out on the stage. She understood, even in her confused state, that the fear stemmed from that centrepiece: the people were not just running because the ground shook beneath them, but because they were repelled by the abhorrent thing that stood before the altar and which had looked at each one of them personally and mockingly invaded the intimacy of their very souls. It had scorned and reviled each man, woman and child, and had *known* each one's cruelness, every sin and iniquitous desire they held. It knew them and made them recognize themselves.

Paula put her arms around the frail shoulders of her mother and led her unsteadily along the row towards the centre aisle. They staggered and nearly went down several times as the ground lurched; it was exhausting, dragging her mother along, pushing her way through those who had become paralysed with terror, fighting off others who were desperate to get by. They made it to the end of the bench and paused, gathering strength to join the mainstream of struggling people.

Somebody collapsed against them and they fell, rolling over the bench behind to crash into the soft earth. Paula scrabbled onto hands and knees, feeling for her mother, a moving jungle of legs passing with inches of her face. She touched her mother's body and tugged at it, but it did not move. Her fluttering hands moved along the shape towards her mother's face: they found it and the mouth was gaping open, the eyes closed.

'Mother!' she screamed and the tremoring earth became still. The surrounding cries of terror quietened with the stillness of the earth. People stopped and looked around. Whimpers came from everywhere, but they were soft, the moans of animals after a harsh beating. Even the hymn singing had stopped. Even the praying.

On the altar, something burned.

Paula knew instinctively that her mother was dead, even though she pushed a hand beneath the old woman's coat to feel her chest. The heart was as still as the air around them. She felt no grief, only a numbness. And in a way, a release.

But the numbness dissipated when she saw Rodney Tucker collapsed against a bench nearby. Hatred seethed within her, a fury that quickly devoured the numbness and sent emotion soaring through her.

And then, just as an uneasy calmness began to settle over everyone, the earth opened.

George Southworth had fled towards the church wall, all dignity shed, naked terror revealed.

Everything had gone so well, his dreams easily within his grasp. The shrine – *his project* – had become a huge success, a fantastic money-spinner. He, and others in the area, those with the foresight to invest, to deal themselves in at the very beginning, were about to see their shrewd business acumen rewarded. Indeed, the rewards had already been made apparent; now they could only increase. The village of Banfield was no longer dying; it flourished and would continue to do so, just as had the French village of Lourdes, now a bustling town, a thriving community that was known worldwide.

But she, that thing, that bloodied monster who had impossibly risen from the dead, had looked at him, just him, and seen the greed in his heart. And she had laughed at it, and had welcomed it, for it was part of the evil that gave her existence.

He was running even before the earth began to tremble. Those around him were too blind to see, too horrorstruck to realize the meaning of this unholy resurrection. He knew, but did not understand how he knew, that this creature was the manifestation of their own evil, that she existed on the power she drew from their own blackened souls. That instigation was this creature's torment: the realization of one's own infinite vileness. The guilt that the Church taught all men to suffer was founded on actuality: the culpability was real because the wickedness had always been there in each and every person. Even in the innocent, the children. Children like Alice.

He brushed by those who could only gaze up at the altar and he fought the weakness and dizziness that assailed him, knowing that catastrophe was to follow this new, obscene miracle.

Vaguely, somewhere in the far distance, he heard the hunched thing speak, one word, perhaps a name, and the echo in his mind was drowned by thunder, a sound so loud, so shattering, *so near*, it seemed to rip into his heart. But he was still moving, staggering among the invalids stretched out on the ground.

Then there were others fleeing with him, screams breaking loose from terrified souls, entreaties from those too crippled to move. A hand grabbed at his leg and he looked down to see a wasted, skeletal man wrapped in a heavy red blanket, begging him with wide, frightened eyes to carry him away from the disorder. He knocked the yellow, withered hand away and staggered onwards, the ground vibrating beneath him, the low rumble seeming to rise up through the soles of his feet to shake him like a rag doll.

It was an eternity before he reached the low wall surrounding the church grounds, and the oscillation had grown more violent. There were others with him, those who realized the exits would be blocked, and they, too, climbed the wall, leaping into the graveyard beyond.

He fell heavily and lay panting in the rough grass, hands clenched into the earth. He was kicked as others scrambled over and a blow caught him on the temple, sending him reeling. Southworth pushed himself back, rolling close to the wall and lying there gasping for breath, cautiously waiting like a dislodged jockey under a jump.

High-heeled boots scraped off his shoulder and he vaguely recognized the American journalist who had been at the convent when Alice's stomach had refused the Communion wafer. He called after her fleeing figure, needing help, too dazed to move; but she was gone, disappearing between the gravestones.

He had no record of time, no knowledge of how long he lay there, for his senses were jumbled, both fear and the knock he had received combining to confuse. He became aware that the ground was no longer trembling and that a quietness had descended. He wiped a palm across his face and found it came away wet; he hadn't realized he had been weeping.

Southworth groaned as the pandemonium broke loose again. The tearing, wrenching sound felt as if the very earth was erupting. Everything shook: the trees, the ground, the gravestones. Lush, fresh soil trickled in rivulets down the tiny pyramid molehills. As he watched, a grey slab no more than eight feet away tilted, then fell. The stone lids on the tombs reverberated; one was jolted in quick shuddering movements so that it slid from its perch, breaking into fragments when it landed, leaving the tomb gaping open.

He had to reach the church. There he would find sanctuary from this bedlam. He tried to rise, but the quaking of the earth would not allow it; he staggered forward, bent, sometimes on all fours like an animal, sometimes flat on the ground, propelling himself with arms and legs.

Figures around him stumbled through the graveyard, falling against the headstones, leaning on trembling tombs for support.

Occasionally, the rolling clouds allowed a glimpse of moonlight, its brightness sparing and soon gone.

A mound of earth near Southworth moved and he stared spellbound, telling himself it was the earth tremors causing the disturbance to the grave. But the soil was being pushed upwards, from within, as though something beneath it wanted to breathe the air of the living once more.

More shifting of soil nearby. An urn containing fresh flowers tipped over. Earth beneath it began to bulge, began to break.

A trickle of soil touched his outstretched fingers and he pulled his hand away, tucking it beneath his chest. He saw the small grave nearby, a child's grave – or perhaps a dwarf's.

A tiny hillock was forming, rising from the flatness around it and, before the moonlight was swallowed by the heavy, thunderous clouds again, little white things pushed through the soil. Little white things that could have been worms. Worms that were stiffened, upright. Five of them. Joined by five more.

Southworth screamed and staggered to his feet. He ran, stumbled, crawled, to the door of St Joseph's, aware of the moving shapes in the ground around him.

He slammed into the old wood, whimpering, his legs drenched and stained with his own excrement, his eyes blurred by tears. He scratched at the wood as if to claw his way through, scrabbled for the metal ring at waist level, twisted it, once, twice, pushed the door open and stumbled inside. He slammed it shut and stood there in the dark church, his back against the door, his chest heaving, gasping for breath.

Until he froze, his lungs half-filled.

And listened to the scratching against the wood outside.

40

Where have the dead gone?
Where do they live now?
Not in the grave, they say,
Then where now?

Stevie Smith,
'Grave by a Holm-oak'

Fenn raised his head from the platform's surface and tried to take in a deep breath. The air was fetid, though, full of corruption and the stink of burning; he choked, his stomach heaving in short gut-wrenching spasms.

He was vaguely aware of the turmoil below, the panic-stricken people staggering towards the exits, earth tremors causing many to fall to the ground where they lay and were trampled. But it was dark out there and virtually impossible to make out more than a confused mêlée of struggling bodies; it was the screams and piteous wails that revealed the true horror.

Somewhere in the channels of his fuddled mind, reason told him he had to get away, that he had to go back and find Sue and Ben and lead them away from the danger, for this abhorrence meant to destroy, to devastate. He had no strength; his muscles felt sluggish even though his nerves were tautly stretched. He wanted to look away from the smouldering bloody monstrosity, but the vision held his gaze, held his debilitated body, held him there as if chains restrained any action.

He heard her speak and there were other voices inside his head that told him he must resist her power. Her strength was *his* strength, was the strength of all those present, was accumulative potency drawn from the evil of others, the negative force torn from the positive, creating an imbalance over them all. But resist. *Resist!* The voices repeated the word and they were the same voices and the same words as in his dreams. Elnor could only exist through the kinetic energy of those living. *Resist her!* She could not govern those who opposed.

Was it mere self-delusion that the voices in his mind and dreams were those of the two dead priests?

Fenn moaned and he tried to *resist*, but the effort was too much. He could not even look away from the disfigured creature. In the church at Barham he had run from his nightmares, refusing to confront them, denying their reality; now he had no option in the confrontation. His will was too weak to leave.

Every person on the stage around the altar was in a state of near collapse. Bishop Caines was on his knees, one hand against the flooring, the other waving feebly in the air in an uncoordinated movement that vaguely resembled the Sign of the Cross. His lips moved ceaselessly, and spittle drooled from them to glisten against his chin. The words were almost inaudible, but they were clear in Fenn's mind.

'. . . *Holy Lord, Almighty Father, Everlasting God and Father of our Lord Jesus Christ.*

Who once and for all consigned that fallen tyrant . . .'

The priest who had been conducting the service lay prostrate on the floor, his arms outstretched as if in supplication. He was motionless and Fenn could see his eyes were rolled back into his head, only whiteness showing; the priest's mouth was open but there was no indication that he was breathing.

'. . . to the flames of Hell.

Who sent your only begotten Son into the world to crush that roaring lion; hasten to our call . . .'

Some of the altar-servers were crouched over, their knees drawn up, foreheads pressed against the rich carpet of the centre-piece, hands tucked around their heads as if to shut away the evil that had manifested itself; others swayed as they knelt, white, draining horror in their expressions, but eyes riveted on the small, unclean figure.

'. . . for help and snatch from ruination and from the clutches of the noonday Devil this human being made in Your image . . .'

Only Molly Pagett stood.

Yet even she was sinking, her arm still raised towards her daughter.

'Aliiiiiccce!' she moaned.

And the malevolent voice hissed back: 'Your daughter is in death, sweet Rosemund. She, our Devil's spawn, is between this place and the underworld, her service to me almost complete. None can save her. Nor save you.' The scarred, bent creature turned her head towards the blackness. 'Nor those who slew me and denied my right.'

'. . . and likeness.

Strike terror, Lord, into the beast now laying waste Your vineyard. Let Your mighty . . .'

'Noooooo!' Molly Pagett stumbled forward, sinking to the floor, moving towards the smouldering thing, both hands reaching out.

And the creature who was Alice, who was Elnor, laughed,

and Fenn saw a shape hanging from a lower branch of the tree, and it was burning and twisting, and its neck was stretched, its feet twitching and turning black, and substance was dripping from its body to fall steaming onto the altar below, and its head was aflame and its flesh burnt, and as it turned it was Alice.

'*. . . hand cast him out, so he . . . he . . . she . . . may no longer hold captive this person . . .*'

With a screech of sheer despair, Molly Pagett lunged forward and touched the charred and rotted body of Elnor, then screamed in pain as rivulets of fire ran along her fingers, along her arms, engulfing her head and shoulders.

There was a silence. A silence that was as terrifying as the clamour preceding it.

Bishop Caines became quiet.

Molly Pagett blazed but did not move.

Fenn felt his senses beginning to fade.

And the image-corpse of the sixteenth-century nun chuckled as thunder suddenly roared and the field began to open.

Paula let go of her mother's body.

The deep rumbling noise reverberated in her head as the earth wrenched itself apart, the cacophony of screams and shouts beginning anew. She watched mesmerized as a gaping wound appeared in the soil; it widened, ran jagged along the centre aisle, sending the petrified crowd clambering back into the rows of benches.

The ground yawned open and Paula saw the blackness down there, so deep, bottomless, an infinity of darkness. Yet, as moonlight fought its way through the massed clouds and cast its glow into the chasm, she saw movement, hands reaching upwards, limbs clinging to the soft, rent earth. Shapes climbing from the depths, figures that were twisted, that moaned and stared open-mouthed at the sky above, tormented souls that yearned for the world above.

Paula closed her eyes, telling herself it couldn't be true, that this was not really happening. She opened them again and saw it was true, it was happening.

There were figures on the edge of the opening chasm, backing away, pushing each other to keep clear of the widening gap. Even in her own terror, Paula recognized two of them.

Tucker was struggling away from the pit, hindered by his wife, who had slipped, one leg over the edge, disappearing into the blackness. She scrabbled at his clothes, desperately trying to cling to him, but he pulled her hands away, afraid she take him with her, knowing he could not drag her weight clear. She screamed at him, imploring him to save her, but he shouted back at her, shrieked for her to let go, slapped at her face, prised at her fingers. She held on with one hand, the other grabbing at the sod beneath her, one knee on the very lip of the chasm. The earth crumbled beneath her heavy body and the material of his coat tore as she fell screaming.

Tucker stumbled back, then righted himself. He stood with hands against his thighs, struggling to recover his strength, soon realizing he had to keep moving back, that the opening was still widening.

He turned just as Paula rushed at him.

Hatred drove her forward, loathing for a fat bastard who had betrayed her, used her, abused her body, and lied, lied, *lied*! Beneath the ground was where he belonged, to wriggle and squirm with the slugs and worms and underground creatures that he was akin to.

She slammed into him and he caught her. But her impetus

was too forceful: he could not keep his balance. He toppled backwards and clutched at her, taking her with him.

Together, locked in screaming embrace, they plunged.

Southworth ran from the door.

He touched every pew with his left hand as he passed, like a child touching every spoke in a railing, an action that had no logic, panic its prompter.

He reached the low rail in front of the altar and slumped against it, whining against the solitude of the church, afraid of the frozen corpses outside seeking entry.

The church began to vibrate. Statues around its walls moved, shifted by the tremor. The rail he clung to became impossible to grip. The cracking of ancient stone rang out like a report from a cannon, jerking his head in the direction of the sound. He watched in fascinated horror as the jagged line ripped across a wall. More ear-splitting sounds and more lines joining the first. Now from the other side of the church. Now from the roof.

Pieces of masonry began to clatter onto the stone floor. Powdered concrete descended as white dust, and the dim lights of the church began to falter, flickering as if candlelight caught by the wind. On – off – on – off. Then, just very low.

His hands were at his mouth, stifling the cries that nobody would have heard over the tearing of old stone. Behind him, candlesticks toppled from the altar; the tabernacle door swung open, revealing the white silk emptiness inside; the huge stained-glass window, donated to St Joseph's by a sixteenth-century nobleman, flew inwards, sending shards of coloured glass spearing through the air.

He gasped as several pieces struck his head, scything through his hair and scalp, leaving fine cuts that quickly oozed with blood. He was fortunate that the rail he clung to protected most of his face and neck.

The turbulence became more intense, the cracking and rumbling sounds deafening. A long, jagged line appeared in the stone floor, running beneath the pews and across the aisle. A gap began to open, a scissure so black it seemed painted. Pews shifted, fell against one another as the cleft became a fissure, the fissure a wide split.

The knuckles of his hands began to bleed as he bit hard; he watched slime-covered fingers appear over the edge of the hole. He bit down until his teeth were grinding against bare bone.

Hands, then arms, filthy with earth and mould appeared. Small black things scuttled out, disappearing into darker corners; something long slithered across the floor and curled itself around the base of a statue. More fingers slid over the edge, more arms reached into the air. More hands and naked, death-discoloured shoulders began to appear.

The door at the far end of the Church began to splinter, pressure from the breaking stone around it forcing it from the frame. It burst open and the dead creatures entered.

Sue felt strangely calm.

'What's happening, Mummy? Why are all the people screaming?'

She held Ben tightly, one hand against the back of his neck, his head tucked against her chest.

'It's all right,' she soothed, stroking his hair. 'Don't be frightened.'

He pushed his head away from her, looking round to see what was going on. 'I'm not afraid,' he said seriously, eyes widening at the spectacle.

Someone hurtled over them, tripping on their recumbent bodies. The figure scrabbled to his or her feet – there was no way of telling whether it was man or woman in the poor light – and rushed on.

Ben sat up again. 'I can see Uncle Gerry,' he said, pointing towards the altar.

Sue pushed herself up, using the overturned bench next to her for support. The ground was still trembling, although not quite as violently as before, and the rumbling sound was now deep down as if in the bowels of the earth. For some reason people were fleeing from the centre aisle, but it was impossible to see why. She followed Ben's pointing finger and gasped when she saw the scene on the altar.

There were bodies dressed in the robes of the Mass littered all over the platform. She recognized the portly figure of Bishop Caines, his sparse, grey hair flat against his forehead, dampened with perspiration; his hand waved uselessly in the air. Not more than two yards from him something was bright with flame. It was a figure, a kneeling figure that did not move, nor squirm, in its agony. Only the head, arms and shoulders were burning, the hands outstretched towards someone who stood just beyond the light thrown from the one remaining lamp. It was just a small black silhouette, a child's figure, standing before the gruesome display, watching, perfectly still, smoke eddies from burst lights swirling around the altar. And dominating everything, towering over the shrine, was the oak tree, its stout lower branches twisted downwards like arms about to scoop up the fallen bodies.

She saw Fenn lying on the steps of the platform. He looked so helpless and afraid.

She stood, bringing Ben up with her.

'Where are we going?' he asked.

'Away from here,' she replied. 'But we have to get Uncle Gerry first.'

'Sure!' he shouted and scampered over the bench.

At once, Sue felt nauseous and dizzy. Her knees began to sag.

'Ben!' she cried out and he was back with her, arms wrapped around her waist, little face peering anxiously up at her.

The dizziness vanished. She swallowed and the sickness was gone. Sue looked curiously down at her son.

She bent close. 'Don't leave me, Ben. Don't let go of me.'

He took her hand and together they climbed over the benches towards the altar.

Sue forced herself to ignore the pitiful cries for help coming from the invalids scattered on the stretch of ground between the front benches and the altar-piece, knowing she could not go to their aid, that she had to reach Fenn, then perhaps together they could carry just one or two away from there. She clutched Ben's hand tightly, not understanding why her strength, her calmness derived from him, just aware that it was so.

She tried not to look at the burning figure and saw that Ben had become fascinated by it. She pulled his head against her hip, a hand covering his face to shield him from the sight, but he pulled her fingers open and peeped between them.

They reached the foot of the steps and began to climb.

'Gerry?' She was beside him, peering anxiously into his face. He blinked his eyes, seeming not to recognize her at first.

'Sue,' he said softly and she breathed a sigh of relied. Fenn suddenly grabbed her arm. 'Sue, you've got to get away from here! Now, right away! Where's Ben?'

'It's all right. He's here. Come on, you're coming with us.'

His head sank against the step. 'No, I can't move. I'm too weak. You've got to go without me.'

She pulled her son up the steps. 'Touch him, Gerry. Hold his hand,' she urged.

Fenn looked at her uncomprehendingly. 'Just get away, Sue. Just go!'

She put her son's hand into his and Fenn looked from her to the boy; then down at their joined hands. His sapped vitality began to return.

Shrieks of agony made all three look towards the altar.

Molly Pagett was slowly rising from her knees, beating at her enflamed hair with hands that were also alight. The sound of her screams struck into them, chilling them.

'Oh God, I've got to help her.' Fenn tore off his coat and climbed the rest of the steps onto the platform. He stumbled forward, coat held before him, ready to be thrown over the burning woman's head and shoulders.

But Molly Pagett was beyond help.

With one last piercing scream she lunged at the dark figure standing just beyond the light. The figure did not appear to move, yet the burning woman's arms did not strike it. Molly plunged off the platform, falling into the darkness to lay writhing in the field below, a fiery rag, the agonized shrieks slowly becoming weak, fading, stopping abruptly when her life was spent.

Fenn groaned and slumped to the floor, rocking back on his heels, his eyes closed, coat held uselessly in his lap.

The small figure stepped forward into the arena of light and stood before the altar, looking up at the tree. Then it turned its gaze on Fenn.

Lightning flashed, freezing the shrine, the field, the church in the distance, in its silvery light. Fenn, whose eyes had opened, felt he was not part of the scene, but hovering somewhere above, viewing from a great height and having no involvement. The jostling, tearing worshippers, the sick left behind, arms upraised beseechingly; the huge black abyss from which crawling things emerged; the church, its tower beginning to crumble, the opening graves; the shrine, the slumped bodies before the altar, the fallen crucifix, the hideous, misshapen tree. The creature who watched him.

The lighting flash expired, a two-second exposure that ingrained an indelible monochrome vision of Hell's chaos on Fenn's mind.

Thunder boomed, a deafening sound that overwhelmed all others and he clapped his hands to his ears in reflex.

Ben tugged at his mother and said: 'There's blood all over Alice's dress, Mummy.'

Fenn stared back into Elnor's knowing eyes and found himself sinking into their softness, a peaceful vortex that drew him inwards to be exquisitely drowned in their depths. He was aware of her delicately beautiful features, the whiteness of her skin, the moist, natural redness of her lips, even though he looked only into her eyes. He sensed the pleasing suppleness of her body, its litheness, its vitality, and the firmness of young breasts which the nun's simple costume could not disguise.

Elnor smiled and his head reeled.

When she spoke, he barely understood her words, so strange was her accent and so low, rasping, was her voice.

'Witness my vengeance,' she said. 'And be, thyself, part.'

And her eyes were no longer soft and brown, but were darkly hollow, deep pits that held him fascinated. Her skin was no longer soft and white, but was charred and torn, the lips burnt away to reveal stumps of blackened teeth and weeping gums. Her body was no longer supple and straight, but was twisted, bent, a warped, scarred figure that in some curious way resembled the malformed tree which towered over her. Her stench clawed at him in putrefying waves. He raised a hand against her, falling backwards, pushing himself away.

Her laughter was insidious, a sly creeping chuckle.

'Why is Alice standing there?' Ben asked his mother.

The laughter grew, filled Fenn's head, swamped his mind. *Must get away*, he told himself. *Must get free of her. O God, Jesus Christ, please help me!*

The platform began to vibrate. His hands were forced from its surface, his body rolling backwards. He turned, tried to get his knees beneath him, toppling over, the splintering of wood sharp against the rumbling noise. The long black rent in the field was widening, the gash growing longer, flowing like a dark river towards the raised altar, stretching towards the shrine.

The nun's clothes were smouldering as she approached Fenn, and her skin was blistering once more. Yet still she chuckled and her lipless mouth mocked him. Broken charred fingers were reaching for him. A streak of lightning cut its jagged way through the sky.

Elnor was almost upon him and her breath was as foul as her body.

He screamed, unable to move.

And she grinned her death's grin.

But then she had stopped. Was looking back towards the tree. Was moaning a low, piteous wail. She straightened and her broken hands clenched tightly at her breasts. Her moans became louder.

Fenn followed her sightless gaze and saw nothing. Then a shimmering.

A glow.

At the base of the tree.

He felt renewed fear, but this was of another kind. The glow became stronger, became bright, like a newborn sun. His hand tried to shade his eyes, but the radiance was too great, too blinding. Yet there was something in its centre. Something standing within its incandescent core.

And in his mind he could hear the voices of the two priests. *Pray*, they urged him. *Pray*.

He blinked. He closed his eyes. He prayed.

Lightning struck the tree and his eyes shot open.

The hunched creature was moving away, shuffling backwards, arms stretched towards the splintered oak. She screamed, cursed, her guttural voice rising in pitch.

The upper branches of the tree were in flame, its trunk torn open, tiny creatures pouring out, maggots, lice, glistening wood leeches. The tree was rotted, dead inside, a nesting place for parasites that fed on dead things.

Thunder, and, almost at once, forked lightning. It struck the tree and every branch became alive with blue dancing flashes, energy pouring through the contorted limbs, seeking earth. The whole of the oak burst into flames and a tearing, rending sound split the air. The tree began to topple.

Hands tugged at Fenn's shoulders. A woman's hands and a child's.

Sue and Ben pulled at Fenn until he was moving with them, running from the platform, away from the screaming creature, away from the falling tree. Hand in hand they jumped from the shrine into the night.

They landed heavily, but the muddy earth was soft, yielding. Fenn, winded, his ankles jolted by the fall, turned to see the small girl standing beneath the descending, screeching inferno, the child who was already dead, slain by a madman, Alice, who now raised her arms as if to ward off the fiery nemesis, yet no longer the child as the flames engulfed her, once again the black, hunched creature who could not defy the greater power. Fenn believed he heard Elnor cry out as the burning tree crushed then incinerated her corrupt and unearthly body.

The centrepiece collapsed, all those sprawled on its surface falling inwards towards the heart of the fire. Soon the whole structure was burning.

Only the crackle of flames could be heard and the weeping of those still left in the field. The earth tremors had stopped. There was no more screaming.

Fenn reached for Sue and Ben, their distraught faces bathed in the warm glow of the fire. He pulled them to him and they huddled together, moving only when the flames of the burning platform came too near.

And then the rain gently began to fall.

41

'Round and round the circle
Completing the charm
So the knot be unknotted
The cross uncrossed
The crooked be made straight
And the curse be ended.'

T. S. Eliot,
'. . . The Curse be Ended'

'Come in with us.'

Fenn smiled at Sue, who was peering in the open car door, and gently shook his head. 'You go with Ben,' he said. 'I'll pick you up later.'

The boy scrambled from the back seat out onto the kerb. Sue leant back into the Mini, one knee on the passenger seat, and stretched across to kiss Fenn's cheek. She tenderly hugged him and then was gone.

He watched as they walked down the long path towards the church entrance, Sue's hair caught by the sun, made golden at its edges, Ben holding her hand, skipping alongside her.

It was a Sunday morning, a bright fresh day, the smell of the sea strong in the air. The church was of contemporary design, elegantly simple, its structure rejecting any solemnity or oppressiveness. More inviting than a couple of churches I could think of, Fenn thought grimly. Few people strolled the streets in that part of the seaside town for, although it was a bright, sunny morning, winter's chill still clung; only those with dogs to be exercised, those who were too lonely to stay indoors, and those attending Sunday services at the many and various Brighton temples and chapels, had left the warmth of their homes. One such person, a dog-stroller, passed by on the opposite side of the road and Fenn caught a word of the front-page headline in the newspaper the man was avidly reading.

It said 'SHRINE' and Fenn turned his head away.

He was tired of their theories, their conjectures, their desperate need for a rationale. The current favourite was that an electrical storm had centred on the field, its lightning destroying the altar-piece, causing the tree to burn and fall, even striking the ground to send shock currents running through the earth. Film, radio and television technicians present complained that electrical interference had jammed their equipment. Even the film in the cameras of the Press photographers had been blanked out, although nobody could quite explain how an electro-magnetic storm could have that effect. The police, receiving severe criticism for not having controlled the panic, had limply claimed that their own communications system had been disrupted by the storm. The shockwaves had caused mass hysteria among the already highly-charged, emotional crowd, causing hallucinations, breakdowns and panic. That was the Number One, highly-rated conclusion. Others were even more fancied but nevertheless not totally rejected: Alice Pagett had acquired some unknown paranormal mental powers and, having no control over them, had upset nature's delicate balance; an underground eruption had shaken the area, frightening the whole assemblage into hysteria (unfortunately no seismographic evidence substantiated the idea); an anti-religious organization had planted a bomb beneath the shrine (probably the same group that had killed the monsignor). More and more solutions, more and more confusion.

Over twenty thousand had arrived at the shrine on that black Sunday and, if there had been any miracle to that day, it was that only one hundred and fifty-eight had been killed in the panic. Many had been crushed to death beneath the trampling feet of their fellow-worshippers; some had suffered heart seizures or fatal fits; others, those on the central altar-piece, or close by, had been burned to death; still others had died in accidents as they had fled the field. Many, many more had been seriously injured and maimed, while the condition of a number of the invalids present had deteriorated to an alarming degree. Strangely, those whom Alice Pagett had cured at other times at the shrine found their illnesses and infirmities had returned, as though the child's death had cancelled the miracles.

Scores of the unfortunate worshippers, clerics and nuns among them, claimed they had witnessed the ground tear itself open. But these people were confused, even weeks later, and their mental state could at best be described as 'unstable'. It was a fact that hundreds, possibly thousands, had blanked the incident from their minds completely; all they could remember was the fierce storm and running from the field.

Speculation im the media was rife, swinging from the wild sensationalism of the so-called popular Press (as if the incident needed any sensationalizing) to the deliberately underplayed scientific and psychological views of the more conservative. Fenn was no longer a part of that particular circus. He had resigned from the *Courier* and refused offers of employment with the large Nationals. He had even refused to answer questions concerning the events of that night. Maybe one day, when his head was clear and his nerves more controlled, he would sit down and write a definitive book on the Banfield shrine. But it would have to be marketed as fiction for who would believe the facts?

He smiled as he remembered Nancy's frantic phone call from the States. Her bosses wanted him over there, were offering him a job on the *Post* – 'name your own figure' – in return for the full story of the shrine. He declined the offer and Nancy had fumed and ranted on the other end of the line. She had been one of the first to flee as soon as she realized 'something bad was going down', mindful and still fearful of what had happened to her at St Peter's. So scared had she been that the slightest hint of trouble had sent her scampering. Unlike most of the panicked people, she had headed directly towards the church grounds, knowing that all exits would be swamped, and had followed a man she thought was Southworth, the hotelier in the village, losing sight of him somewhere in the graveyard. She had used the entrance to St Joseph's as her escape route and had missed the finale. That was why she was so chagrined. Happy to be alive, of course, but pissed that she hadn't witnessed the grand slam. Nancy had urged, begged, threatened, but he refused to join her. She was still in a rage at the end of their conversation, but managed to growl, 'I love you, you fink,' before her receiver clunked down.

He rubbed his temples with stiffened fingers and thought of those who had died in the field. The fat businessman, Tucker, found lying in the mud, his face purplish blue from a heart attack. His chief assistant, a woman whose name Fenn could not remember, lay on top of him as though trying to protect his gross body from the crushing feet of others. She was in a state of shock. Ironically, her mother was found dead nearby, she too having suffered heart failure. Employer and mother, both lost at the same time with the same cause. No wonder she was still in shock. Tucker's wife, also found nearby, could remember nothing, only that she had fainted while trying to escape the field.

Bishop Caines had died, along with other clerics and altar-servers, in the fire. Crushed by the tree, burned by the flames.

George Southworth had been more fortunate, although some might reason otherwise. He had been discovered hiding in St Joseph's, a shivering, slavering wreck of a man. They had to drag him screaming from the church, for he refused to walk down the aisle to the broken doorway. Apart from the cracked door and a shattered stained-glass window (both struck by lightning, it was thought) there was no other damage to the church, even though Southworth insisted it lay in ruins around him.

Then there was Molly Pagett.

He closed his eyes, but the vision of her enflamed body was even sharper. That poor, poor woman. How she had suffered in the final minutes of her life, seeing her daughter shot, resurrected, changed into something unspeakable, then dying in agony. Perhaps it was better she had died, no matter how terribly, for the memory would have killed her just as surely, only death would have been slow and more cruel in its claiming.

Why had Alice – no, *Elnor*! – called her 'Rosemund'? One of the two nuns mentioned in the sixteenth-century priest's chronicle had been named Rosemund. She had been one of the young novices whom Elnor had seduced, one that had been cast out from the church and was said to be living in the forests around the village. Could Molly Pagett possibly have been a descendant of that girl? Or was the creature Elnor, this resurrection, this reincarnation, confused by its own hatred? He would never know, for there were no clear answers.

There was not even a clear answer as to why the young man had shot Alice. His dead body had been found among the others, battered and crushed; nobody would even suggest that he had been torn apart by the mob. The German gun was found nearby, its barrel jammed. His name was Wilkes, and the only abnormality of his typically middle-class background was that he appeared to have, judging by the collected newspaper clippings found in his bedsit, a fascination for the assassin of John Lennon, and the would-be assassins of Pope Paul and Ronald Reagan. If he had been a little older, then perhaps his heroes would have been Oswald, Ray, and Sirhan.

Whatever his twisted reasons were, a trigger-squeeze to fame, a rejection of what *he* believed to be total good, Alice was dead. Perhaps evil had defeated evil.

Elnor had sought her revenge and had claimed much of it. Only the child's unpredicted death had thwarted its completeness, and the shrine had been destroyed as surely as if the hand of . . . Fenn could not accept it. It was too unclear in his mind. He could have imagined he'd seen . . . everything was so confused . . .

Alice's body – what was left of it – had been found beneath the charred remnants of the tree. She had been buried, along with the remains of her mother, in the graveyard of St Joseph's nearby. Curiously, when the site of the shrine had been excavated a week later, the remains of another body had been found buried beneath the roots of the fallen oak.

But this one was centuries old, just a twisted skeleton. It

appeared to be that of a small person, many of its bones broken at the time of death. Burned black also.

The remains had been taken away to be studied by experts who would decide on the date of its origins. Eventually the bones would go to the British Museum where they would be displayed in a glass case for tourists, and those interested in mankind's evolution could come and smile at the grinning skull.

Fenn looked up and Sue and Ben were nearly at the church door. Ben had been distracted and was squatting by the edge of the path, watching something on the ground, perhaps an insect of some kind. Sue was speaking to him, obviously telling him they would be late for the Mass.

What strange power did Ben have? Was it his total innocence that had protected him, that had not let him see what others *thought* they saw, not let him hear what others *thought* they heard?

He had never witnessed Alice's radiance, had never witnessed her levitate. *And he had not seen Elnor.* Nor felt the earth shake, nor watched the ground open. And he was not alone, for other children in the field that night had not shared their parents' and guardians' terror. Yet there were other young ones who had.

Fenn had felt his strength return when he touched the boy; so had Sue. It was as though their weakness had passed through him, the boy acting as a human conductor, and dissipating their weakness into the ground. Was innocence so powerful against such evil?

Whoever said that questions were more important than answers was a fool. Unanswered questions could drive you to insanity.

He forced himself to relax. Outside the windscreen, the

sky was a clear Disney blue, the sun hazy, soft-edged. Even though there was no strength to its glow, it was painful to look at, and he shielded his eyes, resting his elbow on the windowsill. He was reminded of the glow he had seen at the shrine, the glimmering shining at the base of the tree; the one sight more than any other on that terrible night that constantly haunted him. Yet it was not an unpleasant haunting. Somehow it gave him courage. Something more ... Faith?

His hand scraped against his chin and he shifted in the seat in agitation.

Why did it disturb him so? Why, out of everything else that had happened, should this drive him to such distraction? Why had the thing called Elnor been so afraid when it, too, had seen the glow?

And had he really glimpsed the shadowy figure of a white-gowned woman within that radiance?

It couldn't be! He had suffered too many delusions that night! His mind had been filled with too many terrors! His own survival mechanism had suddenly worked against them, creating a different kind of illusion, one that spread calmness, peace, a vision that exuded a quiescent tranquillity.

Yet why had Ben, who had *not* seen the other horrors, asked later who the lovely lady in white was, standing by the tree that night when everybody was screaming and the altar burned down?

Who was she?

Who was she?

What was she?

His eyes were closed, his hand covering them. He opened them, looked towards the church. Sue was leading Ben up the short flight of steps to the open doorway.

He clenched his fist and rapped his knuckles against his

teeth. He opened the car door and strode towards the church gate. He hesitated.

Sue turned and saw him. She smiled.

And he strode up the path to join them. Together they went into the church of Our Lady of the Assumption.

Little Alice, sweet and pure
Come see her if you need a cure
She'll stop your boils and clear your head
And smile sweetly when you're dead.

New Nursery Rhyme